SISTERS AT WAR

TWO SISTERS AT WAR WITH THE NAZIS... AND EACH OTHER

JINA BACARR

Boldwood

First published in Great Britain in 2023 by Boldwood Books Ltd.

Copyright © Jina Bacarr, 2023

Cover Design by Colin Thomas

Cover Photography: Alamy and Colin Thomas

The moral right of Jina Bacarr to be identified as the author of this work has been asserted in accordance with the Copyright, Designs and Patents Act 1988.

Every effort has been made to obtain the necessary permissions with reference to copyright material, both illustrative and quoted. We apologise for any omissions in this respect and will be pleased to make the appropriate acknowledgements in any future edition.

A CIP catalogue record for this book is available from the British Library.

Paperback ISBN 978-1-83751-512-7

Large Print ISBN 978-1-83751-508-0

Hardback ISBN 978-1-83751-507-3

Ebook ISBN 978-1-83751-505-9

Kindle ISBN 978-1-83751-506-6

Audio CD ISBN 978-1-83751-513-4

MP3 CD ISBN 978-1-83751-510-3

Digital audio download ISBN 978-1-83751-504-2

Boldwood Books Ltd
23 Bowerdean Street
London SW6 3TN
www.boldwoodbooks.com

To every woman who felt she must keep silent. That time is no more.

INTRODUCTION

A word of caution. I have written a story some may find disturbing. A story about sexual violence in wartime. A topic ignored in the most part by history, but more timely than ever.

I pray you will come along with me on my journey.

CHARACTER LIST FOR THE PARIS RESISTANCE COLLECTION

SISTERS AT WAR
Characters who appear or are referred to and are also in the following books in the series:

THE RESISTANCE GIRL
Sylvie Martone – French cinema star and Resistance fighter known as 'Fantine'.
Father Armand – kindly priest from Sacré-Coeur.

THE LOST GIRL IN PARIS
Angéline de Cadieux – Roma girl turned perfumer and Resistance fighter working at The House of Doujan – parfumerie
Countess Ester Bulgávari – Hungarian countess working for the Allies.
Professor Oskar Zunz – parfumier and spy posing as the countess's 'uncle'.
Jarnak – works in a pawn shop used by the Resistance as a base of operations.

THE ORPHANS OF BERLIN
Kay Alexander – American candy heiress who rescues Jewish children.

IN ALL FOUR BOOKS
Herr Avicus Geller – the relentless Gestapo man famous for working crossword puzzles.

PROLOGUE
PARIS, 1940

I shall never forget that hot August day when the SS officer attacked me. The horror that took hold of my body, my soul. My psyche. My outlook on life. Everything changed. I changed. Afterward I could no longer look at the world in the same way. I was no longer filled with promise. I'd never bloom from the love of the sun. I was smashed into the dirt and quashed by the heel of a black jackboot. I couldn't move. Couldn't think. I was alone with my pain. Humiliated. Lost. I kept quiet as we women do. As we're supposed to do, I guess. Yet I couldn't go back to the way things were. The city I loved, the city of perfume and flowers, had lost its sweet smell, its vibrant Impressionist pigment gone and replaced by the dull beetle-green of the occupiers. The world I knew ceased to exist. I was an innocent girl no more.

I was shocked it could happen to me.

Late summer started out as it always does, sending Parisians out of the city to escape the heat. That summer, my beloved Paris wept like a spoilt child. Not believing everything we loved was turned upside down, everything we tasted turned bitter. Two million souls had fled Paris last June to escape the Nazis. Refugees clogging the road going south away from the city, carrying their life's belongings piled high on top of motorcars, bicycles, pushcarts, or on their backs, strafed by German aircraft and dragging along despair with each labored step. What they called the Exodus.

I wasn't one of them.

Instead I gathered in the cozy servants' kitchen that morning with Maman and my sister, knitting, chatting as one does about how slow the days pass in summer, staring out the windows misting with a dove-gray dawn.

I sipped my tea, smiling. I felt safe here in the grand house of Monsieur and Madame de Giocomte, descendants of a wealthy Jewish banking family who had settled in France after arriving here from Venice over two hundred years ago with treasures that dazzle the eye. Art, antiques, tapestries. Glorious art that enriches our lives. Maman works for Madame as a seamstress and reminds us every day how lucky we are to grow up in a luxurious three-story house known as Maison des Ombres Bleues. House of Blue Shadows. We call it Maison Bleue, an abode that bristles with art masterpieces hung at every angle in every room. A house named for the deep blue shadows that appear every day in the library at twilight and take on evocative shapes, reminding me of spirits weary from keeping family secrets they can never tell. A place filled with exquisite portraits where luminous faces on the wall peer down at me with warnings in their eyes I'm too blind to see.

I often used to study the portrait of my sister and me when we were young girls of sixteen and fourteen sitting on a Carrara marble bench in the garden bleached white by centuries of young girls sitting their backsides there, making daisy chains and pining for romance. I love the happy glow on our faces, the innocence captured by the artist in angular, colorful shadows. Our youthful joy. Strong lines, and exuberant greens, yellows, and blue.

The flamboyant female artist called the painting *The Beaufort Sisters*.

We call it *The Daisy Sisters*.

I dawdle here this morning, smiling up at the painting after I finish my tea. No one to shoo me away with a disapproving look. Monsieur and Madame de Giocomte have gone off to their villa near Deauville to escape the August heat, even though horse racing was suspended, to spend time with Madame's sister-in-law and her daughter and children. Something they do every summer, and German soldiers wearing armbands with black swastikas weren't going to stop them. They hold to tradition like so many of the Jewish elite in Paris, like nothing happened. They live in a bubble no Nazi would dare penetrate.

I also believed we were untouchable.

And then I found out I wasn't.

1

Ève

I prick my finger on a sharp thorn when I push aside a red rose to get at my unhappy basil. Limp, droopy leaves that look all out of breath stare back at me. I lament their demise while I suck on my finger to dull the pain, mindful one should never plant such a delicate herb next to a sultry rose bush. The rose always wins.

I sigh. *Alors*, I have no place else to conduct my science experiments since I graduated secondary school last June. It's the Nazis' fault, of course. The Occupation disrupted the examination schedule and I won't get the results of my written exams until next month. The oral tests were scrapped, thank God. I pray with all my heart I passed the 'bac'—the baccalaureate examination—so I can get into the university. If so, I start classes on October 1. Meanwhile, I keep doing my experiments in the gardener's shed since I've nowhere else what with the Nazis and their rules and curfew.

They even forced us to set our clocks ahead one hour and operate on German summertime. *What next? Strudel instead of macarons?*

I wave away a buzzing bee, adding to my frustration.

Lucky for me, it prefers the rose.

It's hot and stuffy in the shed today, so I head for the double doors at the back of the grand house, sniffing the green basil leaves, eager to breathe in their deep aroma. Barely a scent. I'm not surprised. Not with the hot, searing sun beating down on the large rectangular garden behind the *grande maison*. The air oozes with a humidity that won't let up.

I pull off my lace collar and wipe the sweat off the back of my neck. It must be well after the noon hour. I was so deep in communicating with my plants, I lost track of time. I do that often, much to the dismay of my older sister Justine.

You see, I'm her live mannequin.

You're never around when I need you, Ève, she's wont to say, teasing me, then pushing back her curly blonde hair from her pretty face. I'd rather be looking through a microscope than in a mirror. I admit standing in the upstairs sewing room in a dress held together by straight pins is *not* my idea of a productive afternoon. I prefer my nose in a chemistry book or, better yet, in a Petri dish sniffing out my latest experiment. I'm not much for fashion, while Justine has an eye for design like that bee has for flowers. She designs her creations for Madame de Giocomte on a fashion doll, a charming rendition of a lady standing more than a third of a meter high with a real-hair blonde wig, painted features, and glass blue eyes that look straight at you. Madame insists the doll belonged to her grandmother in Russia half a century ago.

Now it's Justine's pride and joy.

Then, draping silk, velvet, or taffeta over my tall, lean body, she brings her designs to life. Day dresses. Suits. Gowns. Next, feathers and netting for hats. Justine loves making hats. *A stylish hat gives a woman confidence, Eve.* Not me. I feel silly when she makes me try them on and the feathers make me sneeze.

I'm pondering what pinned-together frock my sister will have me wiggle into today in this heat—most likely that cotton strawberry print I saw her working on—when I hear sounds coming from the library. *Is that Justine calling me?*

No more time to commiserate with my poor basil. I undo the top two buttons on my plain gray dress, wet with sweat. With the basil clamped between my teeth, I pull back my long hair with a ribbon I borrowed from Justine.

Pink velvet.

'It becomes you, Ève,' Justine said the other day, pulling it out of her wicker basket filled with fabric scraps.

'It's *pink*,' I protested, wrinkling my nose. 'Little girls wear pink.'

'Big girls do, too. And lipstick and cake mascara—'

'You mean black shoe polish,' I said, smug. 'You don't have to study chemistry to know that.' I have no time for that female nonsense, but Justine doesn't understand that.

'Oh, Ève. What am I to do with you?'

When I saw how her light eyes turned a deep blue-gray of sadness, I borrowed her lipstick just to see her smile.

'Happy now?' I asked.

She nodded. 'Very. Now for the final touch.' She tied my hair back with the ribbon and gave me a hug. 'There. You look lovely.'

I didn't argue with her, but we both know the truth is I'm not pretty, so why bother? Yet Justine sees something in me I don't and when I asked her what that is, she said, 'You're a strong young woman, little sister, with classic high cheekbones and full lips. You just haven't grown into it yet.'

And with that she was off, teasing me about my experimenting, like how I insist plants speak a silent language they emit through their smell. Vibrant, sharp. Mellow. Sweet. And in some cases, rotting, moldy. A way of communicating their unique place at nature's table, I tell her and, if the table is set correctly, I believe we can harness their essences to cure disease. It's no secret honey was used centuries ago to treat battle wounds and fight infection, and that garlic protects against bacteria. Her eyes widen and her full lips form a perfect *Ooh*, but I don't think she believes me. She'd never say so. Instead she smiles and leaves me be. I feel in my gut I'm right. I studied the work of the British bacteriologist Dr Alexander Fleming last semester at the Lycée Louis-le-Grand, the secondary school I attended on Rue Saint-Jacques. There I came across a fascinating theory about a type of mold that can kill bacteria. My chemistry teacher encouraged me to pursue this line of study. Maman was keen on me becoming a perfumer's apprentice at the famous House of Doujan here in Paris, but I convinced her my heart is into healing, not seduction.

Speaking of the feminine arts...

I'm fortunate Maman doesn't have any interest in marrying me off. Justine, yes. She's her golden child. Talented, pretty, and with the kindest heart. I adore her, too. I wish I could inhale a whiff of her power over Maman, over everyone Justine meets who falls under her spell. She's a marvel with people, empathizing with them and listening to them. No wonder they trust her with their secrets.

Me... I'm more like the ugly duckling without a pond to swim in. Big feet, taller than most girls my age, I hunch over to hide from everyone. I'm fine with that. I have my test tubes lined up on a worktable in the gardener's shed and my experiments to occupy my mind *and* my soul. I want to help people and that leaves no time for romance. I pray with all my heart I passed my exams so I can enter the Sorbonne to study the sciences. Madame de Giocomte is rooting for me, too. She was so grateful to me for helping her cure her migraines—securing butterbur extract for her did the trick—that when Maman showed her my professor's recommendation along with the fact I'd graduated at the top of my class, she promised she'd use her influence to help me get accepted to university.

If I pass my exams.

Now I count the days until I get the test results, my head spinning with so many possibilities, like making scientific discoveries as Madame Curie once did, and pushing the Nazis and the Occupation out of my mind.

Which is why I pay little attention to the sound of a loud motorcar outside racing its engine. It couldn't be the de Giocomtes. They took the train from Gare Saint-Lazare to the Brittany coast and aren't due back for two weeks. *Who, then?* French citizens rarely drive now because we can't buy gasoline. Another annoying restriction the Nazis laid down. Adding to my solitude is the fact the two maids, Lucie and Albertine, who stayed behind left early this morning to line up in queues for bread and cheese. Lucie is a sweet girl with rosy cheeks and red braids, while Albertine is a stern young woman with deep brown eyes. They make up the housekeeping staff since the gardener left for the Free Zone and the chauffeur followed soon after, giving Justine and me the run of the house. Justine loves trying on Madame de Giocomte's posh hats with trailing veils, and Maman is upstairs in her sewing room on the third floor, knitting woolen scarfs for the French soldiers languishing in German POW camps. The incessant heat doesn't stop her. Ever since she saw the lists of young men taken prisoner posted on the window of L'Aide au Soldat, she can think of nothing else.

'Who else is going to help those poor boys if I don't?' she laments, gathering up her blue and green and gray wool for socks she knits with a mother's love even if they're not her own. She's that way and often sits with Madame de Giocomte in the sewing room discussing Madame's charity work, the two women as thick as pea soup when it comes to helping others.

I frown. I believe Maman feels guilty because she has no sons to sacrifice for our country. She mumbles how the boys need scarves to keep their necks warm in winter. Her despair that Paris will still be occupied has transferred to her busy fingers, because she doesn't want to think about how her world has changed. How there will be no more fancy masquerades when Madame changes her costume every hour, each stitch done by Maman, or when Madame invites the corps de ballet to dance in the garden for her guests and Maman sews satin ribbons on snow white slippers for the dancers, the ballerinas giggling and hovering beside her.

She glowed like a fairy godmother.

Now she hides in her room.

Grumbling how she fears the Nazis will drag her from her bed.

Justine and I assure her that won't happen. Yet I can't ignore the sound of... *jackboots pacing up and down in the library*?

I stop short. *Intruders. Oh, God, Nazis? Here?*

Impossible.

The afternoon turns sour like green apples spiked with vinegar when I glance out the long window not covered by a blackout curtain in daytime. I see a big, black Mercedes motorcar parked in the winding driveway, a German soldier leaning against the car, his black boot parked on the running board. I furrow my brow. *What do Nazis want here?*

I sniff the basil, thinking. Could there be trouble at Monsieur de Giocomte's bank? I overheard him telling Madame de Giocomte about the Vichy government doing away with anti-Semitism laws and requiring the Aryanization of Jewish businesses and going so far as to appoint non-Jewish administrators.

But not the de Giocomtes, he told his wife. *We're French citizens and enjoy protection. We're above the law and have nothing to worry about here at Maison Bleue,* he assured Madame and the staff when France surrendered to the Reich in June. The Nazis acted cordially when he presented himself to the *Kommandant* in charge. The German High Command was more interested in confiscating residences on Avenue Foch, now known as Avenue Boche, than on our quiet street hidden off the Rue de Monceau, a street so tiny it's not written on any map.

Still, worry creases my brow.

With good reason. My jaw drops and I crush the herb in my fist when I see two German soldiers loading canvases of paintings into a truck covered with a tarpaulin.

No, that's impossible.

Monsieur de Giocomte's treasures. Renoir. Degas. The Impressionists.

Who let the Boches in? How did they know where to find the paintings?

I race down the long hall toward the library, my mind scrambling like dominos falling one after another faster than my heartbeats. I'm desperate to stop this madness. *Who? Why is this happening?* My brain forces the logic down my throat that I don't want to believe. That an informant—someone the de Giocomtes trust—betrayed them. It could be anyone. A business associate, servant, even a passing acquaintance intrigued by the stories Madame de Giocomte loves to recount with her lady friends over tea in the garden room of the Hôtel Ritz.

My mind bursts into shards of Murano glass, my security shattered when I slide open the heavy oak door to the library. I can't believe what I see. A tall SS officer staring up at a painting. *Our painting.*

The Daisy Sisters.

Justine and me.

My God... no, he can't have it. I won't let him.

In spite of my loud assertions about not indulging in female primping, I *want* to be pretty. And in that painting, I am. The artist made my hair lighter, nose perkier, lips fuller, and emphasized my already prominent cheekbones. I cling to the notion that if I stare at the painting long enough, I *will* look like that girl.

And now this Nazi is taking that from me? *No.*

I panic when the SS officer gives an order in German and the soldier starts to remove the painting. It's not a large painting, and it's set in a simple but elegant frame. That doesn't mean he can just *take* it. *The Daisy Sisters* doesn't belong to me, but I have rights.

'Don't touch that painting, monsieur!' I cry out.

Young, impulsive.

'Mademoiselle dares to question an officer of the Reich?' he says in French, spinning around. 'I can have you shot.'

'You won't.'

I don't know why I said that.

'No?' He raises a brow.

'No. You wouldn't want my blood splattered all over the beautiful brushstrokes, *n'est-ce pas?*'

'Why would you care?'

'It's a painting of *me*, monsieur.'

'You, mademoiselle?' This new information produces a smirk and a step backward. 'Ah... I see the resemblance. You've grown up, mademoiselle.' Before I can stop him, he orders the soldier to remove the painting and stack it with the others in the truck, then he grabs me by the arm and squeezes it tight. I wince. 'Are you the daughter of the family?' he demands.

'No, monsieur, my mother works here as a seamstress for madame.'

'And the older girl with the lovely face and figure,' he drools. 'Where is she?'

'I don't know, monsieur.' I refuse to give up Justine. He holds me tighter, squeezing my arm so tight my eyes bug out, the pain burning my flesh.

'Must I ask you again?'

'*Please*, monsieur, let me go.'

'Since you refuse to cooperate, mademoiselle, I shall take both you *and* the painting as spoilage.' He slams me against the wall, rattling my brains, making my teeth chatter while a shocking, hot pain shoots up my spine. I go numb. He pins me against the wall and I can't move a muscle when he shoves his hand under my cotton dress and forces my legs apart.

His intent is clear. Rip off my dress and then—

But he doesn't. He switches gears. Like a devil teasing his victim with licks of fire. He runs his gloved hand up and down the bare skin on my thighs above my stockings, snapping the garters, taunting me. Panting hard.

'You will find me a good lover, mademoiselle, strong and powerful,' he purrs in my ear. His frightening words reek of a self-confidence that sends chills through me.

I've heard rumors the Nazis are cold, sadistic bastards and not the blonde gods they purport to be on posters plastered around the city. Like the one I saw with a Nazi helping French orphans with the caption, *Have faith in the German soldier*.

I wanted to believe no one could be *that* debauched.

I was wrong.

I know I'll never forget the cold, guttural tones of the major's voice, his eyes marbled with gray and black, his look lustful and void of all humanity when he slides his gloved hand up and down my inner thigh. 'You like chocolate, mademoiselle, smooth and melting on your tongue?' he asks, his eyes glistening as he licks his lips. 'Silk stockings?'

'Let me be, monsieur, I want nothing from you or *any* Nazi.'

Why is he trying to seduce me? To calm me down? Subdue me?

'You disappoint me, mademoiselle. Paris is the city of love. It's your duty to—'

'No, *never!*'

'I want you, mademoiselle, and it will be better for you if you cooperate. Now, *stand still!*' His voice is authoritative, no longer teasing but demanding, hissing ugly words at me and I know I'm lost.

By now I'm screaming, my voice hoarse. The fluttering of fear I felt moments ago explodes into a raging inferno of terror like I've never known before. He abandons his cordial promises and sets his evil will upon me. What happens next is so ugly, so horrible, I block it out, his hands invading my most private places, scalding my skin with his brutal touch until I hear—

'Let her go, monsieur.'

A low, husky voice.

Justine.

Standing in an arc of sunlight, holding the fashion doll, she's a painting come to life, every inch of her womanly and golden and warm. My older sister with the porcelain skin and wavy blonde hair like a Jumeau doll, a creature not of this earth but one who lives in her own special world of silk and chiffon, lace and satin.

No man can resist her.

This girl with a smile as bright as a daisy and just as fragile tries to buck the wind from the east. To save me. Her sister. I'm not surprised. Justine is that way. Outspoken. Daring. We may want different things in life, but we're close. Like two buttons sewn on a sweater. We'd never abandon each other.

And she won't abandon me now.

Her hand to her throat, her eyes wide, she steps forward. 'I repeat, monsieur,' she says, gritting her teeth. 'Take your hands off my sister.' She pleads with the SS officer to let me go, but she doesn't know the price she's about to pay for her courage.

'Your *sister*?' His voice deepens, his interest piqued.

'Yes. She's impulsive and didn't mean to offend you.'

'I'll let her go,' he gloats, '*if* you trade places with her.'

'*Monsieur!*' Shocked, she clutches the doll to her chest.

'It's your choice, mademoiselle. I intend to have one of you.' He looks from Justine to me. 'Or both.'

Justine raises her chin, her steel-blue eyes defiant. 'You wouldn't dare, monsieur.'

'Wouldn't I?'

'This is the residence of Monsieur de Giocomte, an esteemed war hero, a gentleman of business revered by his peers, a well-known and respected Parisian philanthropist.'

'And a Jew.'

He laughs, then releases me. I'm numb, unsure what to do. I can't leave Justine. *I can't.*

'*Run, Ève!*'

'I'm not leaving you, Justine, *I won't.*'

'*Sehr gut.*' The SS officer's blue eyes flash with a mixture of anticipation and amusement. 'You present a tempting proposition, mademoiselle.' He grabs Justine by the arm. She tries to resist, but his grip tightens. 'I want you first.'

'For God's sake, Ève, *run!*' Justine yells.

'*No!*'

'I'm *begging* you, Ève. Don't worry about me, think about Maman.'

'But—'

'Go... and don't look back!'

I nod. Yes, I understand, our dear sweet mother will never recover from the trauma if she sees her daughter suffering an act so vile at the hands of the SS. It makes me retch.

I start up the three flights of stairs, my heart beating wildly, then I hear Justine scream. I turn, see the major fondle her breasts; she resists, he slaps her, she hits him in the face with the doll, he grabs it and tosses it across the room, smashing the doll onto the marble tile floor, its delicate porcelain head cracked, its blue glass enamel eyes closed. Forever.

I must go to my sister.

I race back down the stairs. Justine shakes her head wildly from side to side when she sees me, again her eyes begging me to go. *Run!* Then she pulls her ripped dress across her chest, the lace trimming on her slip hanging in pieces, and in a whisper, she promises to go with the Nazi officer.

Then she lowers her head.

The SS bastard has the nerve to smirk, click his heels and nod in my direction. Then he yells the words that will forever sicken me. 'Heil Hitler.'

Justine gives me one long, last look before he pulls her along behind him, her high heels then his jackboots tapping in my ears like the beats of a funeral drum.

Then silence.

She's gone.

'Justine... No... *No!*'

Knees wobbling, heart pounding, I make my way across the hall, one step at a time, not making a sound, my brain not processing what I saw, not believing, my fingers shaking as I pick up the doll, its head dangling off its shoulders, blonde wig askew.

Its painted smile turned upside down.

I crush the broken doll to my chest, a disturbing scent hitting my nostrils, the SS officer's sweat mixing with my sister's natural perfume. A tightness in my chest so severe grabs me, like the Nazi stomped his boot on me and made my heart stop beating. I hover between a dark place and an even deeper darkness made all the more surreal because I can't cry. I *won't*. Where my world was once filled with the aroma of sweet basil, the prick of an arrogant rose, and a busy bee, the air is now thickened with power and lust and evil.

No tears, not now. Nothing but anguish for the sister I adore, along with a need for revenge as sharp as my anger. Somewhere out there in the city of Paris, this young woman is in the grips of an enemy more evil than I imagined. That this despicable SS officer holds her dignity and her life in his hands, that I can hear her desperate plea for mercy in my mind and I'm powerless to help her.

And that no matter how many times I play the scene back, I know only one thing to be true.

It should have been me.

2

PARIS, AUGUST 1940

Justine

The evil deed is done.

Ripped stockings, my underwear pushed down around my ankles, the buttons ripped from my cotton dress, I lie in the backseat of the black Mercedes with the Nazi flag on the hood. Alone. No one would dare approach the parked motorcar hidden under a green canopy of oak trees near the park. I can't stop shivering while clamping my thighs together to ease the pain in my groin, touching the stickiness between my legs with my fingers, wondering: *Why me?*

What did I do wrong to make me a victim of rape?

I obey the rules of the church, pray to the saints for courage, had saved myself for marriage even when temptation and hot kisses from a young man I fancied begged me to give in to the stirrings within me. Now I can never love *any* man, share his bed, bear his child. I'm ruined in the eyes of God, yet I wonder, *does He know?*

If He does, *how could He let this happen to me*?

I'll never forget the sickening ordeal, the major kissing my lips, my breasts. My skin cold to his touch, I recoiled inwardly and cut off my feelings. I didn't whimper and sigh as he wanted me to; that made him angry and he ripped my stockings from their garters and pulled down my panties. I beat my fists against his chest, praying I had leverage in the motorcar, the black curtains on the back windows drawn to hide his deed, his aide de camp keeping guard, the smell of tobacco lingering in the air. I yelled out. He cupped his hand over my mouth until I quieted down before restraining my wrists with his uniform belt. Still, I wouldn't give in. I yelled out hoarse threats, trying to kick him.

'Be still, mademoiselle, or—'

'I don't care what you do to me.' I swallowed hard. 'I'll not give you what you want.'

'Then you leave me no choice.'

I heard the cock of a pistol and felt the cold metal pressed to my temple. I braced for the inevitable loud *click* before my world went black in a burst of gunfire.

Then—

'If you don't do as I wish, I shall return to the *maison* of the de Giocomtes.' He leaned down, hissing his words between his teeth. 'And shoot your mother *and* sister.'

'No, you wouldn't,' I cried out, alarmed. 'They're innocent.'

'Not if I say they're guilty of attacking an officer of the Reich.' He sucked in his breath. 'Now, shall we both enjoy ourselves?'

Never, I screamed inside, the terror in Ève's hazel-green eyes more vivid than ever in my mind, the wretched fear we both had of seeing our *maman* collapse from despair, that raw emotion making me vow to do *anything* to keep them safe.

I had no doubt the SS officer *would* murder them.

Tightening my gut against the excruciating pain I knew would come, I closed my eyes and prayed it would be over quickly, clenching my teeth. I arced my back when the pain ripped through me, dragging my nails into my palms, my wrists still bound together. I wasn't brave. I cried and sobbed and willed the agonizing burn slicing through me like sharp talons to go away. It didn't. It shot through me so fiercely I choked on my own vomit. All I could do was lie in the backseat of the motorcar and suffer the humiliation made worse when I opened my eyes and realized he hadn't removed his Nazi cap when he entered me. That tightened my resolve not to give him the satisfaction of knowing how much he hurt me.

But there was one thing I couldn't keep him from taking.

My virginity.

It's over but I'm still reeling from embarrassment at how he examined me for disease first, muttering under his breath it was 'necessary', implying Parisiennes have low morals, giving him an excuse to make his conquest without guilt.

Or a condom.

I don't know if he had one or just chose not to use it. He did, however, clean himself afterward with a pristine handkerchief which he tossed onto the floor of the motorcar.

The pungent smell made me gag.

He didn't care. All he was interested in was his own pleasure and reminding me he was in charge.

'You please me very much, mademoiselle, not only your blonde goddess looks, but your Gallic spirit excites me,' he said, his eyes flashing. 'But don't get any ideas about escaping. I *will* shoot you and your *maman* and sister if you try any tricks.'

Then he unbound my wrists, put his belt back on, and left me, slamming the passenger door shut. Hard.

I hear him giving orders to the young driver. I will myself to go numb, wondering, *will I have to endure the prodding of the German driver next*? Will the major let me go then? Oh, God, how can I face Maman? Ève? No, I can't. I won't. I'll make Ève swear she'll *never* tell Maman. The de Giocomtes must never know what happened here today. I pray they'll be too stunned when they return and see their art treasures confiscated by the Nazis to inquire why my eyes are dull, glazed, and why my arms and wrists are covered in bruises.

Then a different thought hits me.

I *am* going home. *N'est-ce pas?*

Long minutes tick by in time to my heartbeat echoing loud in my ears. I'm still alone in the back of the touring car when the driver starts the engine. We're on the move. *Where are we going?* I peek out the window. No, this isn't the way back to Maison Bleue. We're speeding down the boulevard past the Rue Royale, then the Champs-Élysées. A shocking fear hits me, turning my stomach, my legs weak. Does the German soldier have orders to shoot me, then toss my body into the cold waters of the Seine?

I'll fight him, I swear.

I touch my aching groin. I want to go home, nurse my wounds, and forget this ever happened.

Isn't that what we women do in wartime? *Forget?*

What other choice do we have?

If I were to lodge a formal complaint against the major, would I find the courage to *describe* the rape? Answer intimate, revealing and embarrassing questions? Speak loud and clear in a courtroom detailing how the SS officer ripped my slip, my underwear with a vicious urgency, whether I was menstruating, how deep he penetrated me, *then* explain what happened... as if I'm supposed to know? I was a virgin. Would they even believe me? Or press me to tell them what other men I had slept with?

Would they go so far to ask me if I enjoyed it?

Then there's the matter of evidence.

I imagine they'll have a German doctor examine me. He'll look, but he won't *see*. His mind would already be made up by the Reich.

I'm guilty, he'll report, because I don't understand the sexual needs of the SS.

The thought makes me shudder with a dark realization the emotional wounds I harbor will never heal, but will rip open again in a shameless exhibition where my sex life is on display. Where *men* make the final decision of whether or not I was raped.

Where is the justice in that?

We pass the Place de l'Étoile and then onto a side street close to the Arc de Triomphe when suddenly we stop and someone yanks the motorcar door open.

'Get out, mademoiselle, now!'

I clench my fists, forgetting my ripped dress, my blood-stained panties. I'm barefoot, shivering, but ready to fight for my life. I look around. A glimmer of hope lightens my mood. The game's changed. An unseemly woman greets me and the heavy perfume of patchouli makes my nostrils twitch.

Her long nails dig into the flesh on my arm as she pulls me toward the brick building with a grayish-blue roof. Modest in its design, but deceptive. I inhale her perfume mixing with the sweet smell of gardenias pinned in her red hair rolled high on her head and gawk at her tight, blue satin dress and ankle-strap high heels. *Who is she?* No French police in sight, but I find no comfort in that when she grins at me, her smile accented by an upper gold tooth. She assesses my appearance with a trained eye. My ripped clothes stained a bright red... a symbol of lost virtue.

Like I'm a broken doll in need of repair.

'Welcome to Chez Mimi, mademoiselle.'

Une maison close. A brothel.

A poster in German hangs outside on the building. I don't need to speak the language to know this place caters to the occupiers.

No Frenchmen allowed. A despair wells in my heart, sinking my hopes of going home. I can't shake off this new fear that I'll see the Nazi major again. It's eating at me that my ordeal isn't over, but is instead intensifying.

The madam, who I assume to be Mimi herself, chatters on as she ushers me inside the five-story residence that looks ordinary on the outside, but inside I see rich velvet curtains, fancy divans and hanging lamps dripping with crystal. A gold spittoon.

'Don't you get no ideas about running away, mademoiselle. I run a tight ship and if you give me trouble...' She narrows her eyes. 'I've got a houseful of Nazis I can stick on your tail.'

She laughs at her own joke, but I say nothing. I've never seen anything like this place. I'm struck by the black onyx staircase, golden gilding on the walls, portraits of women *en déshabillé* posing in lewd positions, teasing. It's late afternoon and the place is quiet except for two girls dancing together to a jazz tune on the record player. A man aged at least sixty diverts his attention from the girls and looks me up and down, his thick eyebrows crossing, then after a flicker of his droopy eyes, he nods. *A customer? I doubt it. He's French. Then who is he? What's he doing here?* He catches me looking at him and picks up a large round coin off the tip tray shaped like a brass mermaid and tosses it to me.

Instinctively, I raise up my arm and catch it. I wince. It's a token, *jeton*, engraved with a large feather and a capital 'M' on one side and the name and address of the brothel on the other.

I step out of the shock and fear making me numb to the world around me and toss the coin back to him. A sudden urge to strike back—*do something, yell at someone*—gives me courage. 'Keep it, monsieur. I'm not on the menu.'

'You seem wounded, mademoiselle,' he says. His big, bushy dark brows frame deep black eyes. They lock with mine so fiercely

I can't look away. 'Be careful. This hen house is filled with she-wolves.'

Strange creature is the first thing that crosses my mind. Dressed in baggy clothes, he's a big man but his shoulders slump, his hands leaning on a battered wooden cane, faded black beret covering his graying hair. Even in the dim light, two military service medals from the Great War sparkle on his navy coat. An old soldier come in from the cold showing off his decorations as a way of defiance. I admire that, but that doesn't mean I can trust him to help me get word to Ève and Maman that I'm safe. Informants lurk everywhere, ready to turn you in. Besides, the madam made it clear I'm a prisoner here.

I try to dissuade his attention by turning, but he doesn't look away. Yet it's not a salacious stare. Instead I sense he's curious, his eyes softening. I hold my dress together in a modest manner to show him I'm not here of my own free will. I must look a fright: disheveled and violated. When I peek over at the old man, he's not smiling.

He knows. But he doesn't judge.

And that comforts me somehow.

'Don't pay attention to Arsène, mademoiselle, he's harmless.' Madame Mimi laughs. '*Eh bien*, Arsène?'

'If only I were twenty years younger, madame.' He sighs heavily.

'If you were, monsieur, you wouldn't be here. Them Boches would have your arse in a POW camp. Now do your job, old soldier, or you'll find yourself sleeping on the pavement tonight.' She laughs. 'He won't bother you none, mademoiselle, not with all them Nazis we get coming here.'

'Why do you allow the old soldier to stay?' I ask, curious. Something about him fascinates me. It's that voice. A low, resonate baritone.

She pushes me along, her hand against my back. 'Before the war it was routine to give disabled veterans a break and let them go upstairs with a girl. Now, not so much.' She laughs. 'Though I doubt that one is capable of more than a smooch on a girl's—'

She whispers a word in my ear that makes me blush. Arsène notices my discomfort and grins wide, then he pulls himself up with his cane. He can barely walk. Then he turns and grabs the ashtrays and empties them into a canvas bag. The connection between us is broken, and for that I'm sad.

I need a friend.

I shiver as the robust madam huffs and puffs like an overstuffed goose and ushers me upstairs. I make my way up the winding staircase, my legs rubbing together, the skin between my thighs chafed and rough... my groin aching with a tearing pain that gets worse with each step. The smell of my attacker mixing with my sweat, the heat of the day making the odor ripe. I want to gag. I refuse to show weakness in front of the madam and I focus on the loud music coming from the phonograph player echoing off the walls, humming along. Anything to get this over with. Praying I can lie down and die.

You can't. There's Maman... Ève.

The memory of my wonderful life with them needles my brain with a shot of hope. The three of us laughing and slurping up hot onion soup on china that belonged to royalty, feasting on beef that melts like butter, indulging on cream and raspberries when Madame de Giocomte invites us to sup with her in the grand dining room when Monsieur is away on business. She loves the company, she says, and she enjoys having her 'girls' around her.

It was all so glorious and I want it back.

Don't give up. The brothel is garish and grim, but for the moment it's a safe haven and for that I'm grateful. But I'm not staying here. I vow to escape, pray Maman takes me back so I can forget this whole thing ever happened. Because that's the only way... forget, *n'est-ce pas*?

On the third floor, the madam swings open a blue door and pushes me into a plain room with torn wallpaper, a cot, a yellowed chamber pot that smells of dried urine, and a dressing table with a mirror. And a... *dumbwaiter*?

She notices my curiosity and chatters on about the old days when nobility and politicians could dine in secrecy with a girl, the food and wine making its way up from the kitchen in the dumbwaiter without anyone seeing the man's identity, how they were her best customers.

Now it's the Nazis. They want a girl cheap, drink too much, and steal tokens from the tip tray as souvenirs. She rummages through the garderobe then hands me a silk kimono in a bright marigold yellow with white flowers painted on it. It's so thin it's almost sheer.

I'm told to wait here.

Why, I don't want to guess.

She looks me up and down, smirks, then spits on her palm and curls loose hair around her fingers. 'You're a lucky girl, mademoiselle.'

'Lucky, madame?' My voice catches in my throat. The idea stops me in my tracks, puts a spin on this horrible day I never see coming.

'Yes... that Major Saxe-Müllenheim chose *you* as a companion. He's very generous to his girls.'

The game has changed. Again.

I'm more determined than ever he'll *never* touch me that way again. What worries me is, if I refuse him, will he hurt Maman and Ève?

I can't let that happen. I know what I have to do.

* * *

September 1940

'Lucie... *Lucie*... over here,' I call out to the sleepy-eyed young maid hugging her ration card and standing in the bread queue outside the boulangerie. It's 7 a.m. and already the line stretches around the block. I showed up here over an hour ago and hid in a dark doorway and waited until the line twisted and turned like a centipede so as not to attract attention.

Lucie turns on her heel, looking everywhere at once. I see she's wearing Madame's old navy coat with the velvet buttons I refitted for her. A tear comes to my eye. How well I remember when she hugged me and said wearing that coat made her feel special.

Now she's my only hope to get word to Ève and Maman, tell them I'm safe and that they must leave Paris.

I haven't much time before Madame Mimi discovers I'm gone.

It was an absolute nightmare of a week, sneaking out twice already, each time hoping Lucie would show up. I almost didn't make it today. Earlier I creeped past a Nazi officer snoring loud, his trousers tossed on the floor in the foyer. A latecomer, but Madame Mimi turns no Nazi away. As I stepped over him, he roused from his sleep and grabbed my ankle, muttering in German, his sweaty hand sliding up and down my calf. It made me sick. I was ready to yank his hand off me, but the urge to warn my *maman* and sister was stronger. I twisted my foot back and forth until he let me go, then sneaked out the front door, snaking my way in and out of alleyways, headed to what I know is the young maid's favorite boulangerie next door to a spice shop. She's smitten with the taste of cinnamon on her toast.

My pulse raced when I saw her, but I can't be too careful. Madame Mimi has spies everywhere. I found that out when I refused to wear the black garters she insisted the major prefers and tossed them away.

I found them under my pillow with a note:

Do what you're told. I have eyes on you.

'*Lucie!*' I call out again in a harsh whisper.

A morning frost makes her shiver. Or is it because when she turns around she recognizes me?

'Justine... is it you?'

'Yes, I—I...'

What can I say? I was attacked by an SS officer and I escaped from a brothel to ask for her help? No. Instead, I tell her, 'Please tell Maman and Ève I'm safe and they must leave Paris for their own good.'

'Justine... what are you saying?'

'*Please*, do as I ask. Tell them,' I beg her. 'I'll be back here tomorrow to make sure they received my message. Now I must go.'

Then I'm off, running down the alley so quickly I don't allow for her to make the slightest refusal or ask any more questions. I keep going, certain in my heart I've done the right thing even if I never see my *maman* and sister again.

But I should have known it was too easy, too smooth, that it's not only the madam who has spies everywhere, but the major. When I return to the boulangerie, Lucie doesn't show up. Nor the next day. Or the next. When I ask if anyone has seen the girl with the red braids in the navy coat, no one will talk, but the fear in their eyes sends me into a tailspin.

Something's wrong.

'I need to know what happened to her,' I ask, walking up and down the queue of people, mostly women, my heart in my throat. '*Please.*'

Finally, a young girl about twelve calls out, 'A man in a trench coat dragged her away, mademoiselle, and pushed her into a big, black motorcar—'

'Gabrielle, shush... *now!*' yells her *maman*, then pulls her daughter close to her.

My ears are ringing with words I don't want to hear. *Lucie gone... taken by the Gestapo... what have they done to her?*

When I return to the brothel, the madam gives me a wary look —she knows where I was—then she needles me with words of guilt I shall never forget. 'An innocent girl was sent to a prison outside Paris, mademoiselle, because of your insolence.'

I can feel her disgust for my actions, but she doesn't elaborate.

I fall to my knees, my whole body shaking. 'Lucie in prison. No... *No!*'

Yes, it's my fault, my terrible, stupid fault. They took her so she couldn't deliver my message to Maman and Ève. I see the truth now. The major has cut me off from my old life and wants to make certain I won't try to go home and no one will come to find me.

I can't stop the cold shivers, the sweats drenching me through to my underwear. Guilt rides my soul for weeks until I come to grips with the truth. I can't deny it. I can't fight the SS *and* the Gestapo and win.

I must accept my fate, that I have no choice but to do what the major wishes of me.

Or he will make Maman and Ève disappear.

Like he did Lucie.

3

PARIS, OCTOBER 1940

Ève

Weeks after that bleak afternoon when I failed to save my sister, after I come to grips with the idea Justine isn't coming back, I cross the boulevard to the police station. I can't go in. Not yet. I stop for the tenth time to cry. *Get it all out*, I tell myself. Every day I'm haunted by the vivid memory of her assaulted by that SS officer, my emotions running hot and furious and sending me into a bout of cold sweats.

And now Lucie is gone.

She never came home from her shopping. Before I could search for her, a French policeman showed up at Maison Bleue and told Madame de Giocomte her maid was arrested trying to sell stolen jewelry on the black market and is imprisoned in Cherche-Midi and won't be coming back. Madame assured him no jewelry was missing, but he insisted.

Then he left.

My heart was racing so fast I felt dizzy when the gendarme showed up that morning, at first believing he had word about Justine. The news about Lucie set the entire household in a tizzy. We all agreed sitting in the kitchen over tea, with Madame forgoing formalities and joining us in saying a prayer for the girl, that something else was at play. That Lucie was a victim of foul play, but the French police covered it up. Why, we don't know, unless the Nazis are behind it.

I run into a similar situation today.

I dry my face with the back of my hand. I can't make my case for Justine like this. A crying female is nothing but a nuisance in the eyes of the law and is pushed aside as quickly as a broom with short straw. Somehow I pull myself together, knowing it's as much for Maman's sake as my own to find out what happened to Justine.

I still can't look directly into her eyes and God knows if I ever can.

She's dead, Maman laments every morning when she sips her strong black tea then picks up her knitting and scrambles around like a squirrel gathering nuts. Justine's body dumped into a common grave at Père Lachaise holding forty, fifty coffins, common for the poor and unknown.

I don't believe her because I don't want to. I know silently she blames me for what happened and if I dare let that thought cross my mind, does that sorrowful look in her placid eyes say she wishes it were me instead?

She was always determined to make a lady out of me like Justine and for a while I let her think she was winning. I gave up telling her about my dream to get a research grant to study the medicinal properties of plants to heal not only the body but the mind. She'll never understand I don't want her to make my skirts shorter, or try smudging my lips with red wax to make them shine. For what? So a man can press his mouth against mine till my lips bleed? I find no pleasure in that, nor in her nagging about my lack of male companionship, that with so many men dead or in prisoner of war camps, I'll end up alone. Like her.

Maman doesn't say it out loud, but I know that's what she's thinking when she brushes my hair at night. It's a ritual we started when Justine and I were little girls and came to Maison Bleue. Two stools. Justine sitting on one, me on the other. Giggling and laughing in the small sitting room in the servants' quarters while Maman brushed our hair before bed for as many strokes as it took for her to tell us the latest house gossip. This was the only time she felt free to speak in a house where the servants glided on air from one room to the other, quiet and obedient.

My hair still falls down to my waist like it did then and is often tangled from me winding it up on my head, but I don't cut it. I feel guilty.

Two stools. One empty.

Losing Justine was too much for Maman. She stopped brushing my hair. And it's my fault.

Punishing myself seems right somehow. It makes me feel better. Today, however, I'm driven to find answers, not guilt. I have to. I'll never forget the joy surging inside me when I got word I'd passed my exams. Also, the sadness Justine wasn't here to share it with me. I know she'd want me to carry on.

I started my classes at the Sorbonne and I feel obligated to do my best for Maman and Madame de Giocomte and Justine. But the guilt festering in me makes it hard to concentrate. I find some joy at the bottom of a Petri dish, my mind challenged and pushing forward with new experiments, throwing myself into my work. A respite from the heavy burden of losing my sister.

But life at the university isn't what I thought it would be. I can't help but notice the unrest among the students that hangs heavy in the air. I fear something is in the wind with every other word whispered on campus about organizing a 'protest' against the Vichy government.

Speak out against the Nazis? That's insane. They are *the government.*

A pinch in my spine makes me uneasy. I know firsthand what the occupiers are capable of and I want nothing to do with their twisted minds and cruelty.

I stay out of the conversation.

Not easy. My time at the university already started out on unstable legs. It hasn't been that long since women were accepted into the Sorbonne, much less the science programs. I've felt the disapproving glances from staff when I walk the halls, my head high. I keep my distance rather than become the butt of their caustic remarks. I find myself avoiding the outspoken deans making defiant speeches about how women don't belong in the sciences. In their minds I can't think on my own. Yes, the old prejudices still exist, especially among professors hanging on from the Great War. So many young men dropped out to serve in the army and are now POWs, leaving women to make up the majority of students this semester. I want to work hard, think of nothing but work, and pray I get that research grant to study the effects of chemicals and plants on common diseases.

Then I realize all this talk about protest against the Nazis is more than just rumors. I was looking for a quiet place to study when I came upon a secret room in the basement. I was shocked to find students printing a newspaper with subversive writings. *Free France. Liberté, Egalité, Fraternité*. Reading the emboldened words, I felt a national pride surge up in me, my cheeks hot, my curiosity piqued. Then a student—I think his name was Bernard—asked me to join their network. I bowed my head and made excuses. I don't need any trouble. I still have bad dreams about the perverted SS officer who abducted and no doubt raped my sister. But I can't let that stop me from seeking answers about what happened to her. I justify to myself that making an inquiry into Justine's disappearance doesn't fall into the category of speaking against the current government.

That was a week ago.

Since then I've kept to myself, working in the laboratory and distancing myself from other students. I find it difficult to make friends since I don't engage in the usual 'girl talk' about boys and makeup. My sister Justine was my best friend and now she's gone. I admit it's lonely and heartbreaking without her to share my adventures with, but I carry on, spending hours into the night at my studies and blocking out everything political in my mind.

Then this morning I came across that pink hair ribbon Justine gave me in my laundry basket. I still have no answers regarding what happened to her. For weeks all I get when I show up at the police station is, *We're investigating the matter, mademoiselle.*

Lies.

I set about once again to find out what happened to her.

I stop pacing, roll up my sleeves. No more dallying. I make my case again to the police sergeant at the front desk, a man in his forties, seasoned and bored. He's rifling through paperwork and pretends not to see me.

'You've got to help me, monsieur. My sister was assaulted, then taken,' I protest in a direct manner, tears filling my eyes. 'Treated as if she were a thing, not a person.'

He gives me an annoyed look, wriggling his nose like farmer caught too long in the pigsty. He's heard my story before.

'I regret to inform you, mademoiselle, the matter is now closed. No women have disappeared from this district.'

'You're wrong. This is my *sister* we're talking about. She's gone... vanished.'

'I'm busy. Please go. *Now.*'

I stare at him, trying to read his eyes, but he turns away from me. Something's changed since I was last here. His words have a distinct edge to them that tells me the local *Kommandant* saw my report and squashed the investigation.

'Perhaps the paperwork was lost, monsieur,' I insist. '*Please*, take down the information again. Justine Beaufort. Blonde, slender build, twenty years old. She was abducted by an SS officer when he invaded our home and attacked her. He took her with him.'

'Against her will?' he challenges me.

I ignore his question. I can't tell him Justine had no choice but to go with him to save Maman and me. Instead, I say, 'We haven't seen or heard from her since. She'd never leave and then not contact us. I'm telling you, he raped her!'

Snarling, he stands up and sticks his nose in my face. '*Mon Dieu*, mademoiselle, are you a fool? Accusing an esteemed officer of the Reich of such a vile act?'

'I was *there*. I *saw* him assault her. It's *your* job to investigate what happened to my sister.'

'Get out of my office, *now*. I can't help you.'

'You mean you *won't* help me.' My tone is accusing, but I'm not backing down. 'She disappeared into the SS underbelly and I haven't seen or heard from her since.'

The desk sergeant spins around to see if anyone heard my insult, then returns his attention to the paperwork on his desk all stamped with a black swastika. He comes back at me with the same answer I heard before.

'I repeat, mademoiselle, the investigation is *closed*.' He dismisses me like a puff of smoke irritating his eyes.

I repeat what I saw, but he insists what I'm suggesting is impossible, that there have been no reports of assault by German officers. They have shown nothing but 'proper behavior' since the Occupation began.

'Most likely your sister is another bored Parisienne who sold her body to the Boches for perfume and wine,' he says. 'Then she ran off.'

'You're wrong, monsieur. I *saw* the SS officer rip her dress and make cruel, disgusting talk, then drag her outside—'

He cuts me off with a wave of his hand. 'Dangerous talk, mademoiselle, and if the wrong people hear you, they'll label you a political dissident and send you to Drancy.'

Drancy? Since when is it a place for dissidents? I heard the unfinished housing complex outside Paris was turned into a camp for Spanish refugees.

'I guarantee you, mademoiselle,' he continues, 'a German officer would *never* take a Frenchwoman against her will.' He tosses the crushed form into a metal trash container. 'There are Nazi-approved brothels in Paris to satisfy the needs of our German friends.'

Friends? Doesn't he mean occupiers?

'Not how I see it, monsieur.' I grip the sides of his desk. 'More like that Nazi uniform gives them the license to take any woman they want.'

He clears his throat, then threatens to report me to the Gestapo if I don't stop asking questions.

'I assure you, mademoiselle, I can have the German secret police here in minutes to interrogate you.'

'But, monsieur—'

'*Eh,* mademoiselle?' He stands up, challenging me. I'm taller than he is, but that only infuriates him further. I swear he's standing on his toes.

I can't help the disappointment sinking any hope in my heart for justice. *It's not fair, it's not,* I lash out at this weak bureaucrat, a cold rage teeming in my voice, then I go quiet when he picks up the phone, his grim eyes glaring at me, warning me to back down before he makes the call.

I try one last time.

'Her name is Justine... Justine Beaufort,' I say with a fierceness I don't apologize for. 'Don't ever forget it, monsieur. I won't. Nor will I forget how a Frenchman let her down. I hope you can sleep at night, for I'm certain my sister isn't the first woman abused by our German "friends".'

The desk sergeant is puzzled by my relentless questioning, but he's careful not to look my way as he puts down the phone. When he does glance at me, it's a kinder man I see, his lined face softening. 'I wish I could help you, mademoiselle, but it will only get you into trouble if you keep searching for your sister.' He sighs heavily. 'Since she hasn't contacted you or returned home, I fear she is dead.'

I'll get nothing more out of him.

I turn and leave like a wounded dove, its wings clipped. My sister Justine isn't entitled to even a mark of the pen. She's erased. Gone. As if she never existed. Giving her soul no place to go. And her heart broken. That saddens me more than anything, more so because I have no choice but to let go of my quest for justice or face the mental cruelty of the Gestapo... or God help me, physical torture at their hands because I defied them.

But I shall never forget the lovely, passionate, gifted young woman who could be capricious one moment and then quiet the next, absorbed in her designs, then squeeze my hand and tell me she'd always be there for me, her little sister.

And she was.

But I failed her.

I whisper, 'I *will* find a way to avenge you, Justine. Bring you justice.'

Then with a defiant lift of my chin, I pull up the collar on my camel wool coat and head home. The October breeze turns so cold, the brown leaves falling from the chestnut trees shiver before they hit the ground. There's a bite to the air, so cold it warps my face with a sharp sting. I thought I could keep going, wishing Justine would show up and we'd go back to being a family again. Maman, my sister, and me. That we could pretend the rape never happened. That we could survive.

But only if we kept quiet.

I was a fool. I can't hide from what's happening here in Paris, can't go on pretending things are as they were. They're not. I see it everywhere, including Maison Bleue when the de Giocomtes scurried home from their holiday. Madame de Giocomte told Maman and me about how the Nazis started requisitioning villas for their officers, then grabbing the best thoroughbreds from the stables to send to Germany and harassing the population with curfews and laws. She feared for their safety only to return to Paris to find her home looted of its Impressionist works. Every day she looks out the long window, fearing the Nazis will return.

Her husband is a different sort.

The Jewish patriarch of the family, Itzhak de Giocomte, is stiff-backed and traditional and employs a household of trusted servants he knows by name. He's always kind to Maman, asking her if she needs more silk, wool to make Madame de Giocomte stylish, make her happy. That was *before* the Occupation. Before they left for the coast. Since then, I hear him complaining to his wife how the Germans are flush with cash after the French government was forced to pay the costs of the Occupation. *Where to spend it?* He believes they're lured to stealing art by the prospect of a good investment they can resell on the black market or ship back to Germany.

Art.

His art.

I feel a tug at my heart, remembering how his voice cracked, knowing the emotional and financial loss he'd sustained because of the looting. A banker and collector, he's a stern man and he loves his wife but he wears blinders regarding his position since the Occupation. After they returned from Deauville, it was Madame de Giocomte who insisted her sister-in-law and her daughter and children should go to their villa south of Paris to stay safe. But Madame de Giocomte herself chose to return to Paris, still believing their social position would protect her and her husband from further harassment. Still, the damage is done. Monsieur de Giocomte now spends his time locked up in his library in his private rooms upstairs, finishing up the cognac and brandy he hid from the Germans, while Madame plays her cello to soothe her soul. And working in the garden to keep her precious blooms and her hope from withering away.

She worries about her husband's mental health. He still can't believe the Nazis 'confiscated' his collection of Impressionists *and* the avant-garde painting of Justine and me. He had commissioned the artist to paint Madame de Giocomte with her cello, but she was feeling ill that day so she insisted the artist paint Justine and me instead.

How well I remember...

It was a warm, spring day back in 1936 when I heard the muffled voices of two women laughing and talking in the drawing room. When I tiptoed past the half-open sliding door, I couldn't contain my curiosity. Who was this marvelous creature in a purple and gold silk dress, long, shiny beads, and a chic cloche hat with a big white feather? This description is courtesy of my sister Justine, who in all her worldliness of turning sixteen was already a fashion expert. I was fourteen. What did I know? We'd seen the woman arrive in a fancy motorcar with a winged ornament on the hood and blank canvases and a large wooden box I later discovered was filled with paints and brushes.

'She's a famous artist,' Justine whispered in my ear, breathless and excited. Seems Cook spilled the beans. She was all a tither making tea and cakes for the lovely Mademoiselle. 'She's here to paint Madame.'

'*Ooh...*' was all I could say, squeezing Justine's hand. A real artist here at Maison Bleue. *Imagine.*

Giggling, we peeked through the half-open door, taking turns.

'I regret I'm not well, mademoiselle,' we could hear Madame saying, sniffling. 'A terrible head cold. My nose is red and my eyes are puffy.' She sighed. 'I look terrible.'

'You are beautiful, Madame de Giocomte, but I can reschedule if you like when I'm back from Cannes.'

'Did you hear, Ève?' Justine said, sighing. 'She's off to the Riviera.'

'*Ooh...*' was all I could say again.

'I'd like to make a quick sketch of your gown though, madame, before I leave, so I can plan my color scheme.'

'*Bien.*'

'Oh, Ève, look,' Justine said, 'she's drawing Madame.'

'I want to see... *please.*'

'Wait. Oh, she's a wonderful artist.'

'My turn, Justine.'

I admit I got too rambunctious and tried to push the door open a little wider. Oh, no, there it went, the double doors sliding open and two very embarrassed teenage girls tumbling into the drawing room and landing at the feet of the beautiful, dark-haired artist. *Oh-oh, now we're in trouble,* I thought.

'And who are these pretty girls?' she asked Madame, laughing.

'The Beaufort Sisters. They're like granddaughters to me.'

'They're charming.' She looked us over, asking us to stand up, turn around, smile, then: 'I'd like to paint them. Would you mind, Madame de Giocomte?'

'I would be honored.' She turned to us. 'Ready to be famous, mamselles?'

We said *Yes!* at the same time, and so *The Daisy Sisters* was born. Yet I often wonder what would have happened if the artist *had* painted Madame, and the painting of Justine and me never existed?

Yes, I wonder...

Meanwhile, we're all faced with food rationing for meat and bread, though Cook secures fresh eggs and fruit, even chicken, from her cousin in the country. We're surviving, but what happened to my sister shows me what the Nazis are capable of. The Boches call Paris a city of 'love and fashion', but they have no regard for us as a people, only as dolls they can place in a fancy cardboard house, then discard at whim. No one dares to speak up. Why? Because the Nazis treat us like puppets and a puppet has no voice of its own.

I will no longer be a marionette.

I *shall* speak up. I know what I have to do, what's been festering in my mind, but I keep pushing it away. Not any more.

Here in Paris, there *are* others like me who aren't afraid to defy the Nazis, who speak the truth. I want to avenge Justine and I'm willing to risk my life to make it happen because she gave up her virginity to save mine.

It's time for me to return to the basement in the Sorbonne.

And join the fight.

4

PARIS, OCTOBER 1940

Justine

'I hear Her Royal Highness is leaving us today,' pipes a snippy girl with an ivory feather boa wrapped around her neck. I ignore her. She never stops harassing me.

I resume rolling up a pair of silk stockings, feeling guilty since there are few pairs left in Paris, then pack them in a small pouch. Still, I can't help but overhear the whispers around me. *'The major's girl' gets what she wants.* I want to laugh. I'm nobody's girl in spite of what they think. I'm a prisoner here. And now I'm being transferred to *where?* The SS officer's apartment? A humbling and terrifying thought that chills me. That I have no say in the matter. Nor do I understand why Major Saxe-Müllenheim brought me here to 'recover' when he could have any girl he wants.

When I mentioned it to Madame Mimi, she threw her head back and laughed. 'Don't you get it, mademoiselle? The SS officer is obsessed with exerting his power over women, over *you*, possessing them, calling them "spoils of war".' Then she leaned in to me and her familiar scent of patchouli filled my nostrils. 'You're simply the latest female to fuel his needs and desires, *eh bien*?'

She made no mention what those desires are, but I imagine rape is at the top of the list.

'The major is cruel and disgusting,' I told her, then spit on her fancy carpet.

The SS do it, so why not me?

Irate, she grabbed me by the hair. 'Don't be stupid, mademoiselle, the Gestapo is everywhere and you should shut your mouth.'

I've no doubt she's more interested in saving her own hide than mine. She has the routine down pat, insisting I rest, heal, giving me soup swimming with meat and onions and carrots with strong coffee and keeping her clientele away from me, making me suspect I'm not the first girl she's nurtured for the major since the Occupation began. He pays her well, for which she's grateful after being closed for months because of the war. It took some time but the German superintendent-in-charge of 'entertainment' swore all *maisons closes* will be open by Christmas.

'And her not turning one trick since she got here,' snaps another girl, bringing me back to the moment. I shudder at the thought. I don't judge them. I have no right. Only God can see into their souls and judge. I imagine each girl has a story to tell, but they all have the same ending and that's what makes it so sad. All I know is that I'm leaving this morning for God knows where. Madame ordered me to pack my things. Hairbrush, tooth powder, a chemise for sleeping. I'm leaving the flimsy kimono for the next girl. The major sent me new clothes, including leather shoes. A slight tremble makes my hand shake. I'm confident I'm not going to my execution. The Nazis wouldn't waste silk stockings and fine black leather pumps on a corpse.

'I heard an SS colonel offered Madame Mimi *twice* the going rate of twenty francs for her services,' chimes in the first girl, lighting a cigarette, 'but Madame refused him, telling him "the major's girl" has no inspection card.'

Really? I raise a brow. I hadn't heard that story, though I'm aware of the health certificate each prostitute is required to show her Nazi client proving that she's been 'inspected' that week by a doctor.

'You *wish* you were so lucky,' adds Marie, a petite young woman with a seductive black beauty patch on her left cheek but kindness in her heart. She's the only girl who's shown me the slightest bit of humanity since I've been cooped up here. She revealed to me where Madame hides her lavender soap and how to fasten the sanitary towels to a 'fancy' garter belt the girls use when they're 'on the rag.' Except I don't need them.

I missed my monthly time.

Which scares the hell out of me.

Nerves, anxiety, I tell myself. Didn't my menses stop when I nearly failed my exams? It was only because of Ève's tutoring that I passed mathematics. My little sister saved me, taking time to grill me until I got it right. Oh, do I miss her. I have no doubt Ève passed her exams. I wonder how she's doing at the university. She has a brilliant mind. I bet she's running rings around her professors. It never occurs to me to believe otherwise, that she'd drop out because of what happened to me. That she couldn't cope. No, she's strong in mind *and* smart, but I worry what will happen to her if she asks too many questions. I haven't tried to contact her since my 'little talk' with Madame Mimi after Lucie disappeared. I have no choice but to let Ève and Maman believe I'm dead.

I am, aren't I?

Broken inside, no longer a virgin, I remain unfeeling to the world around me. I have no future and the girl I was is no more.

Which makes me no better than the girls here who have no

choice but to service the Nazi officers. I'm still puzzled why this SS major is running his own French version of what the madam calls a 'love camp'. She confirmed my earlier suspicion that I'm not the first woman he brought here when a French physician examined me. 'I won't let that Nazi doctor near "the major's girls",' she vowed, 'him with his dirty spatula poking them everywhere.' All virgins from what I gather that he raped and sent here before deciding their fate. The madam is reluctant to tell me what happened to them. I can only guess, but according to her, the girls that the major rejects are sent to a lower-class brothel for enlisted German soldiers and lost forever in a black hole.

I believe her.

The prostitutes in Madame Mimi's brothel have similar horror stories. Like Marie. She confided to me how she was kidnapped in a movie theater when the woman next to her—Mimi, I assume by the hard look Marie gives her when they're in the same room—jabbed her leg with a hypodermic needle. At first she thought it was nothing. Before she could escape, she collapsed and her male accomplice carried her to a waiting motorcar. She's been here ever since, her life changed forever. She's at the mercy of the madam and must follow the rules, like girls aren't allowed to sit in the window to solicit or she'll be kicked out with only the clothes on her back. She can't walk the streets. Her face is known to local police.

Am I destined for the same?

What makes me fearful is, if I allow the SS officer to take care of me, that makes me a collaborator. No one will believe I'm a prisoner. And what about Ève and Maman? And anyone else who sees me with him, including the de Giocomtes? This wonderful family took us in when we were children, and our widowed mother, after our father died in a street fight.

No, I can't let that happen.

Escape? I still ponder that thought. What's to stop me from running away to the Unoccupied Zone with Ève and Maman, then to Switzerland or Spain? That thought crosses my mind as I pack the new dresses, stockings, intimates, and shoes sent to me in fancy boxes from shops on the Rue de Rivoli and Rue Saint-Honoré. Perfume from the House of Doujan.

No, Ève deserves her chance to study at the university in spite of the Nazis. She'll make a brilliant scientist and I won't take that away from her. And Maman would never leave Madame de Giocomte. Her loyalty to the woman who saved her daughters from poverty and the depravity of those who preyed upon us is above reproach.

How many times have I heard her tell the story of how in 1929, our father, a flamboyant conman who worked the brasseries and gambling when he wasn't acting as the strong arm at the cabarets, tried to help a friend set upon by a gang he owed money to and our papa was killed in a knife fight. Maman nearly died from grief when she lost her man and later we found out Papa owed gambling debts and back rent on our small apartment in the ninth arrondissement on Rue Rochechouart. The landlord tossed us out onto the streets with only our clothes, dishes and pots, a chair with the stuffing sticking out of it, and Maman's old sewing machine, our belongings piled high into a vegetable cart smelling of sweet country onions.

She loved that old black lacquered machine painted with roses and daisies and curly-Qs in white ink. Papa bought it for her to make a christening gown for me when she reminisced about how when she was working in a convent to earn her keep, she learned the fine art of weaving lace and knitting and delicate stitching.

She fell hard for the slick-talking, tall handsome man who helped the priest build the new rectory. Papa Beaufort was a gambler, convincing the priest to invest church funds in a carnival to feed the poor of Paris. Maman was sixteen and worked the kissing booth and had no idea until years later that the handsome man who'd bought all her kisses had also absconded with the church's profits. She made him pay it back, but he never stopped gambling. Her heart wept for this man who was good to her, never abused her, and loved his daughters, but he had a disease. Gambling. And nothing on God's earth could cure him. But he did buy her that sewing machine and she'd always have that to remember him by.

With Maman widowed and penniless with two little girls clinging to her patched skirts, we ended up in the slums in a wooden one-room shack in northern Paris. Maman took in sewing, but she was determined her girls weren't going to live in a dangerous place where vermin crawled out of the woodwork at night to prey upon us. Cockroaches *and* men with unnatural urges that sickened her. So Maman haunted the flea market and the backdoors of the cabarets, begging for scraps of silk, velvet, taffeta, and lace left over from making costumes. She went through the trash behind the design houses like a *chiffonier*, rag picker. Pulling out remnants of rich, soft pieces of smooth spring linen and wintry velvets.

She used her last *sou* to buy spools and spools of thread and basting for the seams and knee-high, pristine white socks and white polish for our old buckled shoes. Then, using her talents, she dressed us up in pretty outfits she made from the fancy remnants. I was so proud when she asked me to help her sew on the red bows and white ruffles and big ivory taffeta sleeves, while Ève built a toy house with the empty wooden spools. 'We're going to have a house of our own someday,' she said, then cried when her spool house fell down. I hugged her tight and assured her someday we *would* have a house.

I never dreamed Maman's fantastical scheme would lead us to Maison Bleue.

To finish off our outfits, Maman let me design big, floppy sun hats using pink and white tulle and soft red ribbons under our chins, then Maman gave us each a white rose to carry which she'd begged off the local flower woman who was touched by her sad story. Then she took us to feed the swans in the Bois at Saint-James pond to show us off—well, pretend to feed them, actually; we had no bread to toss at the beautiful creatures—hoping someone would be so impressed by our outfits, they'd ask her, *Who made the pretty dresses for the little girls?*

And she'd find decent work.

And get her girls out of the slums.

It was a windy day with the trees shaking their leaves hard like a housemaid beating a rug with a stick. Ève and I showed off our dresses, each of us wearing one of Maman's white wedding gloves —I wore the left while Ève wore the right—and we circled the pond like we were dancing on a carousel, doing our best to avoid getting water splashed on our feet from store merchants washing the sidewalk with big pails of water, then jumping back when a horse and wagon raced by. The hardest part was ogling the long baguettes piled up high on a pushcart when a man in a white suit and funny cone hat pedaled past us, the heavenly smell of fresh, hot crisp bread sending our girlish noses into ecstasy.

The truth was, we were so poor we couldn't even afford to smell it.

The afternoon wore on; we wore down. We had some impressed looks from well-to-do, fashionable passers-by, several nice comments, but no takers. Maman was disappointed and so tired from her efforts that she overheated and had to go sit in the shade. She told us to keep walking, that she'd catch up. Ève wanted to go home, but I insisted we couldn't let Maman down. Ève pursed her lips and stuck out her lower lip like she does when she's upset, but she agreed. I know I made her feel bad, but she adores Maman so off we went to try again. We had to. We had no food except for a can of sardines we found tossed away outside a restaurant along with an apple and an orange. We gave Maman the orange and Ève and I split the apple later, grateful it was a whole apple and no one had taken a bite out of it before tossing it away.

Thinking about that apple made my mouth water and I let go of my sister's hand for a moment. Just a moment, giving her time to do what children do... toss stones into the pond, making a swan with a belly the size of a pumpkin angry, *very* angry. The haughty creature waddled out of the pond and hissed at Ève so loud, my little sister squealed in horror and burst into tears. Much to my surprise, a beautiful, elegant woman in her late forties wearing a tailored navy suit, matching kid gloves and a big, feathered hat came to my little sister's rescue and shooed the swan away. She'd been sitting on a bench reading a fashion magazine when she heard Ève scream.

I'd noticed her earlier on our walk, thinking she had such style. Now I knew she was also good and kind, so I didn't hesitate for a second when the capricious wind blew off Madame de Giocomte's hat and it landed in the pond.

Before the pumpkin-bellied swan ripped it apart with its beak, I vaulted over the low wire fence, snagging my dress on the twisted wire, jumped into the water, and snatched up Madame's hat. I waved it over my head like a battle flag. Madame de Giocomte was laughing, clapping her hands together and so was Ève. Maman was horrified when she heard her child scream and came running, then she became angry when she saw my torn dress, then embarrassed... then Madame invited us to tea.

We filled our tummies with strawberry jelly croissants and fresh, cold milk and told her our story.

That afternoon she offered Maman a job as a seamstress.

Madame de Giocomte brought us to Maison Bleue in 1930 when I was ten and Ève was eight. She admitted later she didn't need another seamstress, but Maman's innovation to find work and her devotion to her daughters had touched her heart. A heart that for so long had ceased to beat to a happy rhythm. Madame had lost her own ten-year-old daughter to a childhood disease and later suffered two miscarriages. When she met Maman, our mother was a young woman in her twenties. Madame de Giocomte was enchanted by her strength and ingenuity and determination to keep her little family together. The two women became close, sharing their pain and their hopes for the future, never once letting their different religious backgrounds come into play or their social differences divide them. It was an amazing thing to watch as I grew up, the two of them putting their heads together to solve a housekeeping problem, laughing over tea and cakes, Madame de Giocomte swooning over the pretty dresses Maman whipped up for her, Maman laboring over lace cuffs or working late into the night to finish hemming a gown for Madame while she insisted our *maman* get new leather shoes or have her hair done at her expense.

I soon realized Maman had become the daughter she'd lost.

And Ève and I became her granddaughters. We enjoyed all the grandmotherly spoiling that came with it. Frilly dresses, chocolate and sweets, the best schooling. And dolls. Beautiful dolls that I adored, though Ève was more thrilled when Madame gave her free rein to grow whatever she wanted in the exotic Maison Bleue garden.

Growing up, I was in awe of the woman. Madame Ekaterina de Giocomte was a renowned beauty in her time with ties to a Russian political figure who became her first husband. She met him when she was a young woman barely out of her teens and chosen to play the cello for the Tsar's daughters. She'd been a child progeny and came from a prestigious Jewish family, though her parents were killed in a mysterious accident when their sleigh overturned during a snowstorm outside St Petersburg. The Tsarina insisted the talented young woman stay with them, then Ekaterina fell in love with an aristocrat with a changing political agenda who married her, but it didn't keep her safe. Her husband died protecting her when they were identified as aristocrats and attacked in the streets. She fled to Paris alone with her cello. A woman of intelligence and style who always wore taupe kid gloves and an amethyst brooch reputed to have belonged to her name-sake, Catherine of Russia.

Maman loves to tell the story about that day and how fate and an angry swan changed our lives. Which leads me to now think of *my* fate.

Just then, I see a cloaked figure coming up the backstairs of the brothel, his hands folded into his wide sleeves, his wide-brimmed hat pulled low over his face. His presence causes the hairs on the back of my neck to lift in a holy moment. I recognize Father Armand, a priest at Sacré-Coeur where Maman, Ève, and I attend Mass on the holidays. He's always so busy with the children and the elderly, blessing them and saying prayers, I'm certain he doesn't remember me.

'What brings you here, Father?' I ask.

He looks up and smiles at me, not judging me. By the concern shading his brown eyes a deep cocoa, he believes me to be one of the madam's girls. 'God's work, mademoiselle.'

Then he enters the 'sick room' where a young woman lies ill, a new recruit for the brothel, pretty face and long legs, but when Madame Mimi discovered she had 'the disease', she sent for the police. I heard the girl earlier begging the madam to get a priest before they took her away, that she wanted forgiveness, that she was weak for not fighting harder to fend off the German soldiers who'd raped her, leaving her no recourse but to leave home and end up here.

I peek through the door, the anguish and fear on the girl's face making my heart break. *Why does she have to suffer so for what men did to her?*

I think about Ève and her obsession with curing different diseases—she doesn't think I listen to her but I do—and how if anyone can find those cures, it will be my sister.

Sadly, I'll never know if she does.

With that thought draining hope from me, I hover outside the door, listening to Father Armand comforting the girl, telling her the Nazis can take our bodies but not our souls and that our faith keeps us pure. And God will not judge her.

But people do, I add. People judge... and hate.

My gut tightens.

And that's a living death unto itself.

Which makes me question if I have the courage to seek a way out of my shame, to do what women have done since the beginning of time when the bloom of their youth is ripped from them, to ease the burden for Ève and Maman... and myself, too.

The motorcar to pick me up won't be here for an hour. There's still time, *n'est-ce pas?*

I race up to the attic. I'll find something, do something to end this mental pain, making me deride myself for what happened every day. I'm not ashamed to admit I'm weak, or is it because I'm frightened? Scared out of my wits the major will take me again and again. Even if the first burning pain is now but a haunting memory, the mental and emotional anguish is too much for me to endure.

I'm a sinner and I... no, wait, I'm not the sinner but I'm paying for the sinner's deed.

Where is the justice in that?

Are you listening, God?

He doesn't answer. At that moment, God and I are no longer talking.

And because no one can predict when the debilitating grief that overcomes a woman raped will come, whether it's a day, a week, a year later... the moment when it all comes flooding back and the horror of cold hands ripping you open and his hot flesh touching you *there* in your most private place hits you again and again and won't stop, you believe the only answer is to do something you *know* is wrong. You can't stop yourself. Because the idea of ending that pain is a sugar rush to your brain that promises relief and propels you forward to take that final step.

And for me that time is now.

* * *

'You will suffer a slow, horrible death, mademoiselle, if you swallow what's in that bottle.'

I know that resonate voice, though I'm standing in semi-darkness and I can't see him.

Arsène. The older man who acts as part-bodyguard, part-cleaner in the brothel.

I sneaked up here to the attic to get away from the prattle and arguing of the mesdemoiselles, fifteen 'beautiful girls for your pleasure,' or so boasts the poster on the wall in the foyer. He must have followed me up here to the top floor. Tiny, cramped, filled with odds and ends and boxes overflowing with feathers in purple, blue. Wigs... scarlet, blond.

And a copper-brown glass bottle half-filled with a solution.

I was looking for something, *anything* to end it all. A strong rope, rusty dagger. Then I found the bottle. Poison? Arsenic, perhaps? Why else would the madam store it in the attic? To kill the rats. *Alors*, only the four-legged ones.

'It's arsenic,' Arsène confirms. 'The resident rat chewed off the label.'

I don't know if he's serious or joking. It doesn't matter. It's still arsenic.

'I suspected it was poison. I've seen my sister Ève experimenting with arsenic. Sulfide mineral, I think she said it was. I remember it because of its yellow color.' *Like daisies. Why did I ever think of that?* 'She's a scientist.'

'Your sister would never want you to end your life, mademoiselle.'

'She already thinks I'm dead.'

He takes a step toward me. I move back. He stops. 'Whatever shame you feel, mademoiselle, whatever heavy guilt rattles about in your heart tormenting you like a devil's lament, you're not like the others.'

'Aren't I?' I open the bottle and sniff. Unlike cyanide with its bitter almond smell, arsenic has no smell. It's so hot up here, I'm surprised the bottle doesn't smell like garlic which, according to Ève, occurs when arsenic is heated. Then I smile. Weak. Effortless. But a smile nonetheless. Why I'm remembering my little sister's scientific ramblings right now makes no sense to me.

Unless it's because I'm stalling.

'*Non*, mademoiselle, you've a good, kind heart.'

'You hardly know me, Arsène.'

'I see into your soul, mademoiselle, the way you treat others in the brothel.' He opens the tiny rectangular window to let in air. 'Never talking down to the help, coming to the aid of the tired maids burdened by fear, their backs breaking when they wash the dirty, soiled sheets the Nazis lie on, or how you have a soft word and salve for that girl when the SS officer beat her for pleasure.

You even assist old Arsène when I need a helping hand.' He pulls in his breath, then in a calm, steady voice says, 'Hand me the bottle, mademoiselle, slowly... please.'

'Why shouldn't I end my misery?' I raise the bottle to my lips. *Do I have the courage?* 'Nobody would miss me. It'll all be over then.'

'No, mademoiselle, it would *not* be over. *I* would miss you.'

Arsène pushes the bottle out of my hand so quickly I don't blink when it smashes onto the floor. *Shock... surprise.* I shake my head, trying to focus on what he said.

'No, *no*, I don't believe you. I'm not worth anything to anyone after what the major did to me.'

'It wasn't your fault. You did nothing wrong.'

'It doesn't matter. The guilt twists itself around my soul. I went *willingly* to him. I didn't fight hard enough. I tried to push him away, *I did*—' I break down, tears streaming down my face. 'I had to go with him, *I had to*... or he would have shot Ève and Maman.'

Arsène sets his jaw in a hard line; his body stiffens. He takes a step and leans down toward me and, for a moment, I think he's going to hold me in his arms, but he stops. Why that gives me goose bumps, I don't know. A fatherly gesture, surely. I lost *mon père* when I was a little girl, the story tainted when Maman tells it, a man torn between two loves... her and gambling. He could only have one of them.

I don't think about that now. All that matters is that this old soldier makes me feel ashamed. Not about the rape—I'll never get over that—but about how I'm reacting to it.

'You're right, Arsène, ending it all would be too easy. God would never forgive me, nor would Ève.' I smirk. 'I don't know who I fear most.'

'You need fear no one, mademoiselle. You can't blame yourself for the cruelty and depravity of the Nazi officer. Blame *him*. *He's* the guilty one.'

'No one will believe me. I can't live with the shame.'

'You'd let the Nazi win?' he shouts. 'Is that what you want?'

'No, of course not,' I stutter. 'But what can I do?'

'Fight him, mademoiselle, him and the whole damn Nazi regime. You're not alone in wanting to oust the occupiers and I assure you it *will* happen. Not today, not tomorrow, but soon. The people of Paris aren't blind. It's becoming obvious the Nazis' plan to invade Britain is failing and the Germans can't stop us from listening to the Free French radio broadcasts from London *asking* us to resist.'

Madame Mimi forbids the girls to listen to anything but German broadcasts. *To learn the language*, she says. Poppycock. She doesn't *want* us to know.

'If we give up now, mademoiselle,' he continues, 'we're done. France is done. Do you understand?'

'Yes, Arsène, but I'm frightened.'

'Of course you are, and I'm asking a lot of you. God knows I would take you away from here if I could—'

'You would?' My eyes widen.

His thick brows furrow. 'Yes... I would.'

I think a moment about what he said, staring at the broken bottle of poison while the wheels turn in my scattered brain. *Do I dare ask him to help me get word to Ève?* Or would I be putting him in danger? In spite of his age, I see him as a man strong in his convictions and no stranger to taking risks. I *have* to try. I start to ask him if he can help me when we hear a commotion outside the brothel.

I look out the window and, my God, I see students flooding the street. A steady roar of voices lifted up in protest, shouting en masse for Madame to let them in. When she refuses, they shout louder, some chanting '*Vive la France*', other tearing down the posters tacked onto the building denoting the brothel is for 'German soldiers only' and screaming insults and expletives at the Nazis staring out the ground floor windows.

I start away from the open window when a familiar voice rises above the fray, a strong, beautiful voice that fills my heart with the warmth of a sunny day.

Ève.

I gasp. 'My sister is down there.'

'What?'

'Yes... there she is.' I lean out the window. 'The tall girl in the plain camel coat.' I smile. 'She's wearing the pink ribbon I gave her.'

That brings tears to my eyes.

'*Alors*, mademoiselle,' Arsène whispers in my ear, his hot breath on the back of my neck comforting somehow. 'I told you. You are *not* alone.'

The danger is over in minutes when an SS officer races onto the scene on a motorcycle, screeching his tires and firing his pistol into the air, scattering the students, but it was a beautiful moment. Not just a small victory for the people of Paris, but for me. If only I could have run to my sister, cupped her face in my hands and explained to her *why* I'm here, what happened that day, beg for her forgiveness, but I can't. I know now after what happened to Lucie, the Gestapo could be watching... *waiting* for me to rush to her, then drag her away before my eyes. If I ask Arsène to help, would it be any different? He may be a brave, old soldier with dreams of freeing France from the occupiers, but I can't take the chance of him dying in prison because he tried to help me. No, I'll have to find some other way to get word to Ève.

I shall always cherish seeing her again.

Meanwhile, Arsène insists I go back to my room before Madame Mimi discovers I'm gone. I doubt she'll notice; she's probably more shaken up by the protest. A bit of mirth makes me smile. I imagine her offering free wine to her German customers, sweet-talking them with her raspy voice into needing 'relaxation' of the female kind after their 'ordeal'.

I turn to Arsène. In a moment of relief, I lay my hand upon his forearm and squeeze it. I swear I feel his hard muscle tighten, surprising me. I tell myself the man has strong arms because he needs that strength to pull himself along. I avoid sweeping my eyes across his broad chest, still muscular at his age, or is it because I'm so lonely for the strength and kindness of a man that I see what I want to see?

I chalk it up to my frayed nerves and end our strange conversation.

I can still hear Arsène's words in my head when the major's driver shows up to fetch me, waiting for me in the foyer of the brothel, his head on a swivel, gazing at the 'lovelies' giving him the eye. I get into the motorcar and ask no questions, but not before I look upward to the window on the second floor and see the old soldier looking down at me. Arsène. I blink. Am I imagining it? Or is he standing tall and straight, a determined look on his face? The sun glimmers on his skin, erasing the lines of time. And for a moment... just a moment, I see him as he must have looked as a young man. Strong, defiant. He gives me a salute and I nod.

Then he's gone.

A new sadness enters my heart. I shall miss him.

* * *

In the days and weeks to come, I adhere to my part of the bargain. A bargain with the devil.

The man who raped me. Major Saxe-Müllenheim.

'You look lovely, mademoiselle,' he says in a low, commanding voice, 'with the moonlight glimmering off your skin.'

'Moonlight provided by direct order of the Reichsmarschall,' I say wryly.

He smiles. 'We Germans own *everything* in Paris, even the moon.'

'And everyone.'

'Yes, *everyone*.' He laughs while I feel a growing sense of frustration, wondering when, *if* he intends to force himself on me tonight, groping and pinching.

I'm lying on a blue velvet *méridienne* in the bedroom of the apartment on Rue des Martyrs, my very own special prison. I rarely leave the flat on the first floor. I have a housekeeper who comes on Tuesdays and Thursdays, but other than that, I see no one but the major. He never sits with me on the terrace or dines with me in front of the fireplace. Our encounters always take place in the bedroom. Me semi-nude in a revealing pose; him in full uniform, including gloves, observing every inch of me. I feel as exposed as the young French queen on her wedding night coupling with an awkward sovereign, the event turning into a public spectacle.

With the major as my audience.

I will *not* go willingly into his arms, not now or ever. He's fondled my breasts several times since I moved in here after I left the brothel, but nothing more. Yet. Interestingly, he hasn't kissed me again since that first time, for which I am eternally grateful, but I watch his flashing eyes moving up and down my body, his gaze fixing on my breasts, my nipples peaked and pointing through the skimpy silk dressing gown he ordered me to wear.

I feel sick.

'How many young women did you terrify today with your sexual demands, monsieur?' I venture forth with as much calmness as if I were asking him what he ate for breakfast. I've grown bolder in my repartee on our evening meets, but that doesn't mean I'm not terrified of his unpredictable behavior. The way he can turn on me in an instant. Smiling at me one moment, then snarling and calling me a French slut the next.

That hurt.

But I refuse to let him see me wince.

'If I could choose among all the flowers that bloom in the market at Les Halles, I would still choose you, mademoiselle.' He leans in closer, his penetrating gaze unnerving, but it's the way he ruffles my hair—playful yet possessive—that disturbs me more. As if I'm his pet kitten.

I am, *n'est-ce pas?*

'You flatter me, monsieur,' I say. 'But you don't own me. *Ever.*'

'Mademoiselle is challenging me?' He raises a brow, intrigued.

'You take what you want, but I shall never give back.'

'You will. I have plans for you that go beyond the bedroom. You will discover them in due time, but first—' He fumbles with the silk-covered buttons on my dressing gown, his frustration growing as he speaks. 'Paris is a feast of female flesh that satisfies a man's hunger, but one soon tires of the same fruit, while *you*, mademoiselle, are an elixir for a man's soul that invigorates me when I touch you.'

'It's called *rape*, monsieur.'

'I prefer to call it "submission to the Reich".'

Tossing aside discretion, he rips my gown open, popping the buttons and scattering them onto the hardwood floor, then he drags the sheer material up to my waist to allow himself full access to my lace panty shorts and yanks down my underwear to my ankles.

'You dog! Stop, *please.*'

'And leave me unfulfilled?' he asks, perturbed. 'I order you not to resist.'

And with that, he drops his trousers then parts my thighs with his gloved hands and enters me. I don't stop him. *How can I?*

I sold my soul to keep Ève and Maman alive.

I stiffen and refuse to cry out no matter how painful it is... refuse to give in... refuse to move my hips. I've numbed my body to his touch. Then before guilt can override my shame, he's finished.

The deed is done. Again.

* * *

The days pass as slowly as if I'm a turtle plodding along the winding path of the Seine. I never thought I'd agree to it, but in exchange for a place to live—a small apartment in the ninth arrondissement with a view of the courtyard from the south-facing terrace—food, clothes, and his protection, I accept my role as the major's companion. To think my apartment is minutes away from where I lived as a child with Maman, Ève, and Papa. There's a certain irony that doesn't escape me. That all the years of living at Maison Bleue were merely a lovely dream and I've fallen from grace. That I'm not worthy of anything more than this arrangement because this man wields not only his physical power over me, but delights in playing mind games.

It's the mind games that send shivers through me.

The major hints that he could end our arrangement at any time. I suspect he's trolling for new flesh, but I can't be sure.

Added to this strange arrangement is the involvement of a man named Herr Avicus Geller from the Gestapo. He stops by the apartment when the major isn't here and makes it clear I'll find myself in the women's prison in Rennes if I don't do as I'm told by the major *and* him. Why this is so important I don't know, but I have no doubt this is the secret policeman who took Lucie. I'm just 'the spoils of war,' to quote the major. Surely I'm not worth as much as a Renoir or a Degas—I recognize paintings by these two Impressionists hanging on the drawing room walls—yet he places great value on possessing me. Now this Gestapo man is in the picture asking questions about the paintings, if they were here when I moved in. I tell him 'yes', then he wants to know if the major attends the art auctions at Hôtel Drouot. *How would I know?* By his smirk, he doesn't believe me and my experience just became more terrifying.

I don't trust him. The man snorts like a mad bull, his black trench coat shiny like the animal's skin. No beast smells as foul as he does, interrogating me about the SS officer and where he secured these art masterpieces.

Looting Jewish homes, I speculate, but I imagine he already knows that. He's after something else, something he's not sharing with me which makes me wonder what dirt he has on the major, or more accurately, what he suspects and can't prove. Yet.

Whatever it is, I'm out of it.

In the weeks that follow, I fall into a routine. Go to parties at the Hôtel Ritz—I caught a glimpse of American candy heiress Kay Alexander looking stunning—and the Italian and German embassies, sit next to Nazi generals, sip champagne and laugh at their insipid jokes. Cajole their wives to visit me at the House of Péroline, the hat shop on Rue du Rivoli where the major secures a position for me designing hats. Madame Péroline had to let the last girl go because she was Jewish. It's a sad moment when a girl gets the job she always wanted but with the caveat that she work for the Nazis.

I can't form the word 'collaborator' on my lips. It's too distasteful. Yet I don't see it as collaborating, especially when the major made it clear I had no choice.

To think it started with a turban.

It was a clear fall day when I was so crazed for something to do besides listen to Radio-Vichy and wash out pairs of silk stockings, I took a long walk to the flea market near Rue de Clignancourt and wandered up and down the rows of items spread out on dark blankets on the cobblestones. I was on the lookout for scarves and silk scraps, ribbons, feathers, and cheap beads. Bric-a-brac, fancy paper, even old film posters. With the francs I exchanged with the housekeeper for butter and sugar—the major takes care of my needs... food delivered, coal, even intimates—I came home with an armful of sundry items and began doing what I've done since I was eleven years old.

Designing hats.

Then the major showed up.

'Going somewhere?' he accused me when he found me prancing around the terrace wearing a white turban I'd designed woven with fancy pleats and dripping with beads. It didn't help my nerves when he began caressing the back of my neck, but I refused to let him browbeat me.

'Are you asking me to dinner?' I said boldly. 'The Ritz or Maxim's with your Nazi cronies?'

'I'm dining alone this evening, but I regret I haven't been around to entertain you, mademoiselle,' he smirked, running his hand over my breasts, making me flinch.

'Too busy polishing your boots?'

'I've been securing art for Herr Goering—'

'And your personal collection as well?' I'm reminded of Herr Geller's inquiry about the paintings hanging on the wall here in my apartment. I suspect the major is hiding a dirty little secret, that he keeps certain works for himself; perhaps I can use that to my advantage.

He ignores my snide remark. 'But I'm never too busy to check on my songbird.'

'You can't keep me in a cage if you want me to sing, major.'

'From what I understand, you were attempting to fly away.'

'Monsieur?'

'What did you do with the francs you stole from the housekeeper?'

'I didn't *steal* anything,' I said, indignant. 'I traded food so I'd have something better to do than listen to Nazi propaganda on the radio.'

'*And* look beautiful.'

I let that pass. 'Before you so rudely interrupted my life, I designed hats for Madame de Giocomte.'

I won't give up seeking revenge for what you did to me... to my family... to that poor maid.

'Is this one of your creations?' he asked, picking up a paper *chapeau* I fashioned using a Sylvia Martone poster and striped blue and gray ribbons.

'Yes.'

'Very clever, mademoiselle, how you formed the design with such precision. *Alors*, I had plans for you to work at the Jeu de Paume museum cataloging art since you grew up surrounded by masterpieces, priceless items to be included in the Führer's museum—'

Is that where the de Giocomte art is stored?

'However,' he continued, 'I see you're a woman of many talents.'

If only magic was one of them. I'd disappear in a pouf of smoke.

'I intend to see to it such talent won't be wasted.' He continues without giving me a chance to speak, as he would a subordinate. 'We Nazis have conscripted several shop owners to assist us in our amicable assimilation into French society.' He pulled the turban off my head and my long hair tumbled down to my shoulders.

I stood still, listening to what he had in store for me and I didn't like it.

'I have the perfect job for you working for a milliner on Rue de Rivoli,' he continued. 'The House of Péroline. I will order the owner to hire you to design hats *and* to spy on her customers.'

'*I will not!*' I protested.

He ignored my outburst. 'You will report to me if you hear anything incriminating, or if the conversation gives clues someone isn't "pure" Aryan or is a Communist or planning subversive activities against the Reich.' He cupped my chin. 'Is that understood?'

'And if I don't?'

'Then my little songbird will find herself chained to a wall in a torture room, what the Gestapo call the "kitchens" on 84 Avenue Foch. No food, no water, beatings until she comes to her senses.'

Counterintelligence headquarters for the SS.

He sickens me.

I'm no fool. I knew he wasn't bluffing. What happened to Lucie convinced me the major will resort to Gestapo tactics to get what he wants. Which is why I agreed and glide through my job each day assisting the ladies with a phony smile on my face. I'm still a prisoner. Like the 'gray mice', the German female auxiliary workers, the major insists I don't go out alone and sends a motorcar to drive me to work every day.

No chance of running into Maman or Ève. Or sending them a message. My driver is a young soldier enamored of Hitler *and* the SS officer he serves. More than once I've seen him talking to Herr Geller while the Gestapo man takes notes. I'll get nowhere with him; he'd never let me get close to Maison Bleue.

Even if I did, I doubt Ève would recognize me.

The major insisted my hair be tinted platinum blonde, sending a girl to the apartment on Rue des Martyrs to bleach my hair every other week, cutting it and styling it. She also reshaped my eyebrows and taught me how to apply makeup and sultry eye shadow.

I'm known as 'Rachelle d'Artois'.

Even Madame Péroline doesn't know my real name. I left Justine Beaufort behind along with *The Daisy Sisters* and Maman and Ève. *Why?* Because I'm ashamed of what happened to me and I don't wish to soil Maman's good name. *See*, I tell myself, *I have a new identity and a new address*. Still, I can never contact my girlhood friends or anyone else in my life, including the de Giocomtes, the shopkeepers who know me, even the priests and kind rosary mesdames at the church where I went to pray with Ève since we were children. The Church of Saint Charles de Monceau. I shall miss its intimacy, Ève and I holding hands when we light a candle in Maman's name—she prays for God to help seamstresses—and reflect on how hard she works to give us a good life. And of course, Madame de Giocomte. I miss my little sister most of all. I cried myself to sleep the night I said goodbye to my old self, but I can't look back. Just like France had to change under the occupiers, so did I. Lose the girl I was to survive under the New Order.

I had to disappear.

And I did.

I had no idea then the major had bigger plans for me. That I'm to do his bidding and make myself available to him *if and when* he has needs.

Oh, God, I'd rather die.

Except for watching me undress—shivers covered my skin with goose bumps—he hasn't forced himself upon me again since he was here at the apartment last week. It's the constant fear he *will* make sexual demands upon me again that puts me in a spin and sends me into a cold panic every time he shows up at my door.

I believe that turns him on.

Meanwhile, I look for a sign Arsène was right, that a movement is about, a group of Frenchmen and women willing to defy the complacency that has taken over Paris. That I'm not alone, that I *can* resist and fight the Nazis. I must be very careful lest the major suspects anything. He places a great satisfaction in sneaking up on me, letting himself into the apartment, nuzzling his face in my hair and exerting his power over me by attempting to arouse me. I believe he enjoys the game more than the act since I'm no longer a virgin.

I resist him and that only makes him more interested, as if he intends to break me.

He hasn't. And he won't.

I have plans. Arsène gave me the courage to endure whatever insanity awaits me, whatever trials I face. He ignited the passion in me for the one thing I'm certain neither God nor Father Armand will tolerate.

Revenge.

I will never stop believing it shall be mine.

5

PARIS, OCTOBER 1940

Ève

The day a Nazi lieutenant pokes his nose in my Petri dish is the final straw.

The promise of an extremely cold winter is in the air when I arrive at the Sorbonne after another session at breakfast with Maman throwing accusing glances at me.

'Justine, *mon bébé*, gone. Why didn't you stop her?'

'I tried, Maman.'

'You didn't try hard enough.'

'I did, Maman, you don't understand.'

She threw up her hands. 'Eh, you're not your sister. She would have tried harder.'

After that, I gave up. I'm tired of explaining to my mother I had no control over the situation. That the Nazi threatened me and I believe he would have hurt Maman, too, if Justine didn't go with him. But she doesn't want to hear it.

She wants someone to blame and that someone is me.

I've lost one daughter to the Nazis and the other to the devil, she's fond of saying, shaking her head. She doesn't approve of my work in the laboratory.

How can she? Justine was her golden girl.

And I'm, well, I feel like I disappointed her because I'm *not* my sister. She'd never say that and I don't believe deep in her heart she loves me less. It's just that she doesn't understand me, doesn't know me really, and that frightens her. And makes her frustrated with me. My world is so far out of her scope of how a girl should act, she throws her hands up and cries. It's my fault, too. I'm not easy to know and now the Nazis have created a bigger rift between us.

I hate them.

I couldn't stomach my black coffee after Maman had her say, not that I blame her, and grabbed dry bread. We'd eaten the butter two days ago. I pulled up the collar on my camel coat and raced out of the kitchen, keeping my head down when I saw Madame de Giocomte pacing up and down in the foyer, wringing her hands. She's a good woman and I've never heard her raise her voice to her staff, but I could see something had distressed her. Maman told me it's her sister-in-law, the baroness, how Madame frets over her surly relative during their fittings, that she received a letter from the woman admonishing her for not leaving Paris with her, saying if the de Giocomtes had left for Switzerland the same time as the Rothchilds did, before the Germans occupied Paris, and taken her and her daughter and her grandchildren *and* their art with them, the Nazis couldn't have stolen their paintings and she wouldn't be in fear of finding them on her doorstep.

And my sister, I wanted to add, but Madame doesn't need more problems.

I don't remember a time when Madame de Giocomte didn't roll

her eyes over something her sister-in-law did with her very proper French manners. How the woman and her spoiled daughter never participated in Madame's charity work helping Jewish immigrants barely surviving in the poor Saint-Paul neighborhood of Rue des Rosiers, calling them 'dirty refugees'. *Why help them? They're not even French.* Yet Madame worries about the baroness and her daughter and her four children since the woman's husband—her brother-in-law—died.

Madame is a good soul, encouraging Monsieur de Giocomte to take his sister's husband as a partner into his bank upon their marriage. She doesn't, however, approve of her sister-in-law's ideas about the occupiers. She believes the woman has been seduced by the phony charm of the 'polite' German officers ingratiating their way into Parisian society. It's not a family secret her sister-in-law believes as long as she keeps her nose clean, the Nazis will leave her alone. Madame disagrees and writes to her often, according to Maman, asking her to consider coming to stay at Maison Bleue, believing they'll be safer here.

But after the looting of the de Giocomte's art, the baroness said no. They're better off in their own home. Monsieur de Giocomte agrees with his sister, disputing his wife's gut instinct not to trust the Nazis, which could prove disastrous not just for them but for *all* Jews in France.

It's a nightly topic of conversation between Madame and Monsieur behind closed doors. I can't help but hear their raised voices when I pass by the main drawing room on my way to the library to study. Yes, I'm allowed to use the library. I'm grateful for the freedoms the de Giocomtes allow me and would never betray their secrets.

But I have one of my own.

I was so distraught about Justine I didn't tell them the whole story. I merely indicated that my sister secured a position at a

dressmaker's salon on the Right Bank and with the long hours—
the German wives and female auxiliary workers are crazy for Paris
couture—she prefers to sleep at the salon. Madame de Giocomte
seemed surprised and concerned since she thinks of us as the
granddaughters she didn't have, but she didn't question me. I hate
to hurt her, but until things calm down—will they ever?—I can't
burden her with the truth.

My secret is safe. For now.

Madame no longer frequents the fancy shops on Rue de Rivoli
since Jews aren't welcome there. I hope I won't regret my fib later,
but how can I explain why all Justine's belongings are still here?
Maman refuses to change a thing in our upstairs rooms and she's
too ashamed to tell Madame what really happened.

An SS officer *raped* her daughter.

Then *silence* on our part because we have no choice.

The two go hand in hand—rape then silence—*n'est-ce pas?*

I *want* to believe the outlandish tale I concocted. It keeps
Justine alive in my heart. As for Maman, my phony story removes
any shame about her daughter 'sleeping with the enemy', though
she refuses to believe Justine left willingly to save us.

My mood slides farther down into a slump when I hear whispers this morning from my fellow conspirators that three Nazi officers showed up at the lecture hall earlier. Sniffing around like wild
dogs hunting for prey. I keep my wits about me as I head to the
laboratory, keeping in the shadows lest I draw attention to myself. I
have no idea if the Nazis figured out that the anti-German newspaper we printed and handed out came from here.

Then I see him.

A short, pudgy Nazi sniffing, squinting, bending over my lab
table with its odd assortment of vials and jars holding my chemical
experiments. I'm tempted to kick him in the—

I don't, but when he picks up a round dish I left with a culture exposed to the air overnight, a sulfa drug I'm trying to duplicate that can stop infection on a wound, I don't see the beetle-green of his uniform.

I see red.

'You're ruining my experiment, monsieur!' I call out, not caring if he understands French. The tone of my voice is enough to make him spin around. He sputters in German in a loud and obnoxious manner.

A gangly young man from Alsace-Lorraine—I remember him, his name is Bernard. He asked me to join the student network— translates for me. 'He called you an interloper, mademoiselle, a shrew,' he says uneasily, 'and doesn't believe a girl has the brains to work in the field of science.'

'He said that?' I shrug and place my hands on my hips. 'Well, you can tell him I'm on the verge of making a big discovery in curing an infectious disease and he just ruined it.'

I wish.

I had to say something, but did I have to say *that*? I'm nowhere near making such a discovery, but I believe in my gut it's not far off and we'd be closer to finding a cure if the Nazis hadn't invaded us.

My lab mate translates as the officer introduces himself as Lieutenant Engel, then boasts that Germany is way ahead of us in their work to find a solution to making such a drug. They've requisitioned a company in the Netherlands and have it under constant surveillance. A company where the scientists are working on this new phenomenon called 'penicillin'. And when they're successful, the Reich will own the patent.

Doesn't he mean *steal* the patent?

'You Nazis can take what you want,' I tell him, thinking about my beautiful sister. I *know* Justine, and whatever that major did to her, he could never induce my sister to collaborate with the enemy like some Parisiennes I've heard whispered about. 'But you'll never own it. Anyway, I heard about scientists in England who made a similar drug and have already successfully tried it on infected mice and the rodents survived. What were their names again? I remember one of the scientists was Jewish.'

He laughs, his loud guffaw telling me he considers the idea ludicrous. 'The mice may have survived, but the Jew won't when we invade London.'

What is it with the Nazis and Jewish people?

I feel in my heart I have to defend them.

'I'm actually proud to live in the household of a wonderful Jewish family,' I offer up. 'My *maman* works for them and we've been there for nearly ten years.'

Bernard raises a brow, then translates, 'Lieutenant Engel says that in Berlin, your *maman* would never be permitted to work for a Jew.'

I shouldn't ask why, but I do. 'Oh, *really*? And why is that, monsieur? Or have you gotten your facts mixed up and the truth is they'd never hire a *Nazi*.'

The damn Nazi comes back at me in slow but precise French, which teaches me never to underestimate the Boches. 'If I may, mademoiselle, I shall educate you on the importance of the Nuremberg Laws decreed in 1935 stating that no Jewish family can hire an Aryan maid under the age of forty-five.' He snickers. 'You can't trust them, *n'est-ce pas?*'

I'm tempted to blurt out that sexual innuendo is insulting to every Jewish family, and by the way, why aren't there laws in France that prohibit SS officers from raping young girls?

I don't.

I keep my thoughts to myself. Barely.

'We're not in Berlin, Lieutenant,' I tell him, 'we're in Paris and my *maman* is free to work for *anyone*, even this Jewish family. They're kind people and they've been good to us.' I don't mention I have a sister. I don't want this parasite digging into my background. The stories I've heard about the secret police are real, including student arrests, not to mention we lost our Jewish professors forbidden to teach here or anywhere in the Occupied Zone.

'I'd be careful if I were you, mademoiselle,' the fat Boche says, tickling me under the chin, infuriating me, but I've already said too much and I hold my tongue. 'Hanging out with Jews can be dangerous to your health.'

Then he clicks his heels and with a 'Heil Hitler' salute, he marches out of the laboratory in perfect military rhythm.

And with that ends my encounter with the Nazi I got away with insulting.

Daring or stupid or both describe what I did, but it was enough to impress my lab mate Bernard. He asks me to meet him at the Café d'Harcourt in the Latin Quarter a few days later. I tell him I'm not interested until—

'We're going to harass Nazis, mademoiselle. You want to come?'

* * *

November 11 1940

'*Run, Ève!* The Gestapo have arrested Bernard.'

'My God, *no!*' I cry out, trying to keep my cotton under-slip from falling down. It's old and the cinch tie broke. I wasted time trying to fix it instead of catching up with Bernard. He went on ahead and I lost him in the crowd.

Where did all these Boches come from?

When we started out this morning, we were a few students protesting the Occupation, then we grew into hundreds, then—

I trip over a rock, then regain my balance before I fall and find myself at the mercy of a German soldier pushing and shoving everyone, the crowd growing bigger by the minute. Darkness showers us, obscuring our faces along with a drizzly rain, but it doesn't stop us. We started gathering before nine o'clock this morning, determined to lay fresh flowers at the statue of Clemenceau and pay our respects to the heroes of the Great War, show the Germans we haven't forgotten our history and we're proud to be French.

Even more daring—

We had declared our solidarity against the Nazis occupying our beloved Paris. Some even wore the rosette on their coats or raincoats in red, white and blue. Nothing extraordinary happened for most of the day, a few arrests, students from different fronts clashing, but nothing more. What the Nazis *didn't* know was that we'd passed the word to students from the universities as well as the *lycées* or secondary schools on hastily printed leaflets a few days before.

Skip class and then march to the Arc de Triomphe.

And we did.

By six o'clock the Place de l'Étoile overflowed with thousands of determined Parisians. Most were students, but it didn't matter who you were; when we started singing 'La Marseillaise', you joined in. It was a heady, musical elixir we drank from the cup of freedom, believing we could achieve that freedom by open resistance.

How wrong we were.

The French police lost control of the overflowing group of protestors, striking many with their batons, but the Nazis were experienced in crowd control and cunning in their methods to round up dissidents. *Dissidents?* A crude, humiliating word for what we tried to do. So many demonstrators were schoolchildren, boys and girls still learning math basics, not hand to hand combat. I watched in amazement as big, covered trucks pulled into place around l'Étoile, parking their vehicles and waiting. We stood no chance against them.

Then the signal came.

Wave after wave of armed German soldiers jumped out of the trucks and stormed into the crowd, bayonets fixed. Shoving students to the ground with force, hitting them in the face with their rifle butts, firing shots into the crowd, wounding I don't know how many. What surprised me was they were shooting the legs of the students. To maim us, but not kill. Maim our resistance as well.

But what if a nervous German soldier forgets the order and aims for the heart?

My pulse goes wild, thudding in my ears. I have to escape. *What will happen to Maman if she loses both her daughters?*

I keep running, trampling on crushed flowers dropped by students, grabbing my loose undergarment, praying I can outrun the Boches, my mind racing through numerous scenarios if they catch me. I never should have worn this old half-slip. I'm an easy target for arrest if it slides down my legs and wraps around my ankles.

Whoever thought so many people would show up on Armistice Day to protest the Boches?

I never saw this coming. I should have.

It started when I met Bernard and his friends at the café near the Sorbonne after the German officers invaded our lab. Fighting broke out with the Nazis, punches thrown, the insults tossed. Caught in the middle, I shoved a Boche who pushed me down on the ground. Bernard tackled the Nazi from behind and he dropped his rifle so I could get away. Then we ran and ran, fearing the worst, but all the German authorities did was to close the local cafés.

Afterward we met up in the apartment of a friend of Bernard's, listening to a character named Remi, his voice dark and gritty with the roughness upon his tongue of a man who knows the back alleys, not the pedantic student slang the boys at the university like to show off with. I couldn't help but be fascinated by what he had to say. He spoke so fiercely about how the Boches were stabbing the heart of France that we had to strike back with sabotage... blowing up German depots, derailing trains... that we had no choice or we'd be destroyed like Poland.

I couldn't believe the newsreels I saw at the cinema, how the Nazis had crushed the Polish people, beat them down, their soldiers slaughtered, tortured. Only the lucky survived and the brave.

Could it happen here?

With our faces flushed, hearts beating madly, souls alive with rebellion, we huddled around Remi like children enchanted by a fairy tale gnome spinning gold. How we had to resist against the occupiers like the Communist students who dared to protest the arrest of a professor of physics at the Collège de France. That we were in no danger.

The professor now sat in La Santé prison, but no students were arrested.

Remi's wild enthusiasm rubbed off on us and made us feel like we were invincible. For the first time, we believed we *could* make a difference. Adding to our curiosity, Remi spoke with fervor about an underground movement recruiting partisans, and he wanted us to join him.

How could I resist?

I raised my hand, shouted '*Vive la France*,' and got so carried along with the moment, I didn't pull away when Bernard hugged

me and swung me around in a circle. I was so startled, I couldn't
say a word. My eyes darted from Bernard to Remi to the shouting
students caught up in a frenzy, every second I was in his arms
longer than the second before and sending me into a panic.

No, this isn't happening. I don't like having him this close.

I turned away from the flirting smile he threw my way, this stal-
wart young man who took on a German soldier to keep me safe.

I couldn't flirt back. It wasn't in me.

The truth is, I'm fearful of men, their strength, their power, the
smoldering desire that sparks in their eyes when their need for a
woman is awakened and hungry. I saw it in the eyes of the SS
officer intent on raping me. His square jaw set, his hand grabbing
my arm so tight, I had a big purple bruise on my upper arm as dark
as smashed blueberries for a week. And the consequences that
followed when I ran.

And left Justine at his mercy.

I decided to leave it there for God knows the deepest sorrow
residing in my soul. A sorrow that burns hot and never cools. A
sorrow that makes me weep. For so long there was room for
nothing else, but I pray He allows me to find the courage to accept
the loss of my sister, for there is work to be done.

And I don't need any distractions.

I left the apartment with my head down, my arms hugging my
chest. Left Bernard scratching his head, wondering why I'd shied
away from him. I'm not the girl for him. He sees me as part of the
cause, conjuring up something romantic in his mind that doesn't
exist. I can't change who I am. I want to be his friend, but he wants
more than that. I couldn't, so I raced home to my refuge upstairs
and stared into the mirror for a long time.

I'm plain... *plain*. What can any man ever see in me?

Or is that just an excuse to deaden my heart? I fear the touch of
a man after seeing what happened to Justine. I'm uncomfortable

with the idea of Bernard pushing himself up against me, brushing my cheek with his lips, his excitement rising as the crowd gets bigger, the threat more imminent and creating a strange surge of adrenaline that numbs you to the reality of the situation. Like the students yelling how great it would be if the Germans arrested them. No exams or classes.

Fools.

Didn't they hear the stories of the Gestapo interrogation methods? Putting out their cigarettes on their victims' foreheads, or ripping open their shirts and burning the bare skin on their chests? I have. From a fellow student who experienced such torture simply for being caught with anti-Nazi pamphlets.

I can't think about that now, can't let my fear of the German secret police keep me from finding Bernard. Breathing rapidly, my conscience racing overtime with guilt, I keep searching for him, forgiving him in my mind if he tries to kiss me, but it doesn't happen. I can't find him anywhere. When my breath is gone, I stop, sucking in air, panting. I'm blocks away from the melee, but I failed. The Gestapo have Bernard.

All because of my stupid slip.

Why are we females subjected to such constrictive clothing? Why can't I dress like a man? Then I'd be faster on my feet. If I hadn't been so slow, so painfully awkward in my mode of dress, this wouldn't have happened. We'd be safe now, laughing at the inept French police trying to control the crowd of thousands. We could have escaped together before the German soldiers attacked us like ancient Huns, marauding soldiers following blindly the orders of the corrupt Vichy government.

What makes my stomach plummet is that the boy who brought me here, a kind boy who trusted me, is in the hands of the secret police and on his way to prison.

And again, just like with Justine, it's my fault.

6

PARIS, NOVEMBER 1940

Justine

The one thing I didn't predict would happen during the Occupation was motherhood.

Yes, I'm pregnant.

Sick-feeling, tired, moody, sore breasts.

I feel like a lamb hunkered down in a hen house, hiding where I don't belong because I have nowhere else to go. It's a confusing state I'm in. One moment I'm smiling to myself at the thought of a little one filling my arms, then tearful when I think about the difficult path ahead of me, then frightened I'll never see my baby born if the major finds out I'm with child. He has no reason to doubt it's his child since he knows I was a virgin and he has me under constant surveillance.

Anxiety grips me in the stomach, ballooning to wild proportions that won't go away. I keep hearing in my mind Madame Mimi lecturing the girls to 'be safe', that she heard a Nazi officer boasting he was privy to the Führer's plans to eliminate those racially impure. I can only imagine the fear a Jewish mother-to-be experiences since pregnant Jewish women are high on their list of 'undesirables'.

I find that so horrifying, I can't sleep. Does that mean children born of an SS officer's indiscretion are *also* subject to extermination? The idea chills me.

I haven't told anyone about my pregnancy. Not the major nor Madame Péroline at the hat shop. I dare not confide in her and I often find it difficult to escape a chattering, snooty German wife when I can't hold my breakfast down. And the Parisiennes eager to defy the occupiers by refusing to give up luxuries like a new hat. Why not? Hats aren't rationed. I smile and make small talk with them, then run into the back of the shop and toss up my insides into a battered bucket used for window washing. It's not all bad. I lose myself in my work, wrapped up in the joy of running my fingers over the silky veiling and lace that my employer procures from the black market.

Lace from Belgium, she says, her eyes beaming.

I remind her that Belgium is occupied by the Nazis and that lace most likely came from the shop of a harassed Jewish owner. She hums louder, pretending not to hear me as I tie silk ribbons on a sporty hat I designed, adding the lace veil while trying not to think about the poor shop owner. I want to forget I'm here to eavesdrop on ladies gossiping as they try on hats. As if spies hang out in a hat shop.

Yet the idea intrigues me.

Today when I go to work, Madame Péroline is as nervous as a canary in a new cage, twittering around the shop, dusting hats and fidgeting with the perky bows and talking to herself.

Be pleasant to the German ladies, she whispers, *even if it kills you*.

She sees me watching her and gives me a weak smile. I slightly suspect that she hates the Boches as much as I do, but neither of us can say it. Her husband and son are POWs in a German labor camp, but somehow she came into the awkward if not lucrative position of her shop being chosen by the local *Kommandant* as a listening post. By cooperating with the Nazis, she enjoys the privilege of sending her son and husband letters and boxes of essentials through a network she refuses to reveal.

The shop is empty this morning, so I rearrange the hats in the window for something to do. I'm determined to focus on the pretty *chapeaux* to lighten the heaviness in my stomach. I can't. *Uh-oh, here we go again.* A queasiness rises within me and sticks in my throat, the taste burning and unpleasant. I suck in my stomach, will it to behave, but Madame de Péroline's flittering, birdlike mannerisms get on my already fragile nerves and send me to the back of the shop looking for the bucket to ease my unhappy stomach.

She finds me there, retching up my guts.

She gasps so loud, I choke.

'I'm shocked, mademoiselle. You're with child.' She blows out her breath and feathers fly off her duster. 'Who's the father?'

I swallow hard. 'He doesn't know and if he did, he wouldn't care.'

She waves her duster and more feathers fly around her face. 'You'll have to get rid of it.'

'Madame?' I protest in alarm.

'You heard me.'

'*No!*'

'You *must*. Do what girls *do*, skip rope, take hot baths, ride a horse for God's sake, but *do something!*'

I close my eyes and let out a long, painful sigh. Her harsh words make me angry, but I won't listen to her telling me I can't have my child, that I can't work here and be a good mother.

I *will* find a way.

Madame Péroline pays no attention to my protests. She's in a tither, complaining about how *une affaire de femmes*, women's business, hurts sales. 'What a frightful situation you put me in, mademoiselle. I admit you're a hard worker and your designs sell, but I can't afford to have you taking time off, and Lord, who will watch the child?' She taps her duster against her hand, muttering, 'I'll find a fortune teller who can direct you where to go.'

She explains how the fortune teller passes along my details to a certain mademoiselle who can perform a 'service'.

I shake my head. 'No, madame. I won't do it, *I won't*.'

I stand strong, but my brain scatters while my stomach plummets again into the depths of nausea and I toss up the rest of the cold cabbage soup. Madame Péroline holds her nose and makes a sound that grates on my ears.

'In times of war, mademoiselle, we women must sacrifice.'

'What you're asking me to do is against every belief, every fiber in my being. Against God.' I spit out the words. 'The answer is *no*.'

Not to mention against the law. The *Code de la famille* considers such an act comparable to treason or sabotage.

She huffs and puffs. 'Then I shall terminate you immediately and find another girl more sensible in these difficult times.'

What she means is, she doesn't want her customers asking who the father is. An uneasy arrangement for both of us, but the major introduced me to her and I'm certain she doesn't want to get on the wrong side of the SS or the Gestapo. Madame Péroline isn't comfortable with me being the major's mistress *and* working for her. She's afraid I'll report her little indiscretions to the Gestapo, like adding an 'Occupation Tax' to her hat prices. I don't blame her, though. She uses the extra money to use as bribes for the guards at the labor camp where her husband and son are POWs. She doesn't know the major raped me and I'm too ashamed to tell her.

Which makes me wonder, why is it that I'd rather let her believe I'm playing a woman of loose morals in this drama rather than a rape victim?

Why is rape more shameful?

I have no answer for that.

I wipe my mouth with a scrap of old cotton, then choose my next words carefully. 'What will Major Saxe-Müllenheim say if you let me go?' I begin. She huffs and puffs again, but remains silent. I go on. 'He secured this job for me to assist you in your shop to gather information with the blessing of Herr Geller. *Eh bien,* madame?'

The name of the Gestapo man has the effect I expected. She tugs at the long earrings dangling on her shoulders and her sparse lashes stand straight up. The heavyset man in the black trench coat and Fedora made *me* uncomfortable when the major picked me up, sitting across from me in the Mercedes touring car, working his crossword puzzle. I had the feeling the whole time he was watching me, his eyes boring holes through me, as if he was two steps ahead of me and that worries me. Why is he so interested in me?

'Shall we forget we ever had this little talk, mademoiselle?' Madame Péroline gives me a weak smile. 'Pardon, but I must lie down. I've got a splitting headache and no medicine to cure it.'

I take a step back. I hated using the major's name and his Gestapo cohort. Herr Geller enjoys a reputation not to be trifled with. I found out afterward *he* secured the apartment for me after 'advising' the previous occupant, an Italian woman, the Reich needed her abode and she should return to her country while she still could. Dealing with the man makes me feel dirty, but I have no choice if I want to keep this child and I do.

Oh, God, I do.

'My sister Ève says butterbur extract will help your headache.'

'What does she know? What does *anyone* know in these wretched times?' Madame shoos me away. 'Go, take a walk. Take the rest of the afternoon off if you like while I come up with a plan to deal with your situation.'

'I feel better now, madame.'

'*Go!*' she yells, her eyeballs popping.

I put on a black cloche hat and pull the veil down over my eyes. She'll calm down, but what makes me sad is whatever good feelings I earned with her through my work, I've lost. I'm a willing collaborator in her eyes. I don't tell her I did what I had to because it was the only way to save my family and that we're born of the same cloth.

It's then I realize a rape victim is violated more than once.

Once during the act.

Then for the rest of her life.

It makes me sad to accept that. In spite of the fact a man took me against my will, I want to be happy with my pregnancy. Why must we women suffer at the hands of a man then feel guilty because we want to embrace motherhood at whatever the cost? Maman says it took her a long time to get over Papa's unfaithfulness, not to another woman, but his gambling habit. That didn't change how she felt about her daughters, she said. Though she was glad we didn't share the flaws of the man.

I don't know all the details. I get worked up thinking about it, wondering if there are any good men left in the world.

Putting such thoughts where they belong—not in my heart, but far back in my mind where it's always a rainy day—I leave the hat shop owner to her headache. It's a perfect chance for me to be on my own. The motorcar won't be here for hours to pick me up. When it arrives, Madame Péroline will make excuses, but it will be too late for them to find me. *Bon.* Exactly what I want. I need a friend. I wish I had Ève to talk to, but even if I could go home, she's too young to understand and Maman would sit with her knitting, disapproving.

Madame de Giocomte is a kind woman, but ever since they returned from Deauville, she's been burdened with her greatest fear, a sudden acceleration of what she's known for a while, a quickening of the effects of a partial heart block that affected Monsieur's brain, according to his doctor. Now she must deal with what to do with a husband slowly succumbing to the disease of the mind, his *thought processes deteriorating*, as Ève would say, leaving Madame to assume the role of head of the household, And God bless her, she has her sister-in-law and niece to worry about. And *her* children. She's taken it upon herself to protect them against what she sees as the rising Nazi tide against Jews. Laws that exclude them from French society, taking away their right to teach, practice law, receive medicine, go to the cinema. Next, I imagine the Nazis will dictate what they wear.

So in the end, my heart pining for a sliver of joy in my upside down world, I find myself trekking to the fancy *maison close* near the Champs-Élysées and looking for the one person I can share my troubles with.

Arsène.

* * *

I'm surprised to see the intrepid old soldier standing on the corner of the boulevard not far from the brothel, his beret in his hand, holding it out to passers-by and leaning on his cane, his hunched shoulders and stooped stance making him a heart-wrenching sight. My heart pings with sadness. No one drops a coin into his hat, though he receives pitiful looks and sighs.

I hate seeing Arsène like this. I get my dander up when two German soldiers stop and point to him, laughing.

Damn Boches will never be the soldier he once was.

I hover off to the side. He doesn't see me. I'm tempted to pour my heart out to him, tell him my fears, like the major throwing me out and me ending up on the streets, a sorrowful figure holding my swollen belly, rain drenching me while I try to keep my little one warm and dry. Nowhere to go.

I won't go home. No, *never*.

Yes, Maman and Ève would take me in, of course they would. But I couldn't bear to bring shame upon them or the de Giocomtes.

I carry an SS officer's child.

A lack of courage holds me back from crossing the boulevard. I continue to stare at the scene unfolding before me. Then another thought strikes me. What if Arsène *isn't* the kind soul I believe him to be? What if he rebukes me, assures me there are 'ways' to fix things like Madame Péroline suggested? He works in a brothel; he'd be privy to the girls' secrets. He'd assure me there are women who can help me. The thought sickens me, for never would I deem to succumb to such a horrible thing. Life is too precious, even if this is a child born of rape. It will also be born of love.

My love for an innocent.

It's my baby, too.

And no one can take the child from me.

A precious gift from God I never saw coming. A way to redeem myself in His eyes by being a good mother and protecting my baby. A strange prayer, but I blame myself for what happened with the major, convince myself that it's my fault. I wonder if I'll ever get over it.

I dally a minute longer, feeling better. Just seeing Arsène gives a boost to my spirit. I turn to walk in the opposite direction when I see the young German soldier make a grab for the medals on his coat. I can't believe it when Arsène steps back so quickly I double blink.

What's this?

Before the soldier can try again, the crowd on the pavements thickens, blocking his path. A trio of schoolgirls skips along, giggling, a matron staring at them with disapproval, then an SS officer riding in a sidecar jumps out when the motorcycle driven by his subordinate screeches to a halt. The soldier clicks his heels and gives the officer the 'Heil Hitler' salute, while Arsène takes advantage of the moment and whacks the soldier across the back of his legs with his cane, then turns calmly around and saunters off, whistling.

Fear and mirth erupt in me. The man's either a fool or braver than anyone.

They'll shoot you, Arsène! I want to cry out. *Run!*

Then something unusual happens.

Arsène looks to the right, *then* left before he crosses the busy street. I find that odd. The traffic comes from the *left*. That evokes a fond memory in me. When I was a little girl, Madame de Giocomte hired an English nanny who always looked to the right before guiding us across the boulevard. Funny that should come to me now as I watch him get lost in the crowd, but not before he glances back in my direction.

I step into a doorway. *Did he see me?* Still other things about him simmer in my mind. His quick movements when it suits him, his deep voice, and standing so tall in the window of the brothel without the stoop of an old man.

I mull that over in my mind as the German soldier spins around, unsure who to blame, but the high-ranking officer calls him back, yelling in German.

I turn on my heel and go after Arsène.

It's time I find out who he really is.

* * *

'Where did you get those old medals pinned onto your jacket, Arsène?' I ask him minutes later. I find him sitting at a small table in a café nursing a cognac. 'And don't give me a sad story about your army days sitting in a trench in Verdun. I'm not buying it.'

He grins, not surprised to see me. 'An irascible old fellow named Jarnak sold them to me in a pawn shop on Rue Saint-Jacques.'

His dark eyes sparkle like dew on a raven's wings. He's enjoying this. Which surprises me. I expected him to deny everything.

I make my next play. 'You're British, *n'est-ce pas?*'

Let him stuff *that* under that his phony wig.

He doesn't deny it. 'What gave me away, mademoiselle?'

'The way you looked to the right before crossing the busy street.'

'You're very observant.'

I grin, pleased. 'Madame de Giocomte hired an English nanny to tutor my sister and me when we were small. Grabbing our hands, the girl always looked to the right first when we crossed the boulevard when she took us to the Luxembourg Gardens.' I sit down, study him. 'Who *are* you, monsieur?'

'You know I can't tell you that.'

I push back, 'You must, monsieur. It's terribly important to me.'

'Why, mademoiselle, what are *you* hiding?'

'Nothing. I—I need a friend.'

'How do I know I can trust you? You're "the major's girl".'

Again, that title haunts me.

'Not by choice, Arsène, or whatever your name is. I hate the major and everything he stands for. I wish I could run away from him, but I can't.' My voice is low, gritty. Without thinking, I place my hands over my stomach. 'It's too late for that.'

His brow furrows. 'You carry his child.'

I stare up at him. 'Yes, monsieur.'

'Does he know?'

I shake my head. 'No one knows but Madame Péroline and now you.'

'I think it best we keep it that way. Major Saxe-Müllenheim is unpredictable. I fear for your safety.'

'You do? Why?'

'No more questions, mademoiselle. I must ask you to keep your suspicions about me to yourself, but be aware, I *will* look out for you.' He gets up from his wicker back chair and I'm amazed how tall he is when he makes no attempt to stoop over. 'You've had enough excitement for one afternoon and I must return to Chez Mimi. Madame will need the ashtrays emptied before the customers arrive for this evening's parlor games.'

'What if the Gestapo raids the brothel? Ask you questions you can't answer, find out your papers are forged, for they are forged, *n'est-ce pas*? Don't try to deny it. Even if they don't suspect you, if you even look at a Nazi the wrong way, you could be exposed.'

He grins. 'I doubt that, mademoiselle, brothels sanctioned by the German Superintendent of Culture are *never* raided.' He pays his check and tips his beret. 'I bid you au revoir, Mademoiselle d'Artois. We *will* meet again.'

Then he moves swiftly into the crowd, his cane hanging on his arm, trying not in the least to act like the old soldier.

I sit there, dumbfounded.

Who is he? A downed pilot? Allied soldier? Everyone's heard the stories about the escape lines set up for the men who so valiantly fought at Dunkirk. How the villagers provided safe haven and false identity papers so they could get home to England. But this man didn't return home. He stayed in France. *Why?* Is he what the ladies in the hat shop call a 'resister'?

And where did he learn to speak our language so well?

I'd bet my meat ration for the week—all two ounces—he's a spy. And there's no way he can convince me otherwise.

* * *

How fast my pulse races when I make my way back to the ninth arrondissement through the streets and alleyways, how buoyant I feel stepping over puddles, even lightheaded. Like I can leap into the air like a prima ballerina and pirouette round and round like a spinning top. For the first time in months, I have real hope the Allies haven't abandoned us.

And a friend. *Arsène.*

Thank God I'm back in my apartment when the major's driver shows up to check on me. I'm grateful Madame Péroline covered for me, telling him she sent me home early today because there were few customers. After he leaves, I make myself a cup of tea, going over again in my mind what happened this afternoon with Arsène.

The details of his clever disguise. Bushy dark brows flecked with gray along with an old man's beard with more silver than black, weaving a convincing tale of a soldier from the Great War. He hides his neck with a high collar, but I could see the skin taut, not sagging. Broad shoulders, and I caught a glimpse of a muscular chest in a tight, seaman's sweater under his baggy coat. Yes, Arsène is a much younger man. I wonder what he looks like without that fuzzy gray wig, phony beard and brows, and shabby clothes.

Then I remember the hard muscle I felt tighten when I touched his arm.

And *that* makes me shiver with a feeling most pleasant. Hmm, most pleasant indeed.

I shake uncontrollably when I slide under the woolen blanket at night, fighting the cold as all of Paris is doing. I can't stop thinking about him. I want to trace my fingertips over his face and peel away the mask, moving them over his stubble dotted with a fake gray color and find the smooth skin of his cheeks underneath.

When he leaned down closer to my lips that day in the attic, I could smell the sharp scent of a heavy red wine lingering upon his breath as seductive as a spring rain. But what sends me reeling even now is the heat emitting from his body whenever I'm near him, sending me spiraling downward with a fierce intensity in a moment of breathlessness I've never felt before. *Spinning, twirling*, not in a frightening manner. I can't explain it. My skin burning, heart racing, wanting something I couldn't have.

It's insane, I tell myself, and then laughing at my girlish crush on a man doing everything he can to hide his raw masculinity, his strength, I start taking deep breaths, trying to wrap my head around this whole idea of me falling for a man hidden by a disguise. It's sharp, biting. I take stock of every reason why I shouldn't seek him out again, why I must forget him.

Because I carry a German officer's child.

And I'm forced to act as a Nazi spy for him, working in the hat shop gathering information, though I don't tell the Nazis anything useful. Now even less so, knowing I'd be putting Arsène's life in danger if the major found out.

'Oh, God, Arsène, I know it's wrong, but I need you.'

Not in a physical way, I tell myself—will I ever desire a man's touch on my skin... *anywhere* on my body again? I tighten my fists. I need a friend and I feel in my gut I can trust him. The idea I've tried so hard to repress emerges stronger than ever. I recall the quiet, even tone in his voice when I admitted I was pregnant. He didn't judge me. Didn't hate me. He said nothing.

Then what *does* he want from me?

I smile. No, the question is, what I want... need from *him*.

A chance to redeem myself, find my place in this war that's

turned me from starry-eyed girl designing dresses to lost girl in hell. I'm like a bolt of yellow Chinese silk with a long, jagged tear down the middle. It doesn't change the quality of the silk.

But no one wants to buy it.

Not today or tomorrow. Trim it with lace, the silk is still torn.

No man will want me after being raped by the enemy and I have to accept that. I can cry about it, feel sorry for myself and go about looking for pity. I've done that, not that I'm proud of it, but what I found is it makes me go backward, not forward. I can't live in the past, but I can learn from it. I know in my heart I can be useful in this fight.

Resist the Boches. Really?

Not a popular idea since most Parisians have gone along with the Occupation. Can I blame them? France has been through so much. Depression, regimes changing, workers' strikes, and political unrest. Everyone is holding their breath, not resisting because it's easier this way. Even the Seine barely ebbs and flows along its banks since the Occupation.

But does that mean we *can't* resist?

To think I didn't pay much attention to General de Gaulle's plea from London over the radio on the BBC except for the phrase *the flame of the French resistance must not be extinguished*. Now I understand what he meant. It's up to us, the people of France, to resist, no matter *how* we do it.

If we don't, we're allowing the occupiers to dictate to us how we live. Do I have the right to bring a child into such a world? Oh, it would be so easy to swim along with the tide and do what I'm told, but I can't. I'm ashamed of myself. Look at Ève, demonstrating against the occupiers. Dangerous, *yes*, and brave. Yet I do nothing to make things better for my child.

Am I that much of a coward that my younger sister shows more courage than I do?

Lying in the dark, I huddle under the blanket, wishing I had more heat in the apartment, and a fever rises up in me in spite of the cold. I feel a warm sensation creep up my spine, then the protective embrace of a man's strong arms around me that makes my pulse race.

It's just a dream, but I can't forget it.

No one's here, but my need for the touch of a good man is so strong, the moment is real to me. A beautiful ache that will stay with me even if I can never have such a man.

I dream that man is Arsène.

I'm certain he's working for the Underground, which means he needs intelligence. *Perfect.* I come in contact with the 'gray mice' as well as the wives and girlfriends of Nazi officers. If I push them harder, I can get the women to reveal things to me that seem insignificant to them. *Like when their Nazi husband or lover is returning to Berlin?*

Is the rumor true he may be stationed in the East? Russia, perhaps?

When is he leaving? Traveling by train, is he? And you say you're dining at the Hôtel Ritz? With Reichsmarschall Goering. He's back in Paris? How fascinating.

Yes, *fascinating.* I vow silently I shall have my revenge against the major and the occupiers who have taken so much from me. These lovely thoughts stick to me like I sewed a patch with a big 'R' for '*Résistant*' on my shoulder with Maman's strongest thread made from wiry lamb's wool. No Boche can tear it off. Oh, they can yank and pull and snip it here and there, but they can't take it away from me. I feel strong, confident.

Like Sylvie Martone, the brave cinema star when she starred in the *Ninette* series, getting into trouble every week and using her brains and guts to get out of it.

I whisper '*bonne nuit*' to my dear, sweet unborn baby and close my eyes and make plans to see Arsène again, convince him I'm strong, that I can do the work, that he needs me. That I can enter places he can't, dine with the Nazi High Command, take tea with their wives and gossip with them about their pillow talk with their husbands or lovers.

I'm determined to offer my services to the Allies.

As a double agent.

7

PARIS, NOVEMBER 1940

Ève

My head is bursting with the painful effort of keeping sane after the Armistice Day student demonstration at the Place de l'Étoile. The Nazi regime isn't making it easy. They closed the university and ordered all students to register with their local police station or face severe sanctions affecting not only them, but their families.

I can deal with anything the Nazis throw at me, but I have Maman to think about and I wouldn't put it past the Germans to harass the de Giocomtes on my behalf. Add that they're Jewish and it scares the hell out of me, so I comply, and with more than a dozen skipped heartbeats, I show up this morning as required at the weathered building flying the Nazi flag.

The bitter chill in the air forecasts a winter that will bite your nose off and I'm glad to scurry inside to get warm. Everywhere I look I see stern guards and the frightened faces of students like myself, wondering what danger lurks behind each closed door. I hear the pounding of typewriters, then an occasional exchange of guttural German that grates on my ears as I warm my hands by a working radiator—I didn't know there were any left in Paris. Next I fill out a card listing questions: where I live, my age, my religion. I make no mention I live with a Jewish family. The most annoying question is where I was on that day of the demonstration. I lie to the German officer looking over my card and tell him I was in the laboratory at the Sorbonne working on a chemistry experiment, then I rattle off a list of chemical elements and formulas that have the captain's head spinning. He questions why I was wasting my time in the laboratory.

'So I can compete with the male students,' I snap back.

'Ridiculous, mademoiselle. The Führer has decreed your only concern as a woman is making a home and having children.'

He is kidding, n'est-ce pas?

'We're not living in the nineteenth century, Captain. Why won't you Nazis accept the fact we women are as smart as men?' I press my point with: 'Like the lieutenant who couldn't keep his nose out of my Petri dish.'

'*Pardon*, mademoiselle?' He raises a brow.

'Lieutenant Engel. He kept asking me questions about my work curing disease.'

The sour captain doesn't comprehend my meaning, or won't admit I'm right. I see him tapping his foot, deciding whether or not to believe me. Five long minutes drag by, no doubt his apathy designed to make me sweat.

I do.

But I won't show weakness in front of him, even when he picks up the phone and makes a call. He grunts in German, snorts, picks his teeth, then smirks and turns back to me.

'You're *too* smart, mademoiselle, according to Lieutenant Engel,' he says, hanging up the phone.

'Monsieur?'

'You're a most fortunate young woman. You impressed the lieutenant when he visited your laboratory with your medical knowledge and convinced me you're an honorable student.' He stamps my paperwork with a black swastika, then tells me I must report here every day. 'Now get out of here and find yourself a lover and do something productive for your country. Like making babies.' He raises his hand. 'Heil Hitler.'

I want to tell him he's an arrogant misogynist, but I don't. I say nothing, nor do I repeat the hated Nazi salute. Instead I run back home, a cold wind biting at my cheeks, all the while yearning for Maman's comforting voice whispering in my ear, *Life is bearable, mon enfant, if you follow the bitter with a sweet macaron.*

That was *before* the Occupation. There's little sugar nowadays to make macarons. They started rationing it last month along with milk and cheese, and butter is harder to come by. When you do find sugar, it's so precious it's kept in a cardboard box and hidden away.

I keep walking, but I feel something shift inside me, something discomforting, even frightening. It's not the lack of a sweet treat that sets me on a new course. It's the idea that my name is now on a list... a *Gestapo* list. The secret police can find me anytime, interrogate me, and do what they want with me.

Like igniting a match. Stick your nose too close to the flame and you get burned.

I still feel guilty for not finding Bernard, which is why I sign up to be a patron with a Quaker group I meet outside the police station. Good souls with comforting words and hushed whispers in my ear about *helping female students leave Paris.* I shake my head. I'd never leave Maman and the de Giocomtes, but they do help me look for Bernard. They ask if he's my lover. I shake my head. I shall never be with anyone. I still quiver inside at the idea of a man touching me after seeing what happened to Justine. It scares me too much.

On the appointed afternoon, I bring a small gift of hard candy and soap to Fresnes Prison where several students ended up after the demonstration. I pray I'll find Bernard here. I fidget with the cake of soap, my nails digging into the soft waxy bar, peeling off flakes. I can't stop my curious eyes darting everywhere. I see for the first time what the Nazis do to *résistants*.

Students huddled together in cells, unwashed bodies and long faces. The pungent smell of urine.

It's painful and frightening.

I could have ended up here.

After a long wait in the queue, German officials interrogate me —I'm getting more adept at answering their questions—and let me see the prisoner they assigned to me. The young man I speak with tells me *yes, he's acquainted with Bernard, lanky, outspoken*. How the Nazi guards beat him with their rifle butts and then he disappeared.

I suffer a cold stab to my heart. I feel responsible for the boy, but further questioning of the guard gets me nowhere. I'm told to mind my own business or I will end up here as well.

I leave.

I'm well aware it could happen. I haven't forgotten I'm on the Gestapo list.

Afterward the days melt into each other. I study on my own, walk in the bleak garden behind the *maison* to think in spite of the cold. I miss my sister and blame myself. It's an odd yet disturbing time in my life and for the first time I feel truly alone. Maman says I should get a fish. *I'd forget to change the water*, I tell her. Madame de Giocomte says I should get a pretty bird and offers me a lovely cage from the seventeenth century the Nazis didn't take. It has a golden key to open the tiny door.

Why not you, madame? I suggest, knowing she's lonely and depressed about her husband's deteriorating condition and has a continuous cold. I told her to be careful, praying she doesn't contract pneumonia. I don't want to worry her, so I say nothing. I do encourage her to shop for a pet bird, though we lost most of the bird population due to the oily black cloud hovering over Paris after the Nazis bombed the petrol dumps in the Seine, a distance from the city where the river mixes with the ocean. She nods in agreement. I don't know where she found the winged creatures, but the next day I hear two birds tweeting, their chatter making Madame smile.

But not me.

Head down, I tread along each day in a self-induced bubble of fear, looking over my shoulder everywhere I go, reporting daily to the Commissariat de Police, but not without incident. A formidable event occurred the other day. I overheard a German officer threatening to send a girl to a concentration camp for not filling out her card on the first day. To think the Boches have this much control over our lives sends me deeper into depression and into my own thoughts. I keep my head down and my mouth shut.

The days turn colder, and the leftover yellow and orange leaves are no match for a bitter December wind and are swept away like careless thoughts. I keep up my studies, reading, going to the library, though my experiments suffer because I can't grow any herbs in the garden in the cold. Even the rose bush has given in to its fate. And I haven't seen a bee in months. I'm hungry to learn, but without the hustle and bustle of the lab and the professors and students, the prattle and discussion and arguing that so often fuels creativity gone, I rely more and more on escaping into my books, rarely coming up for air or to eat. When Cook started substituting bran for tasty oats and acorns for coffee—the de Giocomtes don't keep kosher, and like Maman and me, Cook isn't Jewish—I find I have little interest in food except to stave off losing more weight. My dresses are hanging on me.

Each day I become more complacent, more docile... more numb to the presence of the occupiers. In a moment of childhood longing, I stare at the empty spaces on the library wall where the beautiful Impressionist paintings once hung. Renoir, Degas, and Seurat. And where *The Daisy Sisters* greeted me each morning. Where I breathed in life, creativity, and hope in myself. And the future.

All taken away.

By the Boches.

I feel lost.

I shuffle along to the kitchen, yearning for a cup of tea, fully aware my chemistry book is filled with wondrous ideas and experiments, but I don't feel like opening it. Then my brain—so hungry for a creative boost—tunes in to Madame's songbirds tweeting a pretty tune in spite of the Nazis.

They haven't given up, mademoiselle, but you have. Tsk... tsk. Shame.

Then it hits me.

No... no. I *haven't* given up. Or have I?

I slap my hand against my forehead, a stubborn refusal to accept that. Of course. That's what the Boches want. *For us to give up.* The idea infuriates me and I struggle not to throw my book against the wall.

That's their plan. Lull us into a humdrum existence so we move about in a trance, living but not feeling. And it's working. Maman and I barely talk to each other and that distresses me. She still hasn't forgiven me for what happened to Justine. On the upside, Madame de Giocomte and I have become closer, bonding over a hurtful situation, seeing how the two most important people in our world are slowly succumbing to the unraveling of their minds.

Maman never stops knitting and Monsieur de Giocomte has taken to sleeping in the library and never leaving the house.

Madame de Giocomte and I find solace taking tea together in the drawing room most afternoons, discussing the state of affairs and the situation for Jews in Paris. I know she's clinging to the idea the family's status will protect them, but for how long?

I sit at the round Napoleonic table, a cup of tea in front of me and a map of France spread out on the checkered black-and-white marble. However, my mind isn't on escape lines to Spain then Lisbon, but rather on how to protect this woman and the man she loves from what I see as inevitable.

Each day the Nazis put more restrictions on Jews.

Madame doesn't notice my strained look in her direction. She's sipping her tea while adjusting the cuffs on her dark green woolen dress—ivory lace cuffs Maman wove and Justine cut into a pretty shape. *Oh, how I miss those days.* 'I should have insisted to Monsieur de Giocomte we take the train to Toulouse when we had the chance last summer.'

The railroad tracks were bombed, but she doesn't mention it.

'Or found our way to Marseilles,' she laments, 'but Monsieur de Giocomte didn't want to leave his employees in a lurch and I agreed with him.' She sighs. 'Now there's a rumor the Nazis are setting up an anti-Jewish institute here in Paris. What next? Forced emigration?' She's going over in her mind her list of 'What ifs' and beating herself up because she did nothing.

'*Please*, madame, you mustn't blame yourself,' I tell her. I bring the cup to my lips, but my tea is cold.

'I should have asked the Brazilian ambassador for visas,' she continues. 'God knows he's enjoyed many parties here at Maison Bleue. Now it's too late.'

'How were you to know the Nazis would require Jews to register with the police?' I close the map. No need to upset her even more. 'Or that they'd force you to carry an identity card?' No one was more shocked than I when the Nazis stamped the word *Juife* in bold red letters on Madame's passport. *Jew*.

'I know you're right, Ève, but each day I fear we're losing more and more of who we are, that the Nazis are trying to erase us from their world.'

'How can they, madame? Monsieur's family is an integral part of Parisian business and you are the most elegant of ladies in society. France needs good people like you and Monsieur.'

'My sweet Ève, you're so naïve,' she says, laying her hand over mine. 'I saw what happened in 1917 in Russia when there were those who believed they knew a better way to run everyone else's lives. The pain, the bloodshed on *both* sides. I fear the same will happen here, but this time it will be the Jewish people who will pay the price.'

'No, I won't believe that *ever*. I—I would die if anything happened to you, madame.' I'm close to tears in front of her. I can't help it. I've always maintained a distance from this elegant woman with a kind heart, showed her the respect Maman insisted Justine and I display in her presence, though she insists we're the granddaughters she never had.

We're all family here at Maison Bleue, she's fond of saying.

Never more so than at this moment when she grabs me and gives me a big hug, 'Pray for us, Ève, Monsieur and I and every Jew in Paris, because I fear the worst is yet to come.'

'I will, madame, *I will*.'

I hug her back, my heart swelling not only with deep emotion for this woman, but knowing I *must* do more for her. I hate seeing her like this. Her pleasant face and once elegant demeanor have given way to a slump of her shoulders and shaky hands when she picks up her teacup. Still, she keeps up her appearance with her gray-brown hair pulled back in a long roll around her head, more gray than brown these days, and wearing the silk and wool dresses Justine designed for her and Maman sewed. She reminds me of a queen confined to her palace, praying she will never hear the words she dreads.

That her throne has toppled.

The warnings are everywhere. First, the Nazis forbid Jews to re-enter the Occupied Zone, then they decree Jewish shops must display signs declaring they are *une enterprise juive*, then the French police conduct a census poll of all Jews. We both wonder when it will stop, how far they will go to restrict every move of Paris's Jewish population.

The question is: *who will be spared*?

More disconcerting is the fact that the exhilaration we felt during the demonstration I attended at l'Étoile—the thrill of singing the Marseillaise and we students standing up to the Nazis has dissipated like holy smoke on a Monday morning.

We go about our lives like paper dolls. Knocked down by the ill wind that swirls around the city, then blown about with no will of our own.

Still, I pick up encouraging gossip at my daily sign-in at the police station. I catch snippets about scattered resistance by groups here and there, but nothing organized. Pamphlets, newspapers urging the people to resist showing up on kiosks, buildings. Then the Nazis tear them down and haul off the brave coordinators to prison.

No wonder everyday life here in Paris is beyond stressful.

I look out the long window in the library overlooking the street. Empty. A light frost covers the street with the promise of snow. Cold, unforgiving. Even the beautiful linden trees droop like wilted flowers. It's lonely and not pleasant to walk in the streets.

Wait, is that me talking?

What happened to the girl who believed she could make a

difference? I want her back to give me a kick in the boot. Because I know somewhere out there is a place for me in this war.

I can't believe the Underground is dead. I feel in every fiber of my being it still exists, that the hate for the Nazis simmers below the surface in every Frenchman and woman. I feel the tension and anxiety everywhere. When I stand in line for bread, ride my bicycle, or sit at a café, there's a low hum in the air I can hear, feel its vibration. I'm not the only one willing to resist, to fight.

The problem is... *how do I find the others?*

I believed our student show of solidarity would propel the movement. Keep it going, but it didn't. Then I remember the meetings and speeches before the demonstration, the powerful voices of those willing to speak out, how they inspired me—

Remi. He spoke out the loudest. I know the man is a shady character with ties to the criminal underworld, but in these times it's those men who have the cunning and skills to get the job done. I don't trust him but I trust the Nazis less, so I grab my camel coat and hat and take the daring step of heading where I imagine he hangs out.

The dimly lit bars in Montmartre.

And there I find him in a dark, seedy club on Rue Damrémont, drinking and boasting to a girl in black tights and a blue dress slit up the side about his exploits before the war selling the army rifles and ammunition. I also notice dried bloodstains on the floor, cracked wood on the bar, a chair with three legs... all confirming my suspicions about what goes on here. Mayhem, dirty dealings. I avoid the snide glances of men throwing darts, their swarthy looks emphasizing their attachment to the Montmartre underworld.

Then Remi sees me.

'*Zut alors,* mademoiselle, why aren't you in school?' He laughs, so does the girl in his arms.

'The Sorbonne is closed, monsieur.' I try not to gag at the smell of her heavy perfume and whiskey, then say what's on my mind before I lose my courage. 'I want to join you.'

He smirks, then pats his knee. '*Bien*, mademoiselle, there's room for one more.'

I shake my head, my cheeks tinting. '*Mais non*, monsieur, it's not companionship I seek.'

'*Eh*, what then?' he asks, puzzled.

'I want to join your network... and run the Boches out of Paris.'

8

PARIS, DECEMBER 1940

Justine

'I forbid it, mademoiselle, you are *not* spying for the Germans *and* the Underground.'

'Why not?' I ask, looking Arsène square in the eye. 'Because I've been comprised by the enemy?'

'Because you haven't a clue what you're getting into, mademoiselle.'

'Yes, I do,' I insist.

'And how much intelligence have you gathered?' Arsène glares at me, his eyes fierce.

'Well...' I don't have the nerve to tell him I've sourced together little information so far.

But I will, I assure myself.

'Enough to change the course of the war?' he asks.

I lower my eyes. 'Not yet.' Why is he grilling me like this? I don't like it. I take the offensive and stare back at him. 'What Nazi secrets have *you* uncovered in the brothel? The color of Goering's sock garters when he meets with Hitler?'

'Mademoiselle, if you only knew what you're asking could mean your death.'

I shiver at his words. I won't listen to him. He's just trying to scare me.

'I get it. You're afraid I'll be *too* good and show you up, *n'est-ce pas?*' I challenge him.

'You try my soul,' he admits, exasperated. I hit a nerve. 'So, what are you proposing?'

'I have unlimited access to an untapped source of information your people *don't* have.'

'I'm listening.'

'I sell hats to female German auxiliary workers, Nazi officers' wives, and more important, to their mistresses.'

He cocks a brow at my brazenness. 'Go on.'

He's not that impressed.

I add a jaunty sway of my shoulders to ease the tension between us. 'Women talk and share secrets when they get together, trying to outdo each other, vying for the prettiest *chapeau* and the juiciest gossip. A competition, if you will, and I hear every word.'

He cups my chin and in a dead serious tone he says, 'Putting you in grave danger.'

'Isn't *everyone* in Paris in danger these days?' I shoot back.

He has no answer for that.

We've been arguing about my decision to spy for both sides for the past hour and my toes are freezing in my high heel pumps. I nearly lost my nerve, my morning sickness persisting, the cold getting so bad my nose and hands are *always* chilled. What derailed me from looking for him sooner was that I couldn't ditch the bodyguard the major put on my tail. I don't know what he suspects, but today he called him off. I made a beeline to Chez

Mimi to find Arsène using an excuse straight from the Nazi's own book of tricks.

Take the truth and twist it to your advantage.

I have to make Arsène see I'm the *only* one who can do this job. I shudder now as much from the cold in the attic as I do from the cool reception my offer generated from this man.

He heaves out a deep breath, then says what's really on his mind. 'I assure you, Justine, what happened to you with the major and his indefensible behavior has nothing to do with me discouraging you.'

'Doesn't it? You think I'm going to be careless, seek revenge, then slip up because I'm an emotional female?'

'I'm only trying to protect you.'

'You're just like the rest, Arsène, you see me only as a woman who belongs in the kitchen and the bedroom.'

'I never said that.'

'You didn't have to. I can see it in your eyes, dark and heavy depths that won't let you accept the fact this war won't be won only by men. That we Frenchwomen have just as much to lose, if not more.'

'More than a man giving his life for what he believes in?' he challenges me.

'No,' I concede, 'but a woman must be brave even when she doesn't want to be, knowing a careless word and she could lose the enduring love of a husband, father, brother taken by a bullet. Or a different enemy will take her child crippled by rickets and starving to death because there's no milk. Or she's violated by the enemy and suffers the painful shame of rape.'

'I understand how you feel, Justine, but—'

'Do you?' I shrug. 'I never grasped before what my sister meant by prejudice and harassment because she's a girl. How her professors mocked her for her bold ideas because "students in skirts" don't have the brains to think, dream about conquering science, that it's a different planet and women have no right to enter its realm. If only I'd listened to her more, helped her through those tough times, Ève wouldn't be risking her life.'

'And you wouldn't be risking *your* life *and* your child's spying for the Germans?' His eyes widen in surprise that I would dare contradict his judgment.

'That's different,' I counter. Tears prick at my eyes. 'I'm not an innocent like Ève.'

'Ah, *ma chère* Justine, I've known women like you who have the guts to stand up against tradition, but I've also seen what it costs them.'

He goes silent a long moment, his hard expression slipping away and his eyes diving into a distant past. Brows crossed, jaw set and an excruciating memory sparks in his troubled eyes that makes me hold my tongue. I see a different side of him, vulnerable and hurt. It lasts only a few seconds, but it's there nonetheless.

Then he continues.

'The desert can be both beautiful and cruel, mademoiselle. Where the sun beats down so hot and the tempest winds rip through the swirling sands, only the strongest survive. Where the women ride hard and fast beside their men even into battle. Female warriors wearing blue scarves over their faces, only their ebony dark eyes outlined in black kohl visible. Women who will do anything to protect their families... their men... their children. I believe you have the same grit, Justine, but you're up against a sadistic enemy who has no morals, no scruples and who preys on fear.'

'Then I *must* fight them, Arsène. I can't cry all day and do nothing, wallowing in self-pity. I know that now. You've *got* to let me try.'

Arsène's expression shifts. A weak smile, then I see the wheels turning in his brain. He knows I won't give up. 'No, it won't work. It's too dangerous.'

'*Please*. No one pays attention to the shop girl. I'm invisible in their eyes.'

'You're not a trained agent, Justine, gathering intelligence is—'

'A man's job?' I snap back, brows crossed.

Silence.

Between us. Cold. Biting.

He grits his teeth, fighting back what I'm certain is a typical male retort and for that I give him credit, but I'm determined to use my forced collaboration with the Nazis as a bargaining chip to give me *something* to do in this war besides make hats. A year ago I was highly motivated to do just that, design hats for flirting and making a woman feel pretty and powerful in a feminine manner. That's changed. Now I see my hat designs as a silent, provocative defiance. A way to use my talent to take down the Boches.

It's up to me to convince Arsène.

Earlier I persuaded my driver to let me off at the *maison close* with the excuse that Madame Mimi ordered a new turban and needed it without delay. Why? A pipe broke in the building, I said, no hot water and the madam can't wash her hair and she *must* look elegant for her important Nazi guests this evening. More truth than fiction since so many Parisiennes adopted the turban to cover their dirty hair because of the lack of heat to dry it.

It worked.

I popped a white turban into a hatbox, a saucy number I fashioned from a linen tablecloth interwoven with silk strips in blue and gold and accented with gold fringe, then off I went. I didn't have much time. The major expects me to join him later at the Hôtel Drouot. Herr Geller's suspicions proved to be true. He visits the auction house at least once a week to oversee the art for sale he procured from Jewish owners 'forced to sell'. He never mentions the painting he stole of Ève and me. It's like it disappeared through a portal to another world.

Madame Mimi was surprised to see me but delighted when I presented her with the turban. I couldn't fool her. Ever the watchful madam, she pressed me why I was here, but I suspected she already knew, that she's playing a dangerous game. Aligning herself to both sides and waiting to see who survives. I told her I needed materials for the hat shop and wanted to 'borrow' whatever feathers she could spare in the name of the Reich. That my customers stick their noses up at hats decorated with feathers from chickens and ducks. Madame Mimi was so delighted with her new turban, she didn't protest when I raced up to the attic, leaving her downstairs admiring herself in the beveled glass mirror in the foyer.

Arsène followed me up to the attic as I knew he would. He found me stuffing feathers into an empty hatbox to keep up my pretense for coming here. White boas, pink plumes, sapphire blue. I never expected he'd put up such a fight about me working for the Allies.

Finally, he speaks.

'You have no idea what you're getting yourself into, Justine, the loneliness that eats away at you—'

'I have you, *n'est-ce pas?*' I wave a purple feather under his nose.

He doesn't acknowledge my brazen retort, but he doesn't deny it either. 'The long waiting times, the frustration that pulls at every fiber in your being, the worry of not knowing if they got your intelligence and the guilt because lives depend on it.'

'All the more reason to me to try.'

'You're forgetting the most important thing.'

'What is that?' I look at him, serious.

'The bone-chilling fear that wraps itself around you, constantly looking over your shoulder, never knowing if the shadow behind you is a Gestapo man about to stick a knife into your back... a fear so acute *nothing* can take it away.'

'Not even the warm touch of someone who understands what you're feeling?' I dare to lay my hand upon his arm, show him I'm not afraid, that I can also comfort *him*. Again, he says nothing, but the twitch I feel in his muscle tells me I'm not wrong. 'In case you haven't noticed, Arsène, or whatever your name is, the women of France are joining in the fight. Look at my sister Ève, demonstrating with the students from the university.'

He takes off his beret, puts it on again, mulling over his thoughts before he speaks and catches me off guard. 'I admire your sister's courage, but she almost got herself killed at the Place de l'Étoile.'

Alarmed, I step back. I didn't know she was also involved in the Armistice Day demonstration, though I'm not surprised. 'How do you know that?'

'It's my job to know.'

'And you weren't going to tell me?' I accuse him.

'I wasn't sure I could trust you.'

'Oh, and now you are?'

'I'm still not convinced, but it's my duty to watch over you.' He draws in his breath. 'After all, I *did* save your life.'

I blush, remembering the last time we met here when I contemplated drinking arsenic to end my despair. I'll never forget it. 'Nothing you say can dissuade me. I want to do my part.'

'What if you're detained then interrogated by the Gestapo?' He paces up and down, making no effort to disguise his long strides *or* his voice. I swear his masculine scent grows stronger as we speak. His deep baritone fills the attic with a richness that grabs me by my cold toes and wiggles up my spine.

I won't be seduced by this man. Though I want to be... badly.

I stand up taller, chin raised. 'I can handle it.'

He grabs me by the shoulders and stares deep into my eyes. In spite of my resolve to remain calm, I can't look away. 'Do you know what the prisons are like under the new regime, mademoiselle? Torture and starvation, sadistic cesspools where women are stripped and humiliated and brought to their knees in unimaginable ways to serve their Nazi masters...' He leaves his thought unfinished. 'I pray you *never* find out, mademoiselle. The Gestapo makes Hades look like a walk in the Bois.'

'I know the risks.'

Do I? Would I break under torture?

'You're not trained for espionage.'

'*You* could train me, monsieur, teach me what I need to know.'

'No.'

'*Please.* I've picked up techniques from the Gestapo man the major does business with. I see how Herr Geller pretends not to watch you but observes your every move. How he leads people on with wrong information, knowing they will correct him with the *right* information.'

'No.'

I purse my lips. 'You're being unfair. I'm not dealing with hardened criminals or gleaning intelligence from trained military officers, but fussy German Frauen and young French girls starved for attention because their men are hiding in the woods or imprisoned in POW camps. Girls lonely for a virile man to hold them in his arms... stroke their hair... kiss their cheek.'

I don't add I'm also lonely. I must stay strong.

He holds me tight in his arms, his medals poking me in the chest, his beard tickling my face when he cups my chin in his hand and forgets his disguise, lowering his mouth toward mine, then he turns away.

He lets go with a big sigh. 'If I help you, no personal involvement, do you understand?'

I can't stop my racing pulse. 'Yes, I understand.'

He nods. '*Bon*. I can't sanction your crazy idea, but you make a good case. Our network lacks agents who can infiltrate the Nazi hierarchy.'

I grin. 'Then you'll teach me?'

'I'd rather you work *only* for us and not the Germans. It pains me to see you live in constant fear of discovery. I can't emphasize how dangerous the work of a double agent is. You must toss away all scruples, all personal feelings and emotions. Push aside the rage inside you when you see German soldiers gawking at you and flirting, learn to laugh at tense moments that make you sick when a Boche harasses an old Jewish man. Smile when you want to cry. You must learn not to fear death because it's part of the game. And God knows the humiliation you'll feel when a fellow countryman or woman looks at you with contempt.'

I chew on the end of the long purple plume, not wanting to admit I experienced that look of horror from the staff at the Hôtel Ritz when the major took me by the elbow and escorted me to dine with him and his fellow officers just the evening before. The waiter looked away from me with embarrassment written on his face, barely speaking to me when he served my fruit compote, nodding when I requested more coffee and only half filling my cup, then nearly spilling it on me when I laughed nervously when a Nazi officer at our table complained about the service. In his eyes, I not only betrayed France, but every Frenchwoman, for probably no more than a pair of silk stockings.

I don't blame him.

I blame the Nazis.

'I can survive the looks, the taunting, the hatred, Arsène. I have to, not just for France, but for Ève and Maman. And the de Giocomtes. I want to keep them safe. Major Saxe-Müllenheim promised me no harm would come to them, no arrests, no deportation.'

'And you believe him?' he asks, narrowing his eyes.

'Would you?'

'No.'

'But I *do* believe he will set that Gestapo man on my family if I don't do what he asks. I've seen the salacious pleasure in the major's eyes crinkling up at the corners when he introduces me to his fellow officers, his hand placed firmly around my waist, then rubbing the back of my neck. It sickens me, but my strongest asset is the fact I *am* a woman. And I intend to use it to my full advantage.'

He meets my eyes. 'You may be right, mademoiselle, but I don't know of *any* woman working for both sides, yet you give me no choice.'

'When do I start?' I ask with an eagerness that makes him squirm. He's clearly not happy with my decision. He keeps looking at me with a deep sadness that colors his eyes dark and forbidding, haunting. Like I'm a piece of cheese set in a mousetrap.

'Go about your regular routine, mademoiselle. Don't draw attention to yourself... and *don't write down* what you hear. Keep it in your head.'

'How will I contact you?'

'Exactly as you did today. When you have information to pass to me, deliver a new hat to Chez Mimi. Tell Madame it's a gift from the major for her services caring for the women he brings here.' He maintains eye contact with me to make certain I understand. I nod.

'Is there a new "major's girl"?' I have to ask.

'Yes. Her name is Thérèse.'

Thérèse. I can't keep the burning bile from rising up in my throat, closing it up tight. So another girl suffers with me. Another victim. *Is she young? A virgin? Did she have dreams now shattered?* I wish I could reach out to her, comfort her. Being a rape victim is a whole circle of Hell of its own. The pinging in your chest every time the worst moments return like a haunting refrain. The loneliness of having no one to talk to who understands, *really understands* the fear, the disgust you feel.

For the man who did this to you.

For yourself for not fighting back harder.

For wishing you were dead.

Like I do.

It revisits me at the oddest times. When I'm trying to block the wind blowing through my skirts like cold, invisible hands reaching out to touch me between my thighs. A tense moment when a Nazi smiles at me too long. In the dark when it's so cold I shake all over and can't make it stop.

And now there's another girl.

Is there no end to the SS officer's lusty games?

'I'll contact London,' Arsène says, 'not an easy task with the damn Nazis bombing the city every night, then get back in touch with you.' With a deep sigh, he nods toward the tiny stairway leading up to the attic. 'Go. I'll follow you later.'

I head for the stairway, but not before I see him pull out a plain brown wooden rectangular box hidden under two loose floorboards. He opens it and I catch a glimpse of headphones and a microphone. I've never seen anything like it.

'I've had Gertie with me since I ended up in Berlin in 1939.' Arsène explains it's an army field wireless set. *Which* army he doesn't say. 'She comes in real handy these days.'

I'm surprised he lets me see it.

Or is he testing me?

I head down the narrow stairway. I feel energized, but I know nothing can ever be between us. That's why he doesn't remove his mask. Keeps me guessing, keeps me from breaking down barriers between us. That one delicious moment when he lowered his lips to mine, his breathing hot and fast, tells me he feels *something* for me.

I can live with that. I have to. It's a wonderful feeling, my heart less heavy, my soul at peace. I don't even know what he looks like without that disguise, but I feel close to him.

And maybe, *just maybe*, I'm not as lost as I thought I was.

9

PARIS, JANUARY 1941

Ève

I sneak out of Maison Bleue again tonight to attend a meeting in the Montmartre neighborhood at the quieter end of Rue Damrémont. Remi's mistress, who I now know is called Iris, maintains an apartment here. She's a sassy brunette with a past she keeps hidden under her garters, along with the stiletto knife strapped to her thigh. Her place is perfect for our cell to meet, our secret lab filled with chemicals, empty tin cans, wires, dynamite.

A saboteur's delight.

Remi is a genius at organizing and running the Jade Network, and I suspect his craftiness comes from a life of petty crime. The stocky partisan grins with a pirate's smile, his beret pushed back on his head, a dirty toothpick hanging out of his mouth. Word on the street is that he was part of a gang released from prison by the Nazis to do their bidding, but after his sister was raped by German soldiers and she slit her wrists, he took up the cause and formed his own resistance network. The concierge for the building thinks he's a pimp and the cabaret dancer a prostitute, what with men coming and going at all hours.

Which is why I wear a cap and trousers to avoid suspicion.

And that presents a problem.

I let myself out through the servants' entrance by the garden, knowing if Maman sees me she'd forbid me to leave *la maison* wearing trousers, her old-fashioned ideas about how a girl should dress above reproach. On the other hand, I don't know what Madame de Giocomte would say and I'd rather not find out, so I avoid her, too. I wouldn't want to disappoint her seeing how she's done so much for me. I *would* tell her not to give up hope, that there are Parisians fighting to make a difference... for her, too.

I know she's scared for her husband, her sister-in-law along with her daughter and her children.

The rumors we heard months ago about the Vichy government instituting anti-Jewish legislation turned out to be true when Jews were banned from public life in October. Then they defined who is Jewish and who isn't by your grandparents, making Madame de Giocomte nervous since her entire family is Jewish. More sanctions are coming from what I hear in the meetings, changes so subtle the Nazis don't think anyone will notice, though I wonder how far they will go.

Another rumor is they'll freeze Jewish bank accounts by spring. Then what will Madame de Giocomte do? Whatever happens, we will never abandon her. Maman may be strict and old-fashioned, but her loyalty to Madame is something she passed down to her daughters. *No one hurts Monsieur and Madame de Giocomte on my watch.* We owe them everything. Another reason why I'm here tonight to keep a step ahead of the Nazis' next move. We meet in secret since the Nazis forbid public gatherings of more than six people.

I look around the room. Tonight I see at least a dozen familiar faces from the Sorbonne; classes started again in early December and thankfully I don't have to report to the police any more. No one over thirty, most in their early twenties. Guillaume, Yves, Jean, and Coralie, a wide-eyed girl a little older than me. The boys flirt with her and she flirts back until Remi orders the lot to keep their minds on business. No one thinks *I'm* seductive, which suits me fine. That would be like catching a fish in the Seine and calling it a mermaid.

I sit in the corner alone, my long hair bound on top of my head, cap in hand, thinking about the past few months. How Justine's disappearance is my fault. A moment of poor judgment I blame on my youth because I was so naïve about controlling my own destiny. I lunged forward without thinking. Accusing the SS officer of stealing *The Daisy Sisters* was a stupid move on my part. As if any Nazi would listen to reason. I give myself the excuse that back then we weren't yet privy to how far the Nazis would go to control us. They still flashed that false smile of 'wanting to get along'.

But this defiant Nazi SS officer played by his own rules.

What fools we were.

But Maman and I survived. We had to. We had a very cold winter and snow on Christmas. But we had a few moments together without fighting. I was helping her knit socks for the POWs, dropping stitches as I'm wont to do, but it was the togetherness I shared with my mother that counted, not the lopsided socks. Maman lit a candle for Justine and we talked about our first Christmas at Maison Bleue when Justine and I were children, Madame de Giocomte insisting we join the servants dancing, singing, playing games. She always made Christmas for us while she and Monsieur de Giocomte celebrated Hanukkah, all of us indulging in a chocolate yule log with vanilla buttercream frosting. Justine and I jumped into the air, scooping up festoons of asparagus fern laced with three-foot strands of hand-blown glass beads and then wrapping them around each other, giggling.

Two little girls so happy they had a home for Christmas.

I sigh. Deeply. The pain of missing her never goes away. That worries me so. I fear I'll become bitter and lose sight of my mission to free France so what happened to Justine doesn't happen to other women. I can't help but wonder when this is over, *will there be justice for Justine*? Bring her murderer to trial. Yet I won't forget every woman sexually violated by these monsters and seek a measure of redress for them, too.

I can't believe no one will cry out for justice.

I sit quietly, wrapped up in my thoughts while Remi makes the rounds, asking, 'Has anyone seen Michal? Or did the French police arrest him again for brawling with German soldiers?'

Michal is apparently the Polish codebreaker he recruited but he's yet to show up for the meetings. The others grumble, Coralie giggles, which makes me believe she knows something Remi doesn't. I fidget, hoping he never shows. The man sounds reckless, irresponsible when there's work to be done, but Remi seems anxious to find him. Speaks highly of his exploits as a fighter in Warsaw.

I shake my head. That's just like the Resistance leader, playing *him* up and ignoring *me* when I raise my hand and try to ask a question.

As usual.

I keep waiting for my chance to prove myself, but Remi passed me over to be a courier, riding a bicycle to drop off messages. *You're just not innocent-looking, Ève*, he said, *like Coralie with her pink cheeks and girlish curves.*

What he means is, I'm not pretty enough.

So I get the menial work. Cooking, washing dishes, and printing pamphlets while Coralie gets all the exciting jobs. Like acting as the lookout at the Musée de l'Homme while Remi picked up a false identity card for a Jewish lawyer on the Gestapo's list. How she smiled and batted her eyes at Nazi soldiers carousing in the museum while Remi sneaked downstairs to the basement where resisters work printing a newspaper and forging identity cards right under their noses.

Or when Coralie carried a gun in a shopping bag and delivered it to this Polish codebreaker Michal in a jazz cave in the Latin Quarter, right after he was released from a holding cell. She whispered to me how handsome he is... and tall. The girl is starry-eyed over him. I shake my head. No way would I let a man like that get under my skin.

The only time I got noticed was when Remi pointed out I had blue ink on my fingers. A telltale sign of printing pamphlets, he said. *And* a resister. He reminded me if I'm not more careful, he'll send me home to my *maman*. I told him I wasn't a child. I'm eighteen.

He laughed.

I hate how he treats me.

I look around for the only member of our cell who pays attention to me.

Claude.

He's late. I try not to worry, but I can't help it. The making of explosives falls to the bespectacled loner. Tall, gangly, his right hand covered with a tight, black leather glove to mask his scarred flesh, he set up a makeshift lab in Iris's apartment. He doesn't complain when I sit and observe him at work. I hunker down in my chair for hours watching him like I'm at the cinema. I've memorized every step, how to mix the chemicals including mercury, how much dynamite to pack in the tin cans, then adding nails.

And always, *always* handle the stick of phosphorous with pliers when you remove it from the jar of oil. Or it will ignite.

I listened and learned. Claude didn't make it easy, mumbling in an accent foreign to me, keeping his head down, his hands steady, his long fingers moving about in the air like a wizard's, measuring and mixing ingredients.

I was fascinated.

Where Claude gets his raw materials, I never ask. I learned there are secrets a man never shares. That the art of resistance resides deeper in some than in others. In Claude, it's a purgatory bordering on the macabre.

I wiggle my nose remembering the pungent smell of sawdust treated with chemicals that filled the tiny fifth-floor apartment when he put together explosives for his last job. He was quite pleased with his plan, a unique way of expressing his hatred for the Boches. He hid the explosives in horse dung, then left it on a country road the Nazis favor, speeding by in their big Mercedes touring cars. When he heard a driver and an officer suffered serious injuries, I saw him smile.

When he shows up tonight, he's not smiling.

I see his arm in a sling, his left eye red and bloodshot, half-closed. The man is stricken with self-pity, a flask in his hand, the smell of whiskey emitting from him like the devil's brew. He got caught in an ambush, shot in the shoulder, and now his arm is too weak to make accurate calculations. He's drunk, his skills useless, making Remi desperate for someone who knows how to handle explosives for a job coming up. Someone who won't panic. Someone who can slip in and out of the situation without anyone noticing them.

I wave my hand, trying to get his attention, but his eyes gloss over me. I follow him around like a hungry puppy as he goes from student to student, grilling each man to see who has made bombs, who understands what he's talking about, how to carry the explosive without blowing yourself up. Someone here *must* have made an incendiary bomb, he keeps saying, raking his hand through his hair, and it's that someone he needs for the mission.

Dangerous. No moon.

A one-man job.

I push my way in front of him, forcing him to make eye contact with me. 'I can do the job, monsieur. I'm familiar with how to make bombs and handle explosives.' I stand up tall, pull up my coat collar to emphasize my height, jut out my chin.

'*You, ma petite?*' he smirks. 'A scared rabbit would have more luck.'

'Because I'm a girl?' I dare him. The shocked look on Remi's face makes me more determined to prove my worth.

His eyes narrow. 'You dare to challenge my judgment, mademoiselle?'

I set my mouth. 'Yes, monsieur. Watch me.'

I grab metal tubes and the materials I need to put together the incendiary bomb, using the skills I learned from Claude. I work quickly, my fingers moving on their own, my eyes ever watchful when I grab the pliers and place the phosphorous in the center of the cardboard filled with sawdust so the air doesn't ignite it.

Not a sound in the apartment.

All I hear is heavy breathing.

Then joy and relief rip through me when I finish the task, cutting the tension in the air and bringing me a sense of pride I haven't felt in a long time.

I turn to Remi, a big grin on my face. '*Voilà*, monsieur.'

He nods. '*Très bon*, mademoiselle. Perhaps I underestimated you, but if you botch this job—'

'I won't, monsieur.'

He stares at me with a bitter clarity in his eyes, trying to make up his mind, then before he talks himself out of it, Remi draws me a map, then gives me instructions to memorize it then destroy it.

'I assure you, mademoiselle, I'm giving you a chance because Claude is hurt. I still think you're too young for the job no matter how smart you are.'

I'm half listening to him. I feel so excited, I wouldn't be surprised if I didn't bust the buttons on my jacket.

I'm in the game. *Finally.*

10

PARIS, LATE JANUARY 1941

Justine

True to his promise, Arsène watches over me.

And my unborn baby.

The man is a constant factor in my life if not unpredictable. I never know when he'll turn up. Like delivering a crate of black-market oranges and apples to Madame Péroline's hat shop, the nervous owner hustling him into the backroom, but not before he tosses me an orange and teases Madame about the 'pretty new mamselle'. I know it's him by his deep, velvety voice, though his accent is rough and wild like his longish black hair hugging his collar, his thick mustache and stubble on his face.

I don't know whether to laugh or cry.

Or when I was trudging through the December fallen snow, my arms filled with a box of red satin ribbons to make holiday bows for our customers to spruce up their old *chapeaux*. I got stuck in a snowdrift and would have lost my footing if a dashing gendarme in his round black cap and flowing cape hadn't come along and scooped me up in his strong arms.

To protect le bébé, he said, his breath hot on my cheeks.

And this morning when I go to pray at the Church of Saint-Pierre-de-Chaillot near my apartment, I see a priest in flowing black robes lighting a votive candle, a three-peaked black clergyman's hat topped with a black pompom sitting atop his head. He's wearing wire-rimmed spectacles I think, since his face is hidden in shadows, but I'd know that tall figure anywhere and those battered black boots.

He nods toward the confessional. I follow him.

Inside the cramped booth, it's dark and cold but my cheeks burn, my pulse racing.

I wiggle about on the hard wooden bench hugging my buttocks where sinners lean forward, hands folded in prayer, and beg for forgiveness and then go sin all over again.

I'm here to pass along information.

'Arsène, I—'

'Bless you, my child.' He cuts me off, then lowers his voice. 'You were followed, mademoiselle. See if the Gestapo man is anywhere about.'

I creak the door open enough to let the light in and look around. The church is empty. No one hovering nearby. I should have known the major would send that Gestapo man to follow me. Doesn't he have anything better to do? Or maybe the major *didn't* send him and he has his own nefarious reasons for tailing me? Herr Geller knows no boundaries. Not even the house of God is safe from his snooping. I imagine the ancient spirits who have inhabited this holy ground since the eleventh century drove him away.

'We're alone,' I whisper.

I can't keep the anticipation out of my voice, knowing what that means. Precious minutes to soak up the pure joy of being with him. It could be days, even weeks before I see him again.

'You look beautiful, Justine. Imminent motherhood becomes you.'

I adjust my pale gray veil in a typical female fashion of a woman trying to hide her scars, not on my face but on my soul. Even in the darkness of the confessional booth, I blush. For a moment, I let myself think about what he said, tell myself he means it when he says I'm beautiful. A hint of the man underneath I yearn to know better. In some ways, I prefer not knowing what he looks like. Then I can't be disappointed. Why? Because I see him as so handsome and so strong, no man can ever live up to my dream. Yet it's that dream that has softened the hardness around my heart toward men.

'Bless me, Father, for I have sinned.' I lower my voice to a saintly whisper. 'I have information.'

'*Bien*. I got your message.'

Madame Mimi received another new hat today.

I take a breath. 'Frau Befus was complaining about her husband Colonel Stefan Befus after a disappointing trip to Versailles over the weekend.'

I wish I could see his strong profile through the grill. I'm more curious than ever to know *who* he is, feeling a connection deep in my heart that Arsène is the strong fighter I've conjured up in my mind, that need is both a joy and a burden for my soul to carry. As a woman, I want to know him, though it must be from afar. There can never be anything between us.

Again, I face the consequences of my rape. No man wants bruised fruit.

'Go on,' he says.

'He sent her to explore the gardens of the Sun King alone while he spent the afternoon in the dining room of the nearby Trianon

Palace Hôtel in a huddle with two SS officers from Berlin. Curious as to what was more important than being with his wife, Frau Befus broke up their "little party" but not before she caught bits of conversation about plans for Hitler to invade Russia in the summer.' I smirk. 'She's upset the Führer is interfering with her agenda to purchase items for her apartment here in Paris. An apartment *confiscated* from a Jewish merchant.'

I can't keep the disgust out of my voice yet I'm pleased my social tattling paid off, proving my worth. The woman fears her husband will be transferred to a command in the East and will insist she return to Berlin. A tingly feeling creeps up my spine, and an uncomfortable awareness that Maison Bleue could be wrenched from the hands of Madame de Giocomte makes me queasy. In spite of the major's promise to me, is a Jewish home ever *really* safe from the Nazis?

'We know Hitler is considering an operation on the Eastern Front.' He asks, 'Did she say *when* the invasion will take place?'

'June.'

'Are you certain?'

'Yes, Frau Befus has her heart set on attending an upcoming estate sale auction at the Hôtel Drouot but the items she wanted are in a Nazi storage location and won't be available until summer.' I let go with a frustrated sigh. I can't help myself.

'Mademoiselle?'

'I can't believe that silly woman cares more about bidding on a pair of "rare eighteenth-century porcelain cockatoos", to quote her, than her husband's welfare even if he *is* a Nazi.'

I explain how all Paris is going mad attending these daily auctions of art, jewelry, and furniture from looted collections of Jewish owners, eager to buy up what they can before the art works are shipped to Chambord for safekeeping before making their way to storage repositories in Germany.

'And you wouldn't?' he teases.

'No, if I had a husband, I'd... I'd...'

Adore him, love him. Squeeze him so tight he couldn't breathe because I loved him so much. I'd never send him into danger.

'You'd do what, mademoiselle?'

I dip my chin, bite on my lower lip. I can't hide my past from him, but I don't have to let him *all* the way inside my head. Not now... not *ever*? A slow perspiration trickles down my neck. Is it getting hotter in here? Best not to answer his question. 'Never mind, monsieur, because it will never happen.'

'Why not?' I hear his breath catch.

'You know why.'

Again I clam up, push the past into a neat package and ignore his curiosity—more like probing—to see how I'm coping. I don't want to play this game, but I sense we're kindred spirits getting over a major hurt in our lives. I like him, but it's got to stop right here and he knows it.

I ramble on about the German Frau's comments about Aryan racial superiority and how all her husband talks about is enslaving the Russian people and opening up their lands to Germans, all the while insisting *she'll* never move to that barbaric wasteland.

'Keep her talking. See if she knows how many men, tanks...'

I let go with a chuckle. '*Mon cher* Arsène, Frau Befus cares only about hats and how many ribbons she can tie under her double chins.' Then I get serious. 'The major is taking me to the Bal Tabarin cabaret this weekend. Front row table entertaining an important military officer from Lyon. It's the general's first trip to Paris. I shall smile, laugh and tease, and try to find out more.'

I hear him draw in his breath. 'Don't take any chances, Justine, you're playing a dangerous game and with the baby coming—'

'I'm fine, Arsène. The major still has no idea I'm pregnant.'

'You won't be able to hide your condition much longer.'

'I know, but until then, I have these wonderful moments alone with my baby.'

I rub my tummy, rounded and perfect. I think often of the new life growing within me and pray the child will understand how much I want them, that they can be their own person and live their own life, but then I wonder how to keep them safe from the stigma of being a child of rape.

I can't slam the door shut on who the birth father is, though I want to. It's a dilemma I've yet to come up with an answer for.

I have to be honest that sometimes I'm so scared, I wrap my arms around myself and my unborn baby and cry.

'If you fear for your child's safety, Justine, I can ask London to get you out of France.'

It takes me a moment to grasp what he's saying, that my child can be free from danger. He explains to me the English have plans to drop agents into France via parachute and organize secret landing fields here to pick up compromised agents.

It sounds wonderful, but in my bones I know I can't run.

'I can't leave Maman and Ève. I don't trust the major to keep them out of the hands of the French police if I run away. *Or* the Gestapo.'

Anger, a very controlled anger but there nonetheless, colors his voice and sends new fear in me when he tells me to be suspicious of everyone. That I'm in more danger than he's letting on, before his mask slides back into place. Then in a professional manner, Arsène gives me intelligence I can pass along to the major, a combination of misinformation along with valid information about women who frequent the shop. Names and the vague whereabouts of Jewish customers of the House of Péroline. Clients who *left* Paris and are safely over the Spanish border. I'll find the list in the Missal he left in the booth for me. It's written in an invisible ink between the lines on a handwritten shopping list on white paper. Names I'll tell the major I gleaned from the gossip I heard in the hat shop and recorded to give to him. Though I fear the day the major asks me to write something in invisible ink and I can't.

It will take the Gestapo days, *weeks* to check each name.

I don't say what I'm thinking out loud, but I shake all over each time I give the major the intelligence from the Allies written in invisible ink made from chemicals I've never heard of. I wish I could ask Ève for help. My brilliant sister would know what antipyrine is and how to mix it with alcohol to make the ink. Arsène assures me this is the method the Nazis use.

And a toothpick wrapped with cotton wool at the tip to write.

'Also,' Arsène continues, 'memorize these names. Angéline de Cadieux and Countess Ester Bulgávari.'

I repeat the names. 'Where would I find the mesdemoiselles?'

'At the House of Doujan.'

I smile. The famed *parfumerie* on Rue Saint-Honoré where Maman wished me to learn the art of perfume.

How interesting.

'Angéline is Roma and the countess is Jewish. If you hear any information regarding roundups of Roma or Jews, it's vital you warn them.'

Are they members of the Resistance? I want to ask, but don't. The less I know, the less risk in me telling anyone.

Arsène clears his throat. 'I intended to accompany you back to your apartment, but after I saw the Gestapo man following you here, it's best we're not seen together. And be careful, Justine. It's not only very cold in the streets, but the pavements are slippery.'

I know what he's thinking, how easily I could fall.

And lose the child. No, it can't happen, it won't.

'I don't believe God would be so cruel, Arsène, not after all I've done to keep this baby.'

I hear him let go with a deep sigh. 'I shall never be far away, Justine, I promise.'

And with that my time with him is done.

Dipping two fingers into the holy water font at the entrance, I bless myself before I leave the church without a glance backward. I know Arsène is watching me. I feel his eyes boring into my back with every echo of my high heels on the marble. Though he remains in the shadows of my life, he gives me so much more than protection.

He gives me hope.

11

PARIS, FEBRUARY 1941

Ève

The dark, slick metal of the locomotive on the tracks at the railroad yard not far from the Gare de l'Est... greasy, yet wet with mist. It sits on the tracks, its engine smoking. No one is aboard. *Bon.* The train waits for the first light of dawn, then there's the signal from the foreman in the engine shed to begin its journey to Germany. Its railcars are filled with leather goods and shoes. Vital items the Vaterland needs to keep this war going. A last-minute coupling of a railcar containing furniture stolen from Jews was added, according to intelligence from the railway foreman. Remi wanted Claude to put together a fuse and charge and do the job.

He got me instead.

I grit my teeth as I make my way alongside the railway track, my heavy boots kicking up the wet dirt. A sudden rainstorm hit earlier. I spit on the tracks. Knowing the furniture and leather in that railcar come at the expense of weary and hungry Frenchmen, women, and children.

Why does God let this happen?

I keep stalling, my mind reeling, willing myself to remain functional, not lose my courage. I can't allow myself to question what I don't understand about this war—why so many Frenchmen and women have gone along with the Occupation—or let my personal feelings get in the way, a hidden danger to every *résister*.

Tonight my job is to put the locomotive engine out of commission.

No one knows how effective these acts of sabotage will be in the long run. Remi warned me other attempts have failed, that in spite of his efforts, lapses in communication hamper our activities and his network is in need of weapons.

Frustration drove him to give me the job.

I've got plastic explosives hidden under my jacket that Remi shoved into my hand, refusing to say where he got them, giving me instructions the foreman will meet me at a nearby café. He's fearful the Gestapo has been watching the man but he's willing to do this last job before heading to the Free Zone and willing to teach me how to place the charges in a small compartment on the side of the engine then ignite the fuse. Giving us time to escape before the explosion goes off.

Two minutes.

That was the plan.

But the railway foreman didn't meet me at the café.

Was he arrested? Or is his story a phony and he's actually a Gestapo informant? Are the Boches waiting to take me down, toying with me... *watching me*? I'm shaking, hugging the precious charges hidden under my jacket, praying my body heat doesn't set them off prematurely, my confidence waning.

I can't let Remi down.

The workers have left for the day and a deep darkness settles on the railyard. I move in silence between the cars, the dark, looming presence of the enemy everywhere in the railyard, German soldiers patrolling, unaware of a lone figure intent on sabotage.

I blend in, a night creature on the prowl. Wearing men's trousers, a short dark jacket with hidden pockets, a metal-gray cap covering my hair bound on top of my head, I smudge coal dust on my face. Just another skinny little worker the Boches consider irrelevant.

The truth is, I'm scared. Shaking. Nose, hands cold. *What if I drop the charges?* This is my chance to prove myself, give the Germans the stab in the back they deserve for what they did to Justine.

Don't think. Just do your job.

Now that job has changed. Without the foreman's help, I have no idea where to place the charges on the locomotive engine. A compartment on the side, I think. *But where?* I can't see in the dark and I have to keep the charges from blowing up while coming up with an alternative plan. What would Claude do?

Set the explosive charges on the railroad tracks instead, then detonate them.

Yes, of course. Simple, but it will work.

I keep on the move, bent over, head down till I get to the next car. I stop, listen. It's all quiet on this night, except in my brain, my thoughts rattling around and my instinct pushing me to act. I'm as antsy as a tiger reaching through the bars on its cage with big paws, itching to attack anyone foolish enough to get close.

I want to strike *and strike now*. Any second a German patrol could shine a light on my face and shoot me before I finish laying down the explosives.

Another dead partisan, they'll say. *Just a boy*. Pity.

And then spit on my corpse.

I dare not light a match. I don't have a torch and there's no moon tonight. But there *is* light coming from the engine shed emitting a soft glow on the railway line about five meters from me. Someone forgot to draw the blackout curtain. The German sentry is bound to see it, switch it off. *Wait*, I see a shadow racing past the window. *Is that the sentry?*

Did he see me?

I have to hurry, no time to bury the charges beneath the rail or camouflage the firing wire. Instead I place the charge against the track and pray. The explosion won't be as powerful because it's not directed upward, but it'll have to do. My gut is twisted into a tangled knot so tight I can't breathe. I set the second charge on the track, then a third.

I detonate the fuses, then get the hell out and *run*.

I race across the railyard, kicking up dirt, not knowing where I'm going. How can I see in the dark? I stumble, fall, and then cry out like a damn fool when I hit my knee on the track. My cry attracts the attention of the German patrol guard quick to react.

When the sound of bullets whistling past my ear jolts me so bad my heart stops, I expect to feel the impact of lead ripping through my flesh... until a man, tall and strong, throws me to the ground, pushing my face into the dirt.

Where did he come from? Was he the shadow I saw?

'Let me go!' I gag, dirt in my mouth.

'Shut up and stay still unless you want to get us both killed.'

'Who are you?' I detect an accent. *Polish?*

'Remi sent me. *Don't move.*'

I smell the scent of worn leather and a strong whiskey bitter like cedarwood lingering upon his clothes. He holds me tight, his hot breath on the back of my bare neck searing my skin as we roll over and over in the dirt until we're safely hidden under a train car.

God help us if the train starts to move.

We hold our breath, waiting for long, slow minutes as the German soldier checks under the other railcars, shining his torch, looking for me. Lying on my belly, my body sinks into the soft dirt, preparing itself for a final resting place while my mind rebels against it, and my heart... I don't know what it's doing because it's beating so fast I can't think. Only that the damn Boche will be upon us in seconds.

I prepare to fight for my life when—

The explosives go off. *Boom!*

One, two... *three.*

'*Now!*' the man holding me orders, pushing me through and out the other side from underneath the railcar. '*Run!*'

With the screaming Nazi patrol sounding in our ears, we race through the railyard, around the engine shed, past an empty supply truck, then climb the wire fence. God knows I've never moved so fast, my jacket catching on the wire's sharp edges, my hands clawing at the chain links, fingers bleeding.

I struggle to keep going, shivering like a wet mackerel at the end of a fishing pole, when I grunt loudly and make one big push and pull myself up over the top, then fall to the ground on the other side, the breath knocked out of me and—

My cap flying off my head.

My co-conspirator pulls me up to my feet and my long hair comes undone, swirling about my face like a silky veil hiding my nose, mouth but not my eyes. For a tense, drawn out moment we stare at each other. Squinting in the dark, not certain of our next move. We're lucky to escape, but that doesn't mean the German patrol won't find us, especially if they bring in the dogs. Neither of us speaks, each gauging the other's reaction to what is now a moment of truth.

I'm a female.

And that annoys the hell out of him.

'What the— You're a woman!' He takes a step back, his voice echoing with arrogance, but I refuse to back down.

'So?' I push back my hair. 'Haven't you ever seen a woman before?'

He lets out a low whistle. 'Not one in trousers, mademoiselle, with dynamite powder on her hands.'

12

PARIS, FEBRUARY 1941

Justine

I take great care in keeping up my 'pretty mademoiselle' look to prevent the major from suspecting I'm anything but his charming stooge, arranging my hair in soft waves, smearing on thick cranberry lipstick, and puffing out the shoulder pads on my black velvet gown to give the illusion of a small waist.

Mine is thickening each day.

But when he laughs with glee about the arrests of eleven resisters working from the basement of the Musée de l'Homme, I lose it.

Shocked, angry, then scared, I shake from head to toe, and the slender strand of white pearls I'm holding slips through my fingers and falls to the floor. *A gift to make my Daisy Sister smile.* I'm not fooled. He exudes charm when he wants something from me, and tonight he's showing off his French coquette. *Flirt, cajole, but never forget you owe your allegiance to me and you will obey my orders or—*

He leaves the rest unsaid. He *always* leaves the rest unsaid.

I've kept him in the dark about the baby, praying somehow I can get Ève and Maman out of Paris with the help of the Underground. Arsène offered to assist me, but I can't take them without the de Giocomtes, too. Maman would never leave Madame and I wouldn't ask that of her. Our biggest obstacle is getting everyone false identity cards. I'm not certain how the de Giocomtes feel about that and I can't ask them. Still, I must keep to my plan, hope that the opportunity will present itself to leave Paris and that I can make it work. Then the major will have no hold on me and my baby and I can escape his clutches.

Now the hope I embraced earlier in the confessional with the 'priest' turns to a charged tension that sets me on edge. Arsène insists the British are sending in trained agents, but every time the Resistance makes headway, the Nazis round them up, destroy their mimeograph machines, and make arrests. Like the group operating out of the Museum of Man on the esplanade of the Trocadéro.

I was counting on them helping me. According to Arsène, they'd organized escape lines over the mountains to Spain and could secure false identity papers. I'd yet to approach them. Arsène bade me wait for him to clear an introduction since anyone not known to them through family or close friends is highly suspect. Considering my association with an SS officer, he'd have to convince them I'm *not* a collaborator.

Now that hope is gone.

And my heart breaks for these brave *résistants* who face interrogation and worse at the hands of the Gestapo.

I go numb. Oh, my Lord, what if Ève is among the resisters sitting in *La Santè* prison awaiting trial? After what I saw from the attic window of Chez Mimi, she's crazy enough to have joined their group. I shudder, knowing common criminals are guillotined in the prison courtyard, hands bound behind them, forced to fall on their knees, then wait for the axe to fall.

But not students, surely?

I scoop up the pearls, hoping he doesn't notice my nervousness.

He does. A sly smile curls over his lips. *Damn him.*

'Does my pretty mademoiselle feel sympathetic to the *résistants*' plight?' he asks, probing.

'Of course not.' I smile, he smirks.

Then he adds in that superior tone of his, 'You know how dangerous *any* show of sympathy toward political dissidents is viewed by our Gestapo friends.' He grabs me by the ankle. I wince. 'You should be more careful with how you react to such news. I may not be around to protect you.'

I'm not surprised at his warning. He'll do anything to dissuade me from leaving his 'protection.' He loves to gloat.

'I know how important these arrests are to you, Major.' I wiggle out of his grasp. 'I was merely surprised how quickly you uncovered the group.'

'Yes, I was quite brilliant, *n'est-ce pas?*'

I watch him glow in his own words, knowing he's dying to tell me, but he's holding back to tease me. He won't say it, but I know how these arrests pull him out of his discontent, his angry frustration with certain members of the Party, his drive to secure his assignment to Paris.

The major strikes me as a man unfulfilled in his military career, and he's in a crisis.

His next words confirm that.

'I needed this win, mademoiselle. I have no intention of dying on the fields of France and Belgium or Russia.'

He goes on to brag about how hard he's worked to rise in the ranks of the SS. I listen, keeping my thoughts to myself, knowing that his incessant hunt to quash the Underground movement provides not only excitement, but the tool to keep his boots polished and out of the mud.

I also sense bouts of rage erupt when he's at an impasse in his quest and that's when he seeks a woman, a *young* woman to feed his ego. I fitted his needs on that August day before most SS realized how easily they could become art collectors simply by the taking.

He hasn't stopped since.

One collection after another. Art *and* females.

I'm so hungry to free myself from this man and the shame I feel, I resorted to mental tricks. I found the major possesses an ego I can milk when he's had too many cognacs.

It happened a fortnight ago when he showed up at my place in the ninth arrondissement unannounced, drunk and eager to flaunt his masculinity by unbuttoning his officer's jacket and showing off his athletic chest. I turned away, so he took it off and slung it over the wingback chair in the cozy parlor. Then he grabbed my arm and insisted I put on his SS jacket and model it for him, which I refused to do under *any* circumstance. He laughed and pulled me by the hair, yanking it hard and bringing tears to my eyes. He insisted I *would* please him or I'd suffer the consequences. I blurted out I was spilled milk and he should save his antics for his next conquest.

I must have hit a nerve because before I could pour him another cognac, he flopped on the embroidered divan, raked his hand through his military-cut hair, and talked about himself as men are wont to do when they think the woman listening is not important, that she's there merely to serve and assuage his ego. He ranted on about how I should be impressed, considering the circumstances of his birth. How hard he worked for the Party and how disappointed he was they didn't value him.

And how important it is to him to prove his purity as an Aryan.

He sees his way to the top as using Nazi anti-Semitism laws to confiscate important artwork for the Reichsmarschall's personal collection. The rotund Nazi can't get enough of French art and precious jewels.

I didn't know it until then, but the major dreams of being permanently assigned as an attaché to Reichsmarschall Goering's staff and art curate, a lofty aspiration for the illegitimate son of a wealthy landowner. Because it turns out my rapist is himself the *son* of a rape victim. I admit, I'm surprised when he opens up to me.

Then again, I'm not.

He's as drunk as a sailor on a Saturday night.

'My mother was a peasant girl taken by my father against her will.' He lifts a brow, watching my reaction with curiosity. 'I didn't find out until I was sixteen.'

'How difficult it must have been for you.' I shudder, but any urge I have to give *him* sympathy dissipates quickly. Yet I feel great hurt for the woman violated and then forced to keep it a secret.

'I hated my mother for keeping it from me. I grew up believing she was a servant in the manor house while I was raised as the son of the landowner with rights and privileges I believed were mine.' He scoffs. 'How wrong I was.'

That puts my opinion of him in a spin. I should have known he was reared as upper class with his arrogance and good looks. His suave mannerisms, decent French.

'What happened?' I have to ask, not only because I want to, but because he enjoys telling the story, as if it excuses his subversive actions toward women.

'I believed I would inherit the estate,' he says, 'but my father left it to his younger son born to a wealthy woman he later took as his wife, my heritage stolen from me.' He smacks his fist into his palm, not hiding his anger. 'I no longer had the right to be the landowner, the master, the title I earned but lost simply because of my unfortunate birth.'

'You still carry that anger,' I blurt out, taking the offensive against a man not used to having a woman speak to him as an equal. 'But that doesn't change who you are, Major, the bastard son of a man who couldn't or *wouldn't* amend the law of the land.'

'You know nothing about him, mademoiselle,' he yells, dismissing me with a wave of his hand. 'He taught me a man's greatest pleasure was in exercising *le droit du seigneur*, the medieval edict of taking the virginity of any girl before her groom gets to bed her.' He leans into me, the scent of tart lemon and tobacco mixing together and making me want to sneeze. I don't. I hold it in. 'It's served me well, mademoiselle. In Berlin, Warsaw, and now here in Paris.'

I keep silent, while a strange picture takes shape in my mind.

A sadistic portrait of a career officer who conned his way into the university to study art using faked credentials, then the SS. But he never got over the guilt of being illegitimate. That he raped me not for his personal pleasure, but to prove his superior Aryan manhood in the eyes of the Party.

And that makes this Nazi officer more dangerous than I thought.

Smirking, the major pours himself another cognac as I fasten the pearls around my neck. 'I can't tell you how pleased I am at having broken up that Resistance cell. That group of dissidents caused me many sleepless nights and daylong meetings at the Hotel Lutetia with my fellow officers of the Abwehr and the German Service of Information headquartered there. We interviewed anyone we believed had ties to the group.' He gulps down his cognac. 'Until we found our man. A mechanic willing to betray the leader and his followers.'

I cringe, stiffen my body and turn around so he can't see my eyes. *An informant.*

It's all so horrible, but I have to believe that no matter how many of us they arrest, the Nazis will never blot us out. We will go on fighting. *I* will go on fighting. That no matter how many strands of pearls he dazzles before me, I will never be his. True, he took my virginity with his cold hands groping me, his teeth biting me, his flesh hot and needy and driving me mad with sharp pain and making me cry from the utter humiliation.

But I repeat, *I will never be his.*

Why, God, isn't he punished?

I think about reporting him to the French police or the *Kommandant* in charge of German military affairs in Paris. Then I back down. No one will believe me. I hear stories of abuse every day from German female auxiliary workers who frequent the House of Péroline. A 'gray mouse' told me about a friend of hers who worked as a secretary in a government office, how the girl made a formal complaint about a young army recruit who forced her to have sex with him. The *soldat* was severely reprimanded, she said, not for the brutality of the rape, but because he disgraced the Wehrmacht with his undisciplined actions.

I find this idea appalling, even more so when the German girls trying on hats tell me how the officers they go out with love to boast it's their *duty* to perform in bed or they risk jeopardizing their standing in the Party. How SS officers are considered members of a 'racial elite' who have sexual needs that need to be met.

I'll never forget one *Fräulein* who told me her captain bragged that sex without consent isn't considered wrong if the SS officer has what the Nazi court calls 'a sexual emergency,' then she must submit to him.

Even if it means rape? I asked.

She didn't answer me and stormed out of the shop.

Ashamed or angry, I don't know which.

The whole thing disgusts me and pushes my nerves to the limit. God knows what other atrocities Nazi officers like Major Saxe-Müllenheim engage in to prove their manhood to the Party.

I look into the oval mirror and smooth down my gown while the major sips his drink and smiles, his eyes following me with admiring glances that make me uncomfortable. In the end it's more about exerting his power over me than forcing me to have regular sexual relations with him. He hasn't taken me to his bed for weeks. I suspect he's finding his 'release' somewhere else—*the new major's girl, Thérèse?*—and he sees himself more like my savior. Or it could be he's more interested in keeping our relationship more business than pleasure. If so, I don't know what I'll do when he realizes I'm pregnant with his child. That frightens me more than anything. I'd hoped to get Ève and Maman and the de Giocomtes out of France, but with that plan dashed, I've devised a new one to save the life of my child. When that day comes—and it will—I'll appeal to his ego, assure him the baby can 'pass' for an Aryan.

Or is that what he planned all along?

Is violating my body part of a macabre plan I've yet to discover?

'So, mademoiselle, enough about me. I'm eager for any news you have. Any gossip?'

'We haven't been very busy at the hat shop, monsieur,' I lie. 'I have nothing.'

'Too bad. I've been quite busy.' He recounts his day's activities harassing unfortunates with glee. 'I came upon a disgruntled old codger spitting on an SS man and watched him beaten about the head and ears until he bled.'

He cocks a brow. I say nothing. Baiting me, he continues. 'Then later a Jew protesting because a Wehrmacht officer requisitioned his apartment.' He pauses, waiting for my reaction. I refuse to say anything that sounds like I'm in alignment with his enthusiasm. 'The Jew and his entire family ended up in Drancy.'

'*Drancy?*' I repeat.

He refuses to elaborate, but it's a name I'm hearing more often these days from shop owners, salesgirls and the concierge of my building. A gossipy termagant who goes out of her way to spy on me, telling me tales about other 'occupants' sent there. A Jewish teacher, lawyer... and how none returned. According to her, Drancy is a cold, miserable place where life is put on hold until the 'next step.' It's that next step into the unknown that strikes fear into anyone arrested and sent there.

I look over at the major, oblivious to my thoughts while he savors another cognac.

I resist the maternal urge to cradle my belly, to whisper to my child, 'I will protect you.' Instead I take on a cool air, listen to the Nazi officer boasting how he led the investigation at the museum while I play the companion, refilling his drink, not forgetting to sway my hips even if it makes me want to vomit.

It's the only way I can survive.

And by changing the subject.

'Are you telling me this band of resisters operated under the noses of the inimitable Herr Geller and his Gestapo?' I ask, provoking him since I'm aware there's no love lost between the pudgy man in the black trench coat and the major. At first, I thought the two were in cahoots. Now I'm not so sure. I swear the German secret police have no allies in Hitler's army, even the SS. Like they're rivals competing for the Führer's good graces.

Did I really say that?

Am I starting to think like them?

If Arsène were here, he'd say that's a good thing, that to beat your enemy you must think like him. My problem is, I can't stop thinking about *him*. How the sun shines brighter when I'm with him. How my heart beats faster.

Not so with the major.

He can't stop talking about his victory.

The group fancies themselves intellectuals, publishing a radical newspaper called *Résistance*, he explains, his bare hand slipping under my long gown and stroking my leg. He left his kid gloves next to his major's cap in the antechamber. A discreet way of telling me he's the master here. I notice tonight he's carrying formal white gloves and a baton, presenting himself as the consummate officer of the Third Reich. The man's narcissism knows no boundaries.

I suck in my stomach, though it's getting harder to do.

'How long have you been onto them?' I smile, looking over my shoulder and fluffing my hair. It's a cat and mouse game we play. He sneaks up on me and I jump like a timid mouse, then he paws me again and I jump again, turning up the heat in his eyes to keep him interested. It makes me feel cheap and dirty.

Like I'm one of the girls at Chez Mimi.

And in a way, I am.

I have my price and Major Saxe-Müllenheim pays it.

To keep life normal for Ève and Maman—if you can call Nazi marching bands down the Champs-Élysées every day normal, or swastika flags flying from the Eiffel Tower, or armed sentries standing guard at the famous revolving door entrance of the Ritz Hôtel, normal—I flirt, light his cigarette, pour his drink, and listen to him talk about nothing but himself. I not only walk a tightrope with him, but with the Gestapo and my fellow countrymen. In the end, I fear my duplicity will be the end of me. That my motivation for appearing to collaborate to protect my family and my unborn child will be seen as a betrayal of motherhood... and France.

Because the deeper I get *into* the fight, the more I perceive the threat to us all, especially the de Giocomtes. Where once posters declaring a Jewish business was in fact a 'French business' or the owner was a 'veteran' protected them, the declarations were torn down by French police and ripped to shreds.

I fear more sanctions against Jews are coming.

I thank God for Arsène. He's the only one I can trust. My goal is simple, my reasoning sure. Drive the Boches from France and when the Allies experience victory, and they will, this hardened warrior who pierces my soul will not abandon me.

Until then, I continue to fight.

Like now. It kills me, but I cozy up to the major, resisting the male heat emitting from him pushing up against me.

'According to our informant,' he says, stroking my bare knee, 'they started publishing their newspaper last summer with a few followers, then the movement grew to a stronger band of believers who not only print newspapers but commit acts of sabotage.' He grins. 'We arrested the leaders, and those we didn't won't get far. We have the Chaillot Palace under observation day and night.'

'Why?' I ask.

'They held their meetings in the basement of the museum.'

I'll never enjoy strolling by the old building opposite the Eiffel Tower again.

'Were any university students among the resisters?' I have to ask.

'You mean your sister?' He smirks. 'Herr Geller spotted her in the area, but Ève wasn't among them.' The major stands behind me, toying with the clasp on the pearl necklace. 'I kept my word.'

'*Merci*,' I mumble. I give thanks Ève is safe, that he's holding to his part of the bargain to keep the Gestapo away from my family and the de Giocomtes, but—

I wonder if it's a ruse to keep me under his thumb. He's starting to pressure me for more damaging intelligence, hinting the lights are still on at Maison Bleue.

But they could be blacked out with a casual word to Herr Geller.

Permanently.

That troubles me more than anything.

I gaze at my reflection in the long mirror, the black velvet gown fitted with a peplum skirt to hide my growing belly as I enter my sixth month. My once slender figure grows thicker around the waist, my breasts fuller, my skin the shade of a pink dawn. I'm showing... a protruding belly hidden by the gown. I pull a white velvet cloak with black velvet trim over my shoulders, its lushness reminding me of magnificent, soft angel wings wrapping around me. Protecting me.

And hiding my secret.

Leading me to his waiting motorcar with his aide de camp at the wheel, the major doesn't hide his pride in keeping me as his French mistress. 'You look magnificent, Justine,' he whispers low so his aide can't hear him. The man is so disciplined, he uses my given name only when we're alone. Squeezing my waist and making me flinch, he forces me to give him my full attention before I get into the backseat of the vehicle, the shimmering moon overhead adding a mystical light that's ghostly, accusing. I can never forget this is where he raped me. And that's how he wants it. Sliding his hands over my shoulders, his magnetic blue eyes pierce my soul. His hands tighten on me, his grip fierce.

He wants me to know that I'm his and not to forget it.

I attempt to slip out of his embrace.

I can't.

13

PARIS, FEBRUARY 1941

Justine

'Where did you find such a beautiful mademoiselle, Major?' asks the Nazi general seated on my right. 'She's an exquisite creature.'

Front table. Bal Tabarin. Billed as the most 'erotic show' in Paris, the reopened cabaret features half-nude dancers and gourmet dinners for the Nazi elite.

And the secret police.

I spy the hated Gestapo man I know as Herr Geller and his cohort sitting at a corner table drinking whiskey shots. I turn my attention instead to the Prussian aristocrat with a chest filled with medals and a hungry smile. I smile back. *I'll take my 'old soldier with his two pawnshop medals' any day.* According to the major, General von Klum is a member of Hitler's close camp of advisors and has the ear of Goering, something the major intends to exploit. He singled the officer out for his own selfish purposes, informing the general how he scoured the countryside and discovered a warehouse filled with paintings crated up and ready for transport to America, but he got there first—so *that's* where he's been. Resisters, he said, working the area, and the problem is growing. He's stepping up his fight to weed them out and rounding up saboteurs. That sends a chill down my spine.

I listen closely, making mental notes to pass along to Arsène.

He invites the general to what he calls the 'preview' of the paintings and asks him to bring Goering, proposing that he take his pick before the works are sent to Chambord or auctioned off at the Hôtel Drouot. I see what he's doing. Get into the Reichsmarschall's good graces, though he admitted he finds the general distasteful. I can see why. The pompous swine with bushy brows that wiggle on his forehead like a long caterpillar gawks at the dancers in their scant costumes, smacking his lips and boasting he's a royal. Not quite true. The nobility no longer officially exists in Germany, I'm told, but many officers flaunt their ancestry to gain a certain cachet in the occupied countries, deeming to give off an old-world charm of a bygone era to up their chances with a pretty girl.

This Nazi officer has as much charm as an old jackboot.

'Did I tell you how I met Mademoiselle d'Artois, General?' The major winks at the Nazi who can't take his eyes off my swelling breasts and deep cleavage. I find that interesting with the dancers flaunting their assets *sans brassiere*. I wonder what he'd say if he knew *why* my pregnancy-enlarged breasts caught his scrutiny.

'No, Major, but I'm already jealous.'

The general takes my hand, I start to pull away, but the major shoots me a look that says, *Do what he wants... what I want.*

I shiver when the old Nazi plants a wet kiss on my hand.

'I saw a gorgeous painting of Mademoiselle in the art collection of a Jewish banker when I was a guest in their home.' The major smirks. I wince. He doesn't disappoint tonight. Cutting into me with his innuendos and veiled threats about how he fell in love with me and my golden hair, now bleached platinum at his command, and knew I'd be honored to be chosen by an esteemed member of the SS to show him Paris.

'You have no idea how lucky you are, mademoiselle,' General von Klum assures me. I'm surprised his French is more than passable. 'Major Saxe-Müllenheim is a fine officer and he's done a magnificent job securing art for the Führer's collection.'

'Yes, he's quite capable at taking what doesn't belong to him.' I grimace, cold water cutting into my veins when the horror of that August day revisits me. My dress torn... his greedy hands... the fear rippling through me.

I shudder.

No one notices.

The major is too busy spinning a tale that keeps the aging officer with the bushy brows mesmerized. He wants me to 'entertain' the general to secure his place as art curate. Yes, I believe he's interested in art, but another reason rears its ugly head.

The major is a coward.

He finds no glory in battle and has no intention of serving on the Eastern Front which I believe is coming. He's a bully with women, but he can't stand up to his own army.

'I spared no expense in finding the beautiful mademoiselle, *n'est-ce pas*, Rachelle?'

He enjoys calling me that, reminding me I'm no longer the young, innocent girl in the painting. That the pain I bear is invisible to the naked eye. It's our little secret.

'I couldn't escape him, General,' I tease. 'He insisted on me joining him.'

In the back of his Mercedes touring car while he raped me.

'To my delight,' the major continues without blinking an eye, 'I secured Mademoiselle *and* the painting for my own collection.'

'I would enjoy seeing this painting, Major, though seeing Mademoiselle in the flesh is an experience I shall not forget.'

The Nazi kisses my hand again, eyes my bare shoulders and the cold pearls around my neck tighten like a noose.

'And you shall, General,' he says. 'I have it safely under wraps in my hotel for your personal viewing later tonight.' The major directs his gaze at me. 'If Mademoiselle will accompany us.'

'You don't give a girl much choice, Major.' I fidget in my chair, toying with the plate of rare beef. My stomach is rebelling with loud growls. I had no idea where *The Daisy Sisters* was until now. He's baiting me. Tempting me with the painting, an ugly whispering inside my head speculating what's in store for me. Forcible rape. With the general? Is that why he's kept his distance? He's saving me for tonight? This time he'll say I consented because I went with him willingly. As if that makes it right. But it's *not* true. Though no one will believe me, which puts me deeper into a hole. Like the medieval torture *oubliette*. A cell-like hole in the ground where a prisoner is tossed into and forgotten.

I come back with a caustic remark to keep him at bay. 'Same as you did when you marched into Belgium, Poland.'

The major grabs my arm, squeezes it hard. I wince. 'And then Paris, mademoiselle, with her beautiful women at my disposal.'

'So I'm not the only one whose body, I mean, heart you stole?' I whisper in his ear with more than a hint of sarcasm.

'Jealous, *mon amour*?'

'Should I be?' I counter.

'I chose you, mademoiselle, to accompany me tonight.'

I look him straight in the eye. 'So you could show off your conquest to the general?'

'So we can make it a threesome.'

He's challenging me, but I refuse to give him an answer to his disgusting request. He'll never make me cower before him. I resolve to stand up to him, show him he can't break me. All the while perky dancers wearing short, shiny black panties and big white bows tied around their necks rally around our table, tickling the general under the chin, bouncing their bottoms in the major's face, and giving me the cold shoulder. Then the girls run up the staircase backstage leading to the wings. A French comedian jogs into the spotlight and goes into his act, speaking so fast his words roll into a long diatribe I can barely understand, but it soon becomes clear his continuous jokes come at the expense of the Nazi officers in the audience.

Laughing, clapping, shouting for the girls to return.

I grin. They have no idea what he's saying, giving me courage. I want to tell the major what I think of *him* and his sloppy general, barely controlling the urge to toss up the undigested, stolen Nazi beef into his lap. I look around for a way out, an exit strategy as my stomach turns and bile comes up, burning my throat when—

I notice a tall waiter in a tuxedo staring at me and holding a bottle of champagne. How long has he been watching me? He's broad-shouldered, his feet set apart, and I'm more than curious when he steps into the spotlight panning the audience and meets my eyes. He is finely forged steel. He is a man more fantasy than human. He's no ordinary waiter. Deep, dark eyes swirling like a pool of black ink, a thin, sexy mustache giving him a cinema-star look and dark hair slicked back. A handsome face with a strong jaw set in a hard, brutal line. Late twenties. He grips the neck of the champagne bottle like it's a lethal weapon.

My mouth drops.

Oh, my God, it's Arsène.

My heart skips a beat, my stomach rolls. The raw power of this man as I've never seen him before rushes through me, flushing my cheeks. No beard, no bushy brows, but those dark, smoldering eyes I can't forget. I know it's him, judging by his tall frame and the way his muscular body makes the tuxedo jacket strain at the seams. He's more magnificent than I imagined with a powerful body that speaks of incredible strength. His swagger confident, trained. I'd swear he was an ex-soldier, but he's too much of a rogue to follow the precision of military tactics. And where did he master the art of disguise? I'm more curious about him than ever.

I can barely sit still in my seat, squirming when he approaches our table, never taking his eyes off me, the rush of adrenaline in my veins putting my senses on high alert. *Why is he here? And why is he revealing himself to me?*

Am I in danger?

Without taking his eyes off me, Arsène pops the cork, pours champagne into three empty glasses. The perfect waiter. 'Champagne, mademoiselle?'

'Not tonight, *s'il vous plaît*,' I beg off. I lower my eyes to avoid making eye contact with the Resistance fighter and give myself away, but I feel his eyes boring into me. He expected me to say no and moves on to the general, but the major butts in.

'You *must* toast the general, mademoiselle.' The major lifts my chin and eyes blazing with passion meet mine. Passion to control me. 'I ordered the cabaret's best champagne.'

My blood runs hot. I can't insult the general and take the chance of invoking the major's anger. Who knows if he'd hurt my child? I take several sips of champagne, then turn away, pretending to fix my lipstick, the rhinestone gold case holding a cyanide pill should I need it. A sobering reminder from Arsène of the business we're in, how at any time I could face torture, even death. I can't let my temper get out of control and blow my cover, but there's one thing I have no control over.

My lingering morning sickness.

I had no idea it would last this long, and I pray nothing is wrong with my baby. I have no one to ask, no one to confide in except Arsène. A pregnant woman's wobbly insides are of no interest to him, yet he sees I'm in distress and hovers over me, a sour feeling in my stomach churning after the major insisted I swallow the champagne. Not only do I feel queasy and unsteady, but the alcohol sets my head spinning. Is this part of his plan? Get me drunk then hand me off to the general for a night of sexual amusement? I wouldn't put it past him.

The major grabs the glass of champagne and shoves it into my face. 'I *insist* we give the general a proper toast.'

'*Champagne makes me dizzy.*'

Arsène stands behind me, breathing hard. His hands fisting. He can do nothing or blow *his* cover by helping me. I shake my head, taking a peek at him, my eyes begging, 'I'm fine.'

The major puts the glass to my lips then whispers, 'I can have your sister and mother arrested *tonight* if you don't cooperate.' He nods toward the Gestapo men seated nearby.

'No... *please*.'

'Then finish the champagne or risk insulting the general.' He smirks. 'I hear they're turning Drancy into a concentration camp.'

I refuse to give in to the fear jelling in my veins like hot molten lead, my face perspiring, but I can't stop him when he forces the champagne down my throat, making me choke, but he keeps pouring the sweet wine into my gaping mouth.

I hear the Resistance fighter snorting, gnashing his teeth.

I thrash about, praying Arsène doesn't do something stupid.

Finally, the glass is empty. I barely catch my breath. The major laughs, his ego satiated, satisfied, then he turns away from me and toasts the general in guttural German, standing up and raising his arm in the Nazi salute. 'Heil Hitler!'

The Nazi audience takes up the toast, raising their arms. 'Heil Hitler!'

I gag.

'You look pale, mademoiselle.' Arsène moves toward me, his eyes slamming into mine, questioning, desperate. I nod. He takes advantage of the raucous Germans toasting the general and leans down over me, his salty, musky scent filling my nostrils, making my heart race, putting himself between the major and me to protect me. 'I'm getting you out of here,' he whispers. '*Now!*'

He takes my arm, but the major shoves his elbow into the Resistance fighter's gut. Arsène barely feels it and refuses to stand down.

The major says, 'Bring us more champagne.'

'But, monsieur,' Arsène says, gritting his teeth, 'Mademoiselle is turning blue.'

Am I?

There's an edge to his voice that makes the major scowl. He shouts, 'I order you to bring us more champagne or I'll have you arrested for disobeying a direct order.'

Arsène breathes out hard, but he doesn't move.

I fear for his safety. Out of the corner of my eye, I see Herr Geller reach inside his trench coat, his probing stare trying to decipher why the major is shouting at the waiter.

Then wild chaos breaks out when raucous can-can dancers burst through the backdrop double doors, racing down the stairs and onto the stage at Bal Tabarin, squealing like banshees and kicking their legs up high over their heads. Crisp white petticoats, black stockings held up by red garters, bare thighs, and skimpy underwear. The display of so much female flesh is too much for the starved audience of 'proper' SS officers.

Several drunk German officers race onto the stage, grabbing the dancers, twirling them around, hoisting a dancer up into air, another tossing a pretty soubrette over his shoulder. The Gestapo man shouts and calls for order. The general collapses into a chair and a pretty dancer sits on his lap. He laughs, she wiggles her shoulders. No one is paying attention to us. I see Arsène reach inside his tuxedo coat jacket.

He's going for his pistol. What if he shoots the major? He'll never get out of here alive.

I'd die if anything happened to him because of me. I can't wait another second.

I *must* save him.

I rush into the major's arms. 'Take me home, *please!* I'm sick.'

I glance sideways and I see Arsène retreat, then slip into the crowd.

God, please help him escape.

'Have another glass of champagne,' the major insists, 'then we'll go to the general's room at the Hôtel Ritz for a nightcap.'

'No,' I blurt out in a harsh whisper. 'I can't.'

'You'll do as I say, is that understood?'

'I won't go,' I sputter. 'I'm—I'm pregnant.'

'What?' His voice croaks like a frog squashed by a hunter's boot. 'Is it my child?'

'Yes, the baby is yours.'

The words come in a whisper. No one can hear us, the shouting, music, dancers squealing echoing in my ears, the major's face twisting, eyes darkening. I can't tell what he's feeling. Shock? Why he is, I don't know. I can't be his first victim to get pregnant.

'*Whore!*' he yells, then he slaps me hard, turns and storms out.

Knees wobbly, I back up against a table to brace myself so I don't collapse and fall on my belly and hurt my baby. I'm breathing hard; my chest hurts. I can't believe the man's cruelty. The major showed no concern for my condition, no remorse for striking me. As if it's *my* fault I'm pregnant. I wasn't expecting such a show of emotion from him. Why? His mother. She had a child born of rape.

I hold my belly, going over in my head what happened. Did I fall on my stomach? No. but the major knocked the breath out of me. I'm shaking, nerves taut. Any pain? Yes, I banged my right knee but I can still walk. I steady myself, trying to put it behind me, but I feel off balance, like a twirling top leaning to one side then the other. I should have kept it to myself. He'll say I *deserved* him hitting me. When does this guilt stop? *Ever?*

Frustrated and sick, I turn to make my escape, but the major's hasty departure hasn't gone unnoticed. The general dumps the dancer on his lap, then grabs me and twirls me around.

I feel sick. Dizzy.

'Now we can have some fun, mademoiselle.'

I'm going to throw up.

'Leave me alone!'

I put my hand to my burning cheek. I don't want to be touched. I feel dirty, unclean all over again. Humiliated. Curious eyes scrutinizing me, then accusing. I grab my long cloak and drag it behind me. Head down, shivering, somehow putting one foot in front of the other, I make my way to the foyer, empty except for the guard reading a newspaper, when I feel a stickiness between my legs.

Hot. Wetness seeping through my black velvet gown. Oh... God... no.

'My baby!' I cry out, getting the guard's attention, then my knee gives out and I collapse. Sinking to the floor in a puddle of black and white velvet. I try to pull myself up.

I can't.

Before the guard can reach me, the tall shadow of a man crosses under the swaying chandelier overhead, bathing my face in darkness, the man sliding his hands up and down my body... my arms, hands, ribs, and then my thighs.

I hear a loud gasp.

My instincts beg me to pull myself up, fight back, *do something* to save my baby, but an agonizing weakness has taken over my body, leaving me limp. I can't move. I can't even cradle my arms over my swollen belly.

'Arsène, *where are you?* Please help me,' I whisper, because he's the only friend I have, a man who protects me for a reason I've yet to understand, and my mind flashes back to the moment I saw him slip away.

Escape.

If only I could have escaped with him.

Then a darkness deep and black comes to claim me and I can't stop it.

I close my eyes.

And let go.

14

PARIS, FEBRUARY 1941

Ève

'It's not enough to memorize how to make explosives, mademoiselle,' my rescuer insists after we're long gone from the railway yard after escaping the Nazi patrol. 'To be a useful field agent, the work must be stamped upon your brain so deep it becomes a part of you.'

He blows his hot breath into my face, yet I shiver. His eyes penetrate mine with the cold fire of an avenging archangel. I have the terrible feeling he'd rather be anywhere than here with me.

'We made it, didn't we?' I toss back in an attempt to claw my way out of this mess.

He smirks. 'Just barely. You almost got us both killed.'

The man treating me like I'm a schoolgirl caught stealing an apple is Michal Laska. The Polish fighter and codebreaker Remi recruited and the man he sent to intercept the mission when word came the Gestapo picked up the railway foreman and interrogated him at Avenue Foch headquarters. No one knows if he gave up names, but Remi couldn't take any chances and sent the Pole to rescue 'that reckless university student'.

He neglected to mention I'm a woman.

We took refuge in a Roma camp in Saint-Denis in the north-eastern part of Paris not far from the railyard. The smoky remnants of a fire keep us warm as a murky dawn rises over the city, sweeping over the rooftops, waking up Parisians to another day of Nazi rule. The curious refugees from Belgium sniff us, touching my long hair, my man's jacket, then scratch their heads and ask questions, Michal answering them in a tongue that makes them nod, then they go about their business. They're breaking camp this morning to keep one step ahead of the Gestapo, he says, but we're safe here. For now.

That doesn't mean we see eye to eye.

We crash into each other like two railway cars hauling at high speed from opposite directions. My face heats with the passion of feeling the joy of completing my mission and that I struck back at the Boches... for Justine.

I keep tapping my fingers on my thigh, my pulse racing. He's challenging me and it's all I can do to keep up with him. He's strong, fast, and smart. Thinks on his feet, knows the enemy and how to take care of himself in a dangerous situation. I admire that. That doesn't mean I can work with him. If anything, he's the kind of man who terrifies me. Still. I realize my brain has joined the Resistance, but my emotions need work. When he looks at me with those piercing eyes so blue, I can't shake this strange compulsion I have to stand taller, show him I'm not afraid. Of him. Or the Boches. Which is why my need to prove myself is greater than my need to see the logic of *why* he's admonishing me.

'Whatever you think of me, monsieur, I got the job done,' I shoot back.

'I grant that you have guts *and* talent, mademoiselle, but you're green and foolhardy and lucky. *This* time.' He leans toward me. 'I won't always be there to clean up your mess.'

Well, if that didn't put me in my place.

Which only fuels my determination, and my words come tumbling out before I can stop them.

'Fine with me. I don't need *you* or any man to look after me.' My tone is determined, firm. 'I can take of myself.'

He smirks. 'Have it your way, mademoiselle,' he says, his voice razor sharp. 'You're on your own, but don't come crying to me if you get your knickers in a twist with the Nazis breathing down your neck.'

'You're the *last* person I'd call for help.'

'*Women...*' he mutters under his breath, clearly frustrated.

I flinch, my heart racing so fast, I can't swallow. *Bon*. He gave me the answer I want and I should be happy, but I also want something else from him.

Respect.

We've been over this a hundred times since our escape from the railyard, trudging on foot, then convincing a farmer on his way to Les Halles, the great market of Paris, to let us ride in the back of his truck with his crates of vegetables, mostly carrots since they're not rationed. He dropped us off at the Roma camp consisting of six, maybe seven wagons.

Vardos, Michal calls them, never explaining how he knew about the camp, only that he's always on the move, one step ahead of the Nazis. Hiding in doorways, sneaking in and out of apartments where fellow *résistants* have agreed to hide him, showing his forged identity card with a phony French name.

I refuse to back down when this man continues to interrogate me, even if he does have broad shoulders that fill out his leather jacket and set off a long, powerful torso that has me imagining him taking on the German patrol alone. A guerrilla fighter. Seasoned, taut, a man who wouldn't hesitate to take down the enemy with his bare fists.

He scares the hell out of me.

Blue eyes that dazzle you with their clearness; rich, dark hair the color of coffee, and a swagger that implies he knows he's attractive to women.

The sooner I get rid of him, the sooner I can breathe again.

It's not that easy. He grabs me by the arm, his serious blue eyes piercing and sending a sharp response in me that kicks my fear up a notch.

'When Claude recovers from his wounds,' he continues, 'he'll take over the job of planting the explosives once more.'

'Why not *me*?' I protest. 'I can do *any* job a man can. I set off those charges tonight *without* his help.'

'Because, mademoiselle, your recklessness put the entire operation in danger.'

'*How?*' It takes everything I have not to fire back at him that he's being unfair. 'The mission was a success. That's what counts.'

'This isn't a game, mademoiselle. When the foreman didn't show up, you should have aborted the mission.' He releases me, but his anger rises up a notch. 'I can't have a damn schoolgirl going rogue and putting my agents in danger.'

I burn red. 'I'm tired of running errands and washing dishes.'

'Every job is important, mademoiselle,' Michal says, 'part of a lifeline that connects us all together. But one wrong move and if that line is broken—'

I lift my chin. 'But it wasn't.'

'Remi said you were stubborn. You had your orders and you disobeyed them.'

I have no answer. Again, I was impulsive. I lower my eyes, my passion cooled by his words, and I open my mouth to apologize when he hits me with—

'Why can't you be more like Coralie and do what you're told?'

I blink. *Coralie?*

'How *dare* you compare me to her, monsieur.'

'You're right, she's not hotheaded like you.'

'How would you know?' I ask, curious.

'Coralie knows her place…'

He's kidding, right?

'… and puts herself on the line doing her job.'

'And what *is* her job?' I want to know, hiding the jealousy that's suddenly popped into my mind.

'Keeping me informed of what I need to know from Remi and warning me the Gestapo stepped up their surveillance of the rat hole where I'm bunking. I don't want them following me to Iris's apartment and blowing her cover.'

'Oh, I see…'

'So if you're done prying into my personal life, I suggest we come up with a plan to keep the Gestapo off *your* back.'

I grin. There's no stopping Coralie's flirting. Looking at the man's powerful body, I'm not surprised.

'I told you, I don't need your help.'

'*Damn it*, mademoiselle, what don't you get about the work we do? In spite of what I said earlier, you're a member of our network and I'll do whatever I must to keep the Gestapo out of your hair.' He breathes out, hard. 'However, if it was up to me, I'd put you over my knee and—'

'And what?' As the anger tightens in my gut, I straighten my shoulders, asserting myself, not wanting to again be a victim. 'You're just like the Boches. You take what you want.'

He grabs me by the shoulders, his eyes fierce. 'Don't you ever compare me to the Nazis, mademoiselle… *ever*, is that understood?'

What did I say that set him off?

'Yes, monsieur.'

'Good.'

His eyes blaze hot and with his arms holding me, where I trembled before, now I'm not. My anger subsides, surprising me. I see something in his eyes that bears no resemblance to the brutal, ugly arrogance I saw in the German officer who raped my sister. I concentrate on the pool of sadness in those eyes turning from light blue to dark then back again, as if for a moment he let down his guard and then quickly slid it back into place.

I understand that. I also have such moments when I can't control the rage inside me clawing to strike out.

Why?

Because the war never stops to let us grieve. So we put that grief on a shelf and let it sit there, vowing someday to dust it off and deal with it. But we don't. We let it sit there alone and unwanted. It's as if the terror of war is better than facing our feelings.

I study him closer, see if I'm right, but he's closed down his emotions again. I want to reach out, tell him I understand that we have something in common, and whether or not we can work together, time will tell.

Instead I bury my hands in my pockets, go into retreat. For now. He showed me a human side of himself and that makes me respect him, something new for me when it comes to men.

And that new way of thinking frightens me more than his arrogance.

'Be assured, mademoiselle,' he continues, letting me go and checking the pistol in his pocket. *I didn't notice that before.* 'I will do my job, maintain security at all costs, even if you don't, because it means the difference between life and death. Now do I have your word you'll follow my orders?'

I nod at him, mumble a quick, 'Yes, monsieur,' because I have to, but I can't ignore the rolling emotions in my stomach that send me reeling because I don't know how to handle them. I feel a strong attraction to this man in spite of his obvious distaste for me and it's a strange feeling. I don't like it.

He reads my eyes, sees the pain.

'Whatever the Nazis did to you, mademoiselle, no one can change. We all have our secrets that eat at our souls, piece by piece, until we can no longer feel. You hide the truth behind a locked door and throw away the key. And when you want to open that door, you can't.' He glances at me sideways. 'Don't let that happen to you.'

'You speak from experience?'

'Like I said, mademoiselle, we all have our secrets.'

'How do I know I can trust you?'

'You don't, but in our line of business, you learn to trust your gut.'

'Why should I believe you?'

'Because you have no choice. Whether you want to accept it or not, after that stunt you pulled, you're an unknown liability, mademoiselle,' Michal insists. 'You must leave Paris until I can find out what the foreman told the Gestapo, if they tortured the poor sod to the point where he gave up names. *Your* name. Which means you can't go home. The Gestapo may be looking for you.'

'Me?'

'I fear there's an informant in the network, mademoiselle.' He doesn't elaborate, but his eyes meet mine and a shadow crosses his face as if he's mulling over if he can trust me.

'I *can't* leave Paris.' I panic. 'Maman, my classes at the university...'

'Write her a note, tell her you're staying with friends.'

'I spend all my time in the lab, monsieur. I have no one.'

He thinks a moment. 'Tell her you're staying with Iris, that she's a friend from the Sorbonne.'

'She won't believe me.'

'Do you want to fight the Boches?'

'Yes.'

'Then you must disappear for a few days.'

'Where?' I ask.

'To a hunting lodge not far from here outside Marly-le-Roi. My Roma friends will drop us off there. We can ride in the *vardo* with the blue star and the moon in the center.'

I see a man wearing a wide-brimmed hat and smoking a long pipe signaling us over to his wagon.

'All I have are the clothes I'm wearing,' I protest.

Dirty, torn, bloodied from my cut fingers.

'Iris will loan you whatever you need.' He looks me up and down, shakes his head, and is that a smirk on his lips? 'I imagine you don't bother with stockings and dresses or frilly underwear.'

'My underwear is no concern of yours, monsieur.'

'You can wear red garters trimmed with black lace for all I care, as long as you obey my orders.'

Did I see his eyes twinkle? Is that the kind of woman that attracts him? A woman like Coralie? I know there's more to his relationship with her than what he's telling. Why should I care? A man like him would never be interested in a tall, plain girl like me. Of course, I don't care. Do I? Oh, *damn*, the man infuriates me, insinuating I don't have a feminine bone in my body. I do. I just don't know what to do with it. Flirt? *Pffft!* I always put my foot in my mouth. But I do have one talent. I'll show him I can be a good agent.

Oh, will I.

I kick my boot into the dirt around the dying fire, eager to get going.

'I'll come with you, monsieur, on one condition.'

'Mademoiselle?'

'That you call me Ève.'

I see his eyes widen, then crinkle around the corners with respect, a different sparkle in them that makes me almost like him. 'What do you know about codes, *Ève*?'

I blink, surprised. 'Nothing.'

'You'll learn,' Michal whispers in my ear. 'Though you may find working with homing pigeons a messy job.'

'Pigeons?' I ask, wriggling my nose.

'Yes, pigeons.' Then he grows solemn, thoughtful. 'Communication with the Allies is vital in our line of business, and until London can establish a reliable network of wireless operators here in France, we found our feathered friends loyal to the cause.'

Is he kidding? No, there's no mirth in his eyes. He's dead serious.

My world is turned upside down again. My heart has been twisting from one emotion to another listening to this formidable Resistance fighter. Fear, anger, frustration, but now I want to laugh.

And laugh big.

The last thing I expected to do in this war is babysit pigeons.

15

PARIS, FEBRUARY 1941

Justine

What seems like days later, the heavy sleep crushing my brain lets go. I squeeze my eyes open and a vast whiteness surrounds me. Overhead lighting bright and harsh makes me squint. I hate it and want to block it out, block out the whole damn scene at the cabaret. A nightmare I wished had never happened.

Wrapped up in cold, white sheets, I turn over onto my side and curl up into a ball, wanting to forget how awful I feel. My mouth is dry, lips parched. My breasts feel hot and sore. Yet I detect a sweet, citrusy smell wafting in the air. Oranges. Still groggy, I breathe in the pleasant scent, joyful for a moment, then a pungent odor hits me that makes me cough. Urine and sweat.

And disinfectant.

An odd coupling, oranges and disinfectant, then memories of a nurse mixing chilled castor oil with layers of orange juice in a glass revisit me in a strange but pleasant way, reminding me of when

Ève and I were children and the odors we encountered when Maman took us here to keep us healthy. *Compliments of Madame de Giocomte*, she'd never forget to tell the nurse, so grateful she was to Madame for taking us in and seeing to our welfare.

The American Hospital of Paris.

I force myself to calm down, though my vision is blurry due to a headache, and I ache all over. I remember the distinct white columns, long, multi-paneled windows, bright lighting, and the nurses wheeling medical supplies on rectangular trolleys up and down the wards. Gauze, bedpans, even plasma. And the usual hospital smells that make my nose twitch. I start sweating, then shaking. A more recent memory revisits me of when I brought Ève here after she suffered a burn on her arm when one of her experiments blew up. I suffer a bout of nostalgia, so deep is my longing to see my sister, hear her laugh and watch her brows cross when she's in the middle of measuring and mixing, pouring and shaking the vial, then something magical happens with her plants or strange powders that makes her smile.

That was before the Occupation.

Now the hospital serves civilians and soldiers under the umbrella of the French Red Cross. The Nazis have no jurisdiction here, thank God, no German sentries at the entrance, but that doesn't stop my heart from hammering in my chest. I fear the major will show up any second and pull me from my bed.

Would he dare?

I wouldn't put it past him. He takes a sadistic pleasure in humiliating me. I don't know if it's because he suffers from anger over his questionable lineage, or he's just a mean bastard, but the SS officer slapped me so hard at the Bal Tabarin I fell to my knees. And I can never forget he called me a whore. At first, I saw only the injustice in his tantrum, the irony of his hurtful words, then it hit me when I saw the fear in his eyes because he knew that *I knew*.

That he'd let his perfect Aryan mask slip and revealed to me the secret of his birth when he was drunk.

Knowing I'm pregnant by a man taken against my will like his mother is one thing, but fearing I'd reveal his evil scheme, his cast of God knows how many 'major's girls' he's raped and kidnapped, was too much for him.

He bolted.

That doesn't mean he won't come back to claim what's his.

Not me. My child.

And that, I promise you, ma petite, I will never allow. I shall die first.

Fear... nerves... nausea from the putrid smells act like a smelling salt and make me alert. I fumble around until I loosen the sheet and—

My clothes are gone and I'm not wearing underwear. Sterile white gauze is wrapped around my hips, between my thighs. Why am I nearly naked? How long have I been out? What did they do to me?

Panicked, I tug at the overly big, white patient gown that scratches at my neck, then reach down and—

'*My baby!*' I call out, cradling my belly. 'Did I—'

'No, mademoiselle,' says a woman's voice as she comes around the pleated white canvas partition separating me from the other beds in the ward, 'you didn't lose the child.'

Her manner is soft and kind. Brown eyes. Dark hair nestled under a nurse's long headscarf.

'But I was dizzy and—'

'Be assured, mademoiselle, strong muscles in the walls of your uterus help keep your baby safe,' the nurse says, adjusting the pillow under my head. Her name is Edith. She goes on about how the amniotic fluid serves as a cushion. The physician on duty examined me and did several blood tests and although I suffered vaginal discharge, no damage was done. 'You're not to leave that bed, doctor's orders.'

I see something in her eyes that makes my skin prickle with fear.

'What are you keeping from me?' I ask.

Her eyelids flutter and she bites her lower lip. 'Please, mademoiselle, get some rest.'

'No, not until you tell me what's wrong.'

'Nothing to worry your pretty head about, mademoiselle.' She gives me a weak smile.

'You're hiding something, I *know* it.' I feel sweaty, uneasy.

'We'll talk about it later,' she insists. 'I'll bring you broth and tea to settle your nerves.'

She turns, but I grab her arm, '*Please*, Nurse, don't treat me as if I'm soft, weak. I'm not. I'll fight for my child. My baby means more to me than *anything*.'

She lets out a heavy sigh. 'Well, you suffered an unfortunate trauma in your last trimester.' Does she know what happened at the cabaret? The hard slap? Her eyes tell me she does. 'And the doctor is worried you could experience contractions.'

A sudden jolt in my belly startles me. *A contraction?* I smile wide. No, I'm convinced it's just my baby kicking, making her presence known. Yes, *her*. I've decided my child is a girl. I shall name her after Madame de Giocomte for her generosity *and* my favorite cinema heroine from silent films when I was a little girl.

Ninette starring Sylvie Martone.

Catherine-Ninette Beaufort.

'I can feel my baby move.'

Nurse Edith smiles. '*Bon,* mademoiselle, I look forward to seeing you when your time comes. The doctor has made the arrangements.'

'*Merci,*' I say, though I worry the major won't approve and will send me to Salpêtrière Hospital known for treating women with 'hysteria.' How easy for him to have me declared unfit to be a mother and take my child. Or Lariboisière Hospital for the German wounded. My baby surrounded by Nazis.

I shudder at the thought.

'Now get some rest, mademoiselle. I'll bring your broth and tea.'

'No, *wait*. Tell me, how did I get here?'

'A handsome gentleman in a tuxedo carried you into the hospital, demanded I get you a bed, then raced upstairs to Dr Jackson's office on the fourth floor. I assumed he was your husband by the way he took care of you, but he said he was a waiter from the cabaret looking out for the club's interest.' She explains that Doctor Jackson is a staff surgeon. 'Ten minutes later, the doctor came racing into my ward with the gentleman in the tuxedo, the two of them babbling in English and then insisting you receive the best of care.'

'He did?'

A pleasant warmth makes me shiver but it's nothing compared to the sudden jumping in my tummy and this time it *isn't* my baby kicking. It's knowing it was Arsène leaning over me.

'Yes. I overheard Doctor Jackson and the man reminiscing about their "old days" in Algeria.'

'Algeria?' I repeat, puzzled.

'The doctor and his wife spent time in the area.' She sighs. 'I gather the handsome gentleman was stationed there when he was in the Foreign Legion.'

I lean back, a satisfied smile on my lips. That explains where Arsène learned fluent French, his fighting and tactical skills. As I suspected, he's an ex-soldier. I wonder if he was also an intelligence officer and picked up the art of disguise. It would make sense.

I keep staring at the nurse, but it seems I'm looking through her, seeing Arsène looking so dapper in his tuxedo, his dark brows twisted in worry, forgoing caution and risking exposure to save me. I wouldn't be surprised if he commandeered the general's motorcar to get me across Paris from Montmartre to the hospital in Neuilly.

Yes, the general.

An arrogant Nazi through and through, but he just might be my savior.

I fidget with the sheet, pulling the hospital gown tighter around me, then pull my knees up towards my chest and think. I try not to get too cynical because I owe a great deal to the sloppy-kissing aristocrat, *mon cher général*. I could tell by the glint in his eye—and the bulge in his trousers—he took a liking to me and wouldn't be happy if anything happened to me. I can imagine the whispers in the offices of the Abwehr at the Hôtel Letitia wouldn't be in the major's best interest if my lifeless body was found in a back alley in the Pigalle. Too many questions he couldn't or *wouldn't* answer. Still, I wonder, what's the major's plan for me? He wants that post as art curate badly here in Paris. If my intelligence is correct and Germany *is* planning to march into Russia, he'll do anything to avoid being sent to the Eastern Front.

And that means keeping me alive.

I'm safe for now, but for how long?

My baby kicks, begging for attention. She's lively today. I rub my tummy, thinking. *Then why did I faint?*

'At first we thought you were drugged,' Edith offers up. 'You were sweating and unconscious.'

Drugged? Morphine?

I didn't feel a prick on my skin before the major forced the champagne down my throat. He intended to use me as a bargaining chip with the general, but I foiled his plans when I told him I was pregnant. His twisted mind made him abandon the idea, not that he has an ounce of humanity in his bones, but because a woman in my condition is unappealing to his ego.

'Upon closer examination, the doctor found no indication an opioid had been injected, no pinpoint pupils. Just extreme duress and trauma.'

She means the hard slap.

'And my baby?' I whisper. 'Was the child injured?'

She gives me a smile so warm it takes away the chilly fear in me that something could happen to my unborn child. 'You've nothing to worry about, Mademoiselle d'Artois, you're safe with us. We have mutual friends.'

She knows who I am? Does she also know I'm the companion of an SS officer? That I smile prettily under the veil of my outrageous hat? That I flirt with generals at the major's command?

That I'm a broken woman?

Would her attitude change toward me if she did?

I sink down into the bed, pulling the thin coverlet up to my eyes to hide my face. I say nothing. The nurse is off to conjure up tea and broth, a miracle in these troubled times, and I'm left to ponder what she knows about 'Rachelle d'Artois'. She must have found the identity card the major gave me in my purse. I don't deny it. The last thing I need or want is a record of a Mademoiselle Beaufort treated here. As each day goes by, I feel stronger, my belly expanding like a delicate puff pastry, but I'm disappointed Arsène doesn't come to see me, and I can't ask the nurse about him. Makes me sad. I lapse into a bout of melancholy and loneliness. I find myself talking to my baby, telling her she's getting bigger every day.

And how much I love her.

* * *

I convalesce in the hospital over the next two weeks and Nurse Edith never asks me about myself. But then she's so busy taking care of the steady stream of French soldiers brought here from POW camps or skirmishes with the Nazis, she doesn't have much time for conversation. The beds fill up every day with young men burning up with fever or chills, their heads wrapped up in bandages or their arms or legs broken.

Moaning, calling for their mothers.

It breaks my heart. These young men were each once flutters and kicks in his *maman's* womb, begging for attention then as now, but their *mamans* can't hear them. That stirs a need in me to do what I can for them, especially when I notice soldiers disappearing as quickly as they're brought in with sheets pulled over their faces. Men I wouldn't have judged to be at death's door by their wounds.

I find that odd, but I don't dwell on it.

Instead I offer up a prayer for their souls.

And carry on, as I know Arsène expects me to do. I spend my afternoons walking the corridors wearing a drab chenille robe the nurse found for me with a faded, silk chemise underneath and old slippers. I don't ask where she got the robe, but I see brown blood stains splattered on the silk.

I talk to the wounded soldiers, see firsthand our fighting men broken in body but not spirit, the glory of battle blazing in their eyes when they talk about their buddies who didn't make it. The big flakes of snow falling outside the tall, hospital windows echoing the chill in these men's hearts for those who didn't come back. Their passion heated and yet so terribly sad. As if they don't want to go home because they don't want to leave these men behind.

I feel that way about Ève and Maman. Instinct tells me to run as far away from Paris as I can with my unborn child. But I'd never leave them.

nightmare. If you don't keep your wits about

And the de Giocomtes.

I worry about them and their extended family the more chatter I hear in the hat shop about the 'Jewish question'. I made my choice and I shall stick to it, which fuels my courage to continue my work.

Today is no exception. Chatting or holding their hands if the soldiers don't want to talk. Then I see a patient in a hospital gown wandering up and down the women's ward, looking confused. Nurse Edith stops him, and he answers in English. She shushes him and then hurries him back to his bed.

An Englishman. Why am I not surprised the American doctor is hiding downed British airmen? Of course. Arsène is getting them back home via an escape line. That's why several soldiers stare back at me when I try to talk to them. They don't speak French. I ask the nurse to translate for me. I don't try to hide my pregnancy when the soldiers ask about my baby, telling me I remind them of their wife back home. I don't tell them the father of my child is an SS officer. I'm too ashamed.

Will it always be like this?

Then it hits me that I can help Arsène by gathering information from the soldiers which I can then pass on to him. Where they were captured, how many wounded and killed, where they were headed when the attack came. The soldiers are hungry for someone to talk to and that intelligence may help the Allies.

Then someone notices I'm *too* curious and accuses me of being a German spy.

That hurts me.

Deep.

This double life is wearing on my nerves like constant pinpricks poking me, then unraveling my emotions like a woolen sock come undone. Arsène was right. Being a spy isn't a job, it's a nightmare if you don't keep on your toes. I should have been more careful.

Of course, I deny it, but Edith suggests I keep to my bed and ask no more questions. Her stern but kind warning tells me she knows more about me than she lets on. Arsène, of course. I wouldn't be surprised if she's part of the Underground, but she'll never admit it. Again he looks out for me, but a loneliness digs deep into me like I'm being swallowed by an impending darkness that drapes itself over me like a Nazi flag. Heavy, suffocating, and stealing the breath from me.

I suffer the worst night since I was raped.

All my despair comes flooding out. The future I so carefully ignored biting me in the rear. I can't raise my little girl with her growing up with a hole in her heart because she doesn't fit the dictates of society.

I have one hope. Both the major and I have blonde hair and it would be lovely if she has vibrant blue eyes like a Jumeau doll. I'm certain no one will question her French lineage, and why should they suspect anything different? Otherwise that hole in her heart will never heal from the taunts and jeers from the miscreants as well as common folk who don't understand her mother was raped. Humiliated, but she never stopped loving her.

I vow I will never allow *anyone* to imprint ugly smears on my child. I will never tell her the truth about who her father is. *Never*.

This I swear.

16

SAINTE ANNE-GUILLAUME DES LYS, A VILLAGE OUTSIDE PARIS, MARCH 1941

Ève

I loop the small pouch over the pigeon's back and send her off on the mission just before dawn. Inside I tucked a coded message on a piece of paper the size of a cigarette wrapper. A recap of what rail-yards Michal and I hit this week on the outskirts of Paris. The Germans already know because we busted up the tracks into curling ribbons of iron.

But London doesn't.

I'm proud of what I do to drive *les boches* out of France. I move under the cloak of night, laying explosives along the railroad tracks, my fingers fast and sure, setting the charges deep under the railway line just before dawn breaks, burying the fuses so the morning patrols don't find them, then watching from my hiding place when the explosion warps the track and sends the speeding train onto its side, its engine still smoking like a mythical creature helpless and no longer a danger.

And the Germans never see me coming.

I climb down the stairway leading up to the mobile loft, singing 'Good morning' along the way to my crew of a dozen carrier pigeons cooing and flapping their wings. To stay warm. Me, too. I'm dying for a hot cup of whatever we're calling coffee these days. I even miss Cook's concoction of the brew. I often wonder how Maman and Madame are getting along without me, hoping I see them soon. I had no choice but to send them a note as Michal suggested, praying Maman didn't question it but instead smile when she learned I'd made a friend. Meanwhile, it's freezing out here. A lingering cold snap haunts us here in the countryside, making my teeth chatter, but I have hope that spring will burst upon us like a giant daisy dancing in the wind. Till then we suffer freezing temperatures.

When my wooden-soled clogs hit the dirt, I look up and watch the bird making her way as the sky breaks through a flurry of snowflakes.

Flapping her wings. Feathers vibrating and making a piercing whistling sound indicating she's in a hurry to be on her way.

Soaring.

Not toward heaven, but to her home loft in the east of England.

Justine, I call this one. She's a scrappy little pigeon with a half-moon gray marking on the top of her head and a high-pitched coo different from the other homing pigeons. I'd know it anywhere. Like she's doing scales. Up and down. She's done more than half a dozen missions for me since I got here more than two weeks ago and we took over the loft, a wooden structure about five meters high with a small set of stairs and cubbyholes for the pigeon. Every time I send her off I get a lump in my throat, praying she'll return. It's a deep emotion that roils through me, like I'm betting my sister will come home, too. I know that's impossible, but so again is me becoming a Resistance fighter.

And a pigeon handler.

I never dreamed these inimitable birds fly an average speed of eighty kilometers an hour and can travel the distance of nearly five-hundred kilometers. The Nazi troops can't shoot them down because of their speed, but Michal tells me the Germans have no heart and send Peregrine falcons to take them down in flight.

'I'm off to Paris, Ève, for food,' I hear a voice behind me say. 'And whatever pigeon corn I can get for our feathered friends. I'll be back before dark.'

I spin around. It's Michal, satchel slung over his shoulder, smiling, running his hands through his dark hair, long and curling around his neck. A devious tilt to his upper lip, not a snarl, more like satisfaction. He disappeared yesterday for several hours and I didn't ask questions. He looks at me for a moment and almost lets his guard down... *almost*. Then he starts whistling a saucy tune, a sure sign the man went rogue... again. I shake my head. What's his latest scheme? Sneak into the Bal Tabarin because he knows the waiter there? Or hole up in a bar in Montmartre telling stories about how he escaped from the Gestapo by masquerading as a Nazi captain in a dead officer's uniform?

He admitted to me he has a penchant for languages since his father was a language professor at the university in Warsaw before the war and groomed his son to join him on staff, which Michal, of course, rebelled against, but his talent comes in handy on our missions.

I never forgot how his eyes blazed with an anger that looked like Hell itself when I ventured to ask him if he had other family or a girl back home.

His mood turned ugly, his eyes becoming dark and glassy like hard obsidian.

I don't know why Remi believes I can keep the wild Polish fighter in line. In the field, we've developed a mutual respect for each other, we're bonded by something deeper than the cause, a personal pain of loss by someone we love at the hands of the SS. Iris confided to me before we left Paris that Michal bears the scars of not knowing what happened to his father and younger sister in Warsaw when he escaped to the hills to fight the Nazis. Everyone thought he was dead, killed by the Gestapo, including the girl he loved. She believed him lost to her forever, so she became involved in luring German soldiers to their deaths, a 'honey trap', before being caught by the SS and tortured by the Gestapo.

He doesn't know that she told me, but I see it festering inside him. It makes him angry and reckless at times, but it helps me understand the man better, not judge him so harshly when he goes off the grid like an avenging pirate seeking booty wherever he finds it.

And that includes women.

Burying his broken heart in their bosoms.

I see a twinkle in his eye that makes me certain pigeon corn isn't all he's after.

'Is Coralie back from the coast?' I ask.

He raises a brow. 'How would I know?'

'You would,' I insist, then direct my attention back to the sky, but my pigeon has disappeared into the silky blue edged with frost. *Fly high, ma petite.*

'Jealous, Ève?' He cocks a brow.

'Of course not.' I let go with a tiny shiver and it's *not* because of the cold. We're standing near the edge of the thick forest, the bitter wind whistling in one ear and his sensual voice in the other. Remi sent the perky mamselle in pigtails and bows to escort a downed flier to Brittany for pickup. A freckled pilot who needed a pretty, young fiancée to avoid suspicion from the Nazis on the train. She must have returned by now.

'*Bon.* Because it's none of your business, mademoiselle.'

He calls me that to perturb me, but he doesn't flirt with me the way he does Coralie. And that's the way I want it.

'Does Remi know you're coming to Paris?' I ask, heading for the seventeenth-century royal hunting lodge we call home.

'Yes. He secured more corn for us than on my last trip. Not an easy task since it's rationed.'

'How do you know that?' I glance at him, suspicious.

'You *are* the curious one, mademoiselle.'

'Don't try to fool me, Michal, I know what you're about.'

'Do you?' He raises a brow.

'You took the truck and met Coralie in the nearby village while I was working on my code.'

'You make a good spy, Ève. Remi gave me instructions a member of our cell would meet me for updates. I had no idea it would be the pretty mamselle.'

'No? Well, guess what, you can make your own coffee.'

'You're pretty when you're angry, Ève.'

'Don't flatter me, Michal. I'm efficient, smart, and good with explosives. But I am *not* pretty.'

'I beg to disagree...' I hear him call after me.

Rattled by his flattery, I open the double portal to the one-story stone-covered structure, run inside and slam it shut. I'm fighting back tears and something else I won't admit. I *want* him to think I'm pretty. What rips me apart inside is that he's either teasing me or really thinks I am attractive—what am I not seeing in the mirror?—and if so, that scares me more than anything because I can't hide from my feelings any more.

I'm falling in love with him.

I hear him laughing... hard. Then whistling a naughty tune while I steam. *Ooh*, the man is impossible. Best to forget him. Now. Completely.

I go about scooping the barley out of the tin can and heating the water in the pot hung in the fireplace still burning with red and orange embers, working my way into putting him and everything about him out of my mind. And to think I have to share this place with him for a few more weeks. Not the best accommodations. Forests of weeds grow up around the lodge nearly swallowing it up from view. A broken window provided a convenient portal for a large rat to scurry across the oak floor when we first arrived here, but he didn't like human company and hasn't shown up since. Faulty plumbing causes mold in the kitchen which no amount of scrubbing can fix, but elegant wainscoting speaks of the lodge's earlier glory. I couldn't resist poking my head inside the majestic fireplace five-feet deep with a ten-foot beam spanning its breadth. The biggest surprise came when I explored the cellar. I found a maze of dark, narrow alleyways and dusty bottles of red and white wines, even a pre-Revolution cognac dating back to the late eighteenth century.

Which disappeared on Michal's last trip to Paris.

Sold on the black market for supplies.

While he was gone, I explored the cellar alleyways and discovered an escape route via a small wooden staircase leading up to a trap door opening to a clearing in the forest. I wondered if it was used by smugglers or a lonely young royal meeting her lover.

I'm thinking the original owners were from the days before the Revolution.

Maybe they even lost their heads.

Over the years, squatters have made their home here and from the trash and old newspapers left by the last occupants, I'd say the place has been deserted for at least five years.

Whoever they were, they didn't have to put up with an unpredictable Polish fighter who never stops looking over his shoulder. Even when we sleep. We make our beds on the floor on straw pallets with heavy silk eiderdowns—no furniture but we found plenty of bedding in old storage trunks—and the big fireplace to keep us warm. At night it's so quiet I can hear the trees breathe. I think about this war and everything it's meant to us women of France. How we've become politically awakened to this new reality and we're not going back to a world before 1938 where we couldn't have our own bank account, write a check, or our own passport. We still can't vote, but that will come. Meanwhile, we fight the Boches. I hated to leave Maman and Madame, but I'm not the only one making sacrifices in this war. I've heard the stories, like the young woman leaving her child with her mother to join the Resistance... another fighting while her husband is imprisoned as a POW... still another hiding *résistants* wanted by the Gestapo.

War brings strange demands upon us. I believe with my whole heart in what I'm doing and wouldn't change it. I have no doubt down to my toes it's my duty to delay the supply lines, use my brain to make the detonation cords, grenades, and chargers. I learned how to bundle plastic sticks and then set the fuses and plant the explosives on a locomotive to disable it. I studied how to calculate the amount of cyanide needed to poison the enemy, though I pray I won't have to.

I want to use my skills as a scientist to heal, find new cures for the pain and suffering I've seen. Growing up in a *grande maison*, I've watched the progression of life from birth to death and the devastating moments in between. Infection, disease, despair, even depression and the physical effects it has on a body. Before the Occupation, Madame had a much bigger staff and she went so far as to take care of their families, too, when they needed help. I loved tagging along with her on her visits to Saint-Denis or Montmartre or the Left Bank, bestowing flowers and kind words and much-needed francs on grateful relatives.

I can't deny I also brought along medicinal herbs and a watchful eye, keeping alert if I saw anyone who needed immediate medical help. This stood me well in perfecting my observation skills until the Nazis showed up and took *that* from me, too.

Damn them.

But I wouldn't be human if I didn't seek moments of solitude when I stop to think how the old me misses my lab. I was getting so close to isolating an interesting microbe in my quest to perfect penicillin when they closed the university. Now that classes have resumed at the Sorbonne and I'm no longer required to report to my local police station, I should be back at my worktable. Instead I'm writing messages using a simple code Michal taught me where the letters of the alphabet are interchanged and the information sent to London.

A cipher disk.

The agent in England has the paper disk with the same key letter, making it a simple task to decipher the message. It's important work we do. *Résistants* from every corner of France gathering information which is recorded and tallied, then the British agents looking for patterns that tell a story far beyond my messages. It's like a large tapestry on a wall with multi-colored threads woven in and around, up and down, telling a story that will eventually come together, and the Allies will drive the Boches out of France and I can return to my lab and my experiments.

I'm proud to be one of those threads.

But gathering intelligence has its challenges.

We've been traipsing around the surrounding area in a heavy-duty Renault truck Michal found abandoned by the roadside about ten kilometers from here. We talk to farmers, vagrants we give a lift to—after grilling them to make sure they're not Germans —girls and women picking apples, old men baling hay. Fortunately, the truck engine wasn't dried up or 'seized' like the others Michal found left to rust by the disgruntled Germans. It simply ran out of petrol. Easily remedied by the supply Michal stole right under the Nazi's noses. I held my breath when he poured the gasoline into the tank while he explained to me how the manufacturer devised their own brand of sabotage by marking the dipsticks wrong during production so the Boches don't know when the engine is low on oil.

And the trucks stop running.

Which reminds me. *Where is my wild Polish fighter?*

Did he leave for Paris without saying au revoir?

I look around for him. He's nowhere in sight. That's just like him. Rile me up and flatter my ego, then leave me hanging. I refuse to show him I'm interested in him. That's what he wants. I want to do my job, nothing more, but it's like I've got an itch up my spine I want to scratch but can't. Something unpredictable happened to me when we paired up. For the first time in my life, I'm forced to share the same physical space with a man.

A handsome, strong man. Code name: *Archangel*.

I chide him that his code name should be *Babysitter*. He never lets me out of his sight, keeping watch over me with that flirty look. Shooting me that smirking smile with one corner of his mouth lifted and eyes that smolder dark and hot when he doesn't approve of my meticulous but slow process of laying charges on railroad tracks.

I'm a scientist, I tell him. *I'm methodical.*

I don't care if you're Marie Curie's granddaughter. Get in and get out, fast and dirty.

Still, we make a good team even if he doesn't believe guerrilla warfare is women's work. Where Michal heard that strange term baffles me. He let it slip that he admires my chemistry skills and I'm braver than any female he's run into except... Then he clammed up and I knew he meant the girl in Poland he loved, so I kept it to myself.

Without saying it, we've formed an alliance to drive the Boches out of France, but that's as far as our relationship goes. Anything else is too dangerous for me. I haven't gotten over my fear of men and their power over women like me. Women with no skills of seduction or looks. Yet I'm hungry inside for the first blush tinting my cheeks, my breasts, my body responding to a man who would teach me not to be afraid, that I *am* pretty in his eyes. I never trusted a man. How could I after I saw how my *maman* had her heart broken by a man she adored but who loved his gambling more? That she couldn't compete with a deck of cards was humiliating to her. Or after I saw how the Nazis treated women. Losing Justine is a hole in my heart I can never fill. I know I must learn to trust a man if I'm not to end up bitter and alone. I almost did trust someone. Michal. For a time, I thought he might be that man, but he's bound by bonds of guilt that tie him up inside and when he does break free, he's unpredictable.

I sense he knows only too well the cost of letting someone into his life and how quickly it can be taken away by betrayal and a bullet.

I scrape the barley off the sides of the tin can, then spoon it into the filter I've used over and over again and place it into the coffeepot, then pour the hot water into it and set it on a hot brick I keep by the fireplace. I take a moment to warm my hands. I sigh. My skin is rough, tinged red and dry. I swear the temperature is dropping... again. I don't remember a winter this cold *ever*. I put on an old lime-green sweater under my camel coat. I decide not to dawdle any longer on the crazy notion of letting down my defenses around this man no matter how much he gets under my skin and do what I'm supposed to do in this war.

Blow up trains... make the Boches' lives miserable... and set that crazy Polish fighter straight that this flirting between us *has* to stop. For both our sakes. He's still grieving and he won't admit he needs help. Men never do. I see how it's killing Monsieur de

Giocomte, how he hides the pain of seeing his world collapse and he won't let Madame in to soothe him. He shuts her out and that hurts her, her eyes tearful, wetting her long, dark lashes like a perpetual storm is upon her. I pray I can return home soon to help her, though I despair the day when I have to tell her the truth about Justine.

I head outside ready to make peace with Michal with hot coffee and a smile *if* he's playing games and hasn't left yet when I hear a piercing whistling in the forest—

I look up, shading my eyes with my hand, my heart thumping in my chest. Cloudy overhead and the tall forest trees hide the origin of the sound except for a flurry of outstretched wings that shoot across the sky in a zigzag pattern. That puzzles me. Something's wrong. A homing pigeon flies sure and true back to their home loft and patiently waits for me to come and retrieve the message and scatter the extra corn I always carry in my pocket.

Coo... coo-oo. Up and down like scales like the pigeon I call Justine.

Mais non, impossible. She's on her way to England.

Then loud grunting sounds followed by a loud squawk... squawk...

Homing pigeons grunt when they're in trouble. They don't squawk.

That small creature is in trouble.

Justine. She's hurt.

The only reason she'd return here is if she hasn't the strength to make the trip across the channel. I worry about that with all our pigeons. We're low on pigeon food like corn as well as wheat and peas, but we have fruits and vegetables thanks to the farmers we meet, so I made a mixture of apples and carrots and corn for Justine so she had enough strength for her voyage.

No, *something else* made her return home.

I race around in circles, check the back of the lodge. Carrier pigeons have been known to make the journey across the channel though badly injured, but I have an awful dread something happened to her she *couldn't* withstand.

I see nothing, then I head down toward the narrow stream winding into the forest like a watery, magical path, wishing Michal were here, but I can't find him, leaving me to think he's already left for Paris and—

Then I see her.

'Oh... Lord, no, no!'

I no longer feel the cold because I'm chilled inside from the pain of seeing the pigeon lying on the ground, shivering. Her tiny, bloodied body picked over and clawed by a bird of prey.

What fiend did this to her? Nazis, of course. They sent up a hawk or falcon to kill her. I swear I'll rip them apart with my bare hands.

I don't stop to think what that means, that German soldiers are in the area, that I'm not safe, that they could be nearby searching for the pigeon loft. No, instead I can't control my anger when I get down on one knee, unfold her broken wing dotted with drops of crimson. She squeals and barely moves, lying on the hard dirt.

So there also lies my heart. Cold on the ground. Next to her.

The injured pigeon struggles to breathe, the tiny pouch still attached around her neck. I pick her up and gently remove the pouch, tossing it into my jacket pocket, and hug her tiny body close to me, rocking her back and forth.

'I'm here, *ma petite*,' I whisper over and over again. 'I'm here.'

Can she feel my warmth? My heart beating close to hers?

A strange need fills me, something I never expected. A grieving for this brave little bird, and for the first time since my sister was raped and then disappeared, I'm grieving.

For my sister Justine, too. I couldn't cry before. I can now and hot tears well up, my eyes swimming out of focus, but I don't wipe them away. I can't. Don't want to. What started out with the theft of a painting on a hot August day has turned into a personal war I'm waging against the Nazis and I'll not let it go.

Ever.

Until we defeat them.

I rock the pigeon back and forth, never wiping away my tears, never stopping until my grief is spent like draining the stinging poison from a wound, sucking it dry, only now can I stitch my soul back together and heal.

Then I hear a whispery *coo* and she's gone.

I get to my feet, head for the lodge to give her a proper sendoff. A cruel metaphor for the story of the sadistic SS officer who stole my sister when—

The reality I so conveniently tucked away in the back of my brain hits me head on.

Gunfire.

A rumbling hum somewhere in the vast forest behind me, the deep emerald green treetops shaking, their crisp leaves rustling like a cancan dancer's petticoats, then a loud *boom* reverberates what I perceive to be high-powered rifles firing live ammunition at *a deer... rabbit?*

Are you so naïve you think what you heard is a hunter searching for prey?

Nazis.

I run up the stairs to the loft and wave my arms about to scatter the pigeons. They take off, their wings whistling louder than usual. I lay the dead pigeon in her cubbyhole, then race down the stairs. If I set it on fire, they'll know I'm here. I've got to hide in the forest, pray they think the loft is deserted. I race to the cellar of the lodge, grab a torch, head through the underground alleyway then make a swift exit through the secret trapdoor then... *run, run!*

Heart hammering, I run so fast through the forest my chest

hurts. I don't know where I'm going, just that I've to get away, when I see—

A truck.

Our truck.

And an empty petrol can lying on its side.

Michal. *Isn't he on his way to Paris?*

I hear heavy footsteps behind me, then an angry male voice.

'Ève. What the hell are you doing here? I almost shot you.'

Where did he come from? I thought he'd already gone.

'I'm surprised you didn't.' I heave out a cleansing breath, then say in a serious tone, 'I heard gunfire. Nazis?'

'Yes. I was filling the truck with petrol when I heard the loud shouts and fluttering of wings and then I saw two... three hawks attack our homing pigeon.'

I close my eyes. *My poor Justine.*

'How'd they find us?' I ask.

'The routine patrol I saw back there got lucky or...' His voice grows low and husky. 'Coralie was followed yesterday and they picked her up and—'

He leaves the rest unsaid, but the groan coming deep from this throat tells me he's reliving Warsaw all over again and the pain is crushing him. Before I can utter a word to soothe him, he recovers, becomes the soldier again. 'Our cover is blown, but we've still got a chance. It's a small patrol. Four men, two dogs. I lost them about five kilometers back when I waded through the stream, but the dogs will track me here. We have ten minutes tops. We've got to free the pigeons.'

'I did.'

'And... and—'

He stumbles and a widening red stain on his jacket grows bigger.

'Michal... you're hit!'

'It's nothing. I ran toward the commotion to get an idea of what we're up against and the damn captain got off a lucky shot with his Luger.' He bends over, grits his teeth. 'Take cover in the back of the truck while I'll hold them off, then get the hell out of here.'

'They'll take you prisoner.'

'I said *go!*'

I cross my brows. 'I'm not leaving you.'

'*Damn you, woman,* don't you ever obey orders?'

I don't answer him; I'm too busy trying to stop the blood spreading onto his shirt. I take off my belt and wrap it around his middle under his left armpit, then I take off my camel coat and sweater and stuff the sweater under the belt to put pressure on the wound.

'What the hell are you doing?' he demands.

'Saving your life. Stay with me and *don't* pass out.'

'I don't trust you enough to pass out. You'd probably strangle me with that damn belt.'

'Don't tempt me.'

'I won't.'

I can't see the wound and I don't dare open his jacket, but I've no doubt the punctured flesh is filled with skin, cloth fibers, metal fragments, and the like. It's vital I get him to a doctor to prevent infection. Even if it's a clean shot, the wound is contaminated.

'I wish I were back in my lab working on my sulfa experiment, on *any* experiment,' I babble on because I need to occupy his mind when I pull the belt as tight as I can to keep pressure on the wound. It will hurt him like hell. 'Then I'd sprinkle yellow powder on your wound and watch you squirm.'

'Worried about me, mademoiselle?'

'No,' I snip back. 'I just don't want to lose a live guinea pig, even you.'

Then before he can take a breath and come back at me with a

snappy retort, I pull the belt so tight his body jolts... hard. He groans, clenching his teeth, but he doesn't yell out. The man is steel.

'*Damn*, woman, you love torturing me, don't you?'

I smile. 'Somebody's got to keep you in your place.' I check my handiwork. It's holding. For now.

'Finished, mademoiselle?' he groans.

'No. You had no business getting shot, Michal. You're a damn fool for not running.'

'And leave you to the Nazis?' he grunts. 'Don't think I wasn't tempted.'

'Don't be coy,' I say in a soft voice. 'You were leading the Nazis away from the lodge. Away from me.'

He avoids my eyes, smirks as I expect him to do. 'Not you... the pigeons.'

'Oh, so now the pigeons have top billing. *Bon*. I have half a mind to leave you here, but Remi would have my arse if I did.'

I've got to get him help. Fast. He's losing blood and if my class in anatomy serves me well, he could have severed the brachial artery in his arm from the gunshot. Which means he'll bleed out if I don't get help fast.

'I'll take you home to Maison Bleue. Madame knows a Jewish doctor who will come to the house. I'll explain to her the situation—'

'No, it's too dangerous for Madame and your *maman*. Help me into the truck. Can you drive?'

'Of course,' I lie, amazed at the man's tenacity as he hobbles to the vehicle, barely letting me help him climb into the passenger seat. My brain refuses to connect the sudden warmth in my groin to his hard body pressed against mine. He makes me feel emotions I've never felt before. Emotions a girl like me has no right feeling. 'If I can build bombs, I can drive a rickety old truck.'

I've watched Michal drive this piece of junk numerous times. Turn the key... foot on the clutch pedal... pull the levers. *What could be simpler?*

'Then let's go, *now!*'

'Where?' I ask, grinding the gears as we go tearing through the grass and onto a dirt road heading back toward Paris, driving as fast as I can. My eyes swing back away from the city when I hear commands shouted in German, the dogs' vicious barking. Small animals scampering over fallen tree branches as desperate as we are to escape.

'To the American Hospital.'

I turn my head sharply. 'What if you're arrested?'

He makes a feeble attempt to smile.

'I won't be the first Resistance fighter they've hidden, Ève.'

17

PARIS, MARCH 1941

Justine

'Going somewhere, mademoiselle?'

That voice. Sarcastic... cutting.

I spin around. *Herr Geller. Am I ever safe from the Gestapo?*

The American Hospital may have escaped a takeover by the SS, but that doesn't stop the secret police from poking around like curious rats sniffing for their next meal. Nurse Edith warned me to be vigilant, that the Gestapo could be anywhere, even disguised as a patient. I'm not surprised Herr Geller found me. Never underestimate the SS to have the Gestapo do their dirty work.

I find it odd the Gestapo would show up here, making me wonder what the major has on him. An illicit affair? No. Political? No.

Or is the Gestapo gathering evidence *against* the major? And I'm the stooge? Or more precisely, am I the object of Herr Geller's snooping around to get under the major's skin? The means to an end to some disgusting little game he's playing, like those cross-word puzzles of his. I find the whole thing unnerving, but I'm determined to get to the bottom of it.

'Why didn't the major come himself?' I ask, baiting him. 'Or doesn't he know you're here?'

He stands his ground. 'The major is engaged in a meeting at the Hôtel Lutetia, but he's concerned for your safety.'

'I find that difficult to believe. *He* ran out on me at the Bal Tabarin.'

'I gather then the major didn't entertain you and the general later in his hotel room or...' He pauses, taps his fingers on his crossword puzzle. 'Perhaps he has a "secret" apartment for such rendezvouses?'

'No.'

'A place where he's taken you to show off his treasures?'

'*No*,' I insist. 'And if he did, do you think I'd tell you?' He grunts, agitated. *I've touched a nerve.* He doesn't like being challenged.

I loathe the major, but I also hate being tossed between two sick, perverted alley cats like a live fish. The Gestapo man who never breaks a sweat is eyeing me with that piercing look that tells me this won't end well for me if I ask too many questions. He lets me go. For now.

'Don't dawdle, mademoiselle, I'm busy, *very busy*.'

'Do I have a choice?'

'No.' Direct. Final.

I'm half-dressed, standing next to a narrow bed behind the white cloth partition set in a wooden frame, shivering under his scrutiny. Not because I'm embarrassed, but because I'm well aware there are men in this world you don't flirt with, you don't show weakness in front of, and you *don't* talk back to. That bad things happen if you do. I've heard whispering in the hospital corridors about forced labor camps where prisoners are worked to death.

Which brings credence to what the major enjoys boasting about. Camps in Germany and one built last year in the Polish suburbs of a city the Nazis renamed 'Auschwitz'. And harrowing accounts about what happens to women. The torture to their breasts with burning cigarettes makes me retch. I close my ears at that point. I don't want to know any more.

I inch backward slowly into the corner. Why, I don't know. I have nowhere to go. Herr Geller stands behind me in a too-tight, black leather trench coat and Fedora, working that damn crossword puzzle, then looking up and staring at me. Waiting.

He's the biggest rat of them all.

I'm trapped.

So I'm not surprised when he clears his throat to get my attention. Loud, grumpy. I imagine the other patients are hiding under their sheets to escape his scrutiny. The nurse assigned me to a small ward with two other female patients—they removed the empty beds since they're needed in the men's ward—but it's still busy with nurses pushing their trolleys on wheels, counting medical supplies tossed onto a portable table, emptying bedpans, taking temperatures, doing their best to ignore the presence of the Gestapo man.

Herr Geller pays them little attention. He's enjoying the task at hand like the devil dipping his sharp, pointy toenail into a heavenly cloud. His eyes rake over me, from my flimsy black slip barely concealing my blossoming motherhood to my garters and silk-stockinged feet. Nurse Edith returned my black velvet gown to me this morning, the stain in front dried and barely visible, my underwear scrubbed clean, my cloak and black pumps. I'm leaving the hospital with the blessing of the doctor and a word of caution to get as much rest as possible. He reiterated that I'm welcome to have my baby here in spite of the 'unpleasantness', when I was accused of pretending to be pregnant to gather intelligence from sick and wounded men.

And that a 'friend' took care of the arrangements.

Arsène, of course.

It warms my heart how he watches over me, though most likely his support has to do with his work for the Resistance. I'm a valuable asset, but I'm so lonely and hurting after all these months, his tenderness and deep, caring eyes draw me in until I'm breathless, and the energy radiating from him makes me want to open up to him. Talk about the assault. Be honest. Brutal, if I must. Let it go. Like he helped me in the brothel attic. He makes me believe I'll be a good mother and someday... *who knows*?

I stall getting dressed, pondering these thoughts, letting the daydream last a bit longer after I received a hastily-scribbled note from the major this morning advising me a motorcar will come around to take me back to my apartment on Rue des Martyrs where we would discuss 'the situation'.

I raise a brow. *What is there to discuss?* I'm having a child, *his* child, and now he must face the consequences of his primal urges last summer. What makes my insides tighten is that I could easily become the victim of an 'unfortunate accident' and his evil deed will disappear as quickly as a cool breeze on a hot summer day.

Seeing Herr Geller standing at the foot of my bed gives credence to that fear. He never mentioned the Gestapo.

My first instinct was to run, but where would I go?

I have no money, no clothes except those on my back, my baby is due in May, and I have no one I can trust but Ève, Maman, and Madame. And Arsène. I haven't seen him since I've been here. By his absence, I imagine he's leading 'patients' from the hospital to the escape line over the Pyrenees to Spain. Didn't that Englishman with the thin mustache mysteriously disappear yesterday? And the patient with an accent so thick even the nurse couldn't understand him. He was gone two, three days ago.

Which means I'm on my own.

Making me more vulnerable to this surprise attack by the Nazi bulldog, his mouth frozen in a perpetual snarl. I can't stand to watch him staring at me as I dress. I know asking him to leave is out of the question, so I turn my back to him, the only defiance I'm brave enough to show, and slip the long velvet gown over my head. Out of the corner of my eye, I see him wiping his leather glove on the small white table next to my bed, one drawer, one knob, then shaking his head.

'Dirty... like everything French.' He rubs his gloved hands together. 'I assure you, mademoiselle, the hospital where you shall give birth is clean and properly disinfected.'

I spin around, peeved. 'I beg your pardon, monsieur. I'm having my baby *here*. It's all arranged with Doctor Jackson.'

He raises a brow. 'The American physician?'

'Yes.'

He shakes his head. 'No, mademoiselle, you will do as you're told and birth the child at Lariboisière Hospital with a good German doctor in attendance.'

I can't believe this priggish Nazi is ordering me to offer up the most precious event in my life to the demands of the German government like it's a public event. It's so awful, so humiliating, so against God's natural plan for motherhood that I don't think clearly before lashing out at him.

'It's *my* child, monsieur,' I balk, hands on my hips. 'I will have the baby where I wish.'

'Your child belongs to the Reich, mademoiselle. You should be honored to bear a child with Aryan blood.'

The way he says it makes me shiver.

'No... I refuse.' I make my stand. For my baby's sake. 'I'm *not* leaving here until we settle this matter.'

Herr Geller grabs my arm and squeezes it hard. 'We have ways of making you see things our way, mademoiselle.' The sudden surprise flashing in his eyes tells me I've awakened a sleeping devil itching for the taste of human blood. Mine.

'Why didn't the major tell me this himself?' I ask.

'You may be the major's mistress, mademoiselle, but the Gestapo also has an interest in your fate.'

'Why?' I question. 'You're not the father of my child, monsieur.'

'You *are* a quarrelsome bitch, mademoiselle,' he says, ignoring my question, 'and your insolence tempts me to find you accommodations at Cherche-Midi to have your child in solitary confinement.'

'That's a military prison,' I shoot back.

He babbles on about how the Nazis have taken over the prison to house political prisoners. In other words, anyone who doesn't agree with them. Like me.

'I'm a French citizen,' I insist. 'I have rights.'

Even if my identity card is fake.

He laughs, then stuffs his crossword puzzle into his inside pocket. When he opens his coat, I see he's carrying a pistol. I can feel hot sweat oozing between my breasts. Every fear I had is magnified.

'We Germans are in charge now, mademoiselle,' he continues, 'and you have no rights other than those we decide to allow you.' He smirks. 'If you were Jewish, you'd have no rights at all. Not even the right to live,' he says more to himself than to me.

What does he mean by that? Are the de Giocomtes in danger?

'You surprise me, Herr Geller,' I begin, determined not to back down. He's bluffing about sending me to prison. 'The major needs me to be his songbird.'

'Mademoiselle?'

'You Germans are fanatics about showing off your discipline and precision, marching up and down the Avenue des Champs-Élysées every day with bands playing loud music and goose-stepping, yet you can't keep your own officers in line.'

His brows cross. 'What are you suggesting?'

'Major Saxe-Müllenheim raped me. Took me against my will. I was abused. Humiliated. Torn from my family to serve his primal needs.'

The Gestapo man scoffs. 'You're lying.'

'*Am I?* He stole works of art from the de Giocomte family, wonderful people who took me in as a child. Paintings that don't belong to him. And neither does my baby. His unsavory, disgusting act gives him or the Reich *no* say in my child's welfare.'

'Paintings, mademoiselle?'

'Yes.'

By the sudden twitch on the side of his mouth and the way he grips his pencil hard, I'm certain Herr Geller didn't know about the rape *or* the de Giocomte paintings. That what he suspected is true. The major is keeping works of art for himself. Good. Let the major stew in his own juices when the Gestapo man confronts him with my accusation. He'll deny it, of course. But it will cast doubt in Herr Geller's mind about his honor, and when the Gestapo questions the integrity of an SS officer, that plants a seed of a different kind.

That he's not to be trusted.

That doesn't change the Gestapo man's agenda.

'Finish dressing, mademoiselle. I have other matters to attend to other than babysitting a petulant *French* mother-to-be.'

The way he says it makes me sound dirty. The bastard.

I grab my cloak, swish it around in a grand, royal gesture, which infuriates him, then smooth my hair and lift my chin. Sylvie

Martone couldn't have given a better performance, but inside I'm shaking so hard my teeth chatter. Herr Geller starts pacing and I can almost see the steam coming out of his ears. He's debating whether or not to drag me out of the hospital like a common streetwalker. I won't let him degrade me. I'll walk out of here with my head high, my dignity intact even if I have no idea how I'm going to thwart the Nazi order to have my baby under the flag of the swastika.

Chin up, shoulders back, I push aside the white-sheet partition when I see—

Ève?

My jaw drops. *My sister. What's she doing here?*

I hover to the side, creaking my neck, overjoyed to see my sister again even if it is under dire circumstances. Selfish, I know, but oh how I need this. A ray of sunshine after getting drenched by the Nazi storm cloud.

I look closer. Her face is gaunt, making her high cheekbones more prominent. Contoured and striking, like they've been sculpted from an artist's brush. Her eyes luminous with tears she struggles to keep from falling onto cheeks as pale as a snow angel's. It hurts me to see Ève looking drained. She looks thinner, disheveled, and she's wearing trousers, boots, and that long camel coat. She's holding up a tall, handsome man in a brown leather jacket, grubby pants, boots, his longish hair falling into his eyes, his head wobbling from side to side like he's ready to pass out. Then my eyes shift to the leather belt wrapped around his upper body. A bloodied sweater stuffed underneath it to put pressure on the wound—a lime-green sweater. I smile; *yes, it's Ève's*, Maman knitted it. His teeth clenched, the man holds on to Ève and Nurse Edith as they drag him into a room adjoining the ward. There the nurse will clean his wound and apply the dressing. I know because I've watched several patients taken care of this way when they're first brought in. Nurse Edith told me no dressings are done in the ward to prevent cross-infection.

Today it will save this young man's life.

He's out of view of the Gestapo.

For now.

I move the partition back into place. If Herr Geller sees the bloody jacket, he'll question him, and if he sustained a gunshot wound, he'll delight in hauling the young man to Avenue Foch for questioning before he can receive medical treatment. There they'll torture him for hours and with all the blood he lost, he'll die. I can't let that happen. What makes me suck in my gut is the worry and fear I see in my sister's eyes, the way she holds his hand, not letting it go, smoothing his dark, unruly hair out of his eyes, telling him, 'Hold on, Michal. You're safe now.' A tug to my heart sends me over the moon. I hear a tune in my head I never thought would make me hum. *My sister is in love with this young man. My Ève. In love.* A wonder I never dreamed of has taken hold of my wonderfully crazy sister and it makes my heart soar with a happiness I haven't felt since that horrible August day.

I can't let him die. I can't let the Nazis take that love away from her.

I need a plan. But what? Herr Geller and I must walk past the examination room, then down the long corridor to exit the hospital. We can bypass Ève and her young man as long as the secret policeman doesn't get too curious and look in the room, then he'll be safe. Ève, too.

I clear my throat, and the nurse looks around. She sees me. I nod toward the Gestapo man behind the partition, then pull the sheet apart ever so slightly so she gets a peek of the man in the black trench coat. She gasps and Ève turns her head, looks in my direction. I duck behind the partition before she gets a good look at me.

I can't let her see me. *I can't.*

I let out a heavy sigh. She looks so tired, exhausted, it breaks my heart. I would give anything to talk to her, tell her about the baby. To see the excitement light up her hazel-green eyes like glistening dew on a leaf. I need my sister more than ever, but the Gestapo will arrest both Ève *and* the Resistance fighter if he gets wind of something amiss. So I keep quiet, though I'm afraid she saw me.

Yet I can't help but ask, why is my sister here? It's obvious, n'est-ce pas? I saw Ève protesting with the students from the Sorbonne and Resistance fighters. The young man must be a compatriot shot by the Nazis. Somehow, he knew to come here for help.

He didn't know the Gestapo would be here.

I've got to save him.

I look away with tears in my eyes. I wish just for a moment I could grab Ève's hand and squeeze it for courage.

Just for a moment...

'I'm getting impatient, mademoiselle,' I hear behind me, but I don't turn around. I need to compose myself, quiet the gentle kicking in my tummy with a loving rub. 'And you *don't* want me to become impatient because then I will become angry and I will do something you will regret.'

I turn and smile at him. Sort of. 'Have you seen Paris in the spring, monsieur? When the snow melts and a lovely perfume of white gardenias is everywhere?' I ask to throw him off.

Don't panic. Or be too nice. The Gestapo man will know something is wrong.

'I look forward to springtime in your beautiful city for years to come, mademoiselle,' he says, puzzled.

I'm stalling. I pull the partition over to one side to block Herr Geller's view of my sister holding up the wounded man while the nurse covers him with a blanket to hide his bloodied jacket.

Bon.

'You will find as the flowers bloom each spring after the winter thaw that we French are resilient *and* practical.'

He grunts. 'What are you saying, mademoiselle?'

'Allow me to apologize for my outburst, monsieur. The Gestapo is always right.'

My stomach squirms at the lie I'm telling. I pray I won't toss up the toast and porridge and peas I ate earlier for breakfast all over him. I put on my sweetest smile as Nurse Edith hustles my sister and the wounded man into the examination room.

And out of sight.

'Mademoiselle?'

'I shall have my baby at Lariboisière with a good German doctor in attendance as you suggested.' I fasten my cape around my shoulders and pull up the hood to hide my face. 'Shall we go?'

Satisfied and eager to leave this 'dirty French hospital', Herr Geller grunts again like a boar ready to smash through its wooden pen, then takes me by the elbow and we march out of the ward with all eyes upon us. I can't stop breathing hard after my brush with the Gestapo. Hot sweat trickling down my back, flushed cheeks, pregnant, fearful, exuberant, my baby kicking, I silently introduce her to her Aunt Ève. This wild young woman who makes me so proud to see she joined the fight. I pray someday when the world is back to a better place, the two will meet and hug and take walks in the Bois and feed the swans like we did as little girls.

And all the while I wonder...

What the hell has my sister gotten herself into?

* * *

Ève

'Who is the platinum blonde I saw with the Gestapo man?' I whisper, narrowing my eyes. Months of dangerous sabotage work makes me more aware of my surroundings and the people in them. Like that blonde. I crane my neck to peek into the ward and catch a glimpse of the woman from the rear wrapped up in a white velvet cloak and hood. I can't see her face, the secret policeman pushing her along like she's a fairy tale princess chaperoned by a big, ugly toad.

I flutter my eyelids. She looks so much like Justine. *Am I seeing things?*

Mad, crazed. Lonely. I thought I'd patched up my heart so I could go on, seek revenge against the Nazis for what they did to Justine, then seeing that woman ripped it off, leaving me hurting all over again. The resemblance is uncanny. Blonde, captivating, gliding across the hospital polished floor like her feet don't touch the ground, she has that Gestapo man eating out of her hand. Oh, yes, I saw the snide look on his face when he held her by the elbow, his eyes traveling up and down her body, seeing what I couldn't, wanting to possess her.

Justine affects every man like that.

I caught but a glimpse of her. That porcelain doll face that *is* Justine. I swear she's the spitting image of my sister. Lighter hair, fuller figure, which surprises me since no one in Paris gains weight these days, so she must be either a Nazi wife from Berlin... no, *mistress*... or a Parisian collaborator.

Which disgusts me.

I drop my eyes. What was I thinking? It can't be Justine. My sister would *never* be friendly with the Nazis, much less the Gestapo. I pull in my breath and will my heartbeat to slow down, guilt raging in me for allowing a horizontal collaborator to draw me away from attending to Michal. I'm so crazed worrying about him. He's lost a lot of blood. It's a miracle we arrived here.

I never thought we'd make it, but Michal kept talking, not letting the seductive temptation to let go overtake him, keeping focused, rambling on that he's proud of me, how when the threat happened I didn't panic. Instead absorbing the sights, smells, but working past it, my adrenaline pumping. Yet this man refuses to call *himself* brave, but insists he fell back on his training, pushing past the brutal horror of what he's seen. Spilled blood and guts. Men and women reduced to jagged and ripped flesh to get the job done. It makes me shiver imagining the terror that shaped him when the Nazis marched into Poland. He's the most powerful man I've ever known, a slow burn flooding my body when I'm near him. I fight against it. But in the end, I want to be with him.

And the thought of losing him crushes me.

Fear spiked in my veins as I steered the rambling, old truck down the grand boulevards, a heaviness slamming me between the shoulders, then jumping from the vehicle, grabbing Michal, my arms, shoulders pulling at the sockets to get him out of the truck, his body all brawn and muscle, before abandoning the vehicle near the Bois. We dumped the truck at a German depot then sneaked past the guard and made our way here on foot to the hospital, Michal's arm limp and bleeding, dragging himself along with each step. Hugging doorways and ducking out of sight whenever we saw a Nazi patrol. We were lucky. No German sentries or guards at the hospital main gate. I blew out a sigh of relief—

Until I saw the Gestapo man.

And the blonde.

Confident. Pretty. Am I imagining it or did she hustle him out of the hospital when she saw us?

'You speak of Mademoiselle Rachelle d'Artois. She's the French mistress of a German officer. She came here for help when she nearly lost...' the nurse offers up with a nervous twitter in her voice, then attempts a smile. 'It's not important. She's not anyone you need to concern yourself with.'

Before I can press her further, she insists Michal remain still so she can take off his jacket *and* his shirt then clean his wound before the doctor arrives to make his prognosis.

When she grabs the scissors and cuts off his shirt, the bloodied cotton falling around his waist, I never expected the sight of a man's bare chest could send embarrassing heat rippling through me, and *he*, damn him, in spite of his pain, is smirking like a fox with a squeamish hen in its claws.

It's maddening he can do this to me.

I ignore the heat in his eyes and keep him talking. The burning in his arm makes him clench his teeth so tight his eyes crinkle up into slits, those beautiful eyes that smolder like blue fire when he teases me, hiding such pain he won't let me see it.

He smiles instead.

'Haven't you ever seen a man without his shirt, mademoiselle?'

'Of course,' I tell him. 'On a slab in anatomy class... *completely naked.*'

'I could accommodate you if you wish.'

I see the nurse drop her guard for a moment, grin, then insist her patient refrain from speaking as she goes about her work in the precise manner a woman like her has developed over the years, treating him as her patient and not seeing the wildly handsome man I see.

Sweat shines on his bronze shoulders and muscular arms, and my girlish desire for him to hold me in those arms is overtaken by the damage I see to his body. I've crossed the line into a new reality at the sight of the oozing flesh of his jagged wound. Sinewy, ripped skin. Bone. It sends a wave of dizziness through me. I've never seen an open wound like this before.

And it chills my blood cold.

Michal barely sits still to have his wound dressed. He keeps looking around, instinct driving him to assess the situation, check for danger, while the nurse tells us the bullet grazed his shoulder but no main arteries were hit. She *is* worried about the wound becoming infected.

Me, too.

Michal is my partner, nothing more, I keep telling myself, and in spite of the emotions raging through me, the ache to touch him, making anything else out of it is too disturbing, too dangerous.

I turn away. I'll not give him the satisfaction of seeing my discomfort. Or how much I care. That would never do for our partnership. Keep it professional. Nothing more.

'What else do you know about Mademoiselle d'Artois?' I press her, trying to take my mind off this gorgeous half-naked man. I can't let it go how much she resembles Justine even if she doesn't act like her.

'Nothing, mademoiselle, now I must ask you to leave. The doctor will be here any minute.'

She's hustling me out of here. Understandable given the situation, but I can't shake the feeling there's something she's not telling me about the platinum blonde.

Why can't I let it go?

Because she looks like Justine and the pain of losing my sister persists... and always will.

18

PARIS, MARCH 1941

Justine

'That Gestapo man has no right to tell me where I can have my baby.'

I feel like I want to crawl into a hole, curl up into a ball and never come out. My ears still burn with the words *Lariboisière Hospital*. I'm so angry with the major, I'm not choosing my words well, not caring where this conversation is heading, knowing only that I must fight to have my baby where *I* choose. And it's *not* in a den of Nazis.

'You have no say in the matter.' Major Saxe-Müllenheim turns away from the view of the city to look at me. We're standing on the balcony in my apartment, a chilly breeze frosting the air while this 'discussion' between us becomes heated after the Gestapo man leaves. 'You're *my* property along with that painting of you and your sister that you covet so dearly.'

'Property?' I balk. 'Taking my virginity in a seething moment of lust does *not* entitle you to own me nor the painting. Where is it?'

'Hidden away until I deem the time is right to sell it.'

'*Sell it?*' I cry out. 'Where, how?'

'That's of no concern to you. You and the painting are spoils of war.' I refuse to show fear when he runs his hands up and down my body avoiding rubbing my protruding belly. 'I like you, Justine. You're the most beautiful woman I've ever possessed, and there have been many since I arrived in Paris.'

'I assume you had no difficulty ousting Jews from their apartments to house your conquests.'

'You're mistaken, mademoiselle. We Germans merely take over abandoned apartments.'

'*Abandoned?* Don't you mean forced evacuation?' I dare to comment.

He continues as if he can't hear me. 'I never dreamed what effect you'd have on me that first time I saw you, mademoiselle, how the curves of your body swayed me to toss away all caution and take you without protection, then you did a fool thing and got pregnant. Most unfortunate since we have no Lebensborn nursery here in France.'

Lebensborn? What devil's work is that?

'*I* did a fool thing?' I huff and puff, annoyance at his accusation pumping through me. '*You* raped *me*, then took me away from my family. My home. What more do you want from me?'

He glares at me. 'My child.'

'*What?*' I choke and bile burns in my throat. *He can't be serious. Anything but that.*

'If it's a boy, you will breastfeed the infant until a suitable wet nurse can be found and the child will be sent to Berlin to be raised in the SS nursery by a good German mother.'

'You *are* joking,' I insist, my brain spinning at his brazenness.

'I assure you, mademoiselle, the Lebensborn program bestows a great honor on children selected with the right qualifications.'

'And what *are* those qualifications?' I ask.

'The child must have blonde hair and blue or green eyes.'

'And blue blood?' I add with a smirk.

He snickers. 'Your sense of humor amuses me, but you have no idea how important this program is to the future of Germany and the master race.'

'And where do you find these poor innocents?' I admit my curiosity makes me push him further, if only to understand this preposterous idea so I can protect my child.

'I'm pleased to tell you German agents have relocated such children from the territories under our control, children who are racially pure.'

I try to keep from retching. *Damn the Nazis and their New Order.* I find the idea of taking children from their mothers appalling and against God's *natural* order of things.

'What happens *after* you kidnap them?' I dare to ask.

He doesn't deny it and lights up a cigarette and blows out the smoke before turning to me with a big smile on his face. 'The children are adopted into an SS family and educated where they're taught how to be a good German.'

'You're mad.'

He ignores me. 'If the baby is a girl, she will be raised by French nuns in a convent here in Paris until she reaches the end of her first year. Then she'll be sent to Germany and adopted by an SS family where she'll be raised to fulfill her duty to the Reich after she begins her monthlies.'

My chest burns. 'You and your *Lebens*... whatever it is... is insane.'

The idea disgusts me, makes me want to vomit, beat my fists on his chest, kick him, scream at the top of my lungs that I will *never* allow a man to harm my daughter in the same manner he did me.

'Not so, *ma chère* Justine, merely practical. You're a beautiful woman, intelligent, talented. The baby is not pure Aryan blood, but in time the child will become Germanized and will be proud to serve the Führer.'

I fight hard to tamp down my raw emotions. Not show weakness. I can't afford for him to *ever* see me weak.

'You will *never* take my child,' I say in an even, determined voice. 'I won't let you.'

'*My* child. I can and I will.'

'But *why*? What harm can it do if I raise the baby on my own?' I ask, wringing my hands. Anger, then desperation to understand his macabre, monstrous way of thinking eludes me.

'I need you to remain focused on your work here in Paris.'

'You mean *spying, n'est-ce pas?*'

The major shrugs. He refuses to admit he finds my pregnant condition inconvenient since he depends on me to turn over information regarding anything I hear about the comings and goings of the ladies of Paris. *And*, he never fails to remind me, add to his reputation as a *bon vivant* around Paris with a pretty girl on his arm.

'The Jewish names you provided were noteworthy,' he says, 'but the women had left the country before we could round them up and deport them to labor camps in Germany and Poland.' He circles me like a lion surveying his prey *before* the kill, each heavy step of his jackboots becoming a pounding in my ears. 'Your success record is very poor, mademoiselle, and if I didn't have a fondness for you, you'd already be interred in Drancy.'

Again, the mention of Drancy. To frighten me.

'I'm warning you,' he continues, 'if you wish to continue your lifestyle, you must put aside everything to secure intelligence as well as act as a hostess when I require your services.' He stops pacing, looks at me straight on. 'Having a child to take care of lessens your capabilities to perform your duties.'

I cringe. 'You mean entertaining General von Klum.' It's a statement, not a question.

'He's very fond of you, mademoiselle.'

'And if I don't agree to your preposterous demands?'

'I have it on good authority...'

He means the Gestapo.

'...your *maman* and your sister Ève still reside at the *maison* of the de Giocomtes near Park Monceau, though I can't say for how long. Herr Himmler is orchestrating a final solution to the Jewish problem and I assure you, the de Giocomtes are *not* immune. However, they're safe. I promise you.'

Then he goes on about how he intends to explore opening an SS nursery near Paris for children of French mothers, which makes me wonder how many other poor women the major and his cohorts have gotten pregnant.

I go over my options. I have nothing to gain by opposing him. God knows, I tried. I wouldn't put it past him to keep me a prisoner here, then I'd have *no* options. And more troubling, Ève is working for the Resistance, putting her in danger. I can't afford to bring any suspicion down on her that she's anything but a university student.

My hands are tied.

I have no choice but to acquiesce to him... for now. So I listen to the major outline my life with Germanic precision, how I'm expected to go about my daily duties at the hat shop, reporting back to him any suspicious gossip I hear. I shall be rewarded for my efforts by him allowing me to visit my child if it's a girl at the House of Sainte-Veronica de Mornay run by the Sisters of the Praying Hands. If it's a boy, I will be proud to have served the Reich with a son for an SS officer.

And with that, the conversation ends.

The major leaves me with my thoughts, my pregnancy. And my hopes for a joyful motherhood dashed. Smashed like a vase. Broken pieces I can't put back together.

I feel like God has abandoned me.

The days drag on.

I can't sleep, I worry too much about what will happen when my baby is born, using up my energy and sending me into depression, making my cheeks gaunt, though my breasts become heavier, fuller. I'm not as nauseous at last, but I'm lonely. No word from Arsène. I long to tell him about the major's plan to take my child away from me at birth. He'd understand, he always does, and it's the memory of him that keeps me sane. I can't bear to believe he's been arrested. Or... no, I can't. I *won't* think the worst.

The weeks go by, the cold winter turning to spring, and Paris comes out of her cave to welcome the sunshine. I breathe in the sweetness of the flower markets bursting with roses, posies, daffodils, while ignoring the stale smell of warm beer and crushed cigarettes as Nazi officers and soldiers lift the petticoats of Parisian life and revel in what's underneath.

I find each day a little harder to get through than the day before, straining to pull myself out of bed, the pressure on my back and bladder heavy and painful, my ankles swelling, and my belly rounded and full. I'm carrying the child high. *And* I'm craving raspberry macarons which are, of course, impossible to get, so I chew on sweet carrots. I take this as a good sign because according to Madame Péroline, wanting sweet things means I'm having a little girl.

I pray she's right.

Then I'll have a fighting chance to do what I must. I'm going to take a page from the Nazi handbook.

I plan to kidnap my own child.

19

Ève

When I returned to Maison Bleue two weeks ago with a patched-up Michal in tow, the first thing I noticed was that the Louis XIV beveled glass mirror trimmed with gold gilding and embedded with rare gemstones was missing.

The Nazis didn't steal it.

Madame sold the priceless mirror for a fraction of what it's worth to a wealthy client of her husband's former bank, a devout Catholic, to pay Maman, Cook, and the maid, Albertine, to keep the household running.

Her bank accounts are frozen. The Nazis' latest method to tighten the noose around the Jewish people.

Each day I see another piece of furniture missing: a Tiffany lamp, a miniature Greek statue, a rare book sold to Aryan friends eager to purchase items from their collection before the Nazis raided the *maison* and confiscated them for what they call 'safe-keeping'. Madame takes it in stride, commenting it's a small price to pay to keep the family going, keep Monsieur de Giocomte comfortable in his own home while his condition worsens. Some days he doesn't know her at all and asks her if she's his nurse. And each time afterward, I hear her retreat to her music room, cursing the Nazis who did this to her beloved husband before slamming the door and then playing a piece on her cello.

Today is no exception. I open the door ever so slightly to peek through and listen to Madame playing Mendelssohn's 'Overture to a Midsummer's Dream' on her cello as an act of defiance.

The Jewish composer is verboten.

'She plays like an angel,' Michal says, sneaking up behind me.

'That's because she is.'

I admit having him close to me does things to me I never dreamed. Hot, wonderful things. We've never spoken about our repartee at the hospital that morning. I tried to forget it, tried to forget seeing his magnificent body, wanting to touch him, do things to him that frighten me. Making me wish I *was* pretty so he'd see me as a woman like he sees Coralie, but I can't break down that barrier I've put up around myself. Yet I've caught Michal looking at me, his deep, rich voice teasing me with innuendos about how since we're confined to the house, we should get to know each other better. I ignore him. I like him, but I'll not be another notch on his pistol. Instead, I act as his nurse, changing the bandage on his shoulder, reminding him the doctor wanted to keep him in the hospital, but the Polish fighter insisted he wouldn't take a bed away from another soldier who needed it more than he did.

So we came here.

The perfect place for him to take refuge until he's recovered from his wound and gets the full use of his arm back.

I wish we could stand here outside the music room and listen to the beautiful music for a long, long time, but I must hide Michal before anyone sees him. He's been living in the coach house since the chauffeur left for the Free Zone rather than be picked up by the gendarmes and sent to a work camp in Germany. I sneak him food and we talk for hours about his life in Poland, his father's work at the university, how he lost his mother to tuberculosis not long ago. Today I promised to show him the rest of the house while Cook is busy trying to make sweet bread with carrots substituting for sugar. Albertine has gone to queue up for bread and Maman is humming along to Madame's playing as she knits socks in a big wingback chair. Monsieur de Giocomte is snoozing on the divan, oblivious to everything but the silk pillow under his head sending him into his dreams where nothing has changed, his wife's beautiful playing confirming that in his mind.

But I know it has. So does Madame.

She rests her cello against her thigh and waves her bow at me. 'Come in, Ève, and bring your friend, too.'

I smile. I should have known I couldn't put anything past her.

'Have a seat, young man,' she says to Michal. 'You're welcome to stay in my home for as long as you like. My way of thanking you.'

'Madame?'

'I've long suspected Ève is involved in the Underground.' She smiles at me. Warm, not judging.

'You did, madame?' I ask.

'*Mais oui*, my first husband was an aristocrat turned revolutionary in Leningrad, *ma petite,* when he saw the truth of what was going on in Russia. I know the signs. Disappearing at strange hours, out all night, clothes burned or singed with gunpowder residue.'

'I'm sorry for keeping it from you, madame, but I didn't want to alarm you.'

'I'm proud of you, Ève, and you, too, monsieur.'

'Michal.'

'Michal. For fighting to free us from these horrible monsters who won't stop until they've destroyed a culture that's outlasted revolutions and kings.' She tosses a glance in my direction. 'And for watching out for Ève. She and her sister Justine are like grand-daughters to me.'

Again, I feel the guilt coursing through my veins at not telling Madame the truth, although I wonder what she *does* know.

It's time I find out.

'I have a story I must tell you, madame,' I begin. 'About Justine.'

'She's not actually off working in a house of couture, is she?' Madame asks, her voice hard like steel.

'No. That August day when you and Monsieur de Giocomte were in Deauville, the day the Nazi major barged into your home unannounced and looted your beautiful masterpieces—' I pause. 'Justine was raped. We now believe she's dead.'

'*Ohh...*' Her shoulders stiffen, her eyes widen, and her whole body goes rigid like she's been stabbed in the chest. Amazing though, her grip on her cello and her bow remains strong. She doesn't cry out. Instead, her voice finds its own sorrowful requiem as she speaks, sounding like a gutted animal, low and hoarse. And in terrible pain. 'Tell me, please, about Justine.'

I catch my breath, then tell my story. How Justine protected me from the SS officer's assault, then willingly went with him after he tore her clothes. She never came home. Then how I went to the police afterward to report her missing, but they found no record of the assault and refused to investigate her disappearance.

'I can only assume she's dead. Because otherwise surely she would have come home, *n'est-ce pas?*'

The painful experience of hearing the story of Justine affects each of us in the telling. Madame listens carefully, nodding her head up and down. Michal paces the floor, muttering under his breath, his clear blue eyes so filled with anger they burn cold.

And me... I'm relieved somehow. As if I now can carry on.

I make no mention of the blonde I saw at the hospital, for nowhere in my soul do I believe Justine would align her loyalties with the Nazis.

I could never forgive her if she had.

'I, too, found myself, young and vulnerable like Justine,' Madame de Giocomte says after a long silence. 'I was a young widow when a trio of Bolsheviks invaded our home by the Black Sea. My first husband was killed by such men weeks before and I was alone. The servants had long gone, and I was making plans to leave Russia the next day. I told them I would pay them a great deal of money if they didn't harm me, that my husband had relinquished his title only to die protecting me. A gamble, since I had just enough funds to take the train to Paris, but I had treasures given to me by the Imperial Russian royal family, including bejeweled enamel eggs. Then I played for them. Russian folk songs on my cello for hours and hours while they drank bottles of vodka I brought them from the cellar. Soon the barbarians were dead drunk and I escaped into the night. Before I left, I set out a jeweled egg as payment and never looked back.'

'You were so brave, madame,' I stutter.

'Brave, no. Determined, yes. I wasn't going to let them beat me.' She smiles wide. 'It also helped I added laudanum to their vodka.'

A rare smile these days from Madame de Giocomte.

Then she turns serious.

'I think I've always known what befell Justine, I just didn't want to believe it.'

'How, madame?'

'I saw it in your *maman's* eyes when she tried so very hard to fit a dress on me, giving me excuses that Justine would be here if she could, smiling and eager to adjust a pleat or design a new collar, but she was having a wonderful time at the couture house and we wouldn't want to take that away from her, *n'est-ce pas?*' Madame de Giocomte sighs. 'Nor did I wish to take that dream away from your *maman*, so we played our little game every morning after we took tea, pretending all was as it should have been, as it was before the Occupation, like the perfect stitches in the silk your *maman* executes so beautifully—seamless and invisible.' She lets out a heavy sigh. 'I shall miss our game because it gave us both great comfort. I fear that is not the last thing that will change under the occupiers.'

Then, without another word, Madame de Giocomte resumes playing the lovely overture.

Our eyes connect and I feel a new bond form between us. We're both survivors.

* * *

Soon after, another change is in the wind. One that doesn't bode well for Madame with her dwindling funds.

It happens on a day when the occupants of Maison Bleue have settled into a quiet waiting period, waiting for *what* we're not sure, but rumors abound about more roundups, each of us going about daily chores once ordinary that have become feats of ingenuity and endurance.

Getting food, using precious stored firewood to cook food— could next winter be any colder than the last?—making sewing repairs on garments now too big because everyone's lost weight, stuffing newspapers into our old leather shoes, making our own soap, keeping watch for any disturbance outside which could mean unwelcome visitors and sending Michal scrambling back to the coach house to hide.

At first when we hear the *clip-clop* of a horse's hooves and creaking wooden wagon wheels, Michal and I scoop up the map we were studying for our next railway job and stuff it into a book of poems in the library. A loud scuffle outside in the private driveway attracts our attention, then a horse neighing, a woman's boisterous voice giving orders... and *children squealing?*

I rush outside and the fear making my heart race madly turns to mirth.

A heavily made-up woman in her late forties in a tight brown tweed suit and round hat with a stylish fur piece hanging off her shoulder is brushing bits of straw off her clothes and commanding the occupants of the farmer's wagon *covered* in straw to *hush.*

I can't believe what I'm seeing. The last thing Madame needs is the surprise arrival of her widowed sister-in-law, Baroness Floriah Marie Caudebec, and her daughter with her four rambunctious girls with big, frightened brown eyes and runny noses ranging in age from seven to sixteen. Six more mouths to feed. Clothe. Shelter.

But Madame is Madame and there's no end to the woman's generosity. She welcomes them warmly as I knew she would, taking in their story as she instructs Cook to make tea for everyone and offers them the last of the sugar in their tea to allay their fears and dry the tears of the starving children.

They're on the run with no place to go.

The baroness was tipped off by a friend the SS were on their way to confiscate her villa, so she gathered up her brood and they escaped when the baroness bribed a local farmer to hide them in his wagon and take them to Paris. They have no place else to go.

Their identity cards aren't up to date with the new rules and they've had no word from the baroness's son-in-law in a German POW camp for months. They're all alone except for the de Giocomtes.

So they become part of our household.

Echoes of the baroness's grandchildren laughing, running around the house and playing games as if they've not a care in the world tugs at my heart. These children are so innocent and don't understand why their world has changed, why they're barred from playing outside because the baroness fears the Nazis will snatch up her grandbabies. They still laugh, they still cry when they scrape their knee, but now each squeal sends their *maman*, the baroness's dutiful daughter, running to protect them. Children are supposed to believe that adults will care for them, but I see fear in their eyes when their *maman* hugs them too tight or lingers too long at their bedside at nap time till they close their eyes. Children know when their *maman* is frightened but hiding it well. Like I hide my own hurt because Maman blames me for Justine leaving us. I wish I could go back to where we were little girls so I could tell Justine I'm so sorry I couldn't save her, then Maman wouldn't be so sad. Instead I watch the baroness's grandchildren playing tag and sliding down the banister, the oldest daughter, a sixteen-year-old named Delphine, taking charge and apologizing to Madame de Giocomte who assures her grandniece that 'children will be children'. I feel for the girl, seeing Justine in her as she watches over her younger sisters. Her *maman* and the baroness ignore them, more interested in fending for themselves. They see the children more as a nuisance than as precious angels to be cherished and loved.

Madame sees it, too, and goes out of her way to get Delphine a new dress since she's grown out of her old ones, her young body blossoming and making her embarrassed. Maman volunteers to alter an old dress of mine. It makes me happy to see her eyes light up. A turn of events that brings life into this household since we lost my sister. I'm impressed with Madame's aplomb, her calmness in the face of chaos around us, knowing the danger that hovers over the family like a heavy dark cloud.

Just because they're Jewish.

20

PARIS, MAY 1941

Justine

The day I go into labor is also the day I get into a catfight with a Nazi general's wife.

Over a hat.

A blue velvet tricorn hat with an arrow-shaped pin studded with rhinestones. Accented with a long white plume.

I find joy in creating my designs. Like this hat, inspired by the royal equestrienne hats worn by Marie Antoinette and the French court. I linger for a moment in the past, warm as honey and still golden in my mind. Was it so long ago I stood in the library of Maison Bleue and rifled through the old tomes of French history? Neck creaked, staring up at portraits from that fascinating era at Versailles, I often wondered when they knew their world had ended. When a careless remark sent the royal queen to the guillotine. Is anything different under the occupiers? When whispered words of betrayal mean torture or even death.

Frau Befus spots the unique hat when she prances into the House of Péroline on this spring afternoon, sniffing about like a rodent after a piece of cheese. The German woman is obsessed with appearing in a new *chapeau* every day or so on the Avenue des Champs-Élysées to compete in what I call the 'hat parade' of French girls.

I greet her with a 'Bonjour' since she's infatuated with Paris and stumbles through speaking French with gesturing and facial expressions. She asks for Madame Péroline to help her and I tell her she will be back any moment from an errand. Frau Befus pouts. She's spoiled because the milliner fawns over her like a bee to a flower, a droopy flower buzzing around her and catering to her every wish.

I don't.

The German Frau prattles about, running her fingers over satin ribbons, lush velvet, saying she'll wait in that high-pitched voice of hers that sounds like a squeaky bicycle wheel. She gives me a curious eye when she sees how far my pregnancy has advanced, but avoids discussing my 'condition' like it's a disease—she has no idea the father is an SS officer; can you imagine the questions if she did?—and squints at the daisy pattern on the flowing yellow smock Madame Péroline insists I wear for the German customers. I hate it. It makes me sad, reminding me of happier days with Ève, but I wear it over my dress to hide my protruding belly so no one asks me about my condition. Especially French customers who might inquire 'who the father is'. Not much chance of that, though. They dwindle more and more each day. Soon we'll be an *Aryan only* shop.

How depressing.

My head pounding, her shrill voice dissipates my earlier good mood on this breezy morning. Paris in the spring with the smell of gardenias in the air, leaves as silky as a newborn's fuzz on the top of her head, birds chirping outside my bedroom window louder than usual, eager to awaken me, telling me my time is near.

Then Frau Befus descends upon me like a locust.

It's difficult to decide which is harder on my nerves. The German Frau watching my every move or waiting for my baby to come. Being cordial to the woman only makes me more stressed.

'*Ooh...*'

Without warning, my back spasms and sharp pains double me over, then go away just as quickly. *What's this?* I'm not due yet, but I've been feeling these pains more frequently in the past twenty-four hours. I can't stay in that apartment and do nothing. I'm on edge, waiting for the day I give birth. My heart races, wondering when the major will take my baby. In the delivery room? Men aren't allowed, but when did that stop the SS? I'll not give my child up without a fight, but I need a plan: new identity papers for me and the child, money, a way out of Paris. I think about sneaking over the border into Switzerland. I'd hoped Arsène would contact me but I haven't seen him since that night at the Bal Tabarin except for a quick 'confession' at the church.

I replay those lovely moments in my mind often.

It seemed as natural as counting daisies with my sister Ève when we were little girls, then racing into the kitchen to show Cook our bunches of posies and sneak warm lemon cakes just out of the oven. Comforting. Heart-lifting. Just like I felt sitting in the dark space in the confessional and talking to the man behind the grill like he's family, too.

'*Bless me, Father.* Oh, I've missed you, Arsène. I couldn't wait to see you again.'

I heard him draw in a deep breath. 'You flatter me, Justine, but yes, I've missed you, too.'

'I shouldn't say this, but hearing you say that makes my heart sing and my baby's too.' Silly girlish talk, but this man has gotten under my skin. Of course he knows how I feel, but this time I had to say it out loud.

'Someday, mademoiselle, when I have the right to speak to you not as Arsène, we can continue this talk—'

Tears formed in my eyes at hearing this and my heart swelled.

'But for now, I must remain as him in your eyes.'

'I understand.' I didn't and I felt selfish for thinking that, but his next words brought me back to the world we live in. A world at war.

'It's important you know that I received orders to return to London to help launch the "dropping" of the first SOE agents into France.'

I wasn't sure what SOE stands for, but it was welcome news.

'It will be a direct link to England, also supplies and weapons for the Resistance.'

'Thank God *and* the Allies,' I said with joy in my voice.

'Also, I'm concerned about Countess Ester Bulgávari.'

'Oh?' I asked, remembering the name. She's an important contact for Arsène.

'She's playing a dangerous game with a certain Nazi official. Don't hesitate to send her a message at the House of Doujan *parfumerie* if you hear anything that might compromise her or the foreign agent she works with. The professor.'

'The professor?' I asked, more curious than ever about this mysterious countess.

'I'm sorry, but I can't tell you any more.' Silence. As if he was wondering if he'd said too much. Then he changed the subject in a heartbeat. 'Before you go, I want to know how you're feeling after—'

'Our exciting evening at Bal Tabarin?' I teased him.

He laughed. 'Yes, it was quite a night. Quick thinking on your part. I would have taken the major out if he'd hurt you.'

Did he know about the slap? I decided against bringing it up and instead said, 'The baby's fine and Nurse Edith assured me I can deliver my child at the American hospital.'

I said nothing about the Gestapo's decree I have my baby in a German hospital or the major's plan to take the child. My baby comes first and there's no way I'll allow that to happen even if I have come up with an insane plan to prevent it, ride my bike all the way to Neuilly if I have to. Meanwhile, I don't want to worry Arsène. He has a tremendous responsibility to undertake for the Allies. So much is riding on getting those agents over here to help us. In the meantime, I'm on my own.

Afterward when I lit a votive candle, he knelt down beside me and covered my hand with his. It's that moment that has sustained me. Giving me hope through the last trimester of my pregnancy.

All these thoughts go through my mind every day at the shop to the point where I'm so filled with worry and anxiety, my fingers become like mechanical objects, tying, weaving, cutting, trimming, and going through the motions of making hats.

But today is different. Today I have a duty to perform. And this hat is the key.

I unfold thin tissue paper—Madame Péroline insists I use one piece of tissue now instead of three—and set the hat on top, fussing with it as I do, puckering the crown and checking the stickpin to make sure the message hidden under the crown is secure.

I can't fail in my mission.

I grab a round lilac box engraved with a scripted 'P' for House of Péroline, my heart skipping and pounding in my ears. My emotions pick up again. So far my life as a double agent has been mixed at best. I repeat gossip I hear to the major, then I repeat that same gossip to Arsène. Then I myself try to make sense of it. I've learned what I hear can mean nothing, or something, sometimes it's even life-threatening, but it has everything to do with my ability to rearrange the pieces, like in a puzzle. I've tuned my ear to know what to filter out and what to latch onto, how to find the pattern in the snatched words and phrases I overhear, and then stitch them together to glean viable intelligence.

This morning the puzzle pieces flew together in my mind like they were touched by a magic wand. I put together the information the major has been hinting at for weeks. I noticed the last time I saw him he kept taking his gloves on and off, tapping them against his thigh, talking about how the 'Jewish problem' was creating too much paperwork for his staff when they should be cataloging art acquired for the Führer's museum. He was counting on Himmler to step up his plans to 'fix it'. Then yesterday I heard rumblings from a saucy Nazi mistress about how she'll be glad when the building she lives in is 'Jew-free'. And earlier this morning two gray mice—female German auxiliary workers—spilled the beans, with a little prodding. The German female auxiliary workers babbled on in broken French about how they'd worked so hard this week, putting in extra hours gathering names and addresses for the French police to deliver a summons on a *billet vert*, green card, to foreign Jews, mostly Polish men.

'Green card?' I asked. 'What is that?'

'We shouldn't tell. Right, Greta?'

'Well...' said her friend, rolling her eyes. She was clearly dying to dish.

'Please tell me, Fräulein,' I said. 'You know how much I admire your work for the Reich.' I smiled, then placed a straw hat with a wide brim on her head. The prettiest hat I designed for spring. Daises and daffodils made from yellow and golden silk with a sprig of velvet violets.

'There's to be a roundup on Wednesday...' the girl began.

May fourteenth.

'Of Polish and foreign Jews.'

'Why?' I asked.

'For a "status review".'

'Is that bad?' I pretended to be naïve.

'Oh, no, mademoiselle, it is very good news. It means the Jews will finally be arrested and sent to internment camps.'

'Oh, how interesting,' I said, grinning so wide my cheeks hurt, yet inside I'm flipping through emotions from panic to disbelief. It can't be true. My first thought was the de Giocomtes, but they're not Polish. Then another name popped into my head—

Countess Ester Bulgávari.

She's a Hungarian Jew.

Arsène mentioned he was concerned about her, that if I hear intelligence pertaining to her *or* the foreign agent she works with, I should contact her. Is he Jewish, too?

'So, mademoiselle,' the gray mouse was saying, showing off the straw hat to her friend, 'how about a discount for your German sisters?'

My ears burning, I held my gut, trying not to throw up, then wished I had. How dare they call me their 'sister'? A jab to my belly, a punch. Because the only sister I'll ever have is Ève. Who's fighting against the Nazis when I can't even help her. It's a punishment I must learn to live with for not pushing back harder against the major's assault. I think about it every day. Revisiting the worst day of your life is an addictive drug. You want to let it go, but you can't. So I keep blaming myself, a film in my mind playing on a loop, like the celluloid is caught in the projector. Will it ever stop? *Should it stop? Am I as guilty as he is for not resisting harder?*

Tough questions I can never answer, but I must put my feelings

aside. More important is this information. A roundup of Jews
—*foreign Jews*—on May fourteenth.

I sent a message straightaway to the countess at the *parfumerie*
known as the House of Doujan on Rue Saint-Honoré that the
countess's *chapeau* is ready *pour emporter*. Pick up. And I have.

So now that hat is ready for her. The jeweled arrow's long,
slender shape makes it the perfect stickpin to 'pin' a message to the
inside of the hat.

14/5... rafle. Foreign Jews. Male.

May fourteenth... roundup.

I pray the countess shows up soon.

My hands shake and the blushing excitement on my face
catches the German woman's attention as I place the hat into the
box. Before I can cover it with the tissue paper—

'Let me see that hat, mademoiselle. It's so *French*.'

Frau Befus stands guard in front of me like a sentry, demanding
my attention.

'This plain old thing?' I feign boredom. 'It's not stylish enough
for the wife of an esteemed officer of the Reich. No roses or pearls.'

'Let *me* be the judge of that,' she sputters. Raw, catty. She, like
all Nazis, has to prove her superiority with even the most mundane
item. 'I adore the gorgeous blue velvet and that beautiful stickpin.
And with such a lovely white feather.' I wonder what she'd say if
she knew the feather came from a brothel. 'I want it, mademoiselle, *I must have it*.' She clicks her teeth in anticipation, her fat,
pointy chin bobbing up and down like a raven's beak.

'*Pardon*, madame, but the hat is promised to another customer.'

'Who?' she grumbles.

'A countess.'

'It's mine now. *We* are in control, not you French.'

She grabs it out of the box, sniffs it, and then rubs the velvet against her chubby cheek. 'I'll be the talk of Paris when I wear this hat to the next Hôtel Drouot art auction.'

'This hat is *not* for sale, madame.'

I grab the hat back, keeping my voice firm, but my nerves grow taut, my cheeks flushed. I have trouble breathing, but I won't let this selfish woman take what she wants. How any self-respecting human being could 'dress up' for an auction of art looted from impoverished Jewish owners is like tossing a sou at a homeless woman and then stepping on her fingers before she can grab the coin.

It's downright evil.

'And *I* say it *is* for sale,' she insists.

I can't let her have it. It has a hidden message inside. One that could betray both the countess and me.

'I say, *it is not!*'

I can barely keep down the tea and toast I had earlier as this creature keeps tugging on the hat like a snake wrapping its tail around its prey. We're past the point of fashion. Frau Befus has declared war on the House of Péroline and like all Nazis, she will sink to the lowest depths to win.

She jams her heel on my toe.

'*Ohh...*' I cry out with pain, letting go of the hat. And my pride. The woman is a nightmare, a Nazi who will linger in my memory long after we drive the Boches out of France. 'I will make you a bargain, madame,' I say, limping. *Did my baby just kick me? No, a contraction. Am I going into labor?* 'I will give you a hat compliments of Madame Péroline instead. With *two* feathers.' I point out a fancy black hat with lace and a pair of sleek feathers tipped with red.

'Well, it *is* pretty...' the woman says, tempted.

I can see her thinking about it, her fingers loosening on the hat, but before I can ease it out of her grip—

'I've come for my *chapeau*, mademoiselle.'

A stunning strawberry blonde with a voice sweet, yet tart as a Burlat cherry wine glides into the shop. As if she'd arrived in a royal coach, her eyes take in everything at once, leaving me no doubt the woman is used to being in charge. Svelte, elegant, she wears an emerald-green wool suit trimmed with fur, tight at the waist with an enamel clip pinned to her right shoulder, her hands flitting about as if she's leading a church choir.

I know this must be Countess Ester Bulgávari.

'My hat, *s'il vous plaît*.' She looks from Frau Befus to me, smirking. 'I have my motorcar parked out front. I'm in a hurry.'

'Frau Befus was just admiring your hat, Countess.'

I pluck the hat out of Frau Befus's hand while the woman sputters her displeasure in guttural German. I don't have to speak the language to know it's *not* complimentary.

The countess takes the hat from me, studies it, and then looks at me, her eyes asking, *I got your message. What am I not seeing?*

'We at the House of Péroline tailor our hats to our clients. Every hat *holds a special message for its wearer*,' I emphasize. 'Elegance, style. The velvet is a lovely weave from Belgium, but the arrow stickpin is made from cheap rhinestones. It's the war, you know. I'd be happy to replace it with a silk rose and a jade hatpin.' I smile. 'If you will allow me?'

The countess smiles. 'Of course, mademoiselle.'

I shuffle through our box of silk flowers, intending to unpin the message and slip the folded-up paper to the countess, but Frau Befus refuses to be left out of the conversation. She's sweating profusely, her short, permed hair drooping like wet noodles.

'I was here first, Countess, and I want that hat. I will happily swap it for the one I had chosen.'

She makes a grab for it, but the countess pulls it out of her reach. 'Mademoiselle is right, madame,' she says, ignoring her rant. 'The arrow stickpin is gauche, *non?*'

I watch the countess at work, amazed at her poise, finesse. She deftly removes the arrow stickpin and I see her eyes light up. She found the folded-up message tucked inside the hat. She nods toward me, then retrieves it with a magician's sleight of hand. And since the art of deception depends on drawing attention *away* from the trick, she dazzles the German woman's eye with—

'My brooch would do nicely in its place, *n'est-ce pas?*' She unpins a pretty enamel clip and adds it to the blue velvet hat with a flourish. *'Voilà!'*

'Shall I wrap it for you?' I offer, eager to bring this drama to an end.

'Yes, mademoiselle, then I shall be off—'

Frau Befus turns to the countess with such envy that the shop bristles with tension. 'Are you aware, Countess, my husband is a very important general?' she says, not holding back the threat in her irritating voice. 'He's very close to our Führer and has connections with the Gestapo.'

The countess makes a face like she's frightened by her words, but I don't believe it. She knows how to play the game. 'I see you're a woman of excellent taste, madame,' she says sweetly to Frau Befus. 'It will be my pleasure to offer the hat to you. As a gift.'

Smug, indignant, Frau Befus grabs the hat and plops it on her head on top of her *own* hat then storms out of the shop, pushing past Madame Péroline returning from her errand.

'Rachelle, what's going on here?' Madame Péroline calls out to me, astonished to see the German woman flying out of the shop with two hats on her head.

'May I introduce Countess Ester Bulgávari?' I ignore her question as another contraction hits me. Hard.

'Yes, of course, we're delighted to have you visit our shop,

Countess,' Madame Péroline gushes. She has no idea what insane chess game just played out with the Nazi Frau. 'May I show you our latest *chapeaux*?'

'Another time, madame, I'm late for an appointment.'

No, no. I can't let her leave. I had no idea she'd arrive by motorcar. A way out from the horrible conditions that await me if the major gets wind of me going into early labor. The situation is desperate. My contractions are closer together, but it may be *hours* before my water breaks. I can't let this opportunity slip away.

I know. I've just learned this from the countess.

Improvise.

While Madame Péroline is *oohing* and *aahing* over the countess's smart green suit, I sneak into the storage room and pour a glass of water from the pitcher, then hide the glass in my dress pocket under my smock. Then between deep breaths, I waddle back into the shop. I have to make it look real, that I'm getting ready to deliver my baby. When the driver shows up later to fetch me and I'm not here, the major will have his Gestapo goons searching for me. I need a cover story for Madame Péroline that will hold up when he discovers I'm missing.

I manage a smile, a pat on my tummy to reassure my baby she'll have the birthing she deserves. I can feel her moving. She's restless. I sense her excitement, a sudden and thrilling change in my body. Soon I will have a cherished bundle in my arms nursing at my breast. The thought warms me so, lessening the sharp pain in my lower groin. I can't help but gloat.

I will *not* have my child born in that German hospital.

I may not come out alive.

'Help, come quick!' I yell out, doubling over then dumping the water glass hidden in my pocket on the floor between my legs. '*My water broke!*'

Madame Péroline rushes over to me and puts her hand over

her mouth when she sees the big puddle of water. 'You poor child. Where is your driver? We must get you to the hospital, mademoiselle, *tout de suite*.'

'He won't be here until closing, madame. *Please*, I need help.'

'I must think... *think*. *Alors*, the ambulances are so slow, not nearly as efficient as when I drove an ambulance during the Great War,' Madame Péroline frets, feeling my head for a temperature.

'*You*, madame?'

A nostalgic light beams in her eyes. 'How do you think I met my Henri?' Then it's gone. 'You can't take the Métro... of course not... too crowded. I know. I'll send word to the major—'

'*No!*' I cry out, grabbing her arm. She shoots me a surprised look. The countess leans in, concern etched on her face and a slight smile turning up her red lips. I'm not fooling her. 'We can't disturb him. He's—he's on a secret assignment for Himmler.'

'I will drive you, mademoiselle.' The countess is on to my game, and playing along. I don't know her story; perhaps someday when the war is over we shall share secrets over a cup of tea.

'*Merci*, Countess.'

I don't ask how she commandeered a smart silver Peugeot for her own use, and I may never know, but for now it's my magic chariot. I climb into the passenger seat, holding my belly. Another contraction makes me double over. I know she's read the message in the hat when I hear her gasp. Loudly.

'You've done me a great service, mademoiselle,' she says, her hands going from her breasts to her throat. 'I shall leave Paris for Argenteuil immediately to warn my uncle, who is a professor. He's working on new perfumes at the House of Doujan factory located there.'

Her uncle? Hmm...

Then she becomes the confident countess again, though I see

her lower lip trembling. She's clearly aware of the danger and has a great fondness for her 'uncle'.

'Now, mademoiselle, where should I take you?' she asks.

'To the American Hospital of Paris, please.' I lean back, my emotions going from frustration to hopeful anticipation in a moment, and amazement that my time is here. 'Where I intend to have my baby without one *damn* Nazi in the delivery room.'

21

PARIS, JUNE 1941

Justine

The secret birth of Catherine-Ninette Beaufort at the American Hospital of Paris doesn't stay secret for long. The Gestapo man shows up at my apartment a few weeks later snarling like a mad dog in search of a lost bone.

I'm surprised Herr Geller waited that long.

I could have gone into hiding at the brothel, but a crying baby isn't good for business. The girls were for it, but the madam was afraid it would give them ideas about the joys of motherhood. I also think, wouldn't it be glorious to return to Maison Bleue with this beautiful baby in my arms and watch Maman's eyes light up and Ève go wild? Then the fear of them 'disappearing' as poor Lucie did quashed that hope faster than a sugar cube melting in a cup of hot tea. Besides, I had no doubt the major and Herr Geller would find me soon enough and there'd be a price to pay for my insolence.

I'm sitting on the divan breastfeeding my child when the inevitable knock on the door comes. The secret policeman doesn't wait for me to answer. He has his own key. The major gave it to him, of course. He looks. Squints. Sniffs. Ninette's diaper needs changing, but who wants to stop a happy baby from feeding? He makes a crude remark about the smell and it takes all my resolve not to tell him he smells worse.

'Bonjour, mademoiselle, I bid you good day.'

'Since when do the Gestapo wish anyone a good day?' I hold my baby tight against my bare breast, but I don't back down. I refuse to let him hold me in his grip with an overwhelming sense of embarrassment, which is what he wants.

'You know why I'm here, mademoiselle.'

I ignore him. 'Would you mind turning around, *s'il vous plaît?*'

The blood in the Gestapo man's veins is so cold, it's like he can't even blush.

I wait until he does so then fold my blouse over my exposed breast, knowing my bliss is over. I wanted like every new mother to relish the experience, the wonder of birth and seeing your baby for the first time all pink and red and wrinkly, but perfect in your eyes. Holding her to your breast and her tiny mouth latching onto your nipple, the sweet, gentle tug of an infant hungry to reconnect with the softness she's known for nine months, then slowly gaining her independence and feeling secure enough in your arms to rest her tiny head against your shoulder.

And burp. A sign of sublime contentment.

Then you rock her in your arms and sing the lullaby your *maman* sang to you, and the bond is sealed.

Mother and child.

Now it's over.

I can't let her go, yet I fear the consequences more if I don't. I have people to protect. The doctor at the American Hospital who delivered my baby. Nurse Edith who made the arrangements to take me home in an ambulance. The supplies she gave me. Food. Hospital diapers and tiny infant gowns. The Nazis are capable of anything from beheadings to death by torture. As long as I'm alive, Ninette has a *maman* who loves her and will never stop fighting for her.

But things aren't going according to plan. I'd hope to appeal to whatever humanity there is left in the major, but sending the Gestapo to do his dirty work dashes my hopes. *Why am I not surprised?* The SS see themselves as the Nazi elite when in reality they're boy soldiers running around in long pants, but I'm not fool enough to dismiss their power. In the major's case, he has the ear of Himmler, the man behind Lebensborn, created years ago in Germany to increase the birth rate. Babies born from good Aryan stock. At the top of that list? SS officers. I had no idea when I revealed my pregnancy to him he'd get it into his head to create his own version here in France.

'Why didn't the major come himself?' I button up my white blouse trimmed with a scalloped-edged ruffle and black satin ribbon laced through it. Perfect for a nursing mother. I have this ideal of motherhood etched in my brain, how a woman's emotional wellbeing can be enhanced by things that make taking care of a baby quick and simple. So I designed this easy-to-open blouse for breastfeeding. It makes me feel empowered.

And I won't let this scumbag take it away from me.

Which, for better or worse, is where my surprising act of courage to speak my mind to the secret German police comes from.

He clears his throat. 'I'm here on the major's behalf. He's otherwise engaged.'

'Having lunch with Herr Himmler?' I say lightly, but the arrow hits its mark. The Gestapo man flinches. He knows he's the lackey, and he doesn't like it.

'I'm not at liberty to say, mademoiselle. I'm here on a personal matter for the major.'

'Like watching me breastfeed?' I raise a brow, skeptical of his complacency. He's fidgeting with the leather belt on his trench coat and wriggling his nose. He's uncomfortable and my instinct tells me it has nothing to do with my state of undress.

It tumbles out of him in one sentence so quickly, I'm not sure I hear him right.

'You disobeyed a direct order by not having your child delivered in the appropriated hospital with a German doctor in attendance to document the birth, an order which should result in your death, however...' He pauses for a split second as if the words in his mouth are so distasteful he can't say them. 'The major wishes me to inform you it's in the child's best interest to allow you to breastfeed her'—he clears his throat—'as I've evidenced here today.'

I stop breathing for a moment, a cold sweat coming over me. 'Is this your idea of a joke? A cruel game before you drag my baby from my arms?'

'The Gestapo do not joke, mademoiselle.' He heaves out a breath. 'You have been informed, now carry on.' He turns to leave.

'No, wait.' I still can't believe my ears. A moment of gratitude comes over me in spite of the circumstances. 'Tell the major "*merci*", Herr Geller.'

He snickers. 'It's not for your sake, mademoiselle.'

'Then why?' I ask, puzzled.

'We've noticed in Berlin that several babies in the Lebensborn program denied their mother's milk and contact with her did not flourish. They didn't develop normally as we expected.'

When I ask if the mother stays with the child in Germany, he grins and assures me the child is later given to the SS organization to control their education and subsequent adoption.

'*Adoption?*' A new fear surges in me. So nothing's changed. He still holds to his original plan to take my child. I hold my baby tight and she starts crying. I put her over my shoulder and try to shush her as the Gestapo man continues.

'You will retain custody of the child for six months, mademoiselle, then she'll be sent to the convent here in Paris to begin her developmental training.'

'Six months?'

'Children of the Reich must learn at a very young age about our Führer and obedience, mademoiselle. Heil Hitler.'

Then he's gone.

I feel like a condemned prisoner given a reprieve. *Six months to get out of Paris. Take Maman and Ève, too. Is it possible?*

Ninette stops crying. She doesn't like Herr Geller either.

'Don't you worry, Ninette, Maman won't let that nasty Gestapo man take you from me. Not as long as I can breathe.'

I hum the old favorite 'Frère Jacques' as I change Ninette's diaper. A welcome sunlight beams in from the courtyard through my window though the day is cold and crisp. I let go with a shiver, then wrap another blanket around my baby when I hear a knock on the door.

I panic. Did the Gestapo man change his mind? Then I hear—

'Coal man, mademoiselle. Open up.'

A trick? Heating coal is a rarity these days, but my gut tells me to open the door. *That gravelly voice.* Such is the power of hope that it takes me only a moment to make up my mind. I open the door to find a big man hunched over with a large burlap sack over his shoulder, black dust smudged on his face and hands, patched wool jacket, square nose and fuzzy brows.

Arsène.

He was watching out for me and heard every word.

'A visit from the Gestapo can be most unpleasant, mademoiselle,' he says with concern in his voice. 'But you needn't worry. You'll always have a friend nearby.' His eyes dart back and forth between the door and me. We keep our voices low; you can't be too careful even if the Gestapo man has left. You never assume anything.

'You mean when the ugly black rat corners the cute little mouse?' I tease. 'And the big, strong tomcat comes to her rescue?'

'*Très bien*, mademoiselle, you read my mind.' Then a curious smile curves over his lips when he sees my white blouse slip down over my shoulder when I lay Ninette in her cradle.

I eye him warily. 'Do I dare read your mind *again*, monsieur?'

He starts whistling 'Auprès de ma Blonde', avoiding my glance *and* answering my question.

I smother a chuckle. How can I ever be anything but enamored by this dear, wonderful man? No matter *who* he is.

I rock Ninette back and forth in the cradle, an anonymous gift, but it has the countess written all over it with French Baroque scrolling and smooth ivory wood. I have the feeling Arsène delivered the cradle and left it without me seeing him. I can't stop looking at him, wondering if he's brought news from London, if the British plan to drop agents into France is now in play. But my female urges override my politics and I drink him in like he's a modern Ulysses returned. His latest disguise is a remix of similar clothing with a layer of coal dust for effect, but if anything the smudged black on his face emphasizes his strong jaw and dark eyes that push out of the darkness like the sparkle of a lost diamond. I should feel guilty as his overwhelming male presence takes over my full attention as he goes about his work, checking the bin in the cellar and then returning with an empty sack.

I have so many questions.

Time for that later. Time to plan our escape.

Which seems more real now.

He smiles, tips his miner's cap, and then tickles Ninette under her chin. She laughs, just as enthralled with him as I am and coos as babies do when they're happy. So is her *maman*.

My apartment is soon warm and cozy and my heart is overjoyed.

Arsène is back in Paris.

* * *

July 1941

I admit to a certain curiosity as to how the Gestapo found out where Ninette was born. The Gestapo man is no fool, quite clever actually, and I've no doubt the crossword fanatic knew where to find me but played the waiting game before paying me a visit.

For evil reasons of his own. And that's what scares the hell out of me. The secret policeman is as unpredictable as sliding down a rabbit hole.

You never know how deep the hole goes.

The question lays heavy on my mind when I return to work at the House of Péroline, straddling Ninette on my hip since the concierge can't watch her today. The hat shop owner is strangely quiet, hobbling about, dusting the hats and rearranging them in the display window twice a day. When the women walk by and see a different window in the afternoon than in the morning, she insists they think they've missed something and come into the shop. She asks me no questions, but she retains a cool attitude toward me until I can't take her indifference any more.

Which brings up another scenario.

Did Madame Péroline tell them? Did she overhear me tell the countess where to take me?

'I'm sorry I tricked you and then begged the countess to drive me to the American Hospital, Madame Péroline. I didn't want my child born in a Nazi-controlled facility.'

'What's done is done, mademoiselle.' She blows dust off a feather hat.

'I didn't become pregnant by choice.' I pause. I've got to say it; keeping it in is hurting us both. 'I was raped by an SS officer, madame, during the first summer of the Occupation—'

She gasps loudly. 'Oh, my God, mademoiselle, you poor child, I always suspected Major Saxe-Müllenheim to be the father of your little girl. But rape. It's too horrible.' Her mind puts the pieces together. 'That explains so much. Why he acts so controlling and keeps such a close eye on you.'

I shake my head. 'He doesn't care about me, madame. It's now just Ninette he wants.'

I explain to her about the Lebensborn program organized and run by the SS in Germany and how I believe the major is using my child to get on the better side of Himmler to advance his career.

She spits on her clean floor in disgust. 'I never did like the major and his arrogant air. Now I understand why that—that... Oh, I can't talk about it.' Her disgust turns into fear and tears fill her puffy eyes.

'Madame, please tell me.'

'That horrible Gestapo man.'

'Herr Geller.'

She nods. 'He showed up at the shop the day after you went into labor. I ignored him, humming to myself, praying your child was born healthy and chubby. I mean, what could the Gestapo want with me? Then he forced me into a smelly black Citroën and interrogated me at Avenue Foch for hours. *Was mademoiselle in labor? Where did she go? Who took her?* I told them I didn't know where you'd gone and I couldn't remember the name of the countess. I'm terrible with names, I said, especially foreign ones.' She sobs. 'They beat the bottoms of my feet until they bled, then threatened to break my fingers. "But how can I work selling beautiful hats to the Nazi officers' wives?" I pleaded. Finally, they let me go.' She grabs me and hugs me. 'I was afraid if I told them anything, even the smallest detail, harm would come to you and your child.'

'Oh, madame, you were so brave.'

Was interrogating Madame Péroline a big show by the Gestapo man to throw me off course? Or an opportunity to make her toe the line?

Or it could be the man is simply a sadistic bastard.

I vote for the latter.

We hold on to each other, finding comfort in creating a bond between us forged not only in the physical pain we both suffered at the hands of the Nazis, but the emotional torture of an enemy we're united against, occupiers who will never take our hearts, our minds. The strong, unbreakable bonds between women that are stronger than any Maginot Line, more powerful than any weapon, more lasting than their stupid Reich.

In the end, I imagine the Gestapo checked every hospital, but more likely Herr Geller remembered how I fled once before to the Neuilly hospital, patting himself on the back for his 'ingenuity'.

Madame Péroline insists Baby Ninette come with me to work *every* day and sleep in the back of the shop in a big hatbox.

The weeks... then months go by. I make Ninette the cutest pink bonnet with lace and ribbons and watch her get bigger every day with Madame Péroline doting on her and finding bigger hatboxes. Arsène making deliveries of black-market items to the shop, then meeting him in the church confessional. Finding out the Allies are united with us. More agents are coming to France to prepare the way for what he believes will be a land invasion. No one knows when.

Or where.

I can wait.

I have Ninette. And when that happens, I'll be reunited with Maman and Ève.

I'm the happiest I've ever been.

And I don't want it to end.

22

PARIS, 12 DECEMBER 1941

Ève

The warning that the German Military Police have orders to arrest Monsieur de Giocomte comes before dawn on the coldest day of the month. A bitter irony since we enjoyed a mild early December. Now snow gathers on the roof of Maison Bleue and snowdrifts pile up, covering the front marble walkway like an icy barricade.

Four thirty in the morning.

I'm cuddled up under a heavy blanket snoozing with happy dreams of Justine and me when we were little girls. How often we'd sneak down three flights of stairs to the kitchen for macarons while the rest of the house slept. Dreams that come more frequent to me these days as life in Paris becomes harder and harder. I'm just about to bite into a lemon sweet in my dream when I hear a loud knock on my bedroom door.

Startled, I jump out of bed. 'Who's there?'

'Michal,' he whispers. '*Meet me downstairs... now.*'

The urgency in his voice sends ripples of shivers up and down my spine. Is he hurt? A mission gone wrong? Is he alone?

Why is he alone? Aren't we partners?

Earlier I noticed the coach house was dark and I shrugged it off. I didn't want to think he was with Coralie. I try not to care what he does, but I do. All I know is something changed between us that day at the hospital. Something he doesn't want to talk about. His playful teasing stopped. Like me arguing with him about who had the better plan how to complete the mission. Who would take the lead. Which explosive to use. Time of day to hit the target. Sharing the danger equally.

I miss that.

I grab my old chenille robe, wrap the soft belt tight around my waist, and then race down the servants' backstairs, my bare feet tripping over the smooth but cold tiles. I find him waiting for me leaning against the wall in the long corridor outside the library. I don't think about the way he looks at my curves outlined by the thin cotton then turns away. He has a purpose and it has nothing to do with me.

'Michal, what's wrong?'

'The German military commander is stepping up the roundup of Jews. They plan to arrest a thousand today.'

'What?' I'll never understand this persecution of a people I find to be kind, loving and hardworking. A people always on the move to find a better life, according to Madame de Giocomte. A story she told Justine and me when we were little girls after we put pepper in Cook's vanilla pudding. So silly of us, but we said we were sorry and begged her not to toss us out on the pavements and let us stay. She smiled and said she understood what it's like to be afraid of not having a home. How she carried her pillow with her when she was a little girl and she fled with her parents from country to country before they were killed to escape persecution. How much it meant to her to have a familiar place to lay down her head at night.

And now the Boches have taken away that comfort.

I scrunch my toes on the cold tile. *Why today, why now?*

According to Michal, the German military commander needed an excuse to escalate Jewish deportation and found it when someone attempted to kill a German sentry. It wasn't the first attack against Nazi soldiers, but it kicked his plan to eliminate Jews to the next level. He retaliated by threatening to shoot hostages, and word is he intends to fine the Jewish people of France a billion francs—I can't believe such a figure exists—then top it off with this insane plan of deporting a thousand Jews East.

Where, God only knows.

'Monsieur de Giocomte is on the list,' he insists.

'No, it *can't* be true, Monsieur is French.'

'The Nazis don't care.'

'Are you certain, Michal?'

'Yes. I have an informant willing to talk for a bottle of cognac.'

Black market, of course.

'Can this informant be trusted?' I have to ask.

'Yes. He's a tailor forced to work for the Nazi High Command. He's provided me with intelligence more than once.'

'A tailor?'

'Why not? With pins in his mouth and a measuring tape around his neck, he blended easily into the background while the German officer was getting his uniform altered. Seems he wasn't only upset about the rich Paris beef making his jacket too tight—'

'*Stolen* beef, *n'est-ce pas?*' I add.

He grins. 'But the Nazi was also overheard complaining about the upcoming *rafle*, or roundup, of Jews today interfering with his luncheon plans.'

I start pacing, hands in pockets, thinking. It's so hard to

comprehend how this unbelievable harassment of Jews is escalating. I've witnessed firsthand how the Nazis operate in a world of order. At the police station, the Sorbonne. It seems to me they also possess an ugly, sadistic bent that pushes them to inflict cruelty on the innocent, like firing a pistol into a crowd of Jews about to be deported.

And never looking back.

Heartbreaking. But then again, the occupiers have no hearts.

According to Michal, this impending roundup of Jewish businessmen and intellectuals by the German police, *Feldgendarmie*, and French gendarmes going door to door, isn't the norm, putting Monsieur de Giocomte in imminent danger in his own home. How well Michal remembers in Warsaw the Nazis hunting down Jews in packs, arresting them en masse in the ghetto, nursing homes, subway stations, even orphanages.

We've been lucky the de Giocomtes survived the roundups of May 14, mostly Jewish Poles and Czechs, and August 21 when those arrested in the eleventh arrondissement were transported to Drancy.

Word on the streets is Drancy is now an internment camp for Jews. A place where tuberculosis runs rampant and prisoners face starvation along with the daily fear of the Nazis picking Jewish men at random to execute in retaliation for acts of sabotage. My mind spews out terrible thoughts that something *I* did could cause men to die.

Do we stop resisting? Give up? Or continue to fight?

There's no right answer.

I can't control my heart racing madly, my brain stripped clean of logic. All I know is they're coming for this gentle man I respect. What am I to tell Madame de Giocomte? That the day we've all feared is upon us? That every hope we had to survive as a family is gone? Every morning at tea, I see the pain in her eyes ringed by purple shadows and droopy brows. Her husband grows weaker each day, his mind more distant, his voice gone silent as if he's forgotten how, his body losing the suppleness of a man who loved riding horses and tending to his art collection. A man who once counted brushstrokes and dots of Impressionist color splashed across a canvas by Degas or Seurat like some men counted rare coins.

A man now reduced to a number because Berlin wants the French to arrest more Jewish men.

'Why?' I want to know. I go quiet for a moment, not wanting to believe the Nazis could tear my family apart. *Again. It's not fair*, I want to shout.

'Berlin isn't happy with the manner the French police are handling the deportation of Jews. They made new demands to the Vichy government for thousands of Jews to be sent East.'

'Oh, God, how dehumanizing. These are *people*, Michal, not animals. You can't uproot them like turnips.'

'To the Nazis, they're not even that.' He clenches his fists, trying to keep control, trying to make me understand the reality we face regarding Monsieur de Giocomte. 'He'll be taken and arrested if we don't do something fast. The gendarmerie has a quota to meet.'

'Quota?'

'Yes, a thousand Jewish men will be rounded up and arrested today.'

'They *can't* arrest Monsieur,' I say, 'there's no reason. What can they accuse him of?'

'Being Jewish.'

Of course. I could see it coming, but I didn't want to believe it. The looting, sanctions against Jews, Aryanization of Jewish businesses. They were planning this all along. Where will it stop?

'My informant tells me this isn't like any other roundup, Ève,' he continues. 'The men on the list are among the Jewish elite.

Doctors, lawyers, professors, artists, even men who served in the Great War and are highly decorated soldiers.'

A macabre line of reasoning in my mind to arrest men who served their country. But when did anything the Nazis do make sense?

He continues. 'We must move him to a safe location.'

'Madame mentioned having him transferred to Sainte-Anne Hospital where he can get help for his mental condition.'

Michal ruffles his hand through his hair. 'That won't work. The Nazis have turned it into a military hospital. They pushed the patients out onto the streets and left them to starve.'

I struggle not to let my emotions rule. To break down and cry. Leaving those poor souls so helpless is inhumane and indecent. I must keep my mind clear, save the patriarch of this Jewish family who has given us so much.

'What about the hospital at Clermont-de-l'Oise?' I ask. 'Surely the Germans wouldn't starve their patients at every psychiatric hospital.'

'How far from Paris is it, Ève? We don't have much time.'

'It's not even dawn.'

He shakes his head. 'The Nazis love to ring the doorbell when the families are asleep.'

A dull throbbing in my head sets off an alarm. The *maison* hides from the morning under deep shades of midnight, but not for long.

'The hospital is sixty kilometers north of the city.'

'It's too far. We'll never steal... secure a vehicle in time.' He thinks a moment. 'The American Hospital of Paris. Dr Jackson will find him a bed.'

I nod, understanding. No Nazi guards to stop us and a compassionate American physician willing to help Monsieur as he did Michal when he was wounded. I still can't forget the beautiful blonde I saw giving off an air of intimacy with the Gestapo man accompanying her. Her resemblance to Justine was so uncanny. I chalk it up to my passionate longing not to believe my sister is dead. If she *was* this woman working with the secret police, I'd wish she *were* dead.

A thought that sickens me.

I put my personal feelings aside. Have to. The clock is ticking and knowing the Germanic preoccupation for precision, the Nazis won't be late.

I should have seen this coming when six Jewish synagogues were bombed in October, including the shul on Rue Sainte Isaure in the eighteenth arrondissement where Madame de Giocomte goes to pray. We didn't want to believe it. Madame de Giocomte, Maman, and me. Didn't want to believe the wave of arrests would reach our little corner of Paris after the roundup of foreign Jews last May. A shocking revelation when we found out 3,700 Jewish men were arrested and sent to internment camps.

The throbbing in my head worsens.

We also have a moral problem. If Michal and I help Monsieur escape, presumably another Jewish man will take his place to meet the quota. Whether it's a prominent Jew or a Jewish man off the street, another family will lose a father, a husband, a brother. I run this scenario over and over in my mind until I'm so frustrated I break a nail when I bang my hand on the wood paneling. I will never understand why the innocent suffer so and their families the most. Who gives the Nazis the right to choose who lives and who dies?

I have no answer.

I pray God will forgive me for trying to save Madame de Giocomte's husband. Because I can't bear to see her heart break. I'd never forgive myself.

'I'll find transportation, Ève, a motorbike with a sidecar will do,' Michal says, grinning. 'I know where the SS leave their bikes while they're indulging in a night on the town.'

'I'll get Monsieur ready.'

'Don't dress him in his regular clothes, Ève, too likely to draw attention. Ruffle his hair, outfit him in the chauffeur's old overalls and coat, then put the oldest, scruffiest slippers you can find on his feet so he'll blend in at the hospital.'

I nod. I've heard about agents compromised by the expensive labels on their clothes or their footwear.

'No need, Ève, *I* will take care of my husband.'

Madame de Giocomte appears like the family ghost out of the gloom, her face so pale I can almost see through her. She's dressed in a luxurious deep maroon velvet robe, her brownish-gray hair hanging down to her waist in elegant waves, her left hand laying on her breast, her thick gold wedding band sparkling like a holy beacon. Then without another word, she disappears to prepare her husband for his part in this drama.

Even in this time of great fear, Madame remains in control.

Michal goes over with me again what Madame will tell them when the French gendarmes and their Nazi cohorts show up and Monsieur isn't here.

'Ready, Ève?'

'Yes. Madame de Giocomte will tell them Monsieur was admitted to the Clermont-de-l'Oise Hospital. That he's suffering from depression and became confused and fell and hit his head, then pray they strike his name off the list.'

'Good. By the time they check her story, he'll be hidden under face bandages in a ward in the American Hospital while we make plans to get him out of Paris.'

New identity card. Warm clothes. An escort to take him along the escape line over the Pyrenees to Spain.

Is it possible in his condition? A man whose mind plays tricks on him?

It's the only hope we have of saving him, so I push on when Madame leads her husband into the library wearing overalls soiled with oil and grease, a plain gray blanket around his shoulders, his eyes half-closed and his hands shaking. A frown creasing his forehead is the only indication he has any idea what's happening to him.

And he's scared.

Michal pulls up the collar on his coat then he's off. I head for the de Giocomte private rooms in the rear of the mansion and wake up Madame's sister-in-law, the baroness, and her daughter and four girls, then shuffle them into the coach house. The eldest girl Delphine tells her little sisters we're playing a game and there will be treats later if they remain quiet. May God keep them safe away from the main house so we can save the family patriarch from the Nazis.

I sit with Madame and her husband in the library, going over her story several times over the next hour in loud whispers, the two of them holding hands, all of us praying Michal returns soon when—

The doorbell rings.

A loud gasp. At that moment, Madame's eyes possess a wild fear in them that terrifies me. She knows there's no escape for her husband, but she wouldn't admit it until now. That look fuels my courage *not* to give up.

Where is Michal?

He'd never ring the doorbell. The man has an uncanny manner of slipping inside a building like a sheet of paper sliding under a door. I race down the corridor to the rear entrance in the kitchen to find Cook standing by the backdoor with a rolling pin in

her hand, ranting about a man in a trench coat standing outside
with a handgun.

Gestapo.

Is there no end to their dirty methods?

Back to the library, running in my bare feet so numb I can't feel
the cold, I grab Madame's hands in mine, something I'd never
think of doing in ordinary times, and hold them tight. She
squeezes back.

'The Gestapo are guarding the back door,' I blurt out, panting.
'There's no escape.'

Where is Michal?

'We can't let them take Itzhak, mademoiselle,' she begs, her
mouth quivering. '*Please.*'

A crazy idea pops into my head.

'Stall them, madame, tell them you're alone and you wish to
change to receive them properly and will they please wait outside,
while I hide Monsieur in plain sight if they search the house.'

'Where?' she asks.

'In the servants' quarters with Maman.'

The doorbell rings again. More insistent this time.

Madame rubs her hands together then smooths down the
velvet on her robe, wets her lips, then heads to the front door while
I urge Monsieur up the servants' backstairs. He's quicker on his
feet than I imagined, giving me hope he comprehends he's in
danger. I hear two men's loud voices downstairs then Madame's
eloquent tones and doors opening and banging shut as I rouse
Maman from her sleep. She's groggy then wide awake when she
finds out what we've feared for months is upon us.

That Monsieur de Giocomte is in danger of being taken by
German Military Police.

'Where's your knitting wool, Maman?' I ask, sitting Monsieur down into the wingback chair where I sit when I help her with her wool. Where Justine used to sit, too.

I wish you were here, dear sister, you can charm anyone... even the Gestapo.

My heart stops for a moment. An unsettling thought scratches at my brain.

I can't let that thought into my head.

So I ignore it.

'Here's the wool, *ma petite*.' Maman sits down on her rocking chair with a big ball of blue wool while I wind strand after strand of it around Monsieur's big hands as if he's praying.

'Say nothing, Monsieur de Giocomte,' I tell him, but his eyes glaze over. It's too much for him and he's tuned out. I turn to my mother. 'Remember, Maman, he's the old gardener.'

'A man in my room?' she sighs.

'Let them think what they want. I'll go back downstairs.'

It's too late.

A German officer from the Wehrmacht and a French gendarme wearing a cap and cape burst through the door, look around, see Monsieur and Maman. Madame de Giocomte is close behind them.

The French gendarme eyes the three of us then sneers. 'I thought you were alone, Madame.'

'I am, monsieur.' Madame de Giocomte plays her part well, dismissing our presence in an uppity tone and a wave of her hand. 'These are my house servants and my gardener.'

The Nazi grunts his displeasure, then makes a threatening move toward Monsieur de Giocomte, demanding he identify himself. The dear, sweet man doesn't move, doesn't speak. He's gone to us for the moment, his mind choosing to shut down rather than deal with the beast in the Nazi uniform. The Nazi asks again, this time prodding him in the back with his rifle butt.

'*No, stop, please.*' I step between the German officer and Monsieur to protect him. 'He doesn't understand you.'

'Is he deaf?' demands the Frenchman, irritated.

'Yes,' I adlib without blinking an eye, 'since he was a boy. He can't speak.'

No one breathes for a long moment as the German officer reads a name from a list. Monsieur de Giocomte.

I know how Madame didn't give it a second thought when they had to fill out the census the first year of the Occupation listing them as Jewish, believing they were exempt from the Nazis' edicts and laws. And of course, they'd never have to wear a yellow star like the Jews in Germany are now required to do.

It becomes apparent no one is exempt.

'Where is your husband, madame?' asks the French gendarme.

Madame clears her throat. 'He was taken to Clermont-de-l'Oise Hospital two days ago.' She repeats the story we concocted word for word, her voice never wavering.

The French gendarme turns to the Nazi and whispers in German. The Nazi shakes his head and mutters something in German that makes the Frenchman snicker.

'Are you certain of this, madame?' he baits her.

'Yes, monsieur.'

'I see. According to the lieutenant, Monsieur de Giocomte can't be a patient in the Hospital Clermont-de-l'Oise.'

'I assure you, monsieur,' I say, jumping in, 'I saw them take him away in an ambulance.'

Foolish move, but when do I think before I act?

'How interesting, mademoiselle,' says the French gendarme, 'since hundreds of patients were evacuated during the conflict and afterward the Wehrmacht raided the hospital and confiscated their medical equipment, machines, and beds.' The policeman bares his teeth, his smile gleaming with victory. 'This man is no gardener.'

He grabs the wool off Monsieur's hands. 'Smooth... no calluses. This is Monsieur de Giocomte and he's a Jew. He's coming with us.'

'*No,*' I cry out.

The Nazi shouts at me in German, then grabs my arm and pushes me out of the way. Maman cries out, but I won't stand down.

'You can't take him.'

The German policeman ignores me and pulls him to his feet. Eyes glazed, shoulders hunched, Monsieur de Giocomte, even in his dazed state, knows he's in danger and raises his fist, sending his wife to his defense before the Nazi strikes him on the side of his head with his rifle butt.

'Please don't hurt him!' Madame cries out, no longer trying to hide her panic. 'He's done nothing. He's no threat to anyone! He's ill, can't you see?'

'We have orders to take him to the town hall on Rue des Batignolles, madame,' says the Frenchman, 'to answer a few questions.'

'For how long?' I can't remain silent.

'Forty-eight hours, mademoiselle.' The French gendarme turns to Madame de Giocomte. 'You may pack your husband a small suitcase with a change of clothes, madame, two blankets, food, no more than three hundred francs. But no pen or paper.' He raises his cap in a polite gesture. 'You have fifteen minutes.'

He turns to leave, then stops at the doorway and scowls at me. 'If I may give you a piece of advice, mademoiselle, don't lie to the German military police or you'll also find yourself packing a suitcase.'

23

Justine

I never thought anything could be worse in my life than the day I was raped.

The humiliation, pain, shame. *My soul crushed by the heel of a hobnailed boot*. I carried that image around in my mind for months like a dark, heavy cloud hovering over me. Then my Ninette was born and I felt the sun upon my face, the rain wetting my lips. I believed I could go on. Find a life for my child and me.

That hope is gone.

My heart squeezes, my lips go dry, my once happy blue eyes liquid with tears when the Gestapo man and a German female auxiliary worker come to my apartment in the ninth arrondissement on a bitter cold afternoon. Herr Geller wastes no time spitting out the words I dread.

'It's time, mademoiselle, get the child ready. We're in a hurry.'

I feel the earth spinning around me as I pick up my little girl, her eyes big and wild when she sees the black-hearted toad leaning over her. The *fräulein* standing behind him looks puzzled, not understanding her part in this melodrama and reluctant to take the baby from my arms.

'No... *not yet!*' I make my plea with tears wetting my cheeks. 'I need to say goodbye.'

I have to calm the awful fear I see swirling in my child's eyes.

I hold *mon bébé* close to my breast, kiss her forehead and squeeze her tight as I wrap her up in a red and gold plaid woolen blanket. 'Maman loves you, *ma petite*, never forget that... *never!*'

'Make it quick, mademoiselle,' he repeats with a glee in his voice that tells me he's enjoying this moment. 'I'm not accustomed to waiting for *anyone.*'

Even Hitler? I want to toss back at him, but I'm well aware my attempt at sarcasm would land me in a forced labor camp and I'll never see Ninette again.

I'm scared, shivering, but I can't let my child feel me trembling. I knew it would be hard to let her go, but this is so much harder than I ever could have imagined. Cold, chilling. I feel numb. Like sharp icicles piercing my heart.

I hold her tight. I can't let her go. *I can't!*

'You've had enough time, mademoiselle,' Herr Geller blurts out. 'Take the child, *Fräulein, now!*' he yells.

'*No!*' I scream, cradling her in my arms. She's crying. '*Please,* monsieur, not my Ninette—'

Herr Geller snorts. Loud. He's had enough of my stalling. He yanks the child from my embrace then pushes me so hard, I stumble and fall to my knees, the breath knocked out of me. Chest tight, lungs hurting, I can't move when I see him hand my crying baby to the German worker, her eyes filled with pity for me, but fearing the Gestapo man more.

She races out of my small apartment, my baby's wailing echoing in my ears.

Herr Geller turns to me, not making a move to help me.

He tips his hat. 'Good day, mademoiselle.'

I *hate* it when he says that.

Then he slams the door behind him and shuts me out of my baby's life.

I lose it then. I collapse into a heap, tears streaming down my face, begging God to bring her back, but He's run out of miracles today. Even Arsène can't save my baby. Herr Geller's appearance was unexpected today. Planned that way to put me off guard.

Somehow, I crawl over to the window and peer out the glass. Ninette may as well be wrapped up in a Nazi flag instead of red and gold plaid wool when I see them take her away in that ugly black motorcar. Everything in my life feels 'black' today, especially my soul. I hurt inside, torn apart like a summer daisy, petal by petal, each pull ripping my heart into ragged shreds and leaving me naked and bleeding.

My child torn from my breast.

Six months... *six months* was all the time I had to nurse my baby and embrace motherhood. It went by so quickly, the lovely days in the shop working on my hat designs, laughing when my little girl squealed, engaging her with a fancy ribbon or tickling her bare feet with a feather. Even the customers enjoyed watching her gurgling and hitting her spoon against my worktable when I held her in my lap. I know when our French customers—the few we have left—came into the shop, they threw me wary glances, questioning how Ninette was thriving with her chubby cheeks, pink skin, and clear blue eyes. So many babies don't get enough milk now; many mothers fear rickets will be in their child's future.

What they don't know is the price I pay for a healthy baby.

She's not mine.

She belongs to the Reich.

After they take my Ninette, I cry for days. I can't eat. I walk up and down the quay along the Seine, the steady ebb and flow of the river rushing in my ears. *Don't give up. You'll find a way to get her back.*

At least, for now, I know Ninette is hidden among the other French orphans taken in by the Sisters of the Praying Hands at the House of Sainte-Veronica de Mornay. The church house with its velvety green vines hugging the old stone walls is near the residential area housing the workers from the Renault motor works in a southwestern suburb of Paris. Workers bring their children there during the day, while others come to pray and find solace while asking themselves why they must work in a factory manufacturing German tanks and trucks. Does anyone *really* believe the official explanation? That the motor works is under the control of the Vichy government. Otherwise the Nazis would move the factory with the workers facing deportation to Germany and separation from their families.

How well I understand their plight, forced to collaborate with the Boches. I'm careful to keep my head down when I visit my little girl, lest anyone recognize me. I'm grateful the head nun, Sister Eugénie, looks the other way so I can blend in with the other working mothers. Works of sabotage aren't unknown at the factory. Anti-German sentiment runs high among some workers. Which is why only Sister Eugénie knows Ninette is the daughter of an SS officer. She prays for me every day—she has no idea they took my child from me against my will—but the Gestapo is very efficient at bending people to do their bidding, she says, even those who serve God. She admits she's being blackmailed to keep quiet because her father was German and she still has family in Munich.

One word from the Gestapo and they'll be sent to a concentration camp.

I visit Ninette every week. Our bond is still strong, even since I stopped breastfeeding, though that is something I sorely miss. I shall treasure these visits always though, holding her on my shoulder, her sweet-smelling hair tickling my nose, her body warmth heating up my cold heart. Cold since the Gestapo took her from me. When we're together, we're in our own little world, a *maman* duck and her duckling crossing the road to safety one day at a time. But I'm no closer to getting us identity cards and safe passage out of France.

Not surprising.

Arsène warns me not to try to leave Paris yet, that the trains and roads are closely watched and if I'm arrested and sent to Drancy, I could be caught up in the deportation of French Jews. Jewish men from the professions were taken in the last roundup. The 'notables', they called them. A horrible thought shatters my confidence. *What if Monsieur de Giocomte is among them? Non, c'est impossible.* The major promised me that my family—and that includes the de Giocomtes—would be excluded from any visits from the Gestapo.

Yet I know what he's thinking. If I'm foolish enough to run and get caught, the major will take Ninette and denounce me as an enemy of the Reich. Then I'll find myself on a train going East. No one knows where.

I bide my time.

Meanwhile, I look forward to my visits with Ninette and Arsène. *Father Paul*, he insists I call him. I notice he keeps to this disguise. For now. As a priest, it's easier for the three of us to take long walks along the big loop of the Seine. The Renault motor works plant is spread out along the north bank and on the Île Seguin, an island in the river. If Sister Eugénie suspects anything, she honors her vows and keeps it to herself. Still, I don't see Ninette often enough, but when the three of us are together, I'm filled completely. This man I know so little about, a man whose face I've never seen without some kind of disguise. He now wears a wide brim black wool hat when we're outside the church along with his wire-rim spectacles. But it's still a face I know only by his strong jaw and captivating dark eyes that see everything, know everything, that makes me weak at the knees when he touches my arm, places a hand on my shoulder. The arc of electricity that bounces between us is as powerful now as it's ever been.

Does he feel the same way about me?

Or am I merely a double agent in his eyes, an asset he's sworn to protect?

I smile. The soul-melty look on his face when he watches me hold my child and kiss her sweet cheeks gives me the answer I want... and need.

* * *

March 3 1942

The sun has long given up a yawn and bid me *adieu* when the bombing begins.

Loud, thunderous explosions. The windows rattle and my worktable wobbles so hard the dummy head with my latest hat creation shakes back and forth and falls onto the floor. I sit there, stunned. Nearly two years of Occupation haven't prepared me for this seed of hope exploding in me.

Bombing? Here in Paris?

The Allies? I pray it is so.

For months I've done what I can to help defeat the Boches. I pass along intelligence to Arsène and misinformation to the Nazis.

But to *hear* the sounds of what I suspect is the beginning of an Allied invasion brings so many questions. *How, why now?* I heard no word passed from neighbor to neighbor standing in the queue at Les Halles on butter day. Nothing from my gossipy German customers and not a word from Arsène. As if he'd tell me. For security reasons, of course. He often reminds me how important it is I have no contact with other agents to protect me. Still, I wonder how I'd bear up under torture if Ninette was threatened. We women know our children are often held as hostages, which is why many mothers in the Resistance make the sacrifice to send their babies to safety. If only I had that choice, but as long as I'm useful to the major, Ninette is safe. Yet a lingering question haunts me. Would I be strong enough not to give up what I know about the Underground if Herr Geller pointed a pistol at my baby's head? Would God judge me if I did? Then take my child from me, leaving me with nothing? Except an agonizing hatred not just for the Boches, but for myself?

I couldn't live with that.

I shudder thinking about it.

I flinch when I hear a high-pitched cry coming from the showroom as another blast explodes. *Madame Péroline.* She's calling for me. We're working late tonight. It must be after nine. Madame going over the books, lamenting over the deep discounts demanded by the Nazi wives, and me at my worktable fashioning a spring bonnet for another Frau to boast about when she returns to Berlin. As if hats from Paris are magic. If they were, I'd wish with all my heart I could see my little girl tonight and put her to bed and tell her not to cry, that her *maman* is here and will protect her.

I pick up the dummy head off the floor. At first I thought the loud rumbles were thunder. *Another springtime storm?* No. Heavy rain isn't in the forecast until morning. I hold my breath as a second wave of bombing hits, the explosive sounds shaking the tiny hat shop, one after another, and then another. I grab my long woolen coat and run outside to join Madame watching the sky. There's a moon tonight. The night is cold and clear with the bomb blasts echoing the loud beating of my heart. I see the heavens lit up with brilliant white fireballs, so many I can't count them. Flares bursting into life on their slow descent to earth, suspended in the sky like holy beacons over their targets guiding the planes. *Hundreds of them. Whose planes?*

The British?

The Americans?

And why in the southwestern part of the city?

'They're bombing the motor works factory.' Madame Péroline puts her fingers in her ears. She smirks. 'All those lovely trucks and tanks for the German Army blown to bits. *Tsk... tsk.*'

Trucks used to transport enemy soldiers, guns, and ammunition. And round up Resistance fighters, Jews, and anyone else who dares to speak against the Reich.

'Are you *sure* it's the factory, madame?' I ask.

'*Mais oui,* mademoiselle, *look!*'

The blasts and explosions and flares lighting up the sky keep coming. Loud thunder hurting my ears, one after another without stopping, the flares lighting up the sky as bright as day. *Yes*, it makes sense. The Allies are destroying the trucks and tanks to cripple the Boches. There must be hundreds of bombers dropping their loads on the Renault factory.

I taste a fear I've never known before, like catching falling snow on my tongue. Chilling me to the bone.

Oh, my God, no! My baby. Ma petite Ninette. She's hidden away with the Sisters of the Praying Hands.

The abbey sits so close to the Renault factory you can hear the big machines grinding and chewing up steel during the day like an angry black dragon.

I start pacing... can't stop... keep pacing, wringing my hands. I find I have to work hard not to panic, push down the bitter bile rising in my throat. *I can't think.* All I know is a mother's worst nightmare replaces the exhilaration I felt moments ago.

My baby is in terrible danger.

I must go to her.

I grab the bicycle we keep in the storeroom for errands and race down the Rue de Rivoli following the Seine south toward the west. My route leads me past the Place de la Concorde... then the Eiffel Tower... following the loop into the fifteenth arrondissement... then past the Île Saint-German. Curious Parisians hang over their balconies watching the bombing. A few dare to wander outside their apartments. Even the Nazis interrupt their nefarious nocturnal pleasures to watch the bursts of explosions and plumes of ugly black smoke.

I pick up my speed. I ignore my aching shoulders, the stiffness in my neck. I can make it to the religious house in less than my usual forty minutes if I don't stop, if my coat doesn't get caught in the wheel spoke, if I don't get shot because it's past curfew. I don't give a damn. My child is all that matters.

I keep peddling. *Faster... faster.*

The sound of the aircraft engines is getting louder. Why didn't the Germans sound the air raid alert?

I pick up speed when there's a lull in the bombing. I see few searchlights shooting their light up into the sky, their lights flickering on and off. Surprisingly, I hear little anti-aircraft fire from the Boches.

The planes keep coming. *Haven't they done enough?* They wouldn't bomb civilians. *No, they couldn't.* Don't the Allies know blocks of factory workers' apartments lie near the motor works?

What if the bombs miss their target?

Another wave of explosions splits my ears. *Closer now.* For one mad moment I lose control of my senses, my sweaty hands sliding on the handlebars, my foot slipping on the pedal, and the bike swerves to the right. I tip over onto the boulevard. I ignore the pain shooting up my leg, the twinge in my right ankle. I lose precious minutes getting back on the bicycle before I get going again while my mind conjures up a horror I can't bear. If *I* tremble at the loud noise, what does my dear, innocent child feel? Her tiny body shaking, tears clouding her eyes, crying for her *maman* and I'm not there to hold her and comfort her.

I'm not there.

What kind of a mother am I? Allowing that damn Nazi to tell *me* I can't care for my child, that she's not mine to care for, and that his dirty, lustful act means I have no claim on her. *No... no!* I shall no longer be afraid of him. I've withstood the pain, the shame of my lost womanhood, the scorn. I took it all in and carried on because I refused to be a victim.

Yet I *am* a victim.

And for that, I'm ashamed.

No more. *My baby needs me.*

I must bring Ninette home.

If only I could go back to my *real* home to Maman and Ève. But the major took that from me and for that I will never forgive him.

No. Back to my apartment where it's safe... for now.

* * *

When I reach the House of Sainte-Veronica de Mornay, there's a taste of fear and disbelief in the air. An eerie sallow light from the fires at the motor works housed on the tiny island in the Seine joins hands with the brilliant white moonlight, allowing me to see the front portal is smashed in, blown away from the bomb blast. The walls are still standing, but a portion of the roof is caved in.

Children are crying. Nuns call out names, hoping to hear tiny voices answering back from dark corners. The acrid smell of burning rubber from the nearby factory adds to the surreal atmosphere. Smoke hangs in the air. The odor of scorched wood suggests furniture burning, and the smell of gas sets off a different fear.

Is it coming from here or a nearby building?

I start coughing, my lungs hurting. I have to get my child. *Fast.*

I put my coat sleeve up to my face to cover my nose and mouth, my eyes tearing from the smoke. A queasiness makes me light-headed. The bombing has been going on for more than an hour. Smoke billows where bombs fell on the workers' homes, setting fires. Their occupants never stood a chance. Hundreds of civilians must have been killed or wounded.

And this is how the Allies help us?

I can't think... can't feel... all I can do is make my way through the rubble, looking for Sister Eugénie and my Ninette. Star-like flares continue dropping out of the sky. Someone lit torches along with half a dozen tall, white religious candles, hoping to show the bombers this is a House of God.

'Have you seen Sister Eugénie?' I ask a young nun with two toddlers clinging to her black woolen skirts.

'*Non*, mademoiselle.'

I ask her about the gas leak and her eyes widen. She blesses herself and picks up the children, then runs off to get help before another bomb hits. She can't bear to utter the words we both fear. The building will explode and everyone will be lost.

I make my way through the structure... what's left of it... asking again. And again, desperation in my voice. No one has seen the sister. I stumble over broken chairs and smashed dishes and, God help me, I feel a moment of reverence when I find a crucifix shaken off the wall from the force of the bomb and onto the tile floor. I pick it up with careful hands and give it to the first sister I see. She thanks me and tells me God will watch over me.

'*Les bébés,*' I ask her. 'Where have they taken the little ones?'

'The sisters were evacuating the baby ward when a wooden rafter fell and blocked the door.'

'Did everyone get out?'

She shakes her head. 'I don't know. I heard a scream, then—'

Sister Eugénie. It *has* to be her. No one's seen her. And I'd bet my life on it, she has Ninette. She adores *ma petite.*

I can't wait another moment. I run toward the ward, remembering the day I sewed silk flowers in yellow, blue, and pink on the rim of her bassinet so she sees a rainbow every morning when she opens her eyes. She's not talking yet, but I know she wants to and now my baby might be...

Oh, please, God, no. She's an innocent babe born into a world cruel and unjust but You gave her life and filled me with such joy when I was so desperate to find meaning in what happened to me. Please, please don't take her now.

Somewhere in the back of my mind, I hear the nun yelling at me to come back, that I'll be killed. But I don't stop; I find the ward. The entrance is blocked. I try to move the rafter, I grunt, try again, I can't. I bend down, attempt to squeeze through the narrow opening, but it's too small. I peek through the door and see the cots and cribs lined up in the ward. I call out, 'Sister Eugénie, it's just Rachelle... Ninette's *maman.*'

'Mademoiselle D'Artois... *ici.* Here,' I hear a woman cry out. Hoarse, like it's a struggle for her to speak.

'Is Ninette with you?' I have to ask.

'Yes, mademoiselle, she's...' Her voice trails off. *What's she trying to tell me?*

I've *got* to get inside. I glance around the ward and see a broken stained-glass window depicting a saint. I can make out what's left of her, wearing a blue and gold veil and shards of glass scattered on the floor. Perfect.

I jam back through the damaged building and run outside, racing up and down the perimeter, my lungs bursting, my head pounding from the explosions, trying to remember where the ward is. *No, not here.* Another bomb hits the block of houses and the blast nearly blows me away. I drop to my knees, get up and keep going. *Where is the ward? No. Yes, here.* I see what's left of the window with the saint wearing a blue and gold veil, but it's not wide enough for me to crawl through. I look around as another flare lights up the sky and it's bright as day out here. I find a large rock and toss it through the window. The opening is still too small for me to slip through, then two, *three* rocks until I knock out all the stained glass.

Then with a prayer on my lips, I take off my coat and lay it down over the windowsill, climb over it and into the ward. I walk carefully over the jagged glass, calling out the sister's name. Nothing. That's when I break down, moan so loudly God must have heard me and has pity on me when I hear—

'Mademoiselle... *here!*'

I spin around, left then right. *Yes,* I see Sister Eugénie huddled under the landing. She must have crawled under the stairs to escape the falling rafter. I race over to her. The moonlight coming in through the window casts a light on her face and Ninette is lying in her arms. My heart stops.

Mon petit bébé isn't moving.

'Sister, is she—?' I barely mouth the words.

'I promised God I wouldn't let anything happen to her.' She attempts a smile. 'I never break a promise to God.'

I drop to my knees and take my baby from her arms. Her fat cheeks are streaked with dried tears. She must have cried herself to sleep amid the noise and chaos. Her tiny body shivers. From the cold or fear? I comfort her with soft words then, 'How can I ever thank you, Sister? *Oh!*' I see a trail of blood seeping from under the nun's round white collar. 'Sister, you're hurt!'

'It's nothing, mademoiselle.'

Cradling Ninette in my lap, I push aside the nun's holy bib made from starched white muslin and see a deep gash in her chest bleeding profusely. Large wooden splinters splattered about on her torn black habit. When the rafter fell, it shattered into pieces and a chunk of wood pierced her chest.

'I'll get help, Sister.'

She shakes her head, then grabs my arm. 'No, mademoiselle, God is calling me.' She sucks in a deep breath, struggling to breathe. 'Go quickly. *Vite!* Take your baby before the French police show up. Or the Gestapo.'

'Gestapo?'

'Yes, the pudgy secret policeman in the black trench coat.'

Herr Geller.

'He comes here every week to check on Ninette, calls her his "insurance",' she continues, choking, but she's determined to tell me what's on her mind. 'If he gets his hands on her, you'll never see her again.'

'Why?'

She opens her mouth to speak, but can't. I hear a loud rattle in her throat, her eyes go wide, and then a final sigh as if to bid adieu to a life well served before her body goes still.

She's gone.

With a deep sigh on my lips, I close her eyes, then place her praying hands across her chest while holding back tears. She was a good, kind woman who didn't judge me for having the child of an SS officer. I never told her the major raped me, couldn't share such intimate details with a holy woman. But I wish I had. I have the feeling she would have understood.

I pull back, remembering what she said about the Gestapo. *Why would Herr Geller check on Ninette? What nefarious business does he have with my child?* I sensed back at the American Hospital that Herr Geller wasn't fond of the major, as if there was a rivalry between them I don't understand. But I'll not allow him to use Ninette as a pawn. Not that he has any softness in his heart for her. No, he's cold, maniacal. With the ego of a peacock and the heart of a devil.

I look down at my baby nestled in my lap. She's awake, waving her hands about and making noises to get my attention, her pink lips trying to say something, but she can't quite get it out. She keeps trying, then finally I hear her say, 'Maman!'

A beautiful moment I will never forget, her big eyes watching me, blinking back tears. Me, too. I pick her up, hug her tight. I can't believe she's safe in my arms.

I rock her back and forth, muttering 'Maman loves you' over and over when finally, the bombing stops.

The night sky peeking through the damaged roof goes quiet with only the fading sound of the aircraft returning home, leaving behind trails of smoke smudging the dark sky like brush-strokes.

I wrap my baby in my long woolen coat and escape the bombed-out building through the broken window. My knees wobble, my emotions spent. Ninette clings to me, her tiny hands grabbing onto my hair and not letting go. I don't know how I'm going to bicycle back to my apartment with a baby in my arms, but I'm not waiting around to answer questions from the French police or the Gestapo.

Ambulances show up; someone yells they've capped the gas leak, thank God, then using their headlights they rescue the injured. And cover the dead. I say a prayer for Sister Eugénie. I realize then I can't move, my muscles tight. All I can do is stand in the moonlight with my baby in my arms, my heartfelt thoughts guiding the holy sister to Heaven when I hear—

'Justine. *Justine*, over here!'

I turn and see a tall German soldier on a motorbike screeching to a stop, squealing the tires, then revving his engine like he can't wait to hightail it out of here. I'd know that deep, baritone voice anywhere.

Arsène.

He smiles. 'I thought I'd find you here.'

Simple words. Beautiful words from a beautiful man who knows me better than I know myself. He found me, *how*, I don't know, but he did. I can't think about that now. I hand Ninette to him and jump into the sidecar. Then with my baby in my arms, we take off through the streets of Paris, Arsène dodging fallen debris, wailing ambulances... a Gestapo motorcar, French police with their sirens wailing *dee-dee... dee-dee*, all passing us by. They pay no attention to us, but we and others like us are more dangerous to them than the bombs dropped here this evening. For we will never stop fighting, day *or* night.

We are the Resistance.

But at this moment, I'm a mother first.

My baby is safe and I swear I will *never* let her out of my sight again.

24

PARIS, MARCH 27 1942

Ève

Forty-eight hours, they said, and Monsieur would be home.

They lied.

Did I expect any less?

Forty-eight hours stretches into more than three months. No word from Monsieur de Giocomte. No postcard, no official statement from the local French police. *Jews aren't allowed to write*, they said. It's as if Monsieur disappeared into a thick, green forest of lush oak trees populated by ugly trolls with funny mustaches and black foxes wearing swastika armbands. A world of secrets and lost 'travelers', as the men taken that winter day come to be known by the families they leave behind. Word spreads the *rafle* was organized as a reprisal against brazen attacks on Nazi soldiers by Jews, that a Jew shot a German sentry outside the Wehrmacht billet. No proof, but the German military commander sticks to his story and blames *all* Jews to justify the roundup.

Why? What's his end game?

I pick up gossip while waiting in queues for bread about how the more than seven hundred Jewish men rounded up were taken to l'École Militaire riding arena behind Les Invalides before being transferred to a transit camp north of Paris by train.

An unhappy place rife with rumors and discontent. Where we hear Jewish prisoners were housed in barracks built more than forty years ago and subject to harsh treatment. Daily roll calls morning and evening, standing long hours in the heavy rain or under the bittersweet warmth of the sun depleting whatever strength they had left. Royallieu-Compiègne, the place is called. Where the armistice was signed in a railcar ending the Great War.

After the French policeman and his German counterpart took Monsieur away, the *maison* lies in a gloomy state. Madame spends hours staring at old photographs of her husband. Happier times, holidays, their wedding photo. I see her holding them to her breast, whispering soft words, then kissing the black and white glossy photos before hiding them in a book. As if she fears the Nazis will return and steal those, too.

I want to console her, but a wall goes up between us. Not forged in religious or class differences, but in her eyes I'm still a child and she doesn't want me to see her grieving and sad, see her weak. I'd never think that, but her strong Russian roots to appear regal and proud are so inbred in her by her father that she takes on a cold, imperial air and I can't get through to her.

Her sister-in-law, the baroness, on the other hand, announces she's leaving Maison Bleue after the debacle with the Nazi police-man, screaming that her dear brother is lost to her and she has no reason to stay. That her daughter and grandchildren are in danger. I see Delphine trying to quieten the younger ones, pleading with her *maman*, then the baroness, to let them stay, that they have no guarantee any place else is safer and here they're with family. But to no avail. I notice the girl is wearing one of Justine's old dresses, a blue one with a scalloped collar that Maman fixed for her. I'll hate to see her go. She's a good girl. Madame de Giocomte knows it, too. She does her best to dissuade the baroness in that soothing, firm voice of hers she uses in times of turmoil, believing her sister-in-law is safer here than anywhere else in Paris. There's no reason to believe Jewish women and children will be arrested, *n'est-ce pas?*

The baroness refuses to listen. And she's gone in two days.

Where? She won't say. I don't think she trusts us or anyone. We pray she and her daughter and grandchildren remain safe. I say an extra prayer for Delphine.

And then there is Maman. She swears she'll never knit another scarf because it reminds her too much of Monsieur sitting across from her with that glassy stare, holding her wool. Then arrested before her eyes. She weeps every night and again blames *me* for the Nazi interloper and not saving Monsieur de Giocomte. I have no retort. I just accept her disappointment in me, though I lament causing her pain, her pale face growing more gaunt every day.

One good thing: no Nazi has crossed our doorstep since that morning, but I'm not naïve to believe we're safe. The Boches are always planning something to disrupt our lives.

Also, food parcels arrive on our doorstep. Fresh eggs. Even butter.

Michal refuses to talk about it, denying black-market connections, but I know it's his doing. He remains at my side, not treating me like a child with words he knows won't change the deep guilt I feel in my heart. Although he doesn't speak about that night, I know he also suffers because he returned too late with a stolen motorbike to help Monsieur. The next day I saw he had bruised knuckles and a deep cut above his right eye. I grilled him until he admitted he knocked out two Nazi soldiers ganging up on him. I pleaded for him to go back to the American Hospital. He said it's too dangerous, that an informant told him the Gestapo saw him there and was asking about him. Then he disappeared for two days. When he returned, I noticed fresh stitches above his eye, but he refused to elaborate, saying it's better if I don't know.

Meanwhile, we wait for word about the Jewish 'notables' taken that December day. We get troublesome information that comes by way of numerous letters to the Vichy government and the General Commissioner of Jewish Affairs written by mothers and wives of Jewish prisoners in Compiègne as well as Drancy. Letters detailing the appalling conditions, lack of food and horrible hygiene, men dying from hunger and cold. Letters from wives pleading for visits with their husbands and detailing their anxiety.

Then horrible news comes.

The Nazis execute numerous hostages by firing squad at Mont-Valérian fortress. Anywhere from seventy-five to ninety-five men die.

Was Monsieur de Giocomte among them?

I keep the letters hidden from Madame as the light in her eyes dims more every day. We believe Monsieur may be dead, but why hurt her with the terrifying facts?

No matter how much I try to keep everyone's spirits up, there's a hush sitting over Maison Bleue since we lost Monsieur de Giocomte. I find myself tiptoeing and whispering and keeping to myself, taking care not to let Madame or Maman know when I've left the house. Michal still keeps his distance. Any teasing or humor between us is out of the question after the arrest of Monsieur de Giocomte.

It would be like spilling holy water... a careless gesture against God.

I'm more focused than ever on doing my part to bring down the Boches, working with Michal orchestrating acts of sabotage as well as writing and printing anti-Nazi pamphlets, tacking them up on kiosks, and distributing them to students.

I stop going to my classes at the Sorbonne with a heavy heart. I was so keen on studying and doing experiments to advance science and save lives, but fighting the Boches is what matters, for Maman and Madame and every Frenchwoman struggling and making sacrifices to keep her family together in these troubled times. I give thanks I find moments when the sorrow in my heart hides behind a deep shadow. When my head is clear so I can do my part and use my science skills to fight the Nazis. Reading my chemistry books, making better, more efficient bombs. Scouting railyards to get in and out faster. Finding the courage to take chances to take down the enemy knowing I could be caught.

And get justice for my sister. And Monsieur de Giocomte.

Then on this March morning word is passed from one French-woman to another all over Paris that today is the day their men in the Jewish camp at Compiègne are being deported by train and heading East. *Where? Germany... Poland?* No one knows for sure.

The intelligence spreads quickly before Michal's informants get wind of it. I know we have little chance of rescuing Monsieur de Giocomte when we show up at the train station, but I owe it to Madame to give her closure. Women flock to the station, handker-chiefs pressed to their noses, sniffling and crying, hope alive in their eyes as they pray for a last goodbye before the train leaves. A long line of third-class carriages waits on the tracks—Michal heard a rumor the next train leaving for the East will carry the deportees in freight cars like cattle, though I am loathe to believe that—the locomotive engine blowing and hissing steam as if to shoo the women away.

To spare them what no wife or mother or sweetheart should have to see.

Their men trudging along the three kilometers from the camp

with suitcases lighter than when they left home, but hearts heavier. Their long overcoats hanging on their shoulders no longer straight and proud. Hats pulled down low over eyes riddled with fear, each man asking what the next stop holds. No one knows.

I find it hard to believe a transport of innocent Jewish men to an unknown destination is happening today and no one in Paris, save the families of these men, is paying attention. Not surprising. Everyone's mind is on where to find food, even how to steal coal for heating.

But why move these men? For what reason?

To a labor camp?

Which makes me pray Monsieur isn't among them. I know little about the disease of the mind, but my scientific instincts tell me our wonderful Monsieur suffers from a disease that saps not only his energy but erases the functions of his mind, even his memories.

He's not fit to work in a labor camp.

I don't voice my fears to Madame de Giocomte. She's with us when we gather on the platform of the train station, each Jewish woman—and there is a crowd—showing up after 6 a.m. since Jews aren't allowed out on the streets between eight in the evening and six in the morning.

Michal and I and Madame wait for the deportees to arrive, marching by foot from the transit camp flanked by French gendarmes. The deportation was delayed because there weren't any working railway lines available to travel East. I can't help but smile. Michal and I disrupted numerous train routes with explosives placed on the tracks. New and better explosives dropped into France by parachute by the British.

But it's not enough.

Whispers among the women is that this train is the first of many trains.

I try not to think what that means because it's too horrific for my mind to accept.

'There he is!' I call out, grabbing Madame's hand. I can't believe my eyes. Monsieur de Giocomte is alive.

'Itzhak, *mon amour*...' Madame de Giocomte cries out. 'Oh, God what have they done to you?'

The cry from Madame rises above the crowd, the piercing melody of her voice, high-pitched and familiar, reaching the man she loves. Deep in the recesses of his mind, the past is alive, allowing him a moment of recognition denied to him all these months.

I can't stop looking at him, amazed to see the clarity in his eyes, sunken and deep, but so alive. What is this disease that is so cruel it holds the brain hostage to its fickleness, allowing a peek through the door of the mind only to later slam it shut?

He fights his way through the crowd, waving his arms around. 'Ekaterina... Katya, *chérie*.'

I see the tears in Madame's eyes. 'Itzhak, my love.'

Madame rushes toward him, her arms outstretched, while we watch in horror as a Nazi guard appears out of nowhere and strikes Monsieur between the shoulders with his rifle butt, but his love for his wife is so powerful, he falters, but doesn't stumble.

Time is suspended when he calls out, *'Je t'aime.* I love you.'

Then he's swallowed up by Nazi guards surrounding him, dogs barking, pulling at their leads.

But his words of love linger in the air like the sweetest perfume.

The train whistle blows and the long line of railway carriages begins its journey East where deep clouds of despair gather and the sun has forgotten how to shine.

Madame falls to her knees, reaching out for her husband. I start going toward her when—

'Let her be, Ève.'

'I *must* go to her, Michal.'

'She'll need you more afterward. The long nights, the days that drag on forever. She needs to cry it out before she can go on.' He drags in a long breath. 'I saw my *maman* look like that after they took my father away. A day when the rains came down hard and fast. Like her tears.'

Like Madame's.

I say nothing. *How can I?*

For the first time since I came to Maison Bleue all those years ago, I see Madame de Giocomte break down and sob uncontrollably.

25

PARIS, APRIL 1942

Justine

The Saint-James pond area of the Bois de Boulogne hasn't changed since the Occupation. White swans. Vibrant, tall green trees that outshine the Boches' dull olive uniforms. And a peaceful lake that begs for a curious child to toss a stone into its depths.

But I have.

I'm a mother. And a woman in love with a man I can never have. A man whose face I've never seen. A man I know by his artful swagger, the breadth of his broad shoulders that I can lean on, an intoxicating voice that never fails to send a wave of pleasure through me. When the bombing started on that March evening, Arsène knew I'd rush to the church house to find Ninette and I'd need him, whatever happened. In his usual roguish manner that endears him to me, he 'borrowed' a Nazi uniform and motorbike from a drunken soldier. The Boche was found the next morning in his skivvies and socks with a hangover. We laughed about it for days afterward, then, on a more serious note, Arsène filled me in on the bombing details, that according to word passed down from the British Foreign Office to their agents, the RAF attack with nearly three hundred aircraft was not only about taking out the motor works, but to get an idea of the local reaction regarding Allied bombing on French soil. The British fear the Nazis will use the bombing as propaganda to turn the French people... and the Resistance... against the British.

We shall see. On a sad note, no one predicted the high amount of civilian casualties.

Nearly four hundred killed and six hundred wounded. Two hundred homes destroyed. Including the House of Sainte-Veronica de Mornay. I shall never forget the intense moments that night searching for Ninette and the dying words of Sister Eugénie warning me about the Gestapo. I have no doubt she's watching over Ninette from her place in heaven and praying for us.

Which brings home to me that we're still in the thick of it, that there's no easy road to driving the Boches out of Paris, and that it could be years before the Allies make their big move and stage a major invasion of France.

I feel a tear fall onto my cheek when I park Ninette's navy-blue pram next to the lake. My child is in more danger than ever. What if the major insists on taking her to Germany? I'll never see her again. My baby adopted by an SS family, another woman holding her in her arms, teaching her to say... I don't know what the word for *maman* is in German, but Ninette won't understand, she'll be confused, she'll be scared and she'll forget me. *Forget I'm her maman. No, I won't let that happen. Can't.* Most disturbing is, I never say it out loud, but it's always in the back of my mind, so I'll say it once and be done with it.

What if the invasion never comes?

Then we'll all starve. It's no secret the Nazis send our wheat to Germany and then there will be no Paris.

A world without Paris? I can't imagine it. This beautiful sleeping baby has no idea what formidable thoughts haunt her *maman*.

But that's why we fight. It's something in our core, our soul— we French have a soul but the German forces do not—the knowledge that while the Nazis live to hate and destroy, we live for beauty and art. And we can't let them take that from us.

Ever.

Even in the worst of times, Maman, Ève, and I never gave up. A lovely memory floods my heart. Of the day Maman brought Ève and me here in the fancy dresses she made for us from scraps of silk and lace and taffeta. Determined to make a new life for her daughters. Now, like then, my eye catches a graceful white swan gliding over the clear water, its velvet wings spread open wide like an angel's to prepare for landing, its big webbed feet splashing through the water to brake its descent. It's returning home from a journey.

Like me.

I feel like time stops here. There's no war, no rationing, no hunger. I'm that innocent child again so filled with a love of daisies and sunshine. Dreams and the mysteries of life's unknown secrets. My heart still aches for my lost girlhood ripped from me. But as each springtime arrives with the intoxicating scent that *is* Paris, I accept the fact I'm still healing.

Which is why I came here this morning. The major has insisted I meet him later at the Luxembourg Gardens to discuss our 'arrangement', a park noisy and *trés* busy with Parisians pretending life is normal. Not me. That naivety is a luxury I can't afford. The day is fast arriving when the major will pull rank once more and demand I send Ninette away.

Again.

* * *

After the bombing of the Renault plant, it didn't take long for news of me 'taking' my daughter from the destroyed building to reach the major. Everyone was still on edge around the city, I jumped at every noise, but Ninette reveled in being back in my arms, snuggling up to me and sleeping better than I expected. She was napping peacefully when he showed up at my apartment two days later and, in what was less than a five-minute visit without even one kind word about Ninette's welfare or the sacrifice of that sweet nun, Sister Eugénie, grilled me on my plans.

'You have a duty to me, mademoiselle, and to the German government to continue gathering intelligence at the hat shop and act as my companion *should* I request it,' he spouted, bending over my baby's cradle. She didn't open her eyes. Was she pretending to be asleep?

Clever, ma petite.

'Of course, Major, but with the recent Allied bombing, it's not safe for the child to be anywhere but with me.'

My heart skipped a beat when I thought he was going to pick up Ninette and take her. I held my breath, then let it out when he walked away, his hands crossed behind his back, thinking.

'Yes. I agree.'

'Thank you,' I said quietly, relieved.

Of course he dashed any positive feelings I had toward him with his next statement.

'We'll take this up again when my plans to open a Lebensborn here in France come to fruition. Currently, they're on hold.' He turned to me. 'However, there's still the question of who will watch the child. I made inquiries about assigning a German auxiliary worker to work as a nanny.'

'And take the woman away from her duties to the Wehrmacht?'
I widened my eyes in mock protest.

As if I'd trust *any* Nazi with my child.

He arched a brow, amused. 'You have a point.'

'I know the perfect nanny, monsieur. She's loyal, efficient, and adores the child.'

'Yes?'

'Madame Péroline.'

* * *

The milliner was only too happy to have my little girl back in her hat shop. *To boost morale among our ladies,* she said. I think she meant *her* morale, but I said nothing.

I push my rambling thoughts to the back of my mind when the trumpet-y sounds of the noisy swan startle Ninette and she wakes up from her nap and starts crying, her big doll eyes wide. I pick her up and cradle her close to me, her pudgy cheek pressed next to mine.

'Hush, *ma petite*,' I whisper in her ear. 'Maman is here. Maman will always be here for you.'

I pray it's so...

* * *

A jittery fluttering in my stomach belies my confidence. The time draws near for me to meet the major at the Luxembourg Gardens. I don't know why he's so insistent on it. He hasn't seen Ninette since that day he came to my apartment after the Allied bombing, giving me the excuse he's tied up traveling to Berlin, Munich, and Prague with Herr Himmler, organizing secret meetings with another prominent Nazi. *Heydrich,* I think. He mentioned they're working out the details on their 'final solution' to the Jewish problem.

'*What more can they do to those people?*' I asked. From the gossip I pick up at the hat shop, the situation isn't improving. Roundups. Arrests. People disappearing. I shudder every time I think about it. He wouldn't say.

Though he's kept to his word regarding my family and the de Giocomtes to keep them safe. Still, Ninette is better off without him. She's a joy in my life, eleven months old, teething, dribbling, a happy child who laughs when I make funny faces, she can say several words *and* she's walking... wobbling. Bless her, she doesn't give up even when she plops down on her bum. It warms my heart to see her finding her way.

I came here today to find courage, to rediscover that hope we had so many years ago when Maman brought Ève and me to the pond dressed up like live dolls. So desperate we were to find our next meal, Maman had been up all night sewing our dresses until her fingers bled to feed her babies.

And now I do what *I* must to feed *my* baby.

I check the newspaper every day to see where to line up, in what queue to buy the 'item of the day'. Butcher, bread. Milk on last Saturday, thank God. Even then it's a tedious process since you can only line up half an hour before the store opens. The Nazis fear any public gathering larger than two or three people. I like to think it's because they can't count higher than that.

Still, I manage to get by, helped by Madame Péroline's mysterious black-market deliveries of fruits and vegetables. Food is a bonding source of conversation waiting in line, but I find that when I take Ninette for a walk in her pram, whatever hat I'm wearing takes center stage.

Like today.

I exchange words with a mature madame walking her grand

black poodle. She stops and fusses over Ninette, then gushes over my two-piece powder-blue suit. *It's my design*, I tell her, with a matching hat and veil that trails down my back like a princess's long hair. A young girl on her bicycle waves as she races by, then a young mother walking with her twin girls stops to join our chat. She laments about how hard it is to find fresh fruit these days while ogling the string pearls dangling on the crown of my *chapeau* —pearls the major gave me. An enjoyable afternoon that doesn't last long enough in my opinion.

The major sees to that.

The chitchat and laughter come to a halt when a big, silver Mercedes touring car with a small swastika flag flying on the hood screeches to a halt nearby. Out jumps the major, a man used to commanding obedience from everyone, especially women. That arrogance is undeniable in his powerful stride heading toward me, enjoying the attention from the French women who can't take their eyes off this imposing SS officer. What's he doing *here* in the Bois? We aren't meeting until later in the Luxembourg Gardens. The bright afternoon turns dark and gloomy, the lovely spring air I so enjoyed today, the memories that tickled my heart, dissipate like ripples on the lake.

He's angry... *very angry*.

The air bristles with the ugly anticipation every Parisienne dreads and fears... an encounter with a Nazi officer. The woman with the poodle wants no part of it, nor the young mother with the twins. The woman with the poodle goes pale. The mother shields her twins with her full skirt.

Seeing the two women so shaken by the approaching major upsets me more than having to cut our conversation short. They make it a point to turn their faces away, then walk quickly in the opposite direction, eager to escape the scrutiny of the SS while I live with it every day. A disturbing thought hits me.

Have I become so jaded I no longer see the major for what he is? A fiendish sycophant whose only concern is advancing in the Party?

Have I made a deal with the devil to save my family?

The idea horrifies me.

'You're early,' I tell him, putting Ninette back into her pram. She protests by letting out a big wail and attempting to grab my long veil. I shush her, contemplating how he found me. He must have stopped by the apartment and let himself in. When he didn't find me and saw the baby carriage missing, he must have started searching for me.

And Ninette.

'My schedule is not your priority, mademoiselle,' he snarls.

'And since when *is* Ninette your priority?'

'Let's go.' He ignores my brazenness, which tells me this is more serious than I thought. He settles his hands on my shoulders, pushing me forward as I steer the pram toward the waiting Mercedes.

'Get into the motorcar. *Now.*'

* * *

'It's come to my attention your sister Ève is working with the Resistance.'

Fear chills my blood. *Of course. Herr Geller. That day at the American Hospital. He saw Ève and her wounded friend and came up with this wild accusation.*

'You must be mistaken, monsieur.' I stare straight at the major, determined to remain calm. It's a cool day in the Luxembourg Gardens, a bright yellow sun doing its best to dull the chill that's settled on the city, but I feel a cold wind at my neck as I push Ninette's pram back and forth. To passers-by we look like a young couple with a baby sitting on chairs scattered about the park, soaking up the sun.

My throat goes dry.

I should have known Ève wasn't safe from his clutches, but *this*?

'The Gestapo received a tip your sister is involved with a Resistance network responsible for planting explosives and derailing trains at the railyard near Gare de l'Est and other locations.'

'*Ève?*'

'Yes. Don't pretend you didn't know.'

I take an indignant stance toward him. '*I didn't.*'

'I don't believe you.'

'You must. Have I not performed *every* duty you asked of me, monsieur, including not contacting my sister? Your Gestapo friend made certain of that.'

He looks surprised, but doesn't refute my statement. Instead, he says, 'I want you to find out what you can about her "friends" and everything she knows.'

'You want me to *betray* my own sister?'

'It's your duty, mademoiselle.'

'Ève is a student at the Sorbonne. She's studying plants and flowers so she can work for a parfumier,' I lie. I have no doubt my little sister passed her exams. And didn't I see her protesting with other students when I was at the brothel?

'She's studying chemistry, according to a member of my staff, Lieutenant Engel, which qualifies her to make bombs and explosives.'

'Ève making bombs?' I laugh. 'My sister is a bookworm.'

'Don't lie to me, Justine. Must I remind you that I control where you work, where you live, what you eat—'

I nod, my heart racing, but I can't do what he asks. I have to see Arsène, tell him I can't stay in Paris and beg him to help me get my little girl to safety. I can't betray my own sister.

I'd rather die.

'Ève has never contacted you?' He smiles, but it's not to charm me into giving him information. He waves over a photographer bouncing around with his camera shooting pictures. Pretty girls applying lipstick while Germans soldiers ogle them. A Nazi officer reading a guidebook. In German. A female auxiliary worker smoking a cigarette. Wherever I turn, I see the occupiers trying to blend in, like they belong here.

It turns my stomach.

I pray the camera breaks to spare the outside world this hypocrisy of Nazi propaganda that makes France look weak and complacent and us collaborators. I have the sick feeling I'm about to be pulled into this scheme concocted by Goebbels and the German High Command when I see the photographer hurry over to where we're sitting. The major said nothing in the motorcar about his agenda, instead ordering his driver to put the pram into the trunk and get going. I never should have trusted him. I should have known he always has an agenda and it's never good for me.

'I haven't spoken to Ève since...'

I can't finish the sentence. Relive those final moments when I knew I'd lose my innocence *and* my sister on the same day. He knows it, too, and plays that to his advantage.

'Ève and your *maman* are safe for the moment, but I can't keep the Gestapo off their necks much longer.'

I was right about Herr Geller.

'However, if I assured the Gestapo your sister will lead us to a network of resisters, well...'

He pauses while he gauges my vulnerability to his suggestion. I lower my eyes to keep him from reading the expression on my face because it's one of disbelief he'd even suggest such a thing. That would make Ève a collaborator. My sister may be bookish and shy, but she's *not* a collaborator.

He continues. 'Then I can make a deal to keep your *maman* safe.'

'Ève will never do what you ask,' I insist.

'Things won't go well for her if she doesn't cooperate with the Gestapo.'

'But she's done nothing,' I protest. 'She's a student, not a *résistant*.'

'Then she has nothing to worry about.'

Before I can stop him, he pulls Ninette out of the pram and I've never seen her eyes open so wide. She's fascinated and horrified at the same time by this man with his sharp Teutonic features and grinning mouth showing his teeth. I think she fears him as much as I do. Observing her, looking at her hair, eyes, her fair skin, appraising her like art.

It frightens the hell out of me.

It's a comedy of errors where the SS officer finds himself duly matched when Ninette wiggles her nose, then sneezes in his face. Not once, but *twice*. He wipes his cheek, then hands her back to me, his jaw set.

'Take her.'

That's my brave girl. I hug her tight.

'I wouldn't be so hasty in your decision, mademoiselle,' he says. 'If you refuse to assist the Gestapo in their investigation, they will arrest your sister and take her to Avenue Foch to secure the names by other means.'

Torture.

No, I can't let that happen.

My heart pounds, trying to make my case for not helping him, knowing I lose either way, fretting when the photographer insists on me posing with the major with Ninette in my lap. *A happy family scene in the park,* making small talk about Paris in the springtime, knowing this is *exactly* what the major planned to confuse me and make me acquiesce to his wishes.

'I can't just show up at Maison Bleue after all this time.' I put Ninette down at the photographer's request so he can take some shots of her. She walks a few steps, then plops down on the pavement. I reach out to grab her, but the photographer insists he needs more photos. Why is he enticing her with a small blue ball? I don't like this. 'How will I explain where I've been? Why I didn't get in touch with Maman and Ève? She'll know it's a trap.'

'I have a better idea. I consigned three de Giocomte Impressionist paintings to the Hôtel Drouot to be sent to Nice for an upcoming auction at the Hôtel Savoy—'

'You're *selling* the paintings you stole?' My heart pounds and I slowly let out my breath, disbelieving what I heard. It was one thing to think about the de Giocomte paintings huddled together like precious silk stored in a trunk, no one touching them and marring their beauty. But to think *anyone* can purchase a stolen painting and claim it as their own makes me ill.

'Confiscated from Jewish scum. Not stole. And I actually have orders to sell them, mademoiselle. Unlike certain people, I follow orders.'

Why don't I believe him? What happened to the other de Giocomte paintings he stole? Herr Geller was unaware of the major's dirty deed until I told him. Most likely, he made some excuse to the secret policeman, but I wouldn't be surprised if the major kept other paintings he looted from Jewish owners for himself.

'I will add *The Beaufort Sisters* to draw your sister to the auction house.'

My eyes widen. 'You have the painting *here*... in Paris?'

'I couldn't bear to send it to Chambord for safekeeping.' He grins like the devil stepping on an angel's wing. 'Now it will be very useful to complete my mission.'

'How can you be certain she'll see the notice in the *Drouot Gazette*?' The daily sheet lists detailed information including day, time, and room where patrons can bid on the art, furniture, and jewelry up for auction.

'I'm not, but your sister was so protective of the painting, I imagine she follows what items go up for bidding. It's a chance I'm willing to take. I'll list the three Impressionists from the de Giocomtes along with *The Beaufort Sisters* to pique her curiosity. When she shows up to see the work, you'll tell her you also saw the auction sheet.'

'You think Ève is that naïve?'

'The heart believes what the heart wants.'

Ironic coming from a man with no heart... or spine.

'You'll tell her you ran away after I put you up in an apartment on the Left Bank,' he continues, 'and later found your way to Lyon, too ashamed to go home.'

'She'll never believe me.'

'She will. She won't question you when you tell her you came back to Paris because you have a child.'

That does it. I'm not letting him drag my little girl into his ugly scheme.

I stand up, hands on my hips and let him have it, emotions spilling out of me I've kept bottled up so long. I speak before thinking. 'You want me to use Ninette as bait? Have you no feelings for your own daughter? You're just another heartless Nazi!'

I went too far this time.

He raises his hand to strike me—he wouldn't dare, not here—but I'm not taking any chances. I slip out of his reach and see Ninette laugh when the photographer tosses her the blue ball. She reaches for it, but misses and it rolls away from her. She gets up on her chubby legs and waddles after it.

'Ninette...' I call out to her when the major grabs my arm so hard it makes my eyes tear.

'The child belongs to the Reich, mademoiselle,' he says, squeezing me, 'and the sooner you accept that, the easier it will be for you.' He sneers. 'Agreed?'

'You don't care about Ninette, do you?' The awful truth stings my heart like an angry bee. 'All you care about is your damn standing in the Party. That's why you want me to spy on Ève.'

He doesn't deny it. 'Get under her skin, have her invite you to join her Resistance network then report back to me with information and names.'

'I won't do it.'

'No?' He pulls on his black gloves, like a hangman pulling on a noose.

'No. I'm taking my baby and leaving—'

I'm so stunned by his words, his heartless plan, ears ringing with his impudence at taking my baby and using her for his own deceitful purposes, I lose sense of time and place, my heart pounding. I turn around. The photographer is gone. *My God, where is Ninette?* She's disappeared. I panic. Where is my baby? *Where is she?*

'What have you done with my daughter?' I demand.

He smiles. 'You see, mademoiselle, how easily you can lose someone you love?'

'Where is she?' I cry out. '*Where's Ninette?*'

I hear the sound of sturdy leather shoes pounding the pavement behind me. I turn and see the German auxiliary worker I saw earlier holding my baby in her arms. She's not smiling. Before she can stop me, I grab Ninette from the woman, making no excuses, anger heating my face, and I'm shaking all over. Ninette thinks it's a game and waves the ball in my face, but I can't stop the tears filling my eyes.

She's safe. For now.

I turn to the major, standing behind me with his arms crossed, looking smug. 'You *are* a bastard, aren't you?'

He grins. 'So, do we have a deal?'

26

HÔTEL DROUOT, PARIS, FRIDAY, MAY 8 1942

Ève

I keep up a fast pace, taking long strides, my empty satchel bag banging against my thigh as I head for today's art auction at the Hôtel Drouot. It's a typical day in the ninth arrondissement since the Occupation began. Parisians bustling about, pretending everything will go back to normal. That the flowers will smile and not droop, that taxis will honk their horns. That the air of Paris will smell of perfume and not German sweat. Of course, it won't. Like a plucked goose, we shiver under the accusing monocle of the Boches observing us in our nakedness. Taking what they want.

Not today.

I'm taking *back* what the Nazis stole from me.

The Daisy Sisters.

It festers in me, this pain in my heart that never goes away since the day I lost Justine. I've been strong, blending in, taking care not to draw attention to myself. So far, I've obeyed the rules, but today I can't. I found out select paintings stolen from the de Giocomtes are on preview today at Hôtel Drouot when Madame had a dizzy spell. She slumped down onto the divan when she saw the notice in the *Gazette*. Among the official listings of items coming up for auction is a preview from an 'amateur Parisian collector' in Hall I.

Code for 'art looted from a Jewish home'.

The preview consists of tableaux by Manet, Renoir, Degas, and 'The Beaufort Sisters'. They never mention the collector's name, but everyone at Maison Bleue including the staff knows and loves the pieces of art listed on the auction sheet.

It's no secret the Nazis are on a buying spree of French art, that is, stolen art taken from French Jews like the de Giocomtes. Good people. Strong people. Madame de Giocomte says the Nazis buying art is worse than looting because it's a second violation of the artist's soul.

It's personal for me, seeing how it's *my* portrait the Nazis stole. Well, my sister's, too. That terrible day nearly two years ago when the SS officer destroyed our innocence and the sugared life we'd known turned to salt.

Bitter.

Since then the world has turned topsy-turvy, taking from me my dearest heart, the best sister I could ever have. Sharing lemon macarons, going for walks along the Seine arm-in-arm, feeding the swans in the Bois.

My chest tightens. The anger I keep bottled up heats my cheeks when I turn the corner at the crossroads on the Boulevard des Italiens. In spite of the emotions roiling inside me, I resist the urge to spit on the road signs written in German. I've seen men beaten with batons for less. Too many Nazi soldiers milling about and pointing to their Paris guidebooks, poking their noses into our glorious past while destroying our future. A pestilence of evil has taken over Paris, polished jackboots goose-stepping up and down our boulevards, saluting each other like marching wooden soldiers, though they wear an ugly beetle-green, not royal blue and red.

So many rules...

You have to be careful not to stop and stare too long in a shop window... look over your shoulder to see if you're being followed... and not show too much interest in the secret police harassing a Jew on the street.

I pull down the brim on my black felt hat, its scraggly feather tickling my nose. Sunbeams bounce off the pavements like God's bullets, spraying the enemy in the eye and keeping me safe from their gaze. The morning mist obscuring the swastika flags hanging from buildings dissipates slowly as if ashamed.

I keep going.

I know how to act. Keep my head down and my emotions tucked in my pocket. Shoulders hunched, I appear submissive, non-threatening to the German soldiers. Sneering. Loud voices, acting like they own Paris.

They will never own the city I love, I vow, when I approach the auction house, no matter how long they occupy us.

Or me.

I want to sprint down the boulevard but I force myself to act nonchalant and not attract attention. I suck in slow breaths, calming myself when I spy two SS officers smoking and chatting up a young woman outside the five-story Hôtel des Ventes, their chins jutting out like arrogant roosters. SS officers often seek out pretty girls walking on the boulevard, charming them with their lies of sweets and silk stockings. Words that still send chills through me.

Go home, Ève. Forget this crazy stunt of yours... please.

No, Justine, I can't.

You must. I'm dead... murdered. This insane plan won't bring me back. It will only get you arrested by the Gestapo.

You doubt my skills?

No.

Then let me get the painting back. I can roll it up and hide it in my satchel.

No, Ève. You're acting rash, illogical. I beg you. Kill any emotion in your heart... for Maman's sake and mine... and get the hell out of there. Now.

No, Justine, I won't turn back now.

I shiver with a sudden sweat breaking out on my skin. I admit to a moment of doubt, my deep-seeded need for revenge giving way to a sliver of reason residing in my brain conjuring up an imaginary conversation with my sister. I debated *how, what* I could have done to save her from the lust of that SS officer. His need for a woman so predatory, his animal scent filled the library in the empty house, his voice rumbling about wanting a 'fair-haired' mademoiselle. His mood arrogant, the vicious smile stitched onto his face reminding me of an evil dark knight.

I never knew his name, but I never forgot him.

If the devil were straight-backed and blond, it would be him, eyes so clear and blue they have no depth but they can pierce your skin like sharp ice when he stares at you. An SS officer born without a heart. The man who never had a soul. He didn't need one. His arrogance and single-mindedness to the task at hand pushed him through the military ranks, but he's also a man with a surprising and artful eye for the beauty of the brushstroke.

Which is what brought him to the three-story de Giocomte residence.

A deep sorrow builds in me when I replay that day.

I never forgot that face.

Strong Aryan features, Prussian hallowed cheeks, pristine

blonde hair, and pale skin like he never saw the sun rise on a battlefield. And the cunning disposition of a snake that strikes at its victims not because it's hungry, but because it can.

I swore I'd make him pay.

Nearly two years I've waited for this opportunity to take back the painting of Justine and me so Maman can see Justine's pretty face once more, to give her something to smile about instead of seeing her droopy eyed to hide the tears that never dry. For Madame de Giocomte, so she can regain the beauty of the art that graced her home for so many years, art that her dearest husband Monsieur de Giocomte poured his heart into collecting, and bring a piece of him back into her life.

Sadly, we still have no word on where he is since that day at the train station when he and the other Jewish men boarded the third-class carriages and headed East.

Since then, I continue my work with the Resistance.

I don't consider myself brave. I'm not like the others, rough-necked partisans and red-lipstick-wearing mademoiselles who can slide up to a Nazi and cajole information from him one moment and then slit his throat the next. I work under the cover of night sabotaging the railway lines. A job suited for me, my hands smudged with dirt and grime, the smell of pungent chemicals mixing with my sweat.

But today I'm dressed like a Parisienne mademoiselle.

I donned a summer print dress that once belonged to Justine. Even though I'm taller than she ever was, it's still a bit too big. I'm thinner since the Occupation. I slipped on clogs with wooden soles —forget leather; the Germans shipped all the shoes back to the *Vaterland*—and Maman's old Sunday hat with a wispy long feather that keeps getting into my face.

And a semi-automatic pistol.

I gather my courage as I swing past the Nazi guard at the Rue

Drouot entrance to the nearly century-old auction house. I'm going into the lions' den. Collectors without a conscience bid on stolen art without missing a heartbeat because they have no heart. What if I see the SS officer who raped Justine? I need the weapon to protect myself. I took it off a German sentry on the last job we pulled to derail a train. Michal disarmed him, striking him on the back of the head and locking him in the shed. The Nazi didn't see our faces so he can't identify us, then Michal confiscated his rifle, but the German also had a pistol, a Luger. Michal missed it—he seemed distracted—so I hid it in my jacket pocket, knowing the Polish fighter doesn't approve of me having a weapon, that it could be used against me.

'You have more of a chance to evade scrutiny as a student, Ève, but if you're armed and caught by the Gestapo, they'll arrest you as a political dissident and you'll end up hanging from a butcher's hook,' he'd said before I left.

To scare me?

Maybe, but I've earned the right to carry a handgun.

I never stop practicing lessening the risk of detection. I map out the missions then spend hours hiding underneath a railcar on my belly before picking the right moment to strike. I refuse to give up.

I canvas the auction house, gathering intelligence on the de Giocomte art, where it's going... by train, truck... then coming up with a plan to take the painting back.

I hate deceiving Michal, but he's more distant than ever. I want to tell him about *The Daisy Sisters*, but something is pressing hard on his mind and he's not letting me in. I don't think he's seeing Coralie. She found another man and Michal barely noticed.

It's something else.

Could be the letter I saw him reading... no stamp or postmark. He pulls it out at least once a day. I pretend not to notice and chatter on about the rumor Jews must soon start wearing a yellow star, then he gets angry and stuffs it back into his pocket.

I never thought I'd admit this, but I want his approval.

If only I'd had the courage to talk to him. *If only*.

What if I'm making the wrong move?

My throat tightens.

I need no excuse to seek my revenge for what he did.

I pull my hat down over my eyes, my heart pounding as I take in the vast auction house that first opened in 1852. It's a stately building on Rue Drouot that reminds me of a grand dame wearing a too-tight girdle. Sixteen halls, a basement, and a cellar used as a warehouse. I wander around the auction house, looking for Hall 1 on the first floor, taking in the items for sale: antiquities, paintings, jewelry... even furs auctioned off for charity.

What is it about bidding on an item of beauty that drives these collectors into a mad frenzy? I see it like a tragic story I saw in the cinema. A story where the hero is obsessed with the painting of a beautiful woman, pays dearly for the pain of wanting her so bad he spends his last franc, and in the end, once he has her, he has nothing to live for and jumps into the Seine.

The fool.

Am I also guilty of obsession? Of risking everything to get *The Daisy Sisters* back? Am I also a fool? No, if I'm obsessed with anything, it's making that Nazi pay for what he did to my sister.

I can still see the terror blazing on your pretty face, Justine. I will never forget it. I will never stop searching for The Daisy Sisters *and bring you home. Then I can feel whole again seeing your face one more time.*

I wrap my fingers around the Luger hidden in my pocket, ready to use it, my finger sliding on and off the trigger. Nerves, *God, yes*, nerves make my hand slippery.

What if a loud 'Heil Hitler' startles me? Or those cold, dreaded words, 'Your papers, mademoiselle?' make me jump and the gun goes off?

I pray I won't have to fire the damn thing, but if I feel the cold hand of that SS officer crawling up my skirt, I *will* shoot him.

There are three bullets left in the chamber.

I'm no assassin, but I don't hold back the primal need in my bones to seek justice for that day, my heart dark and heavy with a haunting memory. I go out of my way to avoid contact with the Boches, but today's mission leaves me no choice.

Revenge.

27

HÔTEL DROUOT, PARIS, FRIDAY, MAY 8 1942

Justine

'She's here.'

I pull back into a dark corner when I see Ève race into the hall, out of breath, inquiring to the man in the black suit standing behind the high desk if the auction has started yet. He shakes his head and she looks for a seat in the crowded room. The major can't resist creaking his neck to get a better look at the girl who dared to defy him with so much courage. I believe his ego still hasn't gotten over it. He turns away quickly before she spots him. Not the Gestapo man. Herr Geller struts around the hall with his usual bulldog snarl on his lips.

No one dares to leave or be singled out as 'suspicious'.

I pull down the veil on my blue hat. I'm not ready for my sister to see me. Not yet. I want to prepare myself for what I know will be not only an awkward conversation, but a dangerous one.

'You know what you have to do, Justine, or—'

'You don't have to keep reminding me, monsieur. I understand.'

'*Gut*. I expect a full report this evening when I visit you.' He cocks a brow. 'And Ninette.'

I clench my fists, struggling to keep my temper. He enjoys goading me, knowing when it comes to my baby daughter I stuff my emotions into a box and seal it up tight so he can't hurt me. Then he makes a hurtful comment that sets me off and that box explodes, sending me into a tailspin and I lash back at him. He likes that, me fighting back. There are times I ask myself if by fighting back when he raped me did that excite him? Did he enjoy it more? Questions that haunt me because I can't see myself *not* fighting him.

'Why is Herr Geller here?' I ask, keeping my voice calm. He seems disappointed I didn't take the bait. *Bon.*

'The Gestapo have a significant interest in today's auction, mademoiselle.' The major is smiling, but the tone in his voice is anything but approving.

'Besides watching me?' Why am I not surprised the major alerted the Gestapo man? Or did he get his orders from higher up to observe my meeting with Ève?

He smirks. 'Herr Geller has an eye for acquiring valuable pieces for the Führer's future art museum in Linz.'

A lie.

Does the major think I'll run? Where would I go? Paris is filled with his henchmen, both German and French. Still, the hairs stand up on the back of my neck knowing the secret policeman will be lurking in the background.

'What the Gestapo know about art,' I say sarcastically, 'I suspect you could write on the back of a postage stamp.'

'Herr Geller would not be amused by your comment. I advise you to be cautious, mademoiselle. He has the Führer's ear.'

'Which is the only reason *you* tolerate the Gestapo butting into your affairs.' I can't forget Herr Geller's keen interest in the major's pastime of 'safekeeping' Jewish art for its owners.

The major shifts his weight, his mouth twitching. 'I work independently of the Gestapo.'

I can't resist adding, 'Still, he's the sour grape in your wine, n'est-ce pas?'

He doesn't deny it. *Bien*, I found the major's weak spot. For all his blowhard rhetoric and Aryan bravado, for him to get his promotion to remain in Paris, he must kowtow to the Gestapo's request to rout out resisters.

One dirty hand washes the other.

Satisfied he's made his pitch clear... I mean, *threat*... the major mixes with the incoming crowd and leaves the hall before Ève sees him, while I observe her from a dark corner behind a tall Hindu bronze statue with an ornate headdress.

I take this moment in, breathless.

Seeing my little sister makes my heart ache for the old days at Maison Bleue with Ève and Maman. Two little girls playing princesses in the grand house, the daughters of a seamstress showing our sisterly bond by making daisy chains.

Yet seeing her under these circumstances sends me downward into a spiral.

I want to tell her everything, but I can't. Too many lives depend on me... too many secrets in my head. I've worked too long and too hard to take that chance.

And I'd lose my precious little daughter.

I'd rather die than let that happen.

So I remain in the shadows, think this through, and pray she does nothing stupid when I reveal myself to her. If I tell her the truth, she could blow my cover and the Nazis will know every piece of intelligence I gave them is false. *And dear God, what about Arsène?*

His life will be in danger.

I can't reveal to her my role as a double agent, that my allegiance lies with the Allies and not the Nazis, that I retch like vinegar is forced down my throat every time I feed the Boches misinformation, then wait for the hard slap across my face if the major discovers I'm lying.

Do I have the courage to go through with this? I must. I have my daughter to protect and that's more important than anything, *n'est-ce pas*? Then why am I haunted by my own cowardice? I can't let that rule me. I know how much Ève is suffering. When I pressed the major, he admitted my sister went to the gendarmerie asking about me but the Gestapo paid a visit to the local French police and squashed her inquiry. Another reason the major owes the pudgy secret policeman.

I know that Ève believes she could have saved me. She couldn't.

I made the choice to go with the major. I was so naïve believing I could talk the Nazi down.

I couldn't.

I often ask myself what went through Ève's mind raging against the SS officer when he stole the painting of us. Did she act bravely because she was innocent of the Nazis' cruelty toward women? Or did she see the painting as the last vestige of a way of life destroyed?

Watching her come farther into the hall, I see she's different now, how she acts, more sure of herself, more savvy in the ways of the world. If she *is* a member of the Resistance intent on acts of sabotage, my little sister has grown up. Tougher, wiser, stronger. Filled with fervor to rid France of the invaders.

And those who work for them.

Is she a danger to me?

My own sister?

Then—to protect Ninette—I will have no choice but to keep

her out of my life forever. Make her hate me. Despise me so she'll never want to see me again.

The thought catches in my chest, making it hurt. I have to pull myself together, find out what she knows. I can't let her see me soft, vulnerable. I must be tough, not kind. Push her away. I have a plan, too. The major wants me to find out everything I can about the Resistance cell she's working with... names, contacts, places, but I intend to help her escape. I will tell her I'm working with the Nazis even if it kills me, because I know she's working with the Resistance. That she leaves me no choice but to inform the Gestapo if she doesn't take Maman and get out of Paris in twenty-four hours. Yes, she'll have to leave the university, but it's the only way I can save her... and Ninette. If the Gestapo can't find my sister, then Herr Geller will have no reason to hurt my child. I'll tell the major I arranged a meeting place, but Ève never showed up.

Yet my heart tugs. My emotions spin in every direction. I can't stop looking at the sorrowful feather on her hat, droopy and sad. *Maman's hat*. I want to run and embrace her, but I dare not. That terrifying Gestapo man is watching me, waiting for me to betray my sister.

The frenzy of the art auction gets underway, the bidding starts, the crowd shuffles, and the cluttered hall becomes a fast-moving carousel of art and greed and panic. The de Giocomte paintings will be showcased at the end of the auction to whet the appetite of the art dealers going home with nothing to show for their afternoon.

I can't wait that long. Wait for the auction to end and for Ève to see *The Daisy Sisters* and then pretend to run into her and go into my phony spiel. Set up an act of betrayal that will kill my soul and send my sister to her death.

Damn the Gestapo.

I've got to warn her. *Now*.

The first lot goes quickly, including a Louis Sixteenth round table and a cabinet that apparently belonged to Marie Antoinette. The paintings listed in the *Gazette* are up next. Time is running out. I know with heartfelt certainty if I don't get Ève out of here now, get her someplace where we can talk in private, I'll miss my only opportunity to warn her without the Gestapo listening to my every word.

Make her hate me so she'll take Maman and get out of Paris. The de Giocomtes, too. What I've heard from the major about the 'final solution' doesn't bode well for them.

The gentleman in the black suit behind the high desk calls for the next item. His male assistant holds up a small painting by Corot, *In the Garden*.

That gives me an idea.

I see Herr Geller standing in the far corner looking bored, his afternoon reduced to babysitting two troublesome females and cavorting with the 'dirty' French, whom he considers beneath him. He's so bored he's taken to working his crossword puzzle harder than usual. Not surprising. This is a man whose mind moves so quickly, he fills it every minute with intricate and obtuse detail, whether it's mind games found in a puzzle or torturing a prisoner for information.

I will use that obsession against him. Make my play to get Ève's attention. It will take precise timing on my part to find the exact moment to strike. Bid on the painting. Then pray the auctioneer doesn't bring down his ivory mallet on my bid or I've lost everything.

Insane? Maybe, but I have no choice.

I hold my breath, ready to make my brazen move. This is the moment I've waited nearly two years for, to hug my sister, be a family again, tell her I love her. So, just for a moment, however brief, I'm going to enjoy it.

28

HÔTEL DROUOT, PARIS, FRIDAY, MAY 8 1942

Ève

I shudder, trying to shake off the cold sensation that hits me every time I set out on a mission. Today I can't shake it. I'm not in my element, not covered by the ebony darkness that cloaks me in anonymity leaving me free to do my job.

Not here. I'm exposed to curious glances wondering who I am, why I'm here. Cigarette smoke blowing in my face, seasoned art collectors pushing their elbows into my shoulder every time they raise their hand to bid, sophisticated women drenched in expensive perfume and ego. I'm determined not to back out as I study the throng of buyers, looking, wandering around the hall. The collectors consist of thieves, corrupt art dealers, collaborators, but not one Jewish soul among them to buy back what the Nazis took.

The Germans banned Jews from the auctions.

Everyone chattering like magpies with the same goal. Buy up

as much art as they can afford, then move it, resell it on the black market while their money is still worth something. The only investment better than art, I hear one jaded buyer say, is gold, especially with Nazis like Goering driving up the prices. His eyes widen like the portal opening to another world counting his profit. Another says that owning art is better than depositing francs in a bank. Then they laugh.

While inside I cry.

Hearing them reduce the work of the artist to nothing more than a money-making venture makes me angry. The Nazis have reduced the rich culture of France to nothing more than a sou in a worn pocketbook. Worse is knowing the SS officer who took my sister from me could be here, gloating at the spectacle.

I don't care. I'm here to steal the painting back.

I pull down my black felt hat to hide my flushed cheeks. My clunky, cork-soled heels hit the floor hard as I take a seat in the hall, the auction house swarming with eager buyers looking for nineteenth-century Italian landscapes, furniture from Versailles, porcelain vases from China. Everyone is talking about the preview tomorrow of an important *tableau*, painting, by Camille Corot expected to bring a million francs at auction. I'd never chance coming here, but this is for Justine. I shake off the past, for only in the present can I seek my revenge for the pain the Nazis caused my sister, Maman, and me.

According to the *Gazette*, Impressionist paintings and other artifacts from an unnamed art lover will be sold at auction in June at the Hôtel-Savoy in Nice. It's customary to preview the lot the day before for auctions here at the Hôtel Drouot, but the paintings on preview today were requested by an unnamed curator at the Louvre to be added at the last minute to the special collection in Nice of over four hundred works expected to bring record sales.

Why, no one knows, but I'm certain the artwork came from the home of the de Giocomtes and will be previewed here in Hall 1 after the auction.

My nerves are stretched so tight my body goes numb, including my hand. I take my cramped finger off the trigger and try to relax. I'll be here for a while. The room is stuffy, and the odor of dried furniture varnish and paint on canvas is no match for the ripe smell of humanity crushed together. I lean forward, interested in the beautiful furniture pieces up next, eighteenth-century pieces that remind me of Madame de Giocomte's treasures before she sold them. Frenzied buyers make notes on their writing pads, whispering about the next item, estimating it will sell for over a hundred fifty thousand francs.

A small painting by Corot.

The bidding starts.

Fifty thousand francs.

Sixty.

I squirm in my seat, a prickly feeling inching up my spine when I hear a woman's sultry voice call out, 'Seventy thousand francs.'

Three simple words.

Yet I can't get that voice out of my head. The ping to my brain that says *something in my world just changed*, the darkness lifted. My heart thunders in my chest because it *can't* be true. Intuitively I know I shouldn't get my hopes up, but I've lived with the pain of loss for so long, I give in.

I turn around and see who made the bid: a beautiful blonde comes out from behind a tall Oriental-looking statue where she was hiding. Pale blue suit with matching kid gloves and a blue hat with a long, trailing veil. A string of pearls dangles from the crown of her *chapeau*.

She turns and pulls the veil away from her face. Her hair is a shimmery platinum, her eyes deep and sad like she'd lived in the shadows of twilight... until now.

She stares straight at me.

My heart stops.

Justine.

So I *did* see her at the American Hospital. *Why didn't she speak to me then?*

Remember? A Gestapo man was at her side, acting all friendly with her.

I shoot a quick glance around the hall. I see that same man in a black trench coat and Fedora, leaning against the wall, writing on a newspaper, distracted. Bored. That's him, I'm sure of it.

What hold does he have over her?

The auctioneer rattles off his spiel, asking for a higher bid. I can't think... focus. Wondering what happens next. Do I rush over to her? *Hug her?* Not with the Gestapo watching. Wait, he's *not* watching her. For now. *What's her next move?* As if I can think that far ahead. I'm still reeling from this insane moment when—

'Eighty thousand francs...' comes the next bid.

Justine nods toward me, then rushes out of the hall before the Gestapo man looks up from his newspaper, the long veil on her hat trailing after her like the ending of a fairy tale.

I smile.

She wants me to follow her.

* * *

'I see you're wearing Maman's old hat, Ève.'

I blow the long feather away from my face. 'She misses you terribly, Justine. *Dammit, I* miss you. I went to the police and—'

'I know.' She heaves out a long sigh. 'The major told me, but I had to disappear and not cause a scandal for you and Maman. I didn't mean to hurt you. I'm sorry.'

She's been in Paris all along?

'Did he...?' I can't utter the word *rape* out loud. For nearly two years I've gone round and round in my head what I'd say to her if I ever saw Justine again and now all I can ask her is if this Nazi major assaulted her. Like I have to speak in a whisper because rape is never discussed, even with my own sister because the shame that follows its victim is like the stink of a rotting apple. What was once sweet has now turned sour.

'I'd rather not talk about it, Ève. I've made a new life for myself.' I see her eyes darting toward the door like she's waiting for someone to find us. *Down here? In the cellar*. She keeps tugging on her gloves.

'Oh, so you don't want to talk about it. What about me, how I feel?'

She's acting coy, snarly, like she'd rather not be having this conversation, that I'm a bee in her bonnet and she wants me to buzz away. I'm not going.

'Ève, listen—'

'It's been almost two years, Justine. *Two years*. I've been going crazy looking for you, missing you... believing you were dead.'

'I *couldn't* come home. I—I found work in a milliner's shop on Rue de Rivoli. You know I always wanted to be a designer.' She attempts a smile, but that special light she has for me has gone out of her eyes. She thinks I don't notice, but I do and it wounds me. 'Remember how I made you that floppy hat with the wax strawberries and you hated it?'

Trivia. She's hiding something, but what?

'Why are you here, Justine?'

'I have news.' Her voice is flat. Cold.

'Oh?' I say again. I'm getting more uptight by the minute. I thought we'd be hugging each other, sobbing, tears flowing, and gushing with all the emotion I've kept bottled up for so long. It doesn't happen. Instead Justine paces up and down the crowded cellar warehouse cluttered with sewing machines, stacks of dishes, various and sundry lamps, a beat-up old armoire and junk.

'You *must* leave Paris, you and Maman.' She throws another quick look toward the door. 'It's not safe for you here.'

'I have nothing to fear, Justine.'

'I'm taking a big chance meeting you like this. There will be terrible consequences if the major gets wind of me warning you.' She grabs me by the shoulders and the dark fear in her eyes is so intense their blueness turns into deep midnight. I feel her hands trembling. 'Please, do as I ask. *Go.*'

'Oh... my... God, you're serious.'

'Yes.'

'How'd you know I'd be here?'

She doesn't answer me and turns away. I wouldn't doubt if the major is hanging around, spying on us. It's then I realize she manipulated me to meet her here at Hôtel Drouot using *The Daisy Sisters* as bait. And I fell for it. Where would she get that information? Of course. Am I that dense? She wasn't only *raped* by a Nazi, she's working *for* the Nazis. I see it now. Her suit is made from fine silk from Lyon, she boasts, and her shoes are polished leather. *Real* leather. And I'd bet my last franc those pearls dangling from her *chapeau* are real. A present from the SS officer who... Why can't I just say it? *Raped* her.

Do I dare ask her?

Minutes ago I was debating how to steal back *The Daisy Sisters,* risk everything for a chance to recapture that beautiful spirit of hers on canvas and bring her home to Maman and Maison Bleue. Now I must accept that Justine is gone. Yet I can't forget my sister laughing and feeding the swans when we were little girls, jumping into the lake to retrieve Madame de Giocomte's floppy hat. I remember the grand adventures we had at Maison Bleue and how we found a home there.

Then I remember the day of the rape.

And how we both paid the price.

The price of silence. A silence that betrayed us both.

I regard this Parisienne sophisticate wearing elegant blue shoes while we at Maison Bleue stuff newspapers into our worn soles. I don't know her any more. To think I was exhilarant a moment ago, my pulse racing when I jammed out of the hall. It didn't take me long to catch up with her, maneuvering my way in and out of the crowd of anxious art collectors scanning their *Gazette*, flying in and of the numerous halls, sniffing for a bargain. She stands out in that blue suit and hat. How Justine knew her way down here, I don't know, the labyrinth of narrow corridors and steep stairs leading down to the cellar. Paintings, statues, furniture packed together make it difficult to move around, and the lighting is dim and the air stuffy. She tells me this is where they keep the items bid on but not paid for and later auctioned off. Now it's also used to store paintings and *objets d'art* before they're previewed to the public.

She steers me over to an alcove covered by a black curtain. 'I have something to show you.' She yanks aside the curtain and I see—

The Daisy Sisters.

'Ooh...' I pull in my breath, my heart swelling at seeing the painting sitting on an easel, knowing so much has happened since that day, and now my sister is here but something has changed in me.

I can't take the painting.

I'm standing so close to it, I can see the fine, long brushstrokes swirling in our hair, but we're not those little girls any more. One of us is a traitor to France. I can't take the painting back to Maison Bleue. It's marked with a black swastika, even if that sign is not visible to the naked eye.

'The other paintings are in the next storage room, Ève, but I wanted you to see *The Daisy Sisters* before it's shipped to the Free Zone.'

'I don't get it, Justine. You *knew* where the de Giocomte paintings were and you never tried to contact Monsieur and Madame?' I ask, not understanding.

'I *didn't* know, not until the major listed the paintings in the *Gazette*.'

Should I believe her?

Justine runs her hand over the ornate frame, her eyes tearing up. And here I thought she couldn't cry any more. 'I miss Madame playing the cello and Monsieur de Giocomte humming along with her.' Her eyes dim. 'I imagine Madame plays a sad tune now, but perhaps he still hums. I wish I could help, Ève, but these paintings are headed for a special auction at the Hôtel Savoy in Nice—'

'Then you don't know...?'

'Know what?' she asks, curious.

'The French police arrested Monsieur de Giocomte last December and sent him on a train East with more than seven hundred other Jewish men.' My shoulders slump, deep worry for this good man making it difficult for me to finish. 'We suspect he may be dead.'

'Oh, my God, Ève. That's impossible. The major promised. Damn, he *promised* me they'd be safe.'

'Then he's a liar,' I shoot back. 'Why do you stay with him? He raped you! What spell has he cast over you?'

'You wouldn't understand.'

'*Please*, Justine, join us and we'll fight together.'

'I can't, Ève, it's too dangerous... for me... for you.'

'I can't believe you'd stay with that German pig after what he did to you.'

'I have no choice, Ève.'

'We *all* have a choice, dear sister. You're a coward, letting Maman and me believe you were dead when clearly all along you've been cavorting with the Boches. The gendarme at the police station was right but I didn't believe him, couldn't accept you'd stoop so low. I was a fool.'

'And you'd rather tell Maman the truth?' she fires back, and for a moment I see the old Justine. Filled with love for our *maman*, making sure she has her tea, her favorite paisley shawl. 'Tell her I'm the mistress of an SS officer? You know it would break her heart.'

'Her heart's already broken.'

'Dear, sweet Maman. Does she still brush your hair every night like when we were little girls?' I see her eyes go misty again, and for a moment I want to hug her in spite of the pain I feel. In spite of knowing she's betrayed France, betrayed me. I hate her for that, but she's still my sister and for a brief shining moment she was the Justine I once knew.

I make a final plea. 'It's not too late, Justine. Come with me *now*. My friend Michal can hide you—'

'Michal?'

'Don't act surprised. I know you saw me with him at the American Hospital. I thought I was dreaming, but it *was* you.'

'I have to go,' She hugs me tight, catching me off guard. 'I'm sorry, Ève.'

'Why... why won't you come with me?'

'I can't explain, Ève.'

'What's stopping you?'

She clenches her fists. '*Please* don't ask me again.'

'I'm not alone, Justine, there are many like me, Parisians willing to fight to free France from Nazi rule.'

'I'm begging you to give up these ideas, you can't win. They *know* who you are.'

'Who?' I look over my sister coldly. 'What aren't you telling me?'

'Your friends aren't as clever as you think. The Gestapo has ways of turning *anyone* into an informant. Beatings, whips, drownings, finding your vulnerability and turning it against you.'

Is my sister such a victim?

'What happened to you, Justine? Why are you doing this?'

'Because I don't want to see you hurt... or killed.'

'I don't believe you,' I insist, turning these thoughts around in my head. 'You're just trying to scare me.'

'What do I have to do to convince you, Ève? They *know* you're in the Resistance.'

'The Gestapo?'

'Yes. You're in terrible danger.'

I lift my chin. 'I'm proud of what I've done. I'm in no more danger now than I've been in since the Germans occupied Paris. It's what I do.'

'If you don't care about yourself, Ève, then think about Maman.'

'Maman? What does she have to do with this?'

'She's also on their list. The Gestapo will pick her up and send her to Drancy if you don't get out of Paris *now*. The Gestapo *will* find you, then torture you until you give up your friends.'

'You're saying I should collaborate with the Boches, *like you?*' I pause. I hurt her. Her lower lip is trembling, but I can't stop. 'What happened to you is unthinkable, but what you're doing now is heartbreaking.'

'I have my reasons,' she insists.

'Are you still sleeping with the major? *My God, are you in love with him?*'

'I only love France!'

'If you did, you'd fight alongside us.'

'I can't, Eve.'

'Why?'

'You have my answer. I have to go before he finds me.'

'The Gestapo man?'

'Yes.'

'I can't let you leave, Justine.' I move toward her, my hand cradling the pistol in my pocket, my finger tightening around the trigger.

* * *

It feels like hours pass in that moment, though it can only be seconds. 'I'm sorry, Ève, there's more at stake than you know.' Justine gasps when she sees me pull out the pistol. She says in a calm, even voice, 'Give me the gun.'

'I *can't* let you go. You're a collaborator.'

'*Please*, Eve, you don't understand.'

'Give me one good reason why I shouldn't shoot you.'

'I want to tell you, *oh how I do.* To share with you my joy, but I'm afraid you won't understand, that you'll judge me as you already have. I can't take that chance.'

A sudden fear crosses over her face; her pretty skin goes pale. She's said too much and she regrets it.

'Justine, tell me what's going on. *Please.*'

'*Adieu*, my little sister.'

She turns and runs from me, snaking her way through stacked boxes of toys, pots and pans, then pushing over a pile of probably priceless dishes on a worktable and sending them crashing onto the floor. The sound is deafening, dish fragments splattering everywhere. I drop my satchel... shield my eyes... stepping over shards of sharp china piercing my cork soles. I don't stop. I can't.

'*Justine, come back!*'

I didn't want to hurt her, just frighten her. If I had more time, I know I could have convinced her to join the fight. The Nazis have cajoled her into believing she has no choice but to do their bidding, that she's damaged goods. Never. Not in my eyes. Yes, I hate her for collaborating, but there's something else going on. Something that made her eyes soften for a moment, her lips smile. She mentioned her joy. *Joy?*

What was she about to tell me?

I'd seen that look before. On the day of the painting. When Justine announced delightedly that she had found the perfect daisy. 'Look, Ève! Every petal surrounding the golden crown is flawless. What a precious gift from God!'

I experience a brief moment of disbelief as the truth hits me. *Oh, no, it can't be. Could it?* I smile. *Yes.* Her joy came from the worst time of her life when this war put her in an impossible situation and she made the best of it.

Justine had a baby. A child conceived and then born sometime after the SS officer took her innocence. If that was true, whatever she was thinking sleeping with him, a wonderful thing came out of that nightmare. A beautiful child and she couldn't tell me because she thought I'd judge her.

My God, Justine, we're sisters.

I know when there's something wrong with her. She's quieter, like when she used to get frustrated with a design. She would pull her hair straight back, no curls. No lipstick. Wouldn't talk for hours. I got that. We've always had our own language between us, not words, but looks, gestures, eye rolling. Laughing and seeing who could make the longest daisy chain. We've always danced to our own rhythm; it's something you *feel* rather than what you see and hear.

That's why her rape affected me so. It could have been me. It *should* have been me.

And for that, I shall never forgive myself.

Running footsteps echo in the hallway.

I've got to catch up with her. I stumble against the old armoire, bang my knee and my gun explodes, the shot bursting from the barrel and making my ears ring. I shake my head to clear it. *Oh my God, what have I done? What if she's hurt?*

*   *   *

I race down the hallway, don't see her, then I hear a second shot and a woman scream.

Justine.

I stand, chilled, disbelieving, the scent of her perfume lingering and mixing with the smell of gunpowder. I check the pistol. Two bullets left. I only fired one shot. That means someone else fired *after* me.

If I didn't fire that final shot, then who did?

I head into the narrow corridor near the staircase. Empty. I see a blood trail. She's wounded. I must find her, get help. A sickening fear makes my stomach roll.

Is Justine dead?

Do I have my sister's blood on my hands? I can't believe the story of *The Daisy Sisters* ends here on a spring day in May.

Or does it?

I race through the cellar until I find my way up to the ground floor when I hear—

'What happened?' someone asks.

'There's been a shooting. A woman.'

'Here at the Hôtel Drouot? Who is she?'

I mix with the crowd pushing and scrambling every which way, Nazi soldiers racing into the Rue Drouot entrance with bayonets drawn, rounding people up. The crowd protesting. The deafening roar of boisterous German voices shouting orders. Art patrons chattering about a blonde woman shot... bleeding. *Is she dead? No one knows! The Gestapo took her away.*

I take advantage of the confusion when an overzealous art dealer tries to slip past the soldiers with a Chinese porcelain vase hidden under his coat. A Nazi grabs the vase and another soldier strikes him between the shoulders with his rifle butt. The man goes down. The crowd goes crazy, out of control, demanding the soldiers back off.

I duck down and find the right moment to slip away through the Rue Rossini entrance out into the street, pull my hat down over my face and walk at a brisk pace. Back to Maman. Back to Maison Bleue. Back to Michal. But everything's changed. A fervor for revenge that won't be satisfied until I get justice for my sister.

And I have another mission too now. I must find her child. And bring the baby home.

I realize this as another thought begins echoing in my head: *If I didn't kill Justine, then who did?*

The Gestapo? The SS officer who raped her?

I won't rest until I find out.

The fight isn't over.

Somewhere out there is the man who killed my sister. A man who must be stopped. As certain as I am the soul of Paris endures in the hearts of her people, I know the work of the Resistance will go on.

I will go on.

Tomorrow. The next day and the next. I swear.

I *will* find him. And her child.

That I promise you, Justine.

ACKNOWLEDGMENTS

Bringing Justine's story to publication forced me to open wounds I'd buried years ago because you just didn't 'talk about it'.

Sexual violence.

And here I thought it was just me.

According to the US-based CDC (Centers for Disease Control and Prevention), sexual violence is more common than you think. I was surprised to discover that over half of women have experienced sexual violence involving physical contact during their lifetime and one in four women are victims of 'completed or attempted rape'. Also, one in three women has experienced sexual harassment in a public place.

I experienced all three.

My first encounter happened when I was a teenager on a trip to Paris with my parents, walking down the Avenue des Champs-Élysées on a very busy Saturday night when—

Someone in the crowd grabbed me by the crotch.

I was so shocked my heart stopped, but I said nothing. I didn't see the perpetrator because it was dusk and well, I was ashamed.

Like *I'd* done something wrong.

Later when I was stationed in Italy with US Army Special Services, I was visiting Paris with an Air Force buddy when three men tried to kidnap me on Rue Caulaincourt in Montmartre. (You never forget *where* it happened.) It was late, a dark street, and again I blamed myself. I'd lagged behind to window shop and my friend and the French students we were hanging out with went on ahead. The three kidnappers picked me up and carried me several feet toward a dark alley. Panicked, I called out for help. My friends saved me from what I believe could have been sex trafficking.

When I lived in Pisa, Italy, I had the usual encounters with guys following me... flirtatious, fun... until one afternoon when rain was in the air and I was assaulted by a young man who grabbed me around the neck and started choking me. I was terrified... until he made the mistake of ripping my favorite black crepe pants with a knife. That did it. I got so angry I stomped on his foot and used my sturdy Dutch umbrella case to fight him off. I ran all the way back to my apartment and never looked back.

Then I realized my leg was bleeding.

I went to the Army base where I worked and got checked out by a medic, but I pleaded with him not to report the assault. I was certain I'd be blamed and the Army would send me home. So I remained silent.

But the most devastating experience in my life happened when I was in graduate school.

A young man I'd gone out with only once raped me. He was smart, interesting, but I barely knew him. I thought he was joking when he kept insisting we were getting married. Things got really scary when we stopped at his apartment so he could pick up his wallet that he 'forgot' and he forced himself on me. I tried to reason with him, but he was drunk and a third-degree black belt. I was afraid to fight back. Yet I'm ashamed I *didn't* fight harder. When I insisted he take me home, he told me we were driving to Las Vegas to get married.

It was 4 a.m.

I had few options. Go along for the ride and take a chance I could find help, or try to talk him out of it. It was a five-hour trip to Nevada. No, I had to act now.

When he stopped at a red light, I jumped out of his Mercedes and ran to a small motel with the lights on and banged on the front window until the manager let me in and called the police.

I didn't press charges. I just wanted it to go away. Who would believe me? I'd said *no*, but I didn't scream because I feared for my life.

I never spoke about it.

Then when I was researching my new novel about World War Two in France, I realized how little about sexual assault during the war had been covered in fiction. I decided the time was right to talk about it, that women have been silent too long. How sexual assault affects you in your everyday life. The guilt, the shame, the silence.

And *Sisters at War* was born.

The story of two sisters living in Paris in 1940 when one sister is attacked by an SS officer and how the assault affects the lives of *both* sisters.

I couldn't have made this journey without my fabulous editor at Boldwood Books, Isobel Akenhead. She became my champion for this story and brought not only her editorial knowledge and expertise, but put her heart and soul into this book. I shall be forever grateful to her for her belief in me.

I also want to thank Nia Beynon, Publishing / Sales & Marketing Director, who brought me into the Boldwood Books family and is always there for us authors. And CEO and Founder Amanda Ridout, who never fails to astonish me with her energy and innovation in publishing to make Boldwood Books an industry leader and winner of several book awards.

Thank you also to my copyeditor Jennifer Kay Davies and my proofreader Shirley Khan for their help in making the story the best it can be.

And to every woman who was ever afraid to speak up regarding sexual assault, remember, we get courage from each other. You are not alone. We want to hear your stories.

And now you know mine.

ABOUT THE AUTHOR

Jina Bacarr is a US-based historical romance author of over 10 previous books. She has been a screenwriter, journalist and news reporter, but now writes full-time and lives in LA. Jina's novels have been sold in 9 territories.

Sign up to Jina Bacarr's mailing list here for news, competitions and updates on future books.

Visit Jina's website: https://jinabacarr.wordpress.com/

Follow Jina on social media:

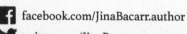

facebook.com/JinaBacarr.author

twitter.com/JinaBacarr

instagram.com/jinabacarr

bookbub.com/authors/jina-bacarr

ALSO BY JINA BACARR

Her Lost Love

The Runaway Girl

The Resistance Girl

The Lost Girl In Paris

The Orphans of Berlin

Sisters at War

Sixpence Stories

Introducing Sixpence Stories!

Discover page-turning historical novels from your favourite authors, meet new friends and be transported back in time.

Join our book club
Facebook group

https://bit.ly/SixpenceGroup

Sign up to our
newsletter

https://bit.ly/SixpenceNews

Boldwood

Boldwood Books is an award-winning fiction publishing company seeking out the best stories from around the world.

Find out more at www.boldwoodbooks.com

Join our reader community for brilliant books, competitions and offers!

Follow us
@BoldwoodBooks
@TheBoldBookClub

Sign up to our weekly deals newsletter

https://bit.ly/BoldwoodBNewsletter

Milton Keynes UK
Ingram Content Group UK Ltd.
UKHW042108230524
443033UK00004B/56